Muffled Echoes

G.K. Parks

Copyright © 2017 G.K. Parks

A Modus Operandi imprint

All rights reserved.

ISBN: 1942710054
ISBN-13: 978-1-942710-05-9

For the real heroes

OTHER BOOKS IN THE ALEXIS PARKER
SERIES:

Outcomes and Perspective
Likely Suspects
The Warhol Incident
Mimicry of Banshees
Suspicion of Murder
Racing Through Darkness
Camels and Corpses
Lack of Jurisdiction
Dying for a Fix
Intended Target
Muffled Echoes
Crisis of Conscience
Misplaced Trust
Whitewashed Lies
On Tilt

BOOKS IN THE JULIAN MERCER SERIES:

Condemned
Betrayal
Subversion
Reparation

ONE

My ears were ringing, and the world spun in dizzying circles. I rolled onto my side, gasping at the sharp pain that suddenly replaced the constant throbbing. Blood ran into my eyes, and I wiped it away with the back of my hand. A burning sensation ran from my fingers to my wrist. Where was I? Grey and green, those were the only two colors I could make out. One was sky and the other ground. I was outside. A vibration shot through my hip, sending a jolt of adrenaline into my system. My phone. It took three tries before my fingers slipped inside my pocket, scraping against the fabric that felt like jagged pieces of glass against my fingertips. I bit back a whimper and blindly hit answer.

"It would have been nice if you called to say you were running late," Agent Eddie Lucca, my new partner at the OIO, said. "Are you even planning to show up at work today?"

"Lucca," I managed to sit up, nearly blacking out in the process, "I need you to come get me."

"Seriously, Parker, I'm not your chauffeur. It's not my job to pick you up and take you to work."

"No, you don't understand." I blinked a few times, hoping to steady the world. "Ping my phone."

"Is this a joke?"

"No. I don't know where I am or how I got here." I tried to swallow, but my throat was devoid of moisture, causing me to gag and choke.

He must have heard the pain in my voice. "Are you okay?"

"I've been better." I tried to get my legs under me, falling face first to the ground. Black bubbles clouded my vision, and I decided not to try that again. When they cleared, I was staring at a concrete curb.

"Parker, are you still there? Come on, Alexis, answer me."

"I'm here," I looked around, not seeing anything except a retaining wall or maybe it was a concrete structure, "wherever here is."

Muffled words came over the line, and Lucca thanked someone. "Alex, what do you see? Describe what's around you."

"A fucking concrete wall. The ground is wet." A stabbing pain shot through my back, taking my breath with it. "It might be blood."

"Shit," he yelled something to someone in the background, "I'm on my way, just keep talking."

"Don't bother stopping to pick up breakfast. I'm not hungry."

"Are you the only one that counts? Talk about selfish." A static burst erupted from my phone. Lucca must have entered the elevator. "I'll be there in two minutes."

My pulse pounded loudly in my ears, and I closed my eyes. The panic was rising, bubbling to the surface. "Bring some forensic experts along. They'll need to protect the evidence before I'm moved."

"Parker, that's not important right now."

"Yes, it is. I don't know what happened, but we need to find out." The phone slipped from my hand, but it landed close enough that I could still hear Lucca's voice. "Do you have my location?"

"Yeah, we're close."

My eyes closed, and for a time, there was nothing but the sound of my heartbeat in my ears. It came with pained exhales, and then a cacophony of sirens broke the rhythm. Doors slammed, and I winced. More sirens. Voices. Someone was close.

"My god," Lucca cursed. "Alex, I'm here. Paramedics are a minute out, just relax." He eased me onto my side. "It's not so bad. You'll be fine." He reached for my wrist, stopping when he saw the condition of my right hand.

"Maintain the crime scene," I hissed. "And no drugs. Don't let them give me anything. I want a tox screening."

He let out an uneasy snort. "Wow, and I thought your cognitive functions might be impaired. Are you sure I can't go grab a cup of coffee while you call the shots?" He brushed my hair away, examining the gash on my forehead, and I grit my teeth. "We'll figure out what happened and find whoever did this, but for right now, why don't you let me take over?"

"Okay." I swallowed, staring at the area around me as numerous people trooped past. Lucca barked orders, and from the frequent flashes going off in the distance, I suspected the area was being photographed. The paramedics arrived, and then everything began to blur. They took my vitals, assessed my injuries, and lifted me onto a stretcher. "Lucca?" I whispered, hoping that he had my back, even though I'd made his life a living hell since the moment I'd been reinstated at the Office of International Operations, a branch of the FBI.

"You're okay. I'm sticking with you," he assured.

The doors slammed on the back of the ambulance, causing me to jump. One of the paramedics reached around to secure the belt on the stretcher, and I panicked. Immediately, my sympathetic nervous system went into overdrive, and the monitors hooked to my chest beeped a staccato rhythm, quickly approaching a crescendo. The paramedic checked the monitor and picked up a syringe. Practically bringing myself to the brink of unconsciousness, I fought against the few buckles that were holding me on the gurney, somehow managing to slip out of them and backing myself into the corner, like a wounded animal searching for a defensible position.

The paramedic moved closer, and I freaked out.

Intellectually, I knew he was here to help, but I couldn't override my instincts. A scream ripped past my lips, and the paramedic took a step back.

"Parker, easy," Lucca said. "No one's going to hurt you." He slowly approached, holding his hands up in surrender. I nodded and collapsed against the seat. "Let's get her to the hospital. Now."

"Sir, it's policy to have the injured strapped down. We don't know how extensive her injuries are. She could—"

"Then light 'em up and roll." Lucca's voice left no room for argument. It was the last thing I heard before falling back into the abyss.

*   *   *

"Thanks for disregarding the rulebook today, boy scout," I mused, struggling to keep my eyes open.

Lucca nodded and bit his lip. He had taken a position in the far corner of the room while I had been scanned, poked, prodded, photographed, and otherwise analyzed. My clothing and other belongings had been taken to the crime lab, and every piece of trace evidence had been collected from my body. Frankly, that was one experience I never wanted to repeat.

One of the few benefits of being a federal agent was that this was being handled internally. At least I didn't have to answer a million questions that some overzealous cop would surely ask. I'd been in and out of consciousness since the ambulance. The medical staff was still determining the extent of my injuries, but I could tell something wasn't right. There was a huge gap in my memory, and I had no idea what happened or how I ended up on the side of the street.

"What do you see?" I asked, forcing Lucca to come closer. "It's not like I have a mirror so describe my injuries."

"Parker," he licked his lips, "this isn't a good idea. You're a victim."

"The last thing I want to be is a victim. This is a case, just like any other, and the first thing we need to do is determine what happened."

"Fine, but for the record, you're insane." He swallowed the lump in his throat and stood at the end of the bed. Except for two strategically placed towels, I was completely exposed. "There's extensive bruising on the side of your right knee. It appears to be a point of impact. Lacerations run around your lower abdomen in a circular pattern." Slowly, I shifted onto my side. "You've been shot?" His voice held surprise.

"Again?" I asked, feeling panicked.

"No, it's a faded scar, at least a year old, I'd guess."

"Let's keep the scar commentary to a minimum, okay?"

"Yeah," he sighed, "why didn't you ask one of the techs to do this instead of me?"

"Why? Does the female body make you squeamish? You're married and have a kid, so you should know what a woman looks like by now." I glanced down to make sure the towels were still in place. Despite the dig, I didn't want Lucca to see the goods either. Unfortunately, I had to focus on something, or I was bound to have a total meltdown. "Continue."

"Extensive abrasions to your left side. They resemble road rash. Then there's a large bruise on your upper back, between your shoulder blades, and what looks like blunt force trauma to your forehead." He backed away from the bed. "And you can see for yourself the condition of your right hand." I met his eyes, but he looked away. "You really don't remember how any of this happened?"

"No." I shuddered. "Is Jablonsky on his way?"

"He'll be here soon. Right now, he's breathing down everyone's neck to get some answers."

"Sounds like Mark." Supervisory Special Agent Mark Jablonsky was my boss, mentor, and one of my oldest friends. It also explained why he wasn't here yet to make sure I didn't escape the confines of the hospital. "Did he send my go-bag? I'd like to get dressed."

"Yeah, he knew it'd be in the trunk of your car." Lucca's brow furrowed. "Your car was parked underneath the federal building in your usual spot. What time did you leave work last night?"

"I don't remember." He gave me a look as if my words proved that I wasn't in any condition to be assessing these circumstances like they were any other case. "Look, you can ask all the questions you want once we get back to the office. Until then, give me a minute to process and remember. The doctor said it might come back, so don't push."

"You're the one that's pushing," Lucca retorted. He went to the door and spoke to someone who handed him a duffel bag. "Don't you think the doctors would prefer you to wear a hospital gown?"

"I've already had every alphabet scan imaginable. It shouldn't matter what I'm wearing since I'm ready to get out of here."

Before I could ask Lucca to give me some privacy, a nurse came into the room. She brought my updated chart and stuck a few images on the lightboard in the corner. Then she ushered Lucca into the hallway, helped me dress, and said a doctor would be in momentarily.

While I waited, my eyes closed, and I lost another indeterminate amount of time. At least that was one way to avoid the medical professionals. The sound of voices woke me, and I pulled myself higher in the bed.

"Alex," Mark Jablonsky strode across the room and stood beside me, "how are you feeling?"

"Not so great."

Mark turned to Lucca. "Give us a minute, kid." Mark and I had been through a lot together. Once Lucca was out the door, Mark turned back to me. "What happened?"

"I don't know. I can't remember anything from last night. Did the tox report come back yet?"

"From the preliminary results, there's no indication that you were drugged. No chloroform, GHB, or rohypnol. They're still looking for less common possibilities, but it doesn't seem likely."

"Then why can't I remember anything?"

"It could be from taking that knock to the noggin'." He frowned at the bandage. "When we found you, you were wearing what you had on yesterday. Do you remember going to a bar or restaurant after work? Did you meet

Martin for dinner or drinks? He was the last received call on your cell phone prior to Lucca phoning this morning."

"I don't remember talking to him." Squinting, I tried to recall our last conversation, but it made my headache worse.

Mark sat on the edge of the bed, quietly studying my right hand. My thumb, pointer, and middle fingers were bloodied and damaged at the tips, complete with torn nails. The space between my thumb and knuckles was badly bruised with a large blood blister beneath the skin. On top of that, my wrist had been severely sprained, so the doctors had bandaged and wrapped the entire mess in a temporary cast. And that was just the tip of the iceberg.

"I spoke to your doctor. You've obviously sustained some head trauma, but the scans came out clean for fractures and bleeds. They aren't certain if the short-term memory loss is due to physical or psychological trauma, but there's a good chance you'll eventually remember what happened."

"Psychological trauma, my ass. I've been through hell, Jablonsky. I doubt that whatever happened last night was any worse than what I've already experienced." I was angry and, admittedly, a bit afraid.

"Until then, the forensic lab is working on the most likely scenario to explain your current state." He patted my shoulder and stood. "We'll figure this out. In the meantime, I've assigned a detail for your protection. A few agents are reviewing your case files and making a list of possible enemies. The techs are combing through DOT camera footage of the surrounding area for some hint as to how you ended up outside that parking garage."

"I can help," I insisted, making another attempt to sit up, but Mark gently pushed me back against the pillow.

"Do whatever the doctor says, and once you're released, Lucca volunteered to take you home and question you."

"I thought he couldn't stand me. Are you sure he volunteered? Maybe he's planning to take advantage of my weakened state and suffocate me."

"Well, I wouldn't necessarily blame him," Mark smiled, "but then he'd have to off the protection detail too. And that would be a lot harder to explain." He crossed the room. "Is there anything you need?"

"Yeah, I need to know what happened."

He nodded and left the room. A few seconds later, Lucca returned to find me struggling to get out of bed. He watched while I wrapped my left hand around the bar and pulled myself up, hissing when the lacerations on my back and torso started bleeding again.

"What are you doing?"

"Getting out of here." I reached for the FBI emblazoned windbreaker that someone left for my use.

"You shouldn't be leaving," Lucca said from the doorway as I fought to get my cast into the sleeve. "The doctors want to monitor you overnight. You could have internal bleeding that they missed or..."

"I don't care. We have work to do."

"You're in no condition to work. You can barely stand. We can handle this."

"You don't even know what this is," I spat, "and I won't be able to relax until I know what happened." My memory was a blur. Blocking out trauma was the body's way of protecting itself, but the horrific things I imagined were sickening. "How long until we get the full toxicology report back?" I wasn't a blackout drunk, so there had to be an explanation for my fogginess.

"Soon. Probably by tomorrow."

"Have a complete copy of my medical report, including the scans and tests, sent to our lab techs. Our FBI field office has a stellar crime lab. They'll be able to determine the most likely cause of my injuries."

"Jablonsky's already done that."

"Great." Teetering, I leaned back so I wouldn't fall forward. "Now go find a nurse and get my discharge papers. I'm not sure I'm capable of tracking anyone down at the moment."

"You should stay here, Parker. The point of this place is to make people feel better."

"A lot of bad things happen in hospitals, so I'd rather take my chances out there." I looked pointedly at the window. "C'mon, you promised to take me home, and I've been assigned a team of babysitters. It'll be fine."

"All right, but if Jablonsky asks, I want plausible deniability."

"Deal."

TWO

As soon as we made it up the six flights of stairs to my one bedroom apartment, Lucca insisted that I get into bed. Normally, I'd protest or make some type of inappropriate quip, but I felt like shit and didn't have the energy to waste. After propping myself up against the pillows and readjusting into the least painful position since none of them were comfortable, I sighed.

"You need fluids," he said, leaving my room and heading toward the kitchen.

"I'm not sick."

"You have no idea what you might have been exposed to or how long you were out cold, so it's not a bad idea to rehydrate." The cabinets opened and closed, followed by the refrigerator. "Really? This is ridiculous." He came back into my room with a glass of water. "How can you call yourself an adult? With the empty fridge and impractical amount of sugary cereals in your pantry, I would have expected to find a futon and a couple of beanbag chairs, most definitely not that expensive living room set. Did you buy it just to appear to be a normal adult human?"

"The furniture's not mine." I squinted.

"Figures," he scoffed.

"You do realize I'm suffering from a head injury, so you could be a little nicer."

"Fine, I'll order dinner since you don't seem to understand the concept of grocery shopping." He handed me the glass and produced a pill bottle from his pocket that I had tried to leave at the hospital pharmacy. "It says take one with food. Do you want it now or when the food gets here?"

"I don't want it at all," I reached for the bottle and put it on my nightstand, "and I'm not hungry."

"My two year old daughter isn't as difficult or stubborn as you." He made a face. "You have to eat, and you need to rest." He pressed his lips together and shook his head. Disappearing from my bedroom, he returned a minute later with one of the chairs from my kitchen table. He took a seat and pulled out his notepad and pen. "What do you want for dinner?"

I snorted. "For a second, I thought you were actually planning to do your job." Rubbing my eyes, I gave in. "The corner deli knows my standing order for soup and sandwiches, and they deliver. There's a magnet on the fridge with the phone number."

"See, that wasn't so hard." After dinner was ordered, Lucca returned to the chair beside my bed. "Whenever you want a break, just say so."

"I'm okay." I looked pointedly at the paper. "Where should I begin?"

"What did you do yesterday?"

"I had a meeting with the district attorney."

"Why?"

"I'm testifying in court against DeAngelo Bard on that drug case we worked. We finished the interview around noon. Then I ran some errands and came to the office. I spent the day analyzing intelligence we collected on that suspected terrorist cell that's been exporting heavy artillery out of the Balkans." I narrowed my eyes. "We worked together on that, but you left before I did."

"I called it quits at five. How much later did you stay at work?"

I shrugged. "Jablonsky might know. His light was on,

but I didn't see him. I wanted to ask him a question."

"About what?"

"I don't remember. It wasn't important. It was something about passport codes." Shaking my head, I couldn't tell if that bit of forgetfulness was the norm or part of the blur.

"Then what happened?"

Blinking, I leaned back against the pillow, gasping at the stabbing pain between my shoulder blades. "I woke up outside." My mind raced through the possibilities of how I ended up there. "Any idea what might have happened? You've seen the aftermath, so what's your best guess?"

He took my left hand in his, turning it over. "No defensive wounds. I don't know what caused the damage to your right hand, but your injuries aren't symmetrical. It could have been an accident." His brow furrowed. "Maybe you fell down the stairs."

"What stairs?"

"I don't know. It was just a guess."

"How about you use the evidence you collected to make an educated guess instead?"

"I will once we analyze the internal cameras at the OIO and figure out what time you left, but since your car was parked in the garage beneath the federal building, you either had a ride waiting or you took off on foot. It shouldn't be that hard to figure out."

"Where did you find me?" I asked.

"You were wedged between a retaining wall and a city parking garage on a dead end street about a mile and a half from work."

"That doesn't make any sense. Why would I go there?"

"You tell me."

"I don't know," I snapped, agitated. "I need a map. What's nearby? There has to be a logical explanation why I would go there."

He softened, realizing that our normal semi-hostile exchanges weren't appropriate at the moment. "Don't worry, we'll figure it out." The doorbell rang, and he went to get the food. "Your only concern is getting better." More drawers and cabinets opened and closed, and then Lucca returned with a foam container of soup and a spoon from the kitchen. "I could drag one of the end tables in here, but I'm guessing you must have some TV trays stashed out of sight, probably with a dozen lava lamps."

"Stop it." I reached for the container, holding it awkwardly with my left hand. "You've done more than enough. Why don't you go help Jablonsky figure out what happened between last night and this morning?"

"I can't go anywhere until your security detail is stationed outside. Plus, someone's supposed to wake you up every few hours."

"I have no plans to sleep." Glaring at the spoon which I couldn't manipulate because of the cast, I took a small sip from the container. "How did this happen?" My head hurt, and I was tired, scared, and pissed. "This is bullshit." I gestured wildly, and he confiscated the soup before I could add second degree burns to my list of injuries. "Do you have any idea how many times I've woken up with no fucking idea where I am or how I got there?" I blinked, fighting to keep my emotions in check.

"Is that rhetorical, or were you some crazy party girl?"

"Twice," I said, ignoring the dig, "and both times I remembered more or less how I'd gotten there once I was coherent. So why can't I remember what happened last night?" My voice sounded desperate to my ears. "I need copies of my medical report and whatever's been pieced together so far."

"All right, after you finish your dinner, I'll see what progress we've made." He bit his lip. "By then, security should be here, so if you need anything, you *will* let them know."

"Great." I held out my hand for the soup. A few sips in, I raised an eyebrow. "Are you on a diet or something?"

"No, I just thought you might need some help to eat."

I continued to glare at him until he went to the kitchen and returned with a sandwich. We ate in silence while I tried to determine what happened last night. After we finished our meal, Lucca took the empty containers into the kitchen and checked to see that the detail was posted outside my door.

"I'll be back in an hour. Two, at the most. If you remember anything or start to exhibit any of those symptoms the doctor warned you about, you will call for help immediately. Is that clear?" he asked.

"Who put you in charge?" I deadpanned.

"Jablonsky, and if anything happens to you, he'll kill me. So don't screw around." Lucca put my cordless phone on the bedside table next to the glass of water and pill bottle. "I mean it, Parker. Stay healthy."

"Yes, sir." I shifted and groaned. "Hey," I stopped him in the doorway, "thank you."

"Don't mention it."

Once Lucca was gone, I eased out of bed, found some pajama shorts and a t-shirt, and took a shower. The water stung my skin, but I had to wash away as much of today as I could. Wiping the steam from the mirror, I stared at my reflection. What the hell happened? After staining my towel with blood, I rebandaged the nasty scrape that covered my left side, attempted to dry the cast that I wasn't supposed to have gotten wet, and went back to bed.

Frustrated that my body wasn't cooperating, I threw the notepad and pen across the room and gave up on the list of facts that I possessed. Instead, I ran through as much of yesterday as I remembered. Even the tiniest detail from the time I woke up to the coffee breaks I took to changing out of my professional attire and into a button-up blouse and a pair of jeans after getting back from the district attorney's office because I didn't like sitting behind my desk in a skirt while reading through threat assessments proved to be unhelpful in determining what happened after I left work.

I reached for the phone, intent on checking the timestamp of my last received call, only to remember that I didn't have my phone. Dammit. Glancing at my nightstand, I realized my gun and credentials were also missing. With any luck, Lucca or Jablonsky would think to return them once they were evaluated for evidence. I flattened out against the mattress, hoping to dull the pain in my head and the ache in my wrist that had begun to radiate up my arm.

Thirty minutes later, I reached for the pill bottle. It was

my only option since the possibility that I had suffered a concussion meant no ibuprofen or aspirin. Swallowing half a dose, I forced my mind to focus on the things I knew in order to avoid the debilitating fear of the unknown. It would be stupid to jump to conclusions, but my rapid heartbeat and slight tremors weren't as easily dissuaded. It was shock brought about by the aftermath of a trauma. Unfortunately, I didn't know exactly what that entailed.

Thankfully, when the pain started to dull, everything else did too. Lucca wasn't back yet, and it was becoming increasingly difficult to keep my eyes open. Oh well, so much for staying awake. I drifted in and out of consciousness, but my painkiller induced sleep was devoid of dreams or thought wisps that might lead to something tangible.

The mattress shook, and I fought to make sense of the world. The lights in my room were still on, and Lucca was seated on the chair placed at the end of the bed. He had taken off his shoes and had his feet resting at the bottom of the bed.

"You said you had no plans to sleep. Who's the current president?" he asked, flipping through the pages inside a manila folder.

"You need to be more specific. There are dozens of countries in this world that have presidents. Some are even elected by popular vote. Obviously, that's not true here, but you get the point." I propped the pillow against the headboard and sat up. "Well, what's the verdict?" I nodded at the file.

"The internal cameras place you leaving the federal building at 7:45 last night. You traveled west, and half a block later, we lose sight of you. For two blocks, there's a blind spot that's been caused by either out of focus or nonexistent cameras. Our computer techs are checking nearby DOT footage, hoping to pick up your trail, but it'll take time." He flipped to another page and read off a familiar phone number. "It's a private number. Who does it belong to?"

"James Martin." Mark knew Martin was the last phone call I received, and he also knew that his old pal and my current romantic entanglement was not a part of whatever happened last night. "I'm sure Jablonsky's already cleared him. Move on."

"Who is he?" Lucca picked up a pen. "There are a lot of calls and texts back and forth between the two of you. Aside from work numbers and your cop friends, he's basically the only person you talk to. Boyfriend? Ex-boyfriend? Bookie?"

"Boyfriend." I shook my head. "He's not involved, so please don't pull him into this. He's already been vetted with a full background check. He's clean. Jablonsky will vouch for him. They go way back."

"You know how it reads. The majority of assaults are perpetrated by someone close to the victim. Most of the time, it's a husband or boyfriend."

"He didn't do this."

"How do you know?" Lucca pushed.

"Because he was at work."

"And he couldn't have just snuck out to meet you? He knew where you were going or at least that you were leaving the office. You were speaking to him when you left." Lucca scribbled a note on the page. "What's his address and place of employment?"

I licked my lips, not wanting to say anything else but unsure of how to get out of it. "Go downtown and read some signs. His name's on the building. And I'm not giving you his home address. Jablonsky has it, so talk to him."

"Jeez, do you expect me to believe that? I'm not the one that hit my head." He studied me for a few moments. "Holy hell, you're serious. Your boyfriend is some big shot mogul?"

"He isn't involved in whatever happened," I repeated, emphasizing each word.

"Well, he does have plenty of means which could afford him opportunity. Clearly, the motive is self-explanatory since he's dating you." Lucca pulled out his phone and began tapping away at the screen. "And he was previously accused of murder, at least by the press. Need I say more?"

"He has no criminal record, and if you keep reading, you'll see that an apology was printed by that particular newspaper for getting the facts wrong. He was a victim, just like the woman he was accused of murdering." The conversation had caused my temper to flare, and I moved to get up and escape the inquisition. "This is not a trial. I didn't do anything wrong, and the few people that I'm close to aren't responsible. So back the fuck off."

"Easy." Lucca put his palms up in surrender. "I'm just doing my job the only way I know how. We start with the obvious and go from there. You'd do the same thing."

"Then let's start with the obvious." I jerked my chin at the file. "What has the forensic lab uncovered?"

"You had wood splinters beneath your damaged fingernails. The wood itself was treated with a varnish, so it had to come from indoors." He flipped to the next page. "Tox screen is negative for drugs, positive for alcohol. Rape kit is negative. No signs of sexual assault. No fingerprints on your body. No real evidence pointing to a clear source for your injuries. Patterns of your lacerations and bruises aren't indicative of any one thing."

Breathing out a sigh of relief, I relaxed. "Well, I guess that's the good news and bad news." Suddenly, the exhaustion seemed to set in as the stress that had been keeping me alert evaporated into the abyss. "Where do we go from here?"

Lucca began speaking, but I was asleep before he finished explaining our next move.

THREE

It was dark. The room was bathed in a menacing red glow. The sounds of footsteps and metal clanging would briefly fill the air, only to be extinguished just as quickly. The echoes didn't carry, and if they did, I couldn't hear them. Everything was dulled, as if I were underwater. Industrial fluorescent light fixtures covered the ceiling, but only a single flickering red bulb at the far end of the room provided any illumination. Twisting from side to side, I tried to determine where I was, but I didn't know.

Voices, two, then three, sounded muffled. A sharp, pleading cry rang out. My heart leapt into my throat. It was a man's voice, begging. The sound was so pitiful and desperate that it made my blood run cold and fear grip my insides. The thud of heavy work boots grew louder until most of the light was blocked out by the hulking figure in front of me.

I tugged frantically to free myself, but my arms wouldn't cooperate. He bent down, placing his hands on either side of my thighs to box me in as he continued to lean closer until I could feel his breath on my neck. Frantically, I struggled to escape. Distance and a weapon were my only thoughts. He began to speak, loud and gruff, but the words were nonsense.

"Get away. Let me go," I screamed.

He shoved my shoulders, pushing me harder into the chair. I jolted backward, hoping to tip the two of us, but there was no give. Managing to kick my left leg up toward my chest, I hoped to use that to leverage him away. My shin came into contact with a gun holstered at his hip. At least now I had additional incentive and a possible plan.

"Parker, stop," the voice growled.

He was too close. Twisting my lower body as far to the left as I could, I raised my knee and hit him solidly in the side, breaking his hold on my shoulders. The momentum carried me backward, and I flipped onto my stomach. His hands were on my hips, and I reached behind me for his gun. Barely, I managed to knock it loose, but his grip tightened. All of my energy was now focused on scrambling to get away.

"Stop. Alex, stop," the voice commanded.

For a split second, I thought I recognized it, but fear was overpowering my rationale, and I continued to fight to get free. Suddenly, the wind was knocked out of my lungs, and then a sharp pain erupted through the middle of my back. I let out a high-pitched whimper, opening my eyes to see the bottom of my dresser. The security detail was in the doorway, and Lucca released the hold he had in order to scoop up the gun that was a foot from my outstretched arm. Carefully, he stood up and took a seat on the edge of my bed. He rubbed his side and stared down at me.

"What the hell just happened?" I asked. My entire body was tingling, and I wasn't sure if I could move. "Did you seriously just knock me to the floor?"

"Why don't you call the paramedics?" Lucca said to the two men in the doorway. "I can handle things in here."

"Agent Parker?" one of them began, wondering if I wanted to be left alone with Lucca and if I was actually okay.

"No need. I'm fine. Everything's fine." I pulled myself to my knees, feeling my muscles shake as I hoisted myself back onto the bed. I narrowed in on their faces, happy to be able to recall their names from the office. "I'm not a morning person, and Lucca found that out the hard way."

"Whatever you say, Parker," Agent Davis said. He and his partner, Agent Samuels, went back outside, exchanging snickers on the way.

"You went for my gun," Lucca declared. "What was I supposed to do? Let you shoot me?"

"Tell me precisely what I did." I took a breath, fumbling to lift my shirt and check my previous injuries to see what new damage had been done.

"I don't know what I walked in on. I showed up to relieve Jablonsky since he stayed the night. I've been in the living room for the last half hour, reviewing the updated file, when I heard noises coming from your bedroom. It looked like you were possessed."

"Well, call a priest next time."

He ignored my remark. "You were thrashing back and forth. I said your name a few times, but you didn't respond. For all I knew, you might have been having a seizure."

"Did you try to restrain me?" Most people knew that wasn't recommended, even on my best day.

"I grabbed your shoulders, and then you tried to break my ribs and went for my gun." He winced, as if for effect.

"I was dreaming, you idiot."

"And you're that tactically skilled when you're asleep? I doubt it." He narrowed his eyes and shook his head. "For what it's worth, I was trying to keep you from swan diving off the edge of the bed," he shook his head, "but you made it obvious you wanted me to let go. So I did."

My side was bleeding again, and I put the hem of my t-shirt in my mouth to free up my one good hand in order to change the dressing. He reached out for the unopened gauze pad and took over since my trembling fingers weren't having much luck.

"Thanks." I studied him for a few moments. Lucca was my partner, despite my protestations to that fact. "You do know that I would never intentionally shoot you."

"You threaten it often enough." He stared for a long time. "What were you dreaming about that had you so frightened?" After telling him about my dream, which made no sense, he sighed. "Okay. Should I even ask if you remember anything from the other night?"

"Not really. I don't know. I can't figure out if that was just a bad dream, my imagination, or something that happened."

"Go get dressed. We'll go over what's been uncovered," he said. "Jablonsky has a few agents compiling your recent closed cases to see who you've pissed off, and he's dividing up your workload among the department. I'll need you to catch me up to speed on this terrorist case and threat assessment you were compiling."

"Sure," I agreed, feeling sheepish for the way our morning started. He rubbed his side again. "Hey, are you okay?"

"Yeah, I'm fine. I only took a knee to the ribs." He untucked his shirt and unbuttoned the bottom four buttons, pulling it up and to the side. Aside from the slight swelling, his ribcage was the color of a blue ink pen.

"Maybe you should reconsider those paramedics," I suggested, wondering how someone could bruise that quickly.

"It's fine. At least I'm not bleeding." He winked and left the room so I could dress.

After slipping into one of the few casual outfits I had in the closet, I marched into the main room of my apartment. My case file was spread over the coffee table, and a stack of materials covered half of my kitchen table. Deciding not to disturb any of it, I poured a bowl of cereal and sat at the counter, watching my partner work. Most days, I hated having a partner. However, today wasn't most days.

"Did you make the coffee?" I asked, gesturing at the pot.

"No, it was here when I got here. Jablonsky must have made it at some point last night. I'd advise against drinking it."

"For once, we're in agreement." Normally, caffeine was my go-to for dealing with most situations, but I was jittery enough already. "Did he leave a note or anything?"

"You don't remember seeing him?" Lucca looked up, raising an eyebrow.

"No." I busied myself with finishing the frosted oats and rinsing the bowl in the sink. "The last thing I remember is you reading my medical report. Apparently, you're excellent at those bedtime stories."

"So I've been told." He took a seat in the armchair next to the couch and waited for me to join him before continuing. "Your clothing and belongings were evaluated for evidence. Your leather jacket is pretty destroyed. There are a lot of deep cuts and scrapes in a continuous pattern. Based on the marks and your injuries, you probably had it unzipped at the time of impact."

"Impact with what?"

He shrugged. "Based on the computer models, the forensic lab seems confident that you hit on your right side and rolled." Spreading out four different photos of my jacket and my bruises, he pointed to each. "Your knee, your side, and perhaps your wrist and forearm took the brunt of the damage. I'd guess it was a vehicle of some sort. It probably threw you off balance, and you rolled off of it. Or it knocked you to the ground, and the momentum kept you moving. It would probably explain the lack of defensive wounds and why your palms aren't scraped. You weren't able to brace yourself."

"What about the wood shards and the head wound?"

"I don't know." He pressed his lips together and assessed me for a moment. "Do you remember a truck or van?"

"No." I searched my memory, but the only insight I could offer was an odd level of concern over a dome light. Strange how the mind works.

"Whatever it was had to be high enough off the ground that the bumper would hit the side of your knee."

"It doesn't feel right. Wouldn't I remember being hit by a car?"

"Not if you hit your head."

"But that doesn't explain the rest of my injuries. What about stovepipes or guardrails or something tall enough to bruise my knee. Maybe there was an altercation, and I was caught off guard and knocked sideways."

"How does that explain the bits of gravel, glass, and tar that were stuck to your jacket?"

"Maybe I was on a rooftop. They use gravel and tar sometimes. Maybe we went through a window or... I don't know."

"Do you remember a rooftop?" His pen was poised over the paper, ready to write anything I said.

"I don't remember anything," I growled, frustrated. "I just have trouble believing that this was an accident. I can't explain how I know this, but this was intentional. It was meant to intimidate and threaten and..."

"And what?" He leaned forward.

"Kill." I squeezed the bridge of my nose. "Yeah, I know. I'm crazy."

"So you escaped?" he asked, and I shrugged. "You climbed onto some roof, fought off your attacker without sustaining any defensive wounds, and then you shimmied down a drainpipe? Or you were escaping, ran into traffic, got clipped by some drunk driving a SUV, and no one came to finish you off because it appeared you were already dead?" He snorted. "Yeah, I seriously doubt that, but it'd make one hell of an action movie."

"This isn't funny, and it's not some stupid joke. Someone did this to me, Eddie. That's the one thing I know for sure."

He flipped through the file again and took a deep breath, rubbing his side. "In that case, we should start calling the hospitals and doctors' offices because whoever came at you probably has more than a sprained wrist and a few bruises."

"Do you believe me?"

"I believe that you believe it. Right now, that's good enough."

While he made some phone calls, I read through the information about my case. Most of it was inconclusive. The DOT cameras hadn't pinpointed my location or destination, and so far, no one knew where I was going or when I ended up next to that parking garage. The forensic lab had speculated as to the most likely cause of my injuries, and the science was sound. But I wasn't convinced since none of the scenarios explained every detail. Then again, reconstructing a crime was never an exact science. It relied mostly on speculation and finding the closest fit possible, but the conclusion the techs reached just didn't fit.

"Dammit, this would be a whole lot easier if I could remember what happened." I slammed the folders onto the table and curled up on one end of the couch. My head ached, and overall, I didn't feel good.

When the calls were concluded, Lucca exchanged the files on the coffee table for the files on the kitchen table. He asked a few questions about recent closed cases, scribbling a list of parties involved that might have an axe to grind. After that, another round of calls was placed, and then he sat heavily in the chair.

"Do you want to take a break? Maybe eat some lunch or get some rest? You're not looking too good."

"Just give me a few minutes."

He went into the kitchen, pulling out a couple of leftover sandwiches from the day before and opening two bottles of water. "Here, you should eat so you can take some pain meds."

"Whatever happened to the guy that was convinced I was a drug addict? I'm starting to miss him."

"Sorry, but he went away after I read your personnel file."

"Well, pretend you didn't. And stop pushing pills, or I'm going to think you're getting a kickback from the pharmaceutical companies."

I took the offered sandwich and took a bite. We ate in silence. I was lost in thought, determined to piece together what happened. My mind replayed my dream over and over, but I couldn't figure out if it was real or imaginary. Placing the empty dish on the coffee table, I sprawled out on the couch and closed my eyes.

"Hey, Parker," Lucca sounded slightly uncertain, "when did those violent nightmares start?"

"When Agent Michael Carver was killed." I set my jaw and faced Lucca. "Then they stopped for a while until different ones took over. Shit happens."

"Have you ever attacked anyone before this morning?"

"I didn't attack you. I was defending myself." At my words, he looked skeptical. "I don't do well with being restrained, even when I'm conscious. You should know that."

"Fine, since you're splitting hairs, did you ever defend yourself while asleep before?"

Remaining silent, I focused on the television, a large screen that Martin had swapped with my smaller TV that was now in his second floor suite along with the rest of my living room furniture and the bulk of my belongings. "Not exactly."

"What does that mean?"

"It means you should mind your own business." I shook my head. "What does this have to do with anything?"

"It was just a thought." Despite the brush-off attempt, I knew he was working on a theory that he didn't want to share. "Have you ever fallen asleep in one place and woken up somewhere else and didn't know how you got there?"

"No."

"Okay, I was just curious."

"The hell you are. What are you thinking? That this entire thing is some kind of PTSD episode."

"I didn't mention a word about PTSD. Any reason your mind went straight there?" he asked.

"Screw you." I stormed into the bedroom and returned with the pill bottle. "Open this."

"I thought you didn't want the meds."

"I didn't, but you gave me a headache, again."

FOUR

Lucca and I bickered most of the afternoon until my body lost the fight against the painkillers. I'd never had a good reaction to medications, even when I was little, and now wasn't any different. May cause drowsiness translated into sound asleep for an extended length of time. However, on the bright side, it meant that I didn't have to listen to Lucca's accusations that this was most likely an accident caused by sleepwalking or something equally moronic. At times, I wondered how he ever made it through Quantico with these harebrained theories.

Opening my eyes, I stared at the fuzzy neon glow from the clock, unable to decipher what the numbers meant. After blinking a few times, I realized it was after midnight. The room was dark, so I almost didn't notice the man seated in the chair beside my bed. He was rolling his tie from end to end into a ball. At the sound of my gasp, he looked up, and briefly, the light caught his eyes, making them appear catlike with green glowing irises.

"Easy, Alex, it's me."

"Martin, what are you doing here?" I asked, relieved.

"I could ask you the same thing, sweetheart," James Martin replied. "Why aren't you at home?"

"I am home," I said without thinking.

Martin frowned, draping his tie over the back of the chair with his suit jacket. It was apparent he'd arrived at my apartment straight from work. "It's my fault, I guess. Until tonight, I didn't realize that it had been nine days since I've seen you. I'm not used to working nights, and I thought we were just missing one another. Why didn't you tell me you moved out?"

"I didn't move out." I patted the spot on the bed next to me, wanting him closer. "I just couldn't stay in your house without you."

"Our house," he corrected. He sat stiffly on the edge of the bed and caressed my cheek. "I was terrified when Mark showed up at the Martin Technologies building this evening. I thought something happened to you."

"Something did, but I don't know what."

"I'm aware." He moved closer, resting his back against the headboard. "I spent four hours being interrogated by Jablonsky before your colleagues decided that I wasn't a threat."

James Martin and Mark Jablonsky had been friends for years, but after my reinstatement as a federal agent, Martin had soured toward his old pal and my boss, believing that Jablonsky had manipulated me into returning to a dangerous job that I hated. Sometimes, Martin's paranoid theory didn't seem that farfetched. Despite the fact that I had made Jablonsky promise to apologize, the two hadn't spoken in a couple of months.

"They shouldn't have done that. Mark knows you would never hurt me. I'm so sorry."

"It's okay. At least he brought me to see you. Frankly, that was the least Jabber could do." Martin let out a displeased grunt. "On the bright side, the agents stationed outside your front door won't let anyone inside without a badge." He brushed his fingers against my arm, afraid to touch me. "I should be relieved they're taking such good care of you now." His hand stopped a few inches from my cast, and he let out an audible exhale.

"Martin, stop. I'm okay."

"That makes one of us." He leaned forward and kissed

me gently. "I love you, Alexis. I'm not supposed to be forced to leave work because you're hurt. And I shouldn't be denied access to you until it's been determined that I'm not the person that hurt you. That's not how life should be." He attempted a smile. "This wasn't on my schedule."

"Tell me about it," I muttered.

"Why didn't you call?" His voice was gentle, careful to avoid a fight. "Jabber said they found you yesterday morning."

I shook my head, unaware of my own reasoning for that decision. "I don't know. I can't figure anything out. It's a mess. Lucca's been hounding me all day. Can we talk about this later?"

"Sure." He slid down in the bed to make me more comfortable. Carefully, he brushed his fingers against the cast. "How long do you have to wear it?"

"Four weeks," I replied, closing my eyes. "Wait," my eyes shot open, "you should be at work."

"You remembered something." There was a teasing tone to his voice. "I'll go back in a couple of hours and teleconference with our German branch. They can adapt. After all, I am the CEO." He sighed. "I hate performing these internal audits, especially now."

"From what I remember, Francesca didn't leave you much choice."

"It's bullshit. She's suing me, so the legal team wants to have everything in order before dealing with actual proceedings. She's making this personal just to bust my balls."

"That's why you shouldn't have done business with your former fiancée," I said matter-of-factly. "I don't care if you were engaged more than a decade ago when you were in business school together; a woman scorned is a woman scorned."

"I didn't do anything to her."

"You broke her heart."

"It definitely didn't seem like it at the time." He gave me an odd look. "Are you taking her side?"

"No," I chuckled, "I never liked her. You could screw her over, and I wouldn't care as long as you didn't actually screw her."

"I'd never," he began.

"I know. I just wish you didn't have quite the past you have." When we started dating, I made it very clear that I didn't want to know about his previous conquests. His relationship history had been limited to his former fiancée, Francesca Pirelli, and his high school sweetheart, but the number of women he'd slept with probably rivaled that of a rock star. At least, that's what I suspected, and I'd learned long ago to never ask a question that I didn't want to know the answer to. "She's claiming sexual harassment and hostile work environment. This is going to be a bloodbath. It won't matter how many internal audits and reviews you conduct. It doesn't look good."

"But she was never a subordinate." Martin switched to work mode which was a relief. "Our companies merged briefly, but when we dissolved our arrangement, she took it personally. She has no reason to be pissed."

"You wanted to use their new tech for your product line. You're arguing over proprietary rights. Of course, she's pissed. You took her bright shiny toy and won't give it back." On my few brief encounters with the woman, I suspected she believed that I had actually taken her boy toy and wouldn't give him back, but that was another story.

"You worked at MT. You know her claims are bogus. It's not a hostile work environment, and I've never sexually harassed anyone. In fact, all the employees are equally paid and compensated. There is no indication of favoritism, sexism, or wage discrimination in any of the branches worldwide."

"That might be true, but you flirted with me," I argued. "Inappropriate comments were made. And I know you've slept with a number of employees. It doesn't bode well. You'd be better off settling."

"Alex," his tone turned harsh, "I don't want to fight with you about this again, especially now." He rubbed his eyes. "The only reason I told you any of this was so you'd be prepared in the event they subpoenaed you."

"And like I told you before, it would be stupid if they use me as a witness. We're in a serious relationship. We live together. There's no way in hell that I'd ever say or do anything that would hurt you. I'm a federal agent. I'd pull some strings and find a way to get out of it, if need be."

"Alex," Martin said my name, but I continued to blabber on about the unlikelihood of Francesca's lawyers finding me of any use in their case. "Alex," Martin said again more urgently, "you remembered."

"Remembered what?"

"Our conversation."

"Oh my god," I felt momentarily overcome with emotion, "that's what we talked about on the phone the last time we spoke." Bolting upright, I flipped on the lamp and reached for the pad of paper. "What time was it?"

"Around eight." In the light, he was able to see more of my bumps and bruises, but he didn't comment. "You don't need to make notes. Mark already has the relevant information."

"Did I tell you where I was going or what I was doing?"

"Alex," he said my name slowly, like he was hiding something, "I don't think—"

"What?" My eyes searched his. "You know something."

He took a moment before saying, "You said you were on your way to meet a police informant."

"Who?"

"I don't know." He hesitated for a moment. "Jablonsky thinks it'd be best to let you remember the details on your own."

"That son-of-a-bitch." I snatched the phone off the nightstand, barely giving Martin time to wrestle it from my grip before I could call Mark. "I have to know what happened."

"Sweetheart, he doesn't know." Martin's eyes screamed out sympathy, and I turned away from the look. Pity was the last thing I wanted right now. "I told him everything I know, and I just told you the same thing. He's checking into it. I wish I could tell you more. I wish I knew. I want to fix this, Alexis. I'd do anything for you."

"I know." Swallowing, I wasn't good with the mushy stuff, and I dropped back to the pillow, placing my casted arm against his chest. "I don't understand why I can't remember, and the possible reasons why terrify me."

He kissed my hair, and we fell silent. My mind considered the reasons I would have needed to meet with a police informant, and I thought about the detectives from the major crimes unit, O'Connell, Thompson, and Heathcliff. But it felt wrong. None of my cases had any overlap with their current cases. The last time Heathcliff and I worked together was a joint venture on the Bard drug case, but I had no reason to speak to an informant about that. Something was missing.

For the next few hours, thought wisps twisted through my mind. The truth was there, buried underneath mounds of useless dribble. How did I happen upon a police informant? There had to be a connection or something that would trace back to the CI's handler. Perhaps a phone call or e-mail message. Fear and dread settled in the pit of my stomach the more I thought about it, but I pushed it away, believing it was part of the terror that I'd been experiencing since this nightmare began.

While recalling the list of open cases that had crossed my desk and tips that had been phoned in, I kept losing my train of thought. My mind had a habit of traveling in wayward directions when I was tired, and the need for sleep was clouding my memory. Eventually, I let my mind and body relax into an uneasy sleep.

Something moved nearby, and I jolted upright. Reaching for my gun, I remembered it was gone and let out an audible growl. Martin turned around from where he was standing in front of my mirror, knotting his tie, and returned to the bed.

"Hey," he whispered, "I'm right here. You're okay." He pressed his lips against the top of my head. "Mark just arrived. He's in the living room. Do you want me to stay?"

"No, you should get back to the grind."

"Okay, but I'll be back later."

"No," I shook my head for emphasis, "we'll conduct a threat assessment. As soon as this is over and I don't have a bunch of bored federal agents outside my door, I'll come home."

"You told me last night that you are home." Martin's

quip was intended to gain reassurance or spark an argument. At the present, I couldn't decide precisely what his goal was.

"Don't be a jackass." I climbed out of bed, and he noticed the small bloodstain on the side of my t-shirt. "I should have known better than to wear white." Turning away from him, I took the bandage off, looking down at the partially scabbed, slightly oozing scrape that covered the length of my side. It was starting to heal, but it wasn't pretty.

"How do you feel?" He buttoned his jacket. "Can I help with anything?"

"I'm fine. I got this." Pulling my t-shirt down, I turned around to face him. "Aren't you sick of playing doctor yet?"

He smirked. "We haven't seen each other in nine days. It would have been nice to play doctor." He leaned down and kissed me. "Promise me that the next time I see you, you'll be in better shape than you are now."

"I'll try."

"That's not a promise." He glanced at the calendar hanging on my wall. "In case you forgot, I'll be back to my regular work schedule in two days."

"Ha ha." I glared at him. "That doesn't give me much time to figure this out and heal. Are you sure you don't need to continue this ridiculous late night schedule?" Truthfully, it was easier when he didn't realize I wasn't around that way he didn't worry about me, and it eased the guilt that I felt for putting him through a lot more than any sane person would typically tolerate.

An annoyed look crossed his face, but I didn't think it was meant for me. "I hope not." Before he could say anything else, there was a loud knock at my door. "Asshole," Martin muttered.

"Parker, are you decent?" Jablonsky called from the other side of the door.

"Am I ever?" I opened my bedroom door. "We need to talk."

"Yes, we do," Mark said. He watched Martin straighten his cufflinks but blocked him from leaving my room. He extended his hand. "Marty," Mark said, "I'm sorry for all of this. Thanks for the help."

Martin stared at Mark's hand for an uncomfortable moment, and then they shook. "You better take better care of your people, Jabber."

Mark nodded. "Agreed."

Clearing my throat loudly, I gave the two overprotective men in my life a dirty look, crossed the hall to the bathroom, and slammed the door. If they wanted to act like macho dickheads, I could act like a prima donna. After stepping into the shower, Martin slipped into the bathroom to say good-bye, catching a glimpse of the extent of my injuries. Fortunately, he was running late, and I was in no mood for any of this. Head injuries were known to cause irritability. Maybe that was my problem.

FIVE

"Marty said you had a breakthrough last night," Mark said when I emerged from the shower with my hair in a towel. "Did anything new come to mind this morning?"

"I kinda hate you. Does that count?"

"I don't think that's new." He held out a coffee cup as a peace offering, but I shook my head. He hid the concerned look, knowing that caffeine was like oxygen to me. "So what did you remember?"

"Nothing helpful," I said, but Mark continued his inscrutable stare until I finally told him about my private phone conversation. "Like I said, it's not useful. What'd you find on the police informant? Does the CI have a name? Do we know who's handling him?"

"Are you certain it's a him?"

I sighed. "No." Taking a seat on the couch, I sifted through the files that Lucca had left behind. None of my cases dealt with the police department or local jurisdiction. "Did you check the call log and my work e-mails?"

"You've been burning the midnight oil again. There's a lot to go through. Lucca's doing his best, but frankly, I'm wondering how we got anything done during those two years that you were on sabbatical."

"Flattery will get you nowhere." Scanning the room for my cell phone, I was focused on finding a new lead. Then I remembered my phone was missing, along with my other personal effects. "Can't you put a rush on my side arm and badge? I'd like to have them back before someone decides I'm not fit for duty. I'd also like my phone back. I should recognize an odd number faster than the computer techs."

"With that wing of yours, you won't be cleared for field work until the cast is off," Mark said, "but that doesn't mean you can't come to the office and help out, if you're up to it."

"You know I'm chomping at the bit to do something productive. So don't give me this 'if you're up to it' crap, or I might start believing that you are being manipulative."

"Marty's still pissed?"

"I'm pissed. How could you drag him to the federal building for an interrogation? Did you handcuff him too?"

"No, it was informal. I knew he'd want to know what happened to you, and it was best to clear him of any suspicion before anyone else started asking questions. You have to believe that I had his best interest and yours in mind." While I went into my bedroom to change into something slightly more professional than running shorts and an oversized t-shirt, Mark boxed up the files that had been deemed irrelevant. "I'm doing this by the book, Parker. Someone did this to you, and when I find out who, their ass is mine. I won't risk getting jammed up because of some procedural issue. If that hurts Martin's precious ego, so be it."

Emerging from my room, I gave my boss a dark look. "You better hope you get to them before I do because, at the moment, I don't give a flying fuck about procedure. I want answers."

"We'll find them." Jablonsky gave my apartment another brief glance and then opened the front door. "I told you that I'd take care of it."

"Yeah, well, tell that to Lucca. He thinks I dreamt the whole thing," I retorted, grabbing my spare keys. I felt naked without a weapon, but hopefully, that would be rectified soon enough.

The drive to the federal building should have been boring, but from the second I climbed into the SUV, my heart raced. Jablonsky's driving wasn't to blame, but the reason for my apprehension eluded me. It was a good thing I skipped the coffee this morning.

"You okay?" Mark asked, glancing at the death grip I had on the armrest.

"Yeah." I swallowed.

"What's wrong?"

"I don't know." I blinked a few times. "Butterflies." I shook my head. "It's nothing."

"If you're not ready," he began, but one look silenced him. "Can you keep it together? Frankly, a meltdown in the office would be understandable, but I wouldn't advise it."

"It's not that. This feels different."

"Well, this is the first time you'll be walking into the OIO as a victim instead of a pain in my ass. That might explain it."

"Just park the damn car." Once I exited the SUV, the pressure in my chest eased and my racing pulse returned to normal. Narrowing my eyes at the vehicle, I fought to recollect what happened. Lucca's theory concerning a possible hit and run came to mind, but I didn't recall being mowed down by a speeding car. "Did forensics come up with any other viable theories to explain my injuries?"

"One thing at a time," Jablonsky said, leading the way to the elevator and pressing the button. "You don't want to overdo it."

"I'm fine. Really." I forced him to look at me, and he realized that I was no longer white as a sheet. "Apparently it's your driving."

"Very funny."

When the elevator doors opened, I expected something to look different, but things were the same. My fellow agents were hard at work, tracking leads, writing reports, and updating our intel. In the last few days, I was the only one who had changed. Jablonsky headed to his office, and I detoured to my desk. Lucca was situated behind my computer, tapping at the keys.

"You replaced me already?" I asked. "That was quick. If

you hand me the back-up nine millimeter in the bottom drawer, that should take care of having to box up my personal effects."

"What personal effects?" he replied, not bothering to look up. "As far as I know, you're the only person who actually uses her work desk for nothing but work."

"You went through my drawers?" I asked, feigning shock. His eyes darted to me for a moment, but he didn't say anything. I knew the answer to that question already. Everything had been searched. My drawers, my computer, my work e-mails, nothing was sacred, which was why I made sure everything at my desk was work-related or completely innocuous. "Then you must have found my stash of hooch."

"Parker," he exhaled, ceasing his typing, "what are you doing here?"

"I want my gun," I repeated, jerking my chin toward the bottom of the desk. "I also want you to get out of my chair."

"Fine." He held up his hands and pushed away from the desk. "Do what you want. It's not like I was in the middle of something."

Taking the seat he just vacated, I glanced at the computer monitor. He was cross-referencing my call sheet and e-mail correspondence with closed cases and recent prison releases to determine who might have been responsible for an attack. Snorting, I unlocked the drawer, removed my back-up nine millimeter, checked the clip, and pulled out my spare holster.

"Did anyone perform a threat assessment?" I asked.

"What does it look like I'm doing?"

"Your due diligence." I smiled and stood. "You can have the chair back now."

"Gee, thanks."

"Anytime." Taking a deep breath, I looked around the room. "Did anyone phone in any threats or tips?"

"No."

"Do you still think that this was unintentional or an accident?" I asked, resting my hips against the side of the desk so I could simultaneously see Lucca's expression and wait for Mark to leave his office.

"Parker," his eyes honed in on my abdomen, "lift your shirt a few inches." Before I could respond with a quip, he added, "Please."

Pulling my shirt up, he studied the scratches along my stomach. "You don't have any bruises in front, just scrapes. That doesn't make much sense."

"Nothing does." I shook off the annoyance. "I take it you're reconsidering your theory."

"I don't know. This morning, I was upstairs with the techs, and from the computer models they ran, it looked like if you had taken a tumble, the bruising would be even, like the scratches." He sighed. "What do I know? I'm sure they can explain how your sprained wrist and bruised knee played a part."

"In other words, you don't know what to think." Normally, I'd enjoy a moment of smug superiority, but this time, I would have preferred Lucca to have an actual answer. "Neither do I," I admitted.

"We'll figure it out, Parker." He offered a tight smile and nodded at Jablonsky, who had just joined us. "Working on the threat assessment, sir."

"Keep me apprised," Mark said, noting my newly acquired weapon. "Feeling better?"

"A little bit," I replied. "Hopefully, the ridiculously intelligent men upstairs can make me feel even better since you boys just can't cut it."

Lucca reddened slightly at my innuendo, probably waiting for the chance to report me for sexual harassment. At this rate, I'd need to see if Martin's legal team did any pro bono work. My brain made a particularly bad joke, and I smiled at my own idiocy. Obviously, things were returning to normal.

"Parker," Jablonsky barked, probably afraid I was having a psychotic episode, "are you coming?" I gave him a wicked grin, and he cringed. "Stop wasting time. We have work to do."

"Yes, sir."

He grabbed my elbow and led me to the elevator. "It's nice to see you're in a better mood than you were earlier, but I'd prefer if it wasn't at my expense." The doors closed, affording us some privacy. "Did Lucca make any progress?"

"Not that I can tell. I think he's abandoned the theory that this was self-inflicted, so that's a plus. But no one has taken credit for roughing up a federal agent, and it looks like he'll be working on that threat assessment for a while."

"Okay." From that single word, I could tell Mark had something on his mind, but he didn't budge. And the ride in the elevator was too short to wheedle it out of him. "Why don't you see what the lab's found and we'll take it from there?"

"Where are you going?" I asked, wondering why he would drag me upstairs and then abandon me.

"I have to give Director Kendall a quick update. I'll be right back." He jerked his chin toward the glass doors. "Go on. They don't bite."

He pressed another button, and the elevator doors closed, leaving me alone with the lab techs and forensic experts. The last time they'd seen me, I'd been naked in a hospital room. With any luck, this encounter would be more pleasant.

"Agent Parker," Thomas Ridley greeted, "your partner warned me that you'd be showing up soon."

"He's not my partner," I grumbled.

Ridley gave me an odd look. "I thought you and Agent Lucca were working together. Didn't he find you that morning?"

"Fine, he's my partner." Letting out a huff, I jerked my chin at the equipment in the lab. "Any idea what happened to me?"

"We have some idea, but our models haven't accounted completely for the extent of the evidence we collected." He stood up from his chair. "Sasha," he called, "hey, Davenport, I'm talking to you." He waved at the woman seated at a desk across the room. "I swear, sometimes I think she does that on purpose."

Davenport pulled earbuds out of her ears and glanced up, offering a smile. "Agent Parker," she said, "nice to see you up and around."

"Yeah, well, they forgot to lock the zipper on the body bag," I joked.

She laughed politely, but I was certain that I could hear aggravation in Ridley's lengthy exhale. Obviously, there must be something wrong with the men that the federal government employs; none of them seemed to understand my sense of humor.

She crossed the room and motioned that we join her at a table. Flipping on the backlight and computer projector, she took a step back and waited for Ridley to take over the presentation. He slipped on a pair of gloves and picked up a metal probe to use as a pointer.

"You are aware that you aren't allowed to work your own case, Parker," Ridley chastised. "However, Jablonsky believes that seeing what happened and hearing a few theories might jog your memory and give us a viable lead. Since this isn't an exact science and we normally don't get to hear an account from the actual victim, this ought to be a learning experience for all of us."

"Just pretend I'm a guinea pig," I said.

"Based on injuries sustained and the pattern of damage," he flipped my jacket over, and I was shocked to see the degree of damage to the leather, "there was an intense impact, followed by a skid, and continued roll at a high velocity."

"Shit." I couldn't help but stare at the practically shredded patches of leather at the side and back.

"If you look at the overlay," Davenport added, flipping on the screen and placing photos of my injuries underneath a see-through photo of my jacket, "the road rash on your side and the deep laceration on your back correlate with the damage to your jacket. However," she added another image while Ridley opened an evidence bag and removed my shirt, "the rest of your clothing is fairly intact, with the exception of a rip on your jeans."

"Which matches up with the bruise on your knee," Ridley said.

"Does that mean anything?" I asked, putting on gloves and rotating my jacket on the table so I could watch the way the deep gashes and scratches in the leather traveled in a fairly continuous circular path.

"The cuts on your lower stomach and back were likely

due to the lack of protective cover surrounding them," Ridley said. He removed my jeans from the evidence bag and stared at the frayed hem at the waistline. "We know for certain that you rolled. There are multiple points of impact — your right knee, your left side, and your right arm. But there are no paint flecks or metal chips which would be indicative of being hit by a vehicle, and the lack of defensive wounds would indicate that you didn't attempt to brace yourself. The trace evidence we found at the site of your injuries is typical of contact with asphalt."

"Meaning?" I asked, growing increasingly more panicked as the presentation continued.

"You were traveling at a high speed and came into contact with the pavement. The initial point of impact occurred on your right side, causing the bruising and sprain to your knee and arm." He focused on my cast. "Did the hospital tell you about spider fractures?"

"They said I have a sprain." I swallowed. "You're supposed to make my day better, not worse."

"In your case, they aren't a big deal," Davenport said. "They're minor. They might have been missed." She opened a file and took out a film, placing it on the lighted portion of the table. "See this depressed area here and these faint lines that look almost like pencil marks?"

"Yeah."

"The lines could be microfractures running from your wrist to your elbow." She shrugged. "Or it could be a shadow or something on the film. They're really not a big deal, but if they are spider fractures, then you hit hard. Not hard enough to sever the bone but pretty damn hard nonetheless."

"The momentum probably made you skip off the ground, like a stone on the water, and you hit again on your left side, this time slower, so the force dragged you until the revolutions began," Ridley concluded. "We see this frequently with motorcycle accidents. Were you on a motorcycle?"

"No." I bit my lip, staring at my jacket and feeling like a stranger in my own skin. "What else could account for it?"

"Extreme sports," Davenport suggested.

"I wasn't wearing skateboarding gear," I snapped.

"Maybe a fall, but angle and trajectory would be difficult, unless it was a sharp incline," Ridley suggested.

"Any sharp inclines near where I was found?"

The techs had pissed me off, and a part of me wanted to walk out of the room and find somewhere safe to hide. It wasn't rational, but Lucca's insistence that I had unknowingly done this to myself while stuck in some fugue state scared the crap out of me. The more I heard, the more confused I became.

"The ramps in the parking garage don't have the necessary slope needed to obtain the velocity at which you must have been traveling. However, a tumble down the staircase might provide the proper angle, but because it isn't a solid line, there would be obvious breaks in the gouges." Ridley pointed to my jacket. "And there aren't." He looked up. "We're baffled, but this isn't even the worst part."

"What is?" I reluctantly asked.

"Underneath your damaged fingernails, we found wood pieces," Ridley said.

"I know. Lucca told me."

"They had to come from finished furniture. We've traced the type of wood and varnish used. It's a match to a popular type of commercially sold tables and chairs."

"So?" I asked.

"It had to come from inside. The wood was pristine. There were no signs of weathering or damage by the elements. But the glass, pebbles, tar, and oil that you were covered in are indicative of any city street. The evidence is contradictory."

"Not if whatever happened began indoors," Jablonsky said from the doorway.

"Tell me you have a lead," I practically begged, hating the pathetic tone in my own voice that earned sympathetic looks from Davenport and Ridley.

"Not yet," Mark said. "We'll get there."

"Did you find anything else on any of my other belongings?" I asked. "Are you finished analyzing my credentials and gun?"

"We recovered your wallet," Davenport said. "You can have that back. It was of no use." She held it out and waited for me to look through it. "Is anything missing? If this was a mugging..."

"Not a mugging. No one took my debit card or credit card. They must have realized what my limit was." Everything else was inside. "What about my gear?"

"What gear?" Ridley asked.

"My nine millimeter, my government ID and badge, and my handcuffs." Closing my eyes, I tried to recall if I had a purse with me, but since my phone had been in my pocket and they had my wallet, I wouldn't have been carrying a handbag. My purse was probably in the trunk of my car.

"We didn't find any of those at our crime scene," Davenport said. She picked up the hospital manifest to make sure they hadn't been cataloged by the ambulance driver or someone on staff. "Nothing was found. Are you sure you had them with you?"

I looked at Mark. "Things just got a lot worse."

SIX

"Notification has been made," Mark said. "If someone tries to impersonate a federal agent, we'll hear about it."

"Maybe," I replied, "but most people aren't going to question an authority figure, and even less are likely to take the time to look at the photo ID. They see a badge, and that's about it."

"At least we have a possible motive," Lucca said.

"Yeah, someone attacked me just to steal my gun and ID in order to perpetrate a murder." I squeezed the bridge of my nose, wincing when it pulled at the scab on my forehead. "Why didn't they kill me?"

"Count your blessings," Jablonsky replied.

Lucca's brow furrowed. "It doesn't make sense. Parker tried to kick my ass the other morning just because I startled her. She wouldn't let some asshole take her shit and walk away. She'd have defensive wounds."

Jablonsky cocked his head to the side. "Or the asshole would be in the hospital." He sighed. "Maybe an opportunistic vulture took them after she was out cold."

"In that case, why didn't he take my wallet and phone?" I asked.

"Phone's traceable," Lucca said, "but he would have

taken your wallet. And why the cuffs? They're not of any real value."

"Unless you want to dress up like a LEO or you're into bondage," I said. "Maybe it's not about committing a murder. Maybe it's about dressing up to play the part." I glanced at the recent cases I'd been working. "It's possible whoever did this wanted access to this building or someplace only an agent could go."

"Perhaps," Lucca didn't look convinced, "but how did they knock you out without a fight." He flipped through my medical file. "You weren't tasered or drugged. Although, you must have been pretty damn smashed the night before since you were barely under the legal limit when the hospital ran the tox screen. Is it possible you left your crap at a bar and this is a total misunderstanding?"

"How incompetent do you think I am?"

"Is that on a scale of one to ten?" he retorted, and Jablonsky cleared his throat before my so-called partner and I came to blows.

"Lucca, go canvas the bars in the vicinity and see if anyone remembers seeing Alex there on the night in question," Jablonsky ordered. Lucca nodded, relieved to abandon the threat assessment for now. Once Lucca walked away, Mark turned to me. "Unofficially, have you been drinking on the job?"

"No." My answer came quickly. It wasn't even something I had to think about. I was professional, and being even slightly impaired wasn't safe.

"I didn't think so," he mumbled, scratching at the scruff on his upper lip. He looked across the room at a few of the agents that didn't seem to be working hard enough. "Henderson, Thatcher, you're going on a treasure hunt. Check out the parking structure where Parker was found and everything in the nearby vicinity. Make sure our crime scene guys didn't miss anything."

As if people around here didn't hate me already, now they had more work to do because of me. Sighing, I slumped into a chair and flipped through the information on my phone. None of the numbers or messages were from an unknown source. Today was supposed to lead to answers, not more questions.

"It's a bust," I said, focusing on Mark who appeared to be deep in thought. "I'm of absolutely no use. I still don't remember anything. I'm fairly certain I didn't join a motorcycle gang or wipeout while practicing for the X-games. Nothing here has jogged any memories. Lucca's right. If this had been an attack, there should be obvious signs of a struggle. At the very least, my knuckles should be bruised."

"You could have been jumped. It happens, even to the best of us. Maybe that one blow to the head was all it took." He frowned at the toxicology report. "Our timeline could be wrong. Just because the last thing you remember was around seven p.m., that doesn't mean that you were attacked right after."

"Then I really could have been anywhere, doing anything." Exhaling, I stood up. "What if this was caused by some kind of mental issue?"

"No," Mark shook his head, "you don't get to pretend that you're Brad Pitt. I have that problem with half the men here."

"Fine, I'll be Ed Norton, the one that shot himself in the head in order to kill off the other personality."

"Parker," Mark growled, "this isn't *Fight Club*. There's another explanation. We just haven't found it yet."

"You're the one that made the reference in the first place." I pressed my lips together, but nothing useful surfaced. "What do you think happened?" He shrugged, but I didn't buy the clueless act. "What did you have to speak to the Director about?"

"Something unrelated." He glared at me. "Leave it alone, Alex."

"Leave what alone?"

"Everything else." He stood up and led me to the door. "You're on medical leave. You have to go for a follow-up consultation before you'll even be cleared to sit behind a desk again. You know that, so why are you poking around in other cases? It was a courtesy that I asked you to come in today." He glanced around the room, finding most of the agents out on assignment. "Give me a few minutes, and I'll have your protection detail take you home."

"It wasn't a courtesy," I argued. "Unfortunately, now we have even more to worry about than we did before." Refusing to leave, I stood in the doorway. "How much of an ass-chewing will I get for losing my gun and ID?"

"It depends on the circumstances. It depends on when and if they're recovered."

"That's a lot of uncertainty. It goes great with everything else." The jaded bitterness was in my voice, and I had the undeniable urge to hit something. "I don't even know what happened. How the hell should I know if I'm even to blame?"

Leaving Mark's office, I returned to my desk, opened the drawer, and took out my car keys. Due to the possible concussion, I probably wasn't cleared to drive, and since I had a protection detail, leaving wouldn't be wise or much of an option. Instead, I figured I'd go to the garage and search my car. Maybe there'd be something inside that would indicate what I planned on doing or who I was meeting.

The elevator ride was brief, giving me a few moments of privacy to think. The only conclusion I reached was that I was angry. This shouldn't be happening. Who the hell loses fourteen hours of her life? Granted, I should be thankful, and truthfully, I was. I was lucky, blessed even. I woke up with fairly minor injuries, no missing kidneys or sexual assault to report. Hell, I woke up with almost all of my faculties in working order. So I had a fourteen hour blank spot in my memory. So what? At least I hadn't suffered any lasting damage. Resolved to look on the bright side of things for once, I went to my car and unlocked the door.

Taking a seat behind the wheel, I checked the cup holder, the center console, and the glove box. There was nothing unusual or indicative of my evening plans. I did a quick check underneath the car seats, and then I searched the back. My subcompact didn't exactly have much of a back seat, and with the exception of my gym bag and towel, it was empty. Hitting my injured side against the car door on my way out, I swore.

Shaking it off, I moved on to the trunk. Mark had taken

my go-bag out of the trunk and brought it to the hospital, but my purse, which I kept in case I made plans after work, was normally in the car. After all, a girl needs a place to keep her handgun when she's out with friends.

The lid lifted, and a sudden uneasiness returned to my chest. My breath caught, and I had trouble swallowing. Nothing sinister lay inside, but my mind didn't agree. The trunk contained my purse, an emergency first-aid kit, and a few other emergency items. A flash shot through my mind of a bloody mass wrapped in plastic. I backed away from my car. My lower back slammed into one of the waist-high, yellow, metal posts near the no-parking area, and a scream escaped my lips. I don't know if it was the utter fear or the pain that caused it, but I found myself crumpled on the ground, gasping.

Time passed, but I wasn't sure how much. It could have been seconds or hours that I remained paralyzed in physical and mental agony. Flashes of a vehicle, blood, and a body went through my mind like rapid-fire. I couldn't discern what was happening or what I was remembering. My side hurt, bringing me back to reality. Physical pain focused my attention, and I remained still, assessing the damage.

"Parker?" Lucca called from across the lot. "Alex?" He sprinted to me with Agent Steve Cooper by his side. "What happened?"

I shook my head, trembling. Words escaped me, and Cooper took my pulse. Lucca went to get help, and Cooper scanned the vicinity for signs of danger. His eyes narrowed in on the growing bloodstain on the side of my t-shirt. Carefully, he lifted my shirt, seeing that I had reopened several lacerations.

"You're pretty banged up," Cooper said. "Did someone do this to you?"

"I walked into the pole," I said, finding my voice. "I hit my side and back. It hurts like a son-of-a-bitch."

Cooper gave me a look. We had worked a case together a little over a year ago when I was nothing more than a lowly private investigator that had been accused of murder. He had been leading the task force that was investigating police corruption and had gotten stuck with me. Cooper was fairly by the book, but he was a stand-up guy that had saved my life once before. I trusted him. I knew he'd never let anything happen to me.

"How bad?" he asked. "Should I call for an ambulance?"

"I'll be fine. It's nothing." I was embarrassed and shaky. Moving to stand up, I pulled myself off the ground using the same damn pole that had reduced me to a whimpering pile of pain.

"It doesn't seem like nothing." He opened my car door and stepped back. "Take a seat." I sat in the car, feeling increasingly stupid as the minutes passed. "Lucca told me what happened, how they found you." He stared into my eyes. "I'm sorry."

I shrugged. "I'm fine, mostly."

"Do you have any idea who might have done it?" he asked, but I shook my head. "What about Vito?"

"The mafia don that threatened to kill me if I returned to the OIO and ratted on him? Nah, the thought never crossed my mind."

"Parker," Cooper said, annoyed by my sarcastic attitude. He must have forgotten that was a cornerstone of my personality. "Are you sure it wasn't him?"

"I'm not sure about anything. I didn't rat on him. I'm not investigating him. I never went back on my word, so he shouldn't have a beef with me." I looked at the elevator, wondering when Lucca would be returning.

"You came back to the OIO."

"Yeah, well, maybe he doesn't know about that." I focused my attention on removing the bandage at my side. "Plus, he wouldn't leave me alive. If it was him, I'd be dead." Pulling the useless piece of gauze free, I said, "Grab that first-aid kit from the trunk, will ya?"

"Sure." Cooper pulled the box out of my trunk and knelt in front of me, but before I could patch myself up, Lucca returned with a medic.

The medic gave me the quick once-over, but I insisted I was fine. The only thing that hurt worse than my bleeding injuries was my ego. The flashes of memory, or whatever the hell it was, had taken a toll, leaving me drained.

"Another panic attack?" Lucca asked.

"It wasn't," I snapped.

"Whatever you say," Lucca replied. "Are you all right?"

"I don't know, okay?" I gave Cooper an uncertain look, afraid he would mention my ties to Antonio 'Vito' Vincenzo in front of Lucca, or even worse, maybe he'd believe Lucca's nonsense that I was mentally unstable and out me to Jablonsky or the higher powers which would result in more psychological evaluations, mandated therapy, and some other form of torment that should have been banned by the Geneva Convention. "It didn't feel like a panic attack. It felt like a sharp jabbing pain in my side and back."

"Then why the hell were you shaking like a leaf?" Lucca challenged. "Did you remember something?"

"Maybe, but it's hard to say for certain. It was more like a memory of fear, muffled echoes of what happened."

"What does that mean?" Lucca asked.

I shrugged. "Forget it."

"Hey, we're here for you," Cooper said. He gave my shoulder a squeeze. "Aren't you on medical leave? Maybe you just need more time to rest and recuperate."

"Sure," I replied.

"Seriously, Parker, if you need anything, just holler. And I mean anything." Cooper gave me a nod and headed for the elevator.

After he left, Lucca offered me a hand up. "I can't leave you alone for an hour without something happening. Honestly, this is getting ridiculous. What were you doing in the garage?"

"Looking for clues. We are investigators. I was investigating."

"Did you find anything helpful? You said you had flashes or something."

"It's hard to explain. It's just a mess of images and feelings." I shut my car door and removed my purse from the trunk before closing the lid. Nothing was inside except the usual items I carried. "How'd your outing go?"

"I came up empty. No one remembers you, and your credentials and gun weren't recovered. We're right where we started."

"Great," I said, unenthused. "For once, I'm actually ready to throw in the towel."

"We're not supposed to make cases personal," Lucca admonished.

"This isn't just a case. It's my life."

"Yeah, which is why you aren't actually allowed to do any investigating. You can answer questions and assist the actual investigators, but that's about it."

"Why do you always have to be so damn by the book, boy scout?"

"I'm not," he tossed a conspiratorial smirk my way and pushed the button for the elevator, "but someone has to do something to keep you in line. Now let's get you home and out of everyone's hair. I have a threat assessment to complete, unless you want to have twenty-four hour bodyguards at your front door at all times. In which case, your boyfriend could probably afford to hire an entire army to protect you, and the two agents guarding you can get back to doing some real work."

"Ha. Ha." I glared at him, knowing that Lucca would make my relationship with Martin another point of contention between us. "The best thing about medical leave is that I won't have to see you every day."

"You will if you want updates on the case," Lucca retorted, enjoying the ribbing.

"Dammit, I really can't catch a break, can I?"

SEVEN

Closing my eyes, I took a deep breath and tried to force my mind to cooperate. I was safe at home. Nothing could hurt me, and there weren't any sharp objects nearby that could randomly decide to attack without provocation, like my car door or that stupid no-parking pole. Why the hell did they even have those in the first place? Was someone really stupid enough to park directly in front of the elevator and block it? Probably. Shaking my head, I berated myself for letting my mind wander into another completely unproductive series of thoughts.

"Focus, Parker," I growled. I shut my eyes again, thinking about the irrational responses I'd had since waking up that horrible morning. I'd reacted badly to being strapped down and being crowded by other human beings, but that was typical. Moving on, I thought about my dream, the car ride to the OIO building, and the brief glimpses of memory that I had upon opening my trunk.

Reaching for the pad of paper, I jotted everything down that might have been a memory. Then I made a second column of the facts that I knew for certain. My credentials, gun, and handcuffs were missing. I had sustained numerous injuries which weren't considered the result of a fight, and my blood-alcohol content had been relatively high, especially since I hadn't been imbibing, at least not that I could remember. The fact was, at some point after my conversation with Martin but before waking up outside, alcohol had entered my system.

Glancing down at my casted arm, I looked at my bandaged fingers. Wood shards had been discovered underneath my fingernails. I must have been inside a bar or restaurant, probably drinking, but how did I end up with splinters like that? Maybe it was modern day torture. Instead of bamboo shoots, I had been subjected to table pieces. No, it didn't make sense. If I'd been subjected to torture, there would be defensive wounds, marks from being bound, or something blatantly obvious.

I looked at my left hand, turning it over to examine my palm and fingertips, but there were no marks. I checked the back, and aside from a slight scrape near my wrist, there was nothing remarkable about it. The other scars on my wrist were old, and no fresh marks or bruises indicated I'd been bound.

What about my alleged meeting with a police informant? I wrote that on my sheet of paper with a large question mark. Who was I meeting? Why was I meeting them? What was it in regards to? No one at the OIO had any idea about this, or if they did, they didn't share that information with me. I hated to think that the people I worked with were intentionally keeping me in the dark, but the little voice inside my head was having issues trusting them completely. These days, I was having trouble trusting just about everyone, including myself.

Picking up the phone, I dialed Detective Nick O'Connell of the major crimes division. Whenever I needed a favor, he was my go-to guy. The fact that he was a first grade detective who was willing to tolerate my pestering didn't hurt matters either. He and his wife, Jen, had become my close friends, and on more than one occasion, I'd confided in him with information that was probably considered privileged. Needless to say, if anyone knew why I was bugging one of the PD's confidential informants, it'd be

Nick.

"Hey, stranger," O'Connell greeted, "don't tell me it's been a month already since our last double-date night. I can't take another jazz club."

"Neither can I," I replied. "So I take it we haven't spoken recently?" Sighing, I should have realized that, but I hoped I'd phoned from my landline or Martin's house. Damn, so much for my wishful thinking.

"No," O'Connell said hesitantly, "did I miss a text or something?"

"No."

"Okay, Parker, what the hell is going on now?"

"I wish I knew." After giving him the abbreviated version of the last few days, I asked, "Have you heard anything about some fed making a request to speak to a police informant?"

"I'll ask around, but I haven't heard anything. If it had to do with major crimes or homicide, I'd know."

"Of course, you would. You'd be the person I asked for the favor," I retorted.

"Well, that narrows it down to a different department, unless you were busting balls at a different precinct. Are you sure the informant is in our jurisdiction?"

"I don't know anything at the moment."

"I'll pass word to the LT. Moretti likes you for some unknown reason. He can ask around. He knows people."

"Thanks, Nick."

"I'll add it to your tab," he teased before disconnecting.

I was almost out of ideas. I turned on my computer and scanned through my recent files. Then I checked my search history. Most of the data dealt with the alleged terrorist cell that I'd been tracking. The group, roughly translated to Shade, functioned out of the Balkans. We had it on good authority that their funding came from the sale of counterfeit goods. While seemingly innocuous, that type of funding often promoted child labor and possibly human trafficking.

Once they had the money, it wasn't uncommon for terrorist cells to purchase military-grade weaponry. Shade hadn't claimed credit for any terrorist attacks or plots yet, but intel suggested that they had ties to other more vocal organizations. The OIO, along with a few other intelligence gathering organizations, were monitoring Shade's activities in the hopes of stopping them before they turned violent. So far, they'd done nothing more than rattle some sabers, but something about their recent behavior had worried me.

My computer contained maps and satellite images of the area they occupied. The OIO had received intel and additional images that showed movement and shipments of some type. The last thing I remembered about the case was checking into overseas shipments that were destined for the United States. Cargo containers often carried contraband and, far too frequently, human cargo.

The ten men thought to be in charge of the terrorist cell had been flagged. That must have been what my passport question for Jablonsky was about. Rubbing my eyes, I jotted down a reminder to ask about that and to pass this intel on to Lucca. He had been assisting on analyzing Shade's movement and terrorist leanings, and since I was in dispose, Lucca should have been made primary on the case.

Other than monitoring Shade's activity and dealing with quite a few other open cases, I was a key witness in the DeAngelo Bard trial. He was the leader of a local gang that I had infiltrated with the help of Detective Derek Heathcliff, another one of my close cop buddies. My computer contained a few files on that case, personal information about Bard and his lieutenants, and my notes and reports. The prosecutor had copies of everything, and I knew Bard was no longer in a position to seek revenge. After his arrest, the gang crumbled. He didn't have the power to make a play against me.

The rest of the information on my computer proved useless, and I reconsidered the possibility that Agent Cooper might be correct. What if Vito realized I was a federal agent again? Would that be enough of an incentive to take a hit out on me? I knew the answer to that question, but Vito was aware that doing anything to me would result in his own destruction. The evidence I had against him would be released, and even if it might not be enough for a conviction, a note from a dead federal agent along with a lot of circumstantial evidence and corroborating accounts would surely bury him eventually. Plus, like I told Cooper, if Vito wanted me dead, I would be. Sure, the mafia boss might have contracted a hit. That would explain my lost credentials and gun, which could serve as verification of the kill, but I wasn't dead. And again, I returned to the lack of defensive wounds.

Tapping my fingers against the desk, I circled back through the possibilities. But aside from the normal amount of enemies a person in my line of work makes, I didn't think that whatever happened was the result of an intended attack, which meant Lucca might be right. This could be an accident.

Playing devil's advocate with myself, I considered a different set of facts. My boyfriend was being sued by his ex-fiancée, and his sexual history and our relationship would be fodder for her attorneys. It was conceivable that a lesser woman might have gotten pissed off and then piss drunk in order to cope with that situation. It was also possible that said woman could have lied about having a work meeting just to have another excuse to stay out late, leave early, or otherwise conceal the fact that she had moved out because she couldn't stomach staying alone in a place where she'd gunned down two assassins and nearly lost the love of her life. Wow, I was a cross between insane and a telenovela. It was no wonder Lucca thought I was unstable; I was beginning to think it was possible.

The light bulb flicked on at my epiphany. If this were any other case, we'd figure out where our amnesiac-like victim had been based on credit card activity. Logging in to my account, I checked, but my last purchase had been at a coffee cart near the prosecutor's office. Dinner at the OIO had been paid in cash. I checked my wallet, knowing that I normally didn't carry more than fifty dollars at a time, and I had almost thirty left. There's no way I could afford to drink to excess. Sure, men often offered to buy me drinks. It was a perk of being female, but I was positive that didn't happen. I wouldn't have let it, regardless of how pissed off I might have been.

Something else about the situation was bothersome, and the familiar twinge circulated through my brain. A CI would want payment for intel. That usually required a hefty cash exchange or paperwork to be filed. I hadn't filed any such documentation with the OIO which meant someone else was footing the bill for the intel.

I dialed O'Connell again, asking if there was a way to see who had filed paperwork on paying CIs. That was a sensitive matter, and one that he doubted he could look into. But he promised to try. That would mean that the cop was with me when we met the confidential informant. I wouldn't have been alone. Perhaps, I had been unexpectedly attacked by the CI or someone else. It would explain the lack of defensive wounds. Hell, it might even explain the drinking to a certain extent, if I needed to sell myself as a civilian. I needed to find the cop. He or she would have the answers.

"Lucca," I said when he answered, "check through the call logs for any PD numbers. I don't think I was alone that night."

"Who were you with?"

"I don't know." Talking to him could be exasperating. "I'm guessing one of our city's finest."

"Don't you have friends over there that can help?" I could hear the snotty tone in his voice, as if being a federal agent automatically meant we were too good to fraternize with the local police.

"I do, but I'm asking you to help. Didn't you mention some crap about being my partner?"

"Sure, when you want something, then I'm your partner."

"Good, you've finally figured out how this works." I sighed. "I have additional information on Shade."

"I'll swing by after work, and you can brief me then, okay?"

"Yep. Can you pass me off to Jablonsky? I need to ask him something?"

"Hang on."

After transferring the call from his desk phone to Jablonsky's office, I waited for the ringing to stop. Mark wasn't one to sit behind a desk all day, but he'd return eventually. Half a second before the voicemail kicked on, he picked up the phone.

"I've been meaning to ask if we ever discussed passport codes in relation to Shade. The men involved have been flagged, but what code are we using? Are they on the watchlist, or do we simply have a warning attached to their names?"

"Parker, you are on sick leave," Mark reminded me, ignoring the question. "That doesn't mean you go home and work on a case."

"This wasn't a case. It's analysis, and I'm not working on it. I happened upon it while searching through my data for what happened to me."

"They have an alert attached to their identities," he replied. "Notifications will be sent if they attempt to travel, and they'll be stopped and questioned. Their bags will be searched."

"What if they travel under an alias or ship their contraband through an intermediary? Do we have a way of monitoring that?"

"Talk me through what you've found," Mark said, giving up on admonishing my behavior.

"They were moving cargo in and out. Large containers. It could be for cargo ships or freight. I don't know if or when they moved it, but the images we received from various other agencies indicate that something big was either shipped in or is getting shipped out. We need to get someone on it."

"You think that the cell members will be at the exchange?" Mark paused, considering my words. "Or were at the exchange?"

"I'm not even sure it is an exchange. They could have taken delivery of something heinous in order to enact some insidious plan. The intel we have doesn't say much, but there was a lot of suspicious activity."

"Did you mention this to Lucca?"

"Yeah, he's stopping by later to discuss it. The last thing I remember from work that night was wanting to ask you about passports, so it must have been in relation to this."

"I'm on it. Now get some rest. I heard about your episode in the parking garage. You need to take better care of yourself."

"I'm clumsy. There's not much I can do about it." I disconnected before he could ask me anything else.

Out of ideas and tired of feeling this frustrated, I sunk onto the couch and turned on the television. There was too much to think about and not enough facts for any of it to make sense. This must be what it felt like to be completely impotent, and I hated it.

EIGHT

The knock at my door roused me from my catnap, and I wondered why the protection detail would even allow someone to knock at the door. Did something happen to them? Just as I was lifting my recently reacquired back-up from the end table, Lucca announced his presence.

"You shouldn't bother to knock unless you're Ed McMahon," I said, tucking the gun into the waistband at the small of my back. "If you aren't here to give me millions of dollars, let yourself in or go away." I opened the door to see Lucca holding a grocery bag. "Great, you brought cash. Let's not report this to the IRS."

Davis, one of the agents assigned to my detail, snickered, and Lucca gave him a dirty look. "Don't encourage her," Lucca said, pushing past me and into my apartment.

I nodded to the two men, who appeared to have been bribed with fast food in order to allow Lucca to enter my home, and shut the door. My "partner" placed a covered casserole dish on my kitchen table and rummaged through the cabinets for plates. Raising a questioning eyebrow, I remained motionless to see exactly what he was planning on doing.

"My wife made this," Lucca said, noticing my stare. "I

told her you were out of commission, and she sent food. The least you can do is grab some flatware so we can get this over with."

Obediently, I picked up a couple of forks, a knife, and a serving spoon, belatedly wondering why I was following Lucca's orders. I sat at my table, and he placed a plate in front of me that he found in my far left cabinet. Then he took a seat across from me and scooped out a large portion of something that faintly resembled lasagna and plopped it onto his plate.

"She's on this vegetarian kick lately," Lucca said. He held the spoon in my direction. "But it's not half bad. I figured you might appreciate a home cooked meal after everything."

"Sure," I stared at him, feeling as if I missed half the conversation. Maybe my condition had deteriorated further, and my short-term memory was worse than before. "Tell her thanks."

I searched my mind for his wife's name, but I didn't possess the knowledge. Thankfully, he didn't offer it, and I was glad that he remembered my rule about keeping his private life private. The fact that I knew he had a wife and a young daughter at home caused enough apprehension for me every time we ended up in a dicey situation. I'd lost my last partner, and I swore I'd never lose another. That's why this new dynamic of considering Lucca to be my partner was so difficult.

"Parker," Lucca said, waving his fork in front of my face, "I didn't just come here to eat dinner with you. You said you wanted to share intel on Shade. Let's make this a working dinner so I can get home at a decent hour."

After briefing him on my suspicions and theories, he made some notes, took the few copied files I had in my possession off my desk, and returned to the table. We ate in silence for a few minutes, but my mind kept drifting back to the questions from earlier.

"Have you finished the threat assessment?" I asked.

He nodded, wolfing down the last few bites from his plate. "Jablonsky has my report. He'll make a decision in the morning concerning your protection detail."

"Do you have any leads?"

"No, as far as we can tell, whatever happened wasn't planned or orchestrated, and since no other threats or attempts have been made since the initial incident, it was either an accident or a random act of violence. I've recommended that the protection detail be reassigned."

Taking a breath, I nodded. Frankly, I didn't like having babysitters, but if I had done this to myself, like Lucca thought, I wanted them outside to stop me from doing something else. "What about identifying the police officer or his confidential informant?"

He gave me a look. "Are you sure James didn't mishear what you said?"

"James?"

"James Martin, your boyfriend," Lucca rolled his eyes, "he's the one that said you were meeting a confidential informant. Is he positive? Because there are no indications that was your intent. You never mentioned it to me. There's no note or file that tracks. No communications. Nothing." His expression softened. "Maybe you just told him that because you had other plans."

I thought about it, knowing that I hardly ever mentioned what I was doing to Martin. On the rare occasions that I did tell him, there was always a reason. Nine times out of ten, it was because I was nervous. But if I was going somewhere dangerous, why wouldn't I have told Lucca or Jablonsky? My eyes traveled to the Tupperware on my table, and I knew why I would have excluded Lucca. And of course, there were plenty of reasons not to tell the boss something, specifically in situations where he was likely to stop me from doing whatever I had planned. In that brief moment of clarity, I knew that I expected to run into trouble that night, and apparently, I did.

"I want to revisit the crime scene," I declared, pushing away from the table.

"It's not a crime scene. We aren't sure a crime ever took place."

"Eddie," I pleaded, "just take me there. You don't have to stay. I just want to see what's nearby. Maybe it'll jog my memory."

"Fine," he packed up the Tupperware and the files and went to the door, "but if Jablonsky has an issue with this, I'm telling him that you said he gave his approval."

"Deal." I smiled. "I like this bad boy persona. It's a hell of an improvement on Mr. Rulebook."

"Why must you break my balls when I'm doing you a solid?" he asked. "Didn't anyone ever tell you not to bite the hand that feeds you?"

"I don't bite. Much."

*   *   *

I stood, staring at the parking garage. It had several levels, two main entrances, and several exits, but it was just a garage. There wasn't anything special about it. Turning around, I surveyed the area. There weren't any bars or restaurants nearby. The closest liquor store was a few blocks away. I wouldn't have come here to drink. Hell, I wouldn't have come here at all.

"You've seen it. Now can we go?" Lucca asked. He'd been impatient since the moment we arrived.

"I'm missing something."

"Parker, it's dark out. What the hell do you expect to see?"

I put my hand up to silence him. Annoyed at the sight of the cast, I let out a growl and brushed the hair out of my face. Choosing a direction at random, I moved down the block, toward the side of the garage. It was unfamiliar, and I hesitated briefly before turning the corner.

Lucca jogged to catch up. "Alex, stop."

"I said you didn't have to hang around. I'm capable of getting myself home, and in the event something goes wrong, well, at least you'll know where to look in the morning."

"Dammit."

He fell into step beside me, silently observing as I marched past the east side of the building and turned again. I came to another cross street at the south side, and for the briefest moment, I felt it. I'd been here before. Halting our procession, I remained motionless, scanning our surroundings in an attempt to recall something tangible. This was a less trafficked street, and as such, there were fewer lights. I remembered tripping over a chain.

"Where did you find me?" I asked.

"Near the western exit," Lucca said.

Without another word, I sprinted toward the opening, stopping at the heavy metal chain that acted as a barrier to prohibit vehicles from entering and exiting. "I was here." I pointed at the chain, resisting the urge to touch it. "I flipped myself over it, I think." It was thigh-high to discourage individuals from ducking underneath it or stepping over it.

Ducking down, I gritted my teeth, feeling every ache and pain in my body while I slid beneath it. Lucca remained on the other side, watching with something akin to horror as I stood up and surveyed the interior of the dark garage. A flash of the cement floor entered my mind, and I remembered scrambling across the floor, hearing my shoes squeak and my feet slide. I teetered slightly, and Lucca slipped under the chain to join me.

"Easy," he said, grabbing my good elbow to steady me. "What do you remember?"

"Scrambling to get out."

"If you wanted out, why did you enter?"

"I don't know." It wasn't making sense. Lucca released my arm, and I took a few steps forward. "I found my way out." Continuing on the path I had probably taken a few nights ago, I moved through the garage, noticing a scattering of cars that became more abundant the closer we came to the actual entrance. Instead of continuing that way, I detoured to a small side exit that was next to the elevator and stopped. "The phone."

On the wall was an emergency phone. The city had installed several, along with cameras, to make neighborhoods safer. The glowing blue light near the phone was an easy indicator, but the phone itself was useless. The cord had been cut, and the glass surrounding the CCTV camera was covered in graffiti.

"Not surprising," Lucca said, but I continued to stare at

it. "Why would you have needed a phone? You had your phone on you. I called you that morning. It's how we found you."

"Did we dust it for prints?" I asked.

"No."

"Make the call."

"Parker," he took a moment to regain his patience, "we know you were here. There must be dozens of prints on that thing. What do you hope to find?" Silently, I continued to stare at him until he removed his phone and asked that our techs make a trip to reexamine part of a potential crime scene. "Happy?"

"Not particularly." Continuing out the exit, I stopped so abruptly, Lucca walked into my back. "Shit," I cursed, "first the damn pole, now you. I thought I'd be safe without inanimate objects around. Apparently, I was wrong."

"Sorry." He took a step to the side. "What are you looking at?"

"Police lights."

"So?" He raised an eyebrow. "There's a precinct a few blocks away. Police cars must come and go at all hours."

I watched the police car pull out of the rear lot and onto the street. It didn't mean anything, but in my mind, it was a beacon. Shaking off the wayward thought, unable to articulate any of this without sounding like a raving lunatic, I asked Lucca to show me where I was found.

Leading the way, we moved farther from the garage exit, and within a few steps, I tripped over the curb, barely righting myself before I went down for the count. Lucca shook his head, removing his keychain that contained a small flashlight. He flipped it on and pointed at a spot a few yards away.

"That's where you were," he declared. "Are we done?"

I walked a few more steps and studied my surroundings. The western side of the lot had limited street access. It was fairly isolated since it was located at the rear of most of the neighboring buildings. It made sense why no one found me. I would have been obstructed by view due to the curb and the retaining wall. At least I'd chosen an out of the way place to pass out. Thankfully, no one found me. That thought reverberated in my skull, and my pulse raced.

"Yeah, we're done," I said, wanting to get as far away from here as possible. It wasn't rational, but I wanted to be back home with the lights on, cozy and safe.

"Great," he said sarcastically, "this was exactly what I meant when I said I wanted to get home at a decent hour."

"Lucca," I began.

"What?" he snapped. "What do you want now?"

"Thanks."

He looked momentarily ashamed, and then he nodded, leading the way around the building and back to where he parked in front of the lot. Once we were on our way back to my apartment, I felt better. The slight panic I felt when we exited the parking garage had abated, and I now had some idea of where to look for answers. Bringing up the search engine on my phone, I keyed in the address, zooming out until I found the nearest police precinct. It wasn't my normal stomping grounds, but it was the closest to the garage. And something told me that it had been the destination I had in mind.

"You tripped," Lucca said. "Do you think that you took a spill and knocked yourself out?"

"Wow, you give me a lot of credit."

"C'mon, Parker, I'm being serious. You were injured. You weren't thinking clearly. Maybe you were trying to get help and didn't quite make it."

"It's possible." I turned to face him. "Did the techs actually agree to print the phone?"

"Yeah, I left a message for Davenport. She'll get it in the morning." He glanced at me. "You remembered the south side of the garage. It'll make it easier to pinpoint where you were based on the direction you were traveling. I'm sure Jablonsky will send some agents to scout the area. It might not be a bad idea if you joined them."

I smiled. "You're starting to believe me."

"I always believed you," he shrugged, "but I'm open to the possibility that it could be an accident since you don't even know what happened." His eyes briefly shot to mine. "It appears that it's starting to come back. I bet you're relieved."

"I will be once everything is back to normal."
He laughed. "You've never been normal."

NINE

The commotion at my front door woke me, and I dragged myself out of bed. Five a.m. What the hell was going on now? Holding the gun in my left, I made it as far as my bedroom door before I recognized the voices coming from the hallway.

"Agent Davis, stand down," I ordered, holding my front door open. "He's not a threat."

"Ma'am," Davis said, not taking his eyes off Martin, "I'm not authorized to allow anyone entry into the apartment."

"We live together," I said, too tired to stand in the doorway and argue. "Call Jablonsky, wake his ass up, and ask for verification." I gave Martin a weak smile. Then I turned around and went back to the bedroom. "Idiots," I mumbled, annoyed by the intrusion.

Five minutes later, my front door closed, and Martin stepped into my bedroom. "Sorry to wake you."

"No, you're not."

He took off his jacket and tie and then searched my drawers until he found a t-shirt in his size. "Mark called earlier to tell me what happened today."

"Fink," I muttered, trying to force my eyes to stay open. "You weren't supposed to come back here."

"I missed my t-shirt," Martin said, changing out of his suit.

"That's mine."

"It used to be mine, but I let you keep it because I like the way it looks on you," he said, giving me a quick kiss. "I also like the way it looks off of you."

"You need to find some new material."

He climbed under the covers. "Are you okay?"

"I will be." Putting my head on his chest, I closed my eyes.

The next thing I knew, someone was banging against my bedroom door. Jumping up, I automatically reached for my weapon, but Martin put his hand on my arm. He brushed the hair out of my face and kissed me.

"Parker, it's time to rise and shine," Jablonsky bellowed from the other side of the door.

"He texted a half hour ago," Martin said, "but I didn't have the heart to wake you." Rubbing his eyes, he sighed deeply. "I guess this is my cue to leave."

"Parker," Jablonsky called, "I'm coming in. You better be decent." My bedroom door opened a crack, and he stepped into my room with one hand over his eyes. "The two of you better not be canoodling."

"How old are you?" I snapped, irritated by the rude wake-up.

Mark slowly removed his hand from his eyes, nodding briefly at Martin. "Get dressed, Parker. I want you on-site today. Lucca said you dragged him to the garage last night, and you remembered something. I want to see what else you might remember." Mark's eyes remained fixed on the back wall of my bedroom. "I'll be waiting in the living room."

"It feels like your dad just walked in on us making out," Martin joked, getting out of bed. "So you remembered something. That's good, right?"

"It wasn't much." Sighing, I went to the closet to find something to change into. "I have the vaguest memory of being inside a garage. It was the closest structure to where I was found, so it's not that impressive."

"It's something," Martin insisted. After shedding the

oversized t-shirt, I felt his hands on my back. "Alex, my god, the bruises weren't this bad yesterday." His fingers brushed against my sensitive skin, and I cringed. "I think you should get these looked at."

"I'm okay."

"I don't think you are."

"I'm fine. I backed into the car door and then a pole. It's nothing." I looked down at the bandage covering my ribs. "See, I'm not bleeding. That's a huge improvement since yesterday." I turned around to face him. "However, you look like shit. You need to go home and get some sleep. A shave and a shower wouldn't hurt either."

"I thought you liked a little scruff."

"Go home."

"Will you meet me there?"

"I'll do my best."

"Do more than that." He finished dressing, but the concerned look didn't leave his face. "I want to know you're okay."

"I am. Plus, I'll be with Mark. He won't let anything happen to me."

"He better not." Martin led the way out of my bedroom. "Jabber," he said, acknowledging Mark, "thanks."

"Sure," Jablonsky said. Once Martin left, he focused his attention on me. "Didn't I tell you to stay home and rest?"

"I was until you woke me up." Giving him an annoyed look, I went into the kitchen and opened the fridge. Finding nothing more than a leftover sandwich, I shut the door. The coffeepot didn't hold any appeal, and I wondered if the conk on the head had altered my personality. "So you get to buy breakfast."

"Fine."

After a short car ride, we arrived at a diner. I was halfway through my egg white omelet before I asked, "Did the techs find any fingerprints on the emergency phone?"

"Tons," Jablonsky said, "just not yours. And none that link to any of the names that Lucca had investigated. Someone did this, but without a motive or a threat, we're flying blind."

"Are you pulling the detail?"

Mark shrugged. "I want you to walk me through whatever you remember. Hopefully, it'll jog something. We'll take it from there." He assessed me for a few moments. "Alex, what do you think happened?"

"I don't know."

"But you're afraid."

It wasn't a question, so I diverted my attention to the rest of my breakfast. When we were finished, Mark paid the check and drove to the garage. He parked inside, and we stepped out of the vehicle. He scanned the area, but there wasn't much to see.

"Let's start where you were found and work backward, okay?" Mark asked.

We moved outside the garage to the place Lucca had pointed out the previous night. "Take note of the nearby precinct," I said, pointing in the direction I'd seen the police lights the night before. "Have we made any progress identifying the CI or his handler?"

"It'll take time, but Agent Cooper is checking into it."

"Well, according to Lucca, I was here. I don't remember how I got here." I turned around, heading back inside the garage and leading the way to the roped off exit on the south side of the building. "I remember tripping over the chain." I swallowed. "I was in a rush to get somewhere."

"Were you being pursued?"

"I don't know." I ducked underneath the chain and stood outside the garage. In daylight, everything looked more sanitized, including the surrounding neighborhood. "I'm not sure how I got to this spot."

"You must have been coming from that direction." He pointed toward the backs of the neighboring buildings. "If you came from the main drag, you would have entered the garage through one of the normal doors," he narrowed his eyes, searching for something, "unless you were observing someone else and wanted to sneak around." His gaze settled on me. "What the hell were you doing?"

"I wish I knew."

"From now on, you won't so much as scratch your ass without my permission. Is that clear?"

Grumbling, I took a few steps toward the nearest

alleyway. From what I could tell, it opened up on another street. "Do you have GPS and a map?" I asked. "I want to know where this leads."

He scrolled through the information and held out his phone. Glancing at the information, I hoped something would set off my internal buzzer, but it was just an alley that connected to another main road. Maybe I needed to see it for myself. Heading down the narrow path, I tried to remember if anything was familiar, but the surrounding brick walls and the smell of garbage and urine weren't unique. It was an alley, just like any other.

A third of the way through, the tight space widened slightly, and a few dumpsters pressed against the wall. Jablonsky stopped, opening one and glancing inside. While he was distracted, I continued on my way, noting the metal doors that cut the monotony of the brick wall. They were exit only, without exterior handles, but I had the vaguest memory of attempting to open a door.

"Parker," Jablonsky said, coming up from behind, "did you find something?"

"No."

"Me neither. Do you want to turn back?"

"Not yet." Continuing farther on our path, we were stopped by a tall, chain-link fence. A padlock secured the door in place, keeping pedestrians from using the alleyway as a thoroughfare. A dumpster stood on the other side, close enough to aid in vaulting over the high fence. Another flash shot through my mind. "I was here."

"Okay." Jablonsky radioed for a thorough search of the alleyway and surrounding areas. "With any luck, we'll determine where you were."

"I know I jumped the fence." I pointed to a piece of cloth that hung on one of the top metal spikes. "I'll bet that matches what I was wearing the morning you found me."

"Do you remember it?"

"Vaguely. It was dark, and I hurt. Everything was spinning." Squinting, I fought against the fuzzy blur that blocked my memories. "I had to escape."

Jablonsky stood in front of me, prepared to catch me if I were to collapse or stop me if I had another freak-out.

"Why?"

Swallowing, I closed my eyes, forcing my mind to find the answer to that question. The sound of gunfire caused me to jump, and I reached for my weapon. Jablonsky grabbed my arm before I could remove the gun from its holster. He didn't look alarmed, and I suspected what I heard had been in my mind.

"What is it?" he asked.

"Gunfire."

"You were escaping gunfire?"

I opened my mouth to speak, but I didn't know what to say. Words wouldn't come. I didn't know what happened then, and I wasn't even sure what was happening now. "My service piece is missing," I said, trying to make sense of things.

"We know. Do you remember what happened to it?"

"No." I shook off the questions and the fog, deciding not to try to force the facts to come to me. "Let's go around and see if I remember anything from the other side of that stupid fence."

"Parker," Jablonsky hesitantly asked, "are you sure you want to do this? Our team can handle it. You're not on the case. You don't have to be here."

"I was here before. I'm the only one that can tell you what happened," I laughed bitterly, "if I remember."

We made our way back to the garage, and Jablonsky insisted on driving to our next destination. Something about my behavior in the alley had changed him from curmudgeonly boss into worried father. Frankly, he was the closest thing I had to a parent since mine abandoned me. It was sweet he was worried. Hell, I was worried, but I didn't think hoofing it for a few blocks would make my problems any worse.

"You called Martin," I said as soon as I was nestled into the government-issued SUV. It was the best distraction I could think of to avoid the reverberating gunfire I kept hearing in my head. Two shots. Then another. "And he actually spoke to you this morning by choice. Does this mean you're friends again?"

"God, Parker, we aren't children. I understand why

you'd be confused though. Marty acts like a child." He chuckled. "Wow, you had him pegged from the first night the two of you met. I should have listened to you then."

"You should always listen to me," I declared, knowing that they were in the process of patching things up, "especially when I tell you I'm fine."

"You're always fine, even when you aren't. Thankfully, Lucca isn't as easily bullied or fooled by your little routine."

"So he blabs to you, and you blab to Martin. I didn't realize that the men I work with were nothing but bored washwomen."

"What happened yesterday afternoon?" Mark asked, illegally double-parking near the opening of the alley. "I want the truth." I pressed my lips together and stared out the windshield. "Off the record."

"I just lost it for no reason. I was searching my car for clues as to my destination, and everything was okay. Then I looked inside the trunk, and it just hit me."

"What did?"

I didn't want to vocalize what I remembered, but it could be important. Or more than likely, I was batshit crazy. "This image of a body, bloody and wrapped in plastic."

"Whose?"

"I don't know. I couldn't see through the blood." I struggled to keep my emotions in check. "It seemed so real, but it could be my imagination or a scene from some movie I watched. I don't know."

"Was that it?"

"Yeah, it startled me, and I backed up. I hit the no-parking post after hitting my side on the car door, and I went down for the count. Lucca kept insisting it was a panic attack, but I don't think it was."

"What do you think it was?"

"A moment of weakness."

"No," Mark chuckled, "I meant the image of the body. What do you think that was? Was it a memory?"

"It might have been a sign that I watched one too many episodes of *Dexter*. After all, I do have a vivid imagination." My denial was more for my benefit than

Mark's. If the macabre image that surfaced in my mind was real, that meant someone was dead and I'd been close enough to see the aftermath. It could be the reason I was running and why I was injured. "Didn't you say I shouldn't jump to conclusions?"

"I might have, and if I didn't, it's sound advice. You should follow it." Mark opened the car door. "Now let's check out the rest of the alley."

TEN

The other half of the alley was ordinary. Aside from the fence in the middle, there was nothing memorable about it. On the way out, Jablonsky thought he spotted a possible blood trail and requested an evaluation by our already overworked crime scene technicians. He was determined to make progress, even though I was ready to give up.

It was mid-afternoon by the time we headed back to the car. The lab techs had found some blood drops that had seeped into the concrete. Samples were taken for comparison, and the piece of cloth that hung from the top of the fence had been retrieved for further analysis. If anything, they'd determine that I was in the alley.

"We'll be able to update our parameters," Jablonsky said. "Our primary objective at this point is to determine where you were. Once we know that, it'll be easier to figure out what happened and who's responsible." Before I could voice a protest, he gave me a stern look. "It's basic investigation techniques. We work most cases like this. See, you're not so special."

"What should I do in the meantime?"

"Go home. Go to Marty's. It doesn't matter, just go somewhere safe." He held the car door open, and I hoisted myself into the SUV with my good arm. He shut the door and went around to the driver's side. "If it were solely up to me, I'd leave the detail in place. I know you hate having them outside your door, but it'd make me feel better. Unfortunately, it's been over seventy-two hours. There's no basis to keep them at your beck and call. However, if anything changes, I'll have them back there so fast, you'll think they never left."

"Thanks." I stared out the windshield. "You said Cooper was checking into the police angle."

"He volunteered," Jablonsky said. "Why?" He shifted his gaze to me, but he knew the reason for the question. "I've contacted OCU, but they don't think Vito's behind this. Do you really think he'd make a play for you just because you've been reinstated?"

"I don't know. Sure, when Director Kendall offered me my job back, I thought accepting would be suicide because of the threat, but Vito went completely silent after that. Some time passed, and when I finally agreed to return, the threat didn't seem real anymore. But anytime something happens, the first thought that runs through my mind is: 'This is it. Vito's making good on his threat.' I'm starting to feel like a dead man walking."

"Alex, I wouldn't have asked you to return if I thought his threat was credible. We took measures to safeguard against a retaliatory attack and a preemptive strike. You should be safe."

"Then why did you contact OCU?"

He took a deep breath. "It doesn't hurt to be thorough." He glanced at me, knowing that whatever happened had spooked me. "Don't make any rash decisions, Special Agent Parker. We're still compiling intel. We have a case to work."

"Funny, I'm not authorized to work any cases since I'm on medical leave." I focused on the buildings that passed by. "Call if you make any progress or if you need help determining Shade's next move, but other than that, I intend to take advantage of my downtime."

"The hell you are," Mark griped. He knew me better than that. "Just promise you'll stay out of trouble."

"Absolutely," I said, stepping out of the car as soon as it

came to a stop in front of my apartment. "You know where to find me if you need me."

"Well, at least Marty will be happy."

*   *   *

Martin's estate was large, secluded, and definitely too quiet for my current state of mind. By the time I packed a bag, grabbed the remaining sandwich from my fridge, and contacted Marcal, Martin's personal valet and driver, to give me a ride to the house, Martin had already left for work. And he wondered why I chose to stay at my place for the duration of his company's internal audit. Rolling my eyes, I dropped my bag in the second floor guest suite, which was a recreation of my apartment, and put my pill bottle on the kitchen counter.

I hadn't taken any in the last two days, and I considered flushing the contents. But maybe I'd fall on hard times and need to hock the painkillers on a street corner. It was a distasteful joke, and I scolded myself for thinking it. Far too often, things like that actually happened. Addiction was rampant in this country, especially since the pharmacy-grade narcotics were far superior to most of the street-level shit. It was depressing to think how far we'd fallen as a society. Well, even Rome fell, so whatever. I wasn't in the business of philosophical discourse or political ideology; I was paid to enforce the laws as a tool of the man or whatever the modern day hippies were calling the federal government. Wow, I needed to stop watching movies from the 1960s.

Restless as always, I performed a preliminary walkthrough of the estate, avoiding most of the third floor and the ghosts that resided there. The fourth floor housed our bedroom and Martin's office. The place was pristine, and I indulged in a shower and a change of clothes before returning to the main level. The second floor contained the living room, kitchen, and dining room. However, I'd been given the run of the downstairs office, so to show my gratitude, I decided to do something productive.

"Dammit," I swore, annoyed by my practically illegible

writing, "it had to be my right wrist. God forbid it was my left." Erasing the chicken scratch on the whiteboard, I tightened my grip on the marker and started over.

On the first board, I jotted notes about the flashes and dreams I'd had since the incident. On the next board, I listed the limited number of facts we had. Then I chronicled the items that were undergoing analysis. Lastly, I struggled to remember the evidence that had been collected and catalog it appropriately. Since I wasn't allowed access to my own case, or any case, I didn't have copies of the files or information that Lucca and Jablonsky had brought to my apartment during their preliminary investigation. Luckily, I remembered most of it.

Picking up the phone, I dialed the hospital, hoping they could supply facsimiles of my medical records. Of course, it was after five, so the records office was closed to civilians. Without my OIO credentials, I'd have to wait until tomorrow. Frustrated, I scanned through my handiwork, shut my eyes, and screamed. Why was this so complicated?

Dropping into a chair, I leaned back, forcing myself to see the forest amidst all the damn trees. Think logically. Getting up, I went to the board, writing numbers next to the facts and memories until I had a decent narrative.

It was after seven when I left the OIO building in order to meet with a confidential informant. At some point, I was indoors, presumably consuming alcohol. The meeting went badly. Maybe a man was leaning over me, and I felt trapped. Something happened, and I ran outside to escape or possibly get help. I went through the alleyway, hopped a fence, darted into a parking garage, came out on the other end, and lost consciousness.

"Great, too bad I don't remember any of it." My eyes honed in on the facts that weren't included. "When did I lose my weapon? *Where* did I lose my weapon?"

Aggravated, I swept the items off the desk with my casted arm and went in search of car keys. Martin had a fleet of vehicles in the garage. After grabbing a set for one of the few automatics, I climbed behind the wheel, intent on coming up with a destination. When nothing useful surfaced, I decided to return to the scene of the crime.

Evening had settled, bringing with it a growing darkness. I drove past the garage, turned onto a cross street, and drove toward the mouth of the alleyway. No crime scene tape or government-issued cars were in the vicinity, so the techs must have concluded their work for the day.

Parking beside a hydrant, I gave the luxury vehicle a look, knowing it would be targeted by traffic cops. Reminding myself not to be long, I opened the door, hoped the vehicle wouldn't be towed, and took off down the block. It was a street like any other, but maybe the dark would make the surroundings seem familiar. It didn't. It looked like every other street. I passed a liquor store and stopped.

Opening the door, the smell of spirits and aged wood hung in the air. A wave of nausea hit me, and I stepped outside, seconds away from vomiting. Breathing through my nose, I forced my stomach to obey my commands. Apparently that leftover sandwich had spoiled. The cool air helped to settle the sudden queasiness, but I returned to the car anyway.

What the hell is wrong with you now, Parker? Swallowing a few times, I prayed that I wouldn't be sick. After a few minutes, I started the car. Something wasn't sitting right, and I had a feeling it was more than just the sandwich.

More annoyed than when I left, I took a sharp left and headed to the nearest precinct. Finding a visitor space in the back with the patrol cars, I slid into the spot and studied the surroundings. None of it was familiar. As far as I knew, I'd never been to this precinct before. After a few minutes of internal debate, I decided to let the officers inside know just how crazy I was.

"Can I help you, ma'am?" the desk sergeant asked.

"I hope so." I gave her a winning smile, unsure how to pose the next question. "Have you received any inquiries from the FBI or OIO recently?"

Her eyes shot up, assessing me quickly to determine if I posed a threat or if I was a lunatic. "I'm not sure," she said, uncertain if she wanted to give an actual answer. "May I have your name?"

"Federal agent Alexis Parker. I'm with the OIO." I smiled again, hoping that she wouldn't ask to see my ID.

"Right." I knew what that tone meant. "Why don't you just wait over there, Agent Parker?" She pointed to a chair in the corner.

Resisting the urge to insist I wasn't a nut job, I slowly removed my wallet and handed her my license. "I'd show you my credentials, but it's a long story. If you want to verify my identity, call Agent Jablonsky." I gave her his number and my ID number. "I'll be right there." Pointing to the chair, I offered a pleasant smile and took a seat. Damn, I should have left a note for Martin that way he could spring me from the loony bin if the men with butterfly nets were called.

"Okay," the desk sergeant said, lifting up the phone. I didn't know if she was playing along, calling for back-up, or if she actually intended to phone Jablonsky. Mark would be pissed that I wasn't keeping out of trouble, but he expected as much. I'd hate to disappoint him. "Give me a second." A few minutes later, she waved me back to the desk. "What do you need, Agent Parker?" She handed back my license, eyeing the cast on my arm.

"I know this sounds insane, but bear with me. I was supposed to meet with a police informant a few nights ago. There was an incident. I'm not entirely sure what happened, but circumstances led me to believe that this might be the proper precinct. Is there any way you can check and see if I issued a request or who the informant's handler is?"

She looked thoroughly confused and rather wary. "I'm sorry. Access like that is kept under lock and key, and unless you can provide the CI's name or alias, there's nothing I can do."

"Thanks, anyway."

Feeling dejected, I returned to the car. A few plainclothes officers were standing nearby, smoking and examining my ride. One of them snuffed out the butt and sauntered over.

"Nice wheels," he said. "Can I help you with something?"

"Not really."

"Are you sure you're okay?" he asked, noticing my bruises and scrapes. "Did someone do that to you?"

"I'm fine."

He narrowed his eyes. "Did you file a report?"

"Yeah, but I don't know who did it." I unlocked the door and tried to step past him. "I was hoping to make some progress, but I hit another dead end."

He stood in front of me, continuing to push the issue. "What's your name? I'd be happy to look into it."

"Here," I pulled out one of my cards and handed it to him, "ask your pals if anyone remembers speaking to me. We were collaborating on a case. If something surfaces, I'd appreciate a call."

He read my name. "That's a fancy ride for a fed. I didn't realize you were paid that well." His tone had gone from concerned flirtation to cold and arrogant. "Guess that's why you came to ask the real cops for help."

"You got me," I said sarcastically. "You know we can't find our asses with both hands and a map."

He snorted, stepping to the side. "That's what I've heard."

"Yeah, that's what I figured." I got into the car. "Have a nice night." I closed the door and put the key in. With any luck, Officer Arrogant would ask around or, at the very least, retell the story to his buddies. Maybe my name would ring a bell with one of them.

ELEVEN

By the time I got home, Martin was back from work. Confused by this turn of events, I gave him an odd look and took a seat across from him at the kitchen table. He was on the phone, taking notes and otherwise wrapped up in some ongoing corporate crisis. Sometimes, I wondered why I'd been so unhappy in the private sector. Things were safer, and the pay was better. Unfortunately, I hated it. I never learned how to do things the easy way; although, from Martin's half of the conversation, he'd disagree on business being easy.

"Thanks, I'll get on that," Martin said. He hung up the phone and leaned back in the chair. "This is fucking bullshit."

"Tell me about it."

He looked up, as if he hadn't noticed my presence until now. "Hey," he smiled, "you're here. Are you staying?"

"I made a promise, didn't I?"

"Not that I remember." He dropped the pen and scratched at his stubble. "Was I supposed to shave?"

"I like you either way, handsome."

His eyes danced, enjoying the compliment. "Why are you being so nice? Did you scratch the car?"

"No," I shrugged, "but those douche bag cops might have drooled on it." I shook my head before he could ask a follow-up question. "Aren't you working nights?"

"Days, nights, nonstop. Frankly, it's hard to tell at this point." He glanced down at the legal pad. "This is a shitstorm, but the evaluation of the international offices concludes tonight. Luc's handling the Paris branch for obvious reasons."

"Sure, your VP ran that place. He knows how to get things done, but isn't that a conflict of interest?"

"Don't you start, too." He glared at the paper. "Luc isn't the problem. Francesca's the problem."

"Bitch."

Martin grinned. "You've been dying to say that."

"Well, it's true." I yawned and put my head on top of my arms.

"How are you? We haven't really had much chance to talk."

"It's been a long day." I didn't want to have another conversation about what I couldn't remember. I'd been going over it all day. I didn't have it in me to do it again. "I'm home. That's all you need to know."

"Do you want to go to bed?" It was early, but he knew I was beat.

"Are you trying to seduce me?" I teased.

He smirked, running his fingers through my long brown hair. "Sweetheart, if I was, you wouldn't be asking. You might be begging."

"Cocky bastard."

"Come on," he gently nudged my arm, "you need your rest. The sooner you recover, the sooner I can seduce you."

*　　*　　*

My eyelids felt heavy. I wanted to sleep, but something told me I shouldn't. I had to keep my eyes open. I had to focus on what was important. I blinked a couple of times, but it was getting harder and harder to force my eyes to remain open. The room was bathed in a red glow, and I stared down at the tile floor. Something felt wrong.

"Martin?" I called, but there was no answer.

I moved deeper into the room, noting the sink and a drain in the floor. The red glow was coming from a light in the upper corner of the room. When did he get that? I wondered, continuing my search. The sound of metal scraping caused me to pause. I tried to turn, feeling dizzy and faint. Hold it together, Parker, my internal voice warned.

Gruff male voices echoed against the hard surfaces, and my eyes shot upward. Anger and annoyance were being conveyed by a demanding voice, but I couldn't make out the words. I forced my eyes to lift upward. My vision was blurry, but I made out a gloved hand and a gun. My gun.

"No," I screamed, struggling to move. It wasn't until that moment that I realized I was being restrained. I twisted and turned, tugging and pulling to get free. I had to stop the gun from firing.

For a brief moment, my vision focused on a man, helpless and bound. He let out a pitiful scream, muffled by a gag. Clawing to get free, I threw everything I had into knocking the gun from the shooter's hand. Somehow, I got a hand free, and I grabbed for the gun. Bang, bang. The weapon discharged twice, and I was backhanded so hard that my head knocked into the countertop. Before I blacked out, I heard another shot and saw blood trickle toward the drain.

Waking with a start, I looked down. I was covered in blood. My hand and cast were red, and I shoved the covers aside, finding my clothing soaked in the coppery stickiness. Turning to the side, I was alone in bed.

"Martin," I screamed. "Martin?" Leaping out of bed, I tripped over the tangled covers, landing hard, but I was only down for a second before dragging myself off the ground and racing into the attached bathroom, terrified of what I would find. "Martin." I kept calling his name, flipping on the light with a shaking hand. The only thought in my mind was he was dead.

The bathroom appeared empty, but some areas were obscured from view. Cautiously, I continued moving forward while my mind considered the possibilities of a shooter being present. The room was clear, and in a brief moment of clarity, I realized it had been a dream. That calm was shattered when the reality of my blood-drenched hands crashed through my forethoughts. Oh my god, I killed him.

The sound of rushed footfalls sounded behind me, and I spun, slipping on the floor and landing in a heap. Someone was here.

"Alex," Martin burst through the door, and I dug my heels into the tile, pushing myself backward, "sweetheart, I'm here." He looked about as terrified as I felt. "Hang on, we'll get help. You'll be okay." He moved toward me, but I continued to scoot backward, studying every aspect of him.

"Are you okay?" I choked out.

"Yeah," he looked confused and frightened, "but you're not. Let me help you."

"Don't touch me," I snapped, seeing the fear grow on his face. "Oh, god." I continued scrambling backward as far from him as possible, stopping only when my back hit the shower door.

"Okay," he held up his hands, "I won't touch you." He leaned back on his haunches, keeping his distance. "Sweetheart, you're scaring me." That much was apparent by the look on his face. "Talk to me. How did this happen?"

"I thought," I fought to steady my voice, "I thought someone shot you."

"Nightmares," he said, nodding. His eyes continued to search my face. "It was just a bad dream." His gaze settled on my bloody hands and shirt. "That's a lot of blood."

I shook my head, gazing down at my trembling hands. It was a dream. A part of me knew it, but waking up to the blood, I thought I had killed him. It was my gun that was fired. Where did the blood come from? Why was I covered in blood?

"Whose blood is it?" I squeaked. My world had been turned upside down far too much for anything to make sense. "Did I do this? Did I kill someone?"

"Alex," he scooted closer, "it was a dream. You must have ripped a stitch or something."

"Stay back," I insisted, feeling the panic rise. I was a

monster. A killer. I'd taken lives, two in this house alone. After tonight, I was certain that number was higher. "You weren't in bed. I thought..." I couldn't say anything else.

"I'm sorry. I couldn't sleep. I went downstairs to get some work done. Had I known this would happen, I never would have left you." He watched as I pulled my legs to my chest and hugged my knees. "Please, you need help." That was the understatement of the century. "You're bleeding," he said patiently, nodding at my side.

"Just give me a minute," I said, fighting to process the irrational fear and incongruent thoughts that my mind kept supplying. "Just leave me alone."

He sat back, leaning against the vanity. Reaching over, he flipped the switch for the towel warmer but remained on the floor across from me. I don't know how long it took before my breathing stabilized or he decided it was safe to attempt to approach me again, but at some point, he doused a washcloth with water and eased his way over to me.

Wiping the blood off my hands and chest, he resisted the urge to lift my shirt which was still slightly wet and stuck to my skin. Instead, he rinsed the washcloth again and gently ran it against my neck and face.

"Alex," he whispered, watching as I continued to tremble, "talk to me."

"I thought I killed you. When I realized it was a dream, I thought I shot you."

"Sweetheart, let's get off this floor and get you checked out."

"No." It was the middle of the night, and in my sleep deprived state, I was paranoid that any sane medical staffer would have me committed. The scariest part was I figured I deserved it. "There's something wrong with me."

"You'll be okay." His voice was soft and soothing. "You must have been thrashing about like you normally do, and you probably ripped open your side." The way he said those words convinced me he wasn't actually feeling as calm as he was pretending to be.

Shaking my head, I curled up on the floor, and he scooted closer, lifting my head onto his thigh. He was safe, and that was enough. Other than that, I didn't want to move. I didn't want to face reality because I was afraid that I no longer had any idea what that was. Reaching for the warmed bath towel, Martin took it from the rack and draped it over me. Then the two of us remained on the bathroom floor for the next few hours.

I must have dozed off at some point because when "Bruiser" Jones, Martin's bodyguard, entered the bathroom, I almost jumped out of my skin. Bruiser had his gun drawn, but he tucked it away with one look from Martin.

"Jones, tell Marcal I need to speak to him," Martin said, "and wait for me in the bedroom."

I sat up, stiff and sore. Until now, I'd been numb. The physical pain was a relief. It was a tether to reality, and I couldn't help but wonder if I hadn't had a complete psychotic break a few hours earlier.

"Martin," I looked at him, desperately wanting to apologize and explain my erratic behavior, but I had no excuse, "I'm a mess."

"We'll figure this out." He ran his thumb across my cheek and kissed me. "Stay here. I'll be right back." He stood, giving me a tentative glance before leaving the bathroom and pulling the door closed behind him.

Standing, I went to the sink to wash up. The side of my shirt was caked in blood and a few smears streaked from the side upward. Other than that, the damage appeared to be contained. In my hysteria, it seemed far worse, but it still wasn't good. Washing my hands, I ignored the theory of not getting the cast wet. Quite frankly, I wanted it gone. Why couldn't this entire ordeal be nothing more than a nightmare?

Shutting the water, I dried my hands and attempted to pull my shirt free. Apparently, the blood had dried and congealed, bonding whatever was left of the bandage and my t-shirt to my skin.

"Ouch." I stopped tugging on the cotton, afraid of reopening the wound and relapsing into the hysterical insanity.

From beyond the door, I heard Martin's voice. "Have

Rosemarie clean the room. If we need new carpeting or a mattress, get it done. I want everything cleaned or replaced by the time I get home. I don't care what it costs or what it takes, just do it."

Great, it sounded like Martin was covering up my crime scene. A horrific thought coursed through my brain that I had actually committed a murder last night, and he was covering it up. But I knew how illogical that was. No one was here last night, and the three people that worked for Martin were all alive and well. Obviously, the blood was mine. It all made sense. The thing that didn't was the fact that my mind wouldn't accept that the dream was nothing more than a dream.

"It was real," I said when Martin stepped back into the bathroom with my clothes.

"Alex," his patience was wearing thin, "you had a bad dream. You must have tore at your side. I know you're scared, but it's over. It's morning. You're okay." He didn't understand my point, and he was tired of dealing with me. He reached for the hem of my shirt, carefully lifting it as high as it would go. "Soak it in water. It might help loosen it." He pulled gauze and tape from underneath the cabinet. "Get cleaned up and get dressed. I'll be waiting downstairs."

"Where are we going?" I asked suspiciously.

"I have to go to work, and there isn't a chance in hell that I'm leaving you alone. So you're coming with me."

"Martin," I protested, but I had no argument to make.

"I spent the night on the bathroom floor, worried sick over you. So shut up and do this for me." He took my face in his hands and searched my eyes. "Honestly, are you okay now?"

I nodded. What was wrong with me couldn't be fixed by Martin or a doctor. I needed to talk to Jablonsky. There was a lot more to my memory gap than either of us realized. With any luck, the team had made some progress since yesterday afternoon.

TWELVE

The bedroom looked like the site of multiple homicides.
The sheets were streaked in blood, and the carpet was
stained where I'd taken a tumble. No wonder Martin had
wanted the room cleaned. He had tried to cover up the
bloodbath by pulling the covers over the bed and placing a
towel on the floor, but my curiosity had gotten the best of
me.

"Miss Parker," Bruiser said from the doorway, "did you
lose something?"

"My mind."

"It happens to the best of us."

Before becoming Martin's bodyguard, Bruiser had seen
action in the Middle East. He'd been a navy corpsman, but
originally, he intended to become a SEAL, allegedly
washing out on the last day of training. I'd seen his
shooting scores and had practiced some hand-to-hand
techniques with him, and I wasn't quite convinced that he
couldn't have been a SEAL. Mark Jablonsky had
thoroughly vetted him, and Bruiser was one of the few
candidates that I had approved to replace me as Martin's
personal bodyguard.

"Can you do me a favor and stay close to him," I asked.

"Sure." He studied me for a moment, but he didn't ask what happened or what led to the room of horrors. "Is there anything else I can do?"

"I wish there was." I checked the bedside table for my back-up, remembering that it was downstairs. I'd never been more relieved to have left my weapon somewhere in my entire life. "Shall we?" I gestured to the door, but he waited for me to exit before following me down the stairs.

*　　*　　*

Upon arrival at the Martin Technologies building, I was greeted by Jeffrey Myers, the head security guard. He had been of great assistance when I worked as a security consultant here, and we were friendly.

"I haven't seen you in an age," Jeffrey greeted, tapping a few keys on the computer to reactivate my old MT ID card. "Are you here for more consulting work?"

"No," I glanced at Martin who was waiting at the elevator, "but apparently today's bring your girlfriend to work day."

"Damn, no one bothered to tell me," Jeffrey said. He handed back my ID "You have the usual run of the place." He nodded at Martin who was holding the elevator door. "I'll see you later."

"Thanks." I strode across the lobby and into the waiting lift.

We didn't speak until the doors opened on the seventeenth floor. Martin led the way down the corridor and swiped his card through the slot, unlocking his office. Holding the door, he pressed his hand against the small of my back, and I shuddered.

"Sorry, I forgot." He sounded exhausted. "Look, if you would rather see a doctor or get checked out, that can be arranged. The company has a physician on retainer. I can have someone contact him."

"Martin, go to work. I'm all right." Taking in the changed appearance of his office, I realized things were a lot worse than he'd made them out to be. "You have enough to deal with. I need to make some calls and get things sorted out. Just stick me in an empty room somewhere, so I can stay out of everyone's way."

"Nonsense, I have meetings. You stay put." He jerked his head toward one of the leather couches. "You should be comfortable here. I know how much you adore a nice sofa." He smirked. "Charlotte's down the hall if you need anything."

"Charlotte?"

"Luc's assistant. Her office is the next one over. You can't miss it. She's at your beck and call."

"I'm sure she'll love that."

He looked at his watch, rushing around the desk and rummaging through the filing cabinet. "It's her job." He looked up for a moment. "You can always bug Jeffrey if you prefer." He went to the door. "Try to get some sleep. You've had a rough night."

"So did you."

He made a noncommittal sound and continued down the hallway, letting the door shut behind him.

I stared at the opaque glass wall that separated his office from the hallway. He'd shifted the clear glass to solid white to hide his psychotic girlfriend from the rest of the world, or so I thought. Truthfully, I was happy for the peace and solitude.

Taking a seat on the couch, I gave the pillow an odd look. It wasn't normal to have a bed pillow on the couch, and briefly, I wondered if Martin had asked Charlotte or some other assistant to ready his office for my arrival. But then I noticed the rack of suits against the far wall. Either Tom Ford had one hell of a sale and specially delivered Martin's new purchases, or Martin hadn't been home in the last week. Moving into the lavatory, I spotted his travel case and a few essentials. The building had showers in the executive washroom. The trash was emptied nightly, but a few delivery receipts littered the edge of his desk.

"Looks like I'm not the only one keeping secrets." He hadn't been home, which was why he didn't know I hadn't been home. It also explained why he'd been acting so guilty and showing up at my apartment. After last night, I regretted returning to his place or telling him that I would.

"Damn, aren't we dysfunctional?" I asked the empty room.

While dialing Jablonsky, I mentally prepared for what I was about to say. Just breathe, Parker, I reminded myself, feeling an uneasiness settle in the pit of my stomach. Mark would know what to do. He always did.

"Parker," he said, having read the caller ID before I could say a word, "we haven't made much progress yet, but the techs have shifted their focus to a different set of DOT cams. Since we have solid evidence that you were in that alleyway, you must have been on that street. They believe they'll be able to locate you, but it'll take time. We should have something promising in the next few days, maybe sooner."

"Mark," I swallowed, "I remembered something."

"That's great."

"No, it isn't." I took a deep breath. "I think I killed someone."

"What?" A door slammed in the background. "What the hell did you remember? Is this about that plastic-wrapped corpse? We haven't found a body. There was no evidence to support any of that. The only blood and DNA on your body belonged to you."

"What about GSR?" I asked, fearing the answer.

"They didn't test for it. There were no indications of a gunshot."

"But you haven't recovered my piece."

"Parker, listen to me, whatever you're about to say. Don't say it. This is a matter that should be discussed in person. I will come to you. In fact, I will meet you at Marty's when I finish up here. Is that understood?"

"I'm at the MT building now."

"What the hell are you doing there?"

"Martin was afraid to leave me alone."

"Holy shit," Mark swore, "just keep a lid on this until further notice. Make sure Martin does the same. I don't need to worry about damage control. Right now, the less I know, the better. I'll see you soon."

He hung up before I could say anything else. I dropped the phone to the table. Shit. Shit. Shit. There was nothing I could do. I had no idea who the victim was. My memory was vague. The image of the man was brief. I could hear his panicked whimper clearly, but his face was a blur. The only real clarity was my weapon firing. Was that why I was running? Where did I ditch the gun? And what about his body? It was in the trunk of a car, but my car was at the OIO. Someone else was there and knew exactly what happened. Maybe I had an accomplice, or I was an accomplice. Did I witness a cop kill his CI? My head spun, and I pressed my palm against my pounding temple, desperately needing to lie down. Easing onto the couch, I let the myriad of questions and the ache in my head swirl around until it was replaced by nothingness.

The sound of agitated voices woke me. At first, I couldn't understand the words, and it took longer than it should have before I realized they weren't being spoken in English. Luc and Martin were having an argument, and from the sounds of it, Luc had reverted to his native tongue. As far as I could tell, Martin was holding his own. Pressing deeper into the couch, I hoped to disappear. I had a splitting headache, and it was getting worse by the minute. Eventually, an accord was reached, and Luc walked out. The silence made the ringing in my ears seem that much more pronounced, and I buried my head deeper into the pillow when the sound of rapid typing replaced the ringing.

When I woke again, I took a deep breath, enjoying the scent of Martin surrounding me. He must be close, I thought, opening my eyes to the sight of his office. He had placed his suit jacket over me like a blanket and was standing near the windows, drinking a scotch. He must have heard the shift of the leather because he turned around, offering a weak smile.

"Hey, beautiful."

"What time is it?" I asked.

"It's almost six. I didn't want to wake you." He moved across the room, taking a seat on the coffee table in front of me. "How are you holding up?"

"My head hurts. My sanity is questionable, and Mark is probably waiting for us at your house."

"They said it was likely you sustained a concussion,"

Martin said matter-of-factly. He leaned closer to brush the hair out of my face. "What the hell are we going to do with you?"

For a brief moment, I was hit by the scent of alcohol on his breath and thought I'd be sick. "I love you, but lose the scotch."

He gave me an odd look. "That's new." The pained expression on my face was enough to stop his questions and get him to move the glass to the other side of the table. Then he went into the bathroom, brushed his teeth, and came back with a breath mint. "Is that better?"

"Yeah, sorry."

"Apologize to the eighteen year old single malt that I won't get to finish." He winked. "Obviously, I must think pretty highly of you."

"You've been sleeping in the office."

"And you've been sleeping at your apartment. I don't think either of those points is relevant at the moment." He narrowed his eyes. The green orbs looked concerned. "Alexis, what happened last night? This morning, you said it wasn't a dream, and I've seen what your nightmares can do. That has never happened before. What's going on?"

"Do we have to talk about this here?" I asked, glancing around the completely empty room.

"Yes, because we are not going anywhere until I know what's wrong with my girlfriend. You scared me last night."

"I know. I saw the look on your face. You were just as convinced as I was that I could hurt you."

"Bullshit. I was terrified for you. Why the hell were you afraid of me?"

"I wasn't."

"You wouldn't let me get near you. It took over two hours before you were calm enough for me to approach. I would never hurt you, sweetheart." He reached for me, testing to see if I would cringe. "But someone did. I know it. I've seen the way you've reacted afterward." He swallowed, not needing to elaborate further. "You said this morning that it wasn't a dream. I didn't comprehend what you meant because I was wrapped up in my own shit, but I haven't been able to get your words out of my head all day.

Luc's pissed that I've been zoning out during our meetings. You can't keep me in the dark. What did you remember?"

With that tiny amount of prodding, I unloaded everything onto him. My deepest fears, my speculations, and the terrifying memories and dreams. "I told Mark," I said, collecting myself. "That's why he wants to meet at your place. He must agree with the conclusion I reached, and he probably wants to get as much of the story as possible before taking official action against me."

"Alex, you didn't murder anyone," Martin said with a level of certainty that I didn't possess. "Of that fact, I'm sure." He pressed his lips together, staring at my cast. "Would you have even been able to shoot someone in your condition?"

"It could have happened before this did," I speculated. "Regardless, I'm a decent shot with my left."

"Well, if you did fire on someone, it would have been in self-defense."

"A bound man isn't much of a threat."

"Then you didn't shoot him." Martin moved onto the couch, and I hugged him tightly, even though it hurt. "Do you trust Mark and your team at the OIO to straighten this out?"

"I guess."

"Should I hire some people to investigate quietly? I have the resources, and if it means we'll end up having a peaceful night's sleep one day sooner, I'm game."

"Not yet, let's see what Mark has to say first."

My boss would not be pleased that I had spilled the beans to Martin. He'd be even less pleased that Martin would intervene on my behalf if he thought it was in my best interest. So much for mending their relationship. However, at the moment, their sensitive egos were far less important than my mental health.

THIRTEEN

"Run through it one more time," Mark insisted. "I'm not seeing the connection that you keep making. Why do you think someone's dead?"

"I've seen the body. I heard his scream." Taking a deep breath and lowering my voice, I said, "I know he was shot. It was my gun."

"You don't know anything, Parker." Rolling his eyes, he pushed away from the table. "You said it yourself; this could be nothing more than your fucking ridiculous imagination getting the best of you."

"It isn't."

"What's your proof? We don't have a body. We don't have your gun. We don't have a crime. The only thing we have is one nut job agent who woke up in the middle of nowhere. Do you want to know what the evidence actually suggests? Do you?" he bellowed.

"What?"

"That you ditched work with enough foresight to know that you wouldn't be in any condition to drive, and you went out on a bender. The tox report supports that conclusion, and your injuries could be the result of dangerous, drunken behavior."

"It's not true."

"Maybe it should be." Jablonsky's eyes conveyed a look that I'd only seen a few times before. It was the 'leave it alone, you're better off not knowing' look. "However, it'll be important to keep the investigation open until we're positive that you were not targeted. I take threats against my people very seriously."

"You know me. You know my instincts are spot on. If I say something happened, it did." I blinked back the irrational tears that threatened to fall. "I can't keep doing this. Last night," I gulped down some air, "it was bad, Mark. I can't go through that again."

"Parker," he grasped my hand, "I never said I didn't believe you. I'm telling you that you don't know what you're talking about, and until there is proof, you shouldn't speculate. Do you understand my meaning?"

"Yeah," I pulled my hand free and sat back, "but it's counterproductive. I need to work toward the truth, not toward the spin that we might have to put on it. I don't have the energy to do both."

Jablonsky steepled his fingers and stared off into the distance. "You wouldn't shoot a defenseless man. Even if someone threatened you, you wouldn't do it." His eyes narrowed on my cast. "You don't remember pulling the trigger. From what you said, you tried to stop the shooter. When you woke up and saw the blood, that's when you assumed that you shot Marty. You need to backtrack to actual memories, not pseudo-memories or whatever. What did the room look like?"

"Everything had a red glow. It originated in the upper corner of the room. There was a drain in the floor. The floor was tile. Everything seemed red, but it might have been white or some light color. Probably white. There were a lot of shiny surfaces, metallic, maybe." Squinting, I tried to recall the room, but all I remembered clearly was the desperation, the shots being fired, and blood moving toward the drain.

"Hey, eyes over here." Jablonsky leaned forward, forcing me to focus on him. "Think hard for a second. The man you saw get shot and the corpse in the trunk, are they one and the same?"

Concentrating hard, I couldn't be sure. "You think two people were murdered?"

"I'm not sure anyone was murdered." The leave it alone look resurfaced. "Let's get back to what we know that isn't a potential memory or nightmare. You told Marty that you were meeting with a confidential informant. I don't know any cop worth his salt that wouldn't have been at that same meeting. With any luck, the reason for your missing weapon and credentials is because you stowed them somewhere before the meet to keep from spooking the CI."

"That would make sense."

"Hell, you might have ordered a drink or two while questioning the CI just to hide the federal agent stink. It's possible time got away from you." Mark stood, giving the whiteboards I'd filled another glance. "Honestly, it's very possible nothing heinous went down. It's also possible things went sideways, and you stumbled into something you shouldn't have seen. We will get to the bottom of it, but being a self-proclaimed killer isn't the way to go."

"I wasn't planning on waltzing into some precinct and turning myself in," I retorted, annoyed.

"Yeah, well, you did waltz into a precinct and stirred the water to see what would surface." He gave me a look. "Don't do that again."

"Why?"

"Just don't." He narrowed his eyes at the cast again before heading for the door. "You're gonna say no, so I'm ordering you to talk to one of the shrinks at work. They've dealt with trauma victims and PTSD patients. They might be able to help."

"I thought you wanted me to keep a lid on this."

"Doctor-patient confidentiality," Jablonsky said, pausing in the doorway. "You said you wanted the truth. There it is."

"Jack Nicholson said it better."

"You can't handle it. Night, Parker," Mark called, exiting the room. "I'll see you tomorrow at the office."

After he left, I stared at the boards. He hadn't helped the way I thought he would. Instead, he made me afraid of uncovering what really happened. He knew something, but he wasn't sharing.

I made a few calls, first to Agent Davenport and then to Lucca. Davenport said they were working on routing the new set of DOT footage through the facial rec software in order to pinpoint my location, but it wasn't done yet. And Lucca had no news to report. I considered phoning Det. O'Connell but didn't want to stoke the fires after Jablonsky's warning. Plus, Nick would call if he had something.

Focusing on my cast, I wondered what Jablonsky had been pondering. Rereading the notes on the whiteboard and what I recalled from my medical records, I had a thought. Going into the kitchen, I searched the drawers for something to saw through the plaster. At home, I had box cutters and screwdrivers in my kitchen drawers. Unfortunately, Martin only had practical items like silverware in his.

Locating a pizza slicer, I spun the sharp wheel with my pointer finger, shrugged, and went to the table. At first, I applied pressure at the end of the cast, near my elbow, and attempted to saw through it, but that quickly proved useless. Maybe I could crack it open. Lifting the pizza cutter in my left, I made sure it was lined up, afraid that I'd miss and cut my arm open. In one swift stroke, I brought it down lightly, not making a significant impact. With the practice swing out of the way, I intended to try again with more force, but Martin grabbed my wrist before I started on the downswing.

"Whoa," he pried the kitchen utensil out of my hand, "what are you doing?"

"I want it off." I held out my casted arm. "Get it off."

"Alex," he sighed, probably convinced that he was dealing with someone mentally disturbed, "you're going to slice through your arm doing this." He put the cutter in the sink and shook his head. "I have tools downstairs. I can get it off, but it is on for a reason."

"I don't care. This is more important. Trust me."

He stared into my eyes. "I do." Returning with what looked like a chisel, he sat across from me at the table.

"This might hurt. Are you sure?"

"Yeah," I nodded, "I need to see my hand, and I can't exactly do that with these bandages and this stupid cast. It's a sprained wrist. I'll put a brace on it and call it a day. It's no big deal."

After cracking the plaster, Martin sawed off the rest of the cast with enough skill to make me think he'd done it before. My freed arm immediately throbbed upon release, but I ignored it, pulling off the bandages. Even though it'd been several days, the bruising on my hand between my thumb and pointer finger was substantial. I stared at it, realizing for the first time what caused it.

"And they say those aren't defensive wounds," Martin scoffed. "Unbelievable." Gingerly, he lifted my hand, concentrating too hard on my torn nails, deep scabs, and black bruise to notice my wince. "You were clawing at something."

"A wood chair or table," I said, piecing together the facts with my broken recollection. Turning my hand over, I stared at my palm, knowing the web between my thumb and finger had been pinched on both sides. "In order to prevent a loaded weapon from discharging, you can shove your hand between the hammer and pin to keep it from firing. The military teaches that with disarming techniques. Quantico taught us that too."

"You weren't the shooter," Martin said, realizing what he was observing. "You were trying to disarm him."

"Or not get shot in the face," I said, feeling the tender spot on my forehead. The damage to my fingernails, the spider fractures, and my sprained wrist convoluted the telltale injury. "That disarming technique isn't recommended because the pressure could easily tear tendons and seriously mess up your hand. If that's what I tried, I didn't have another choice."

The phone rang, and Martin checked the display. "I have to take this. Are you okay here?"

"Yeah." I realized I had a lot more to think about.

"Just the same," he went to the sink and picked up the pizza slicer, "I'm putting this away." He shoved it into a drawer and answered the phone, heading for the stairs.

"One more night of hell."

Picking up a pen, I scribbled down the new set of facts. When my head hurt from thinking too much, I picked up my prescription bottle, swallowed a pill, and locked myself in the second floor guest suite. I wouldn't risk another nightmare or Martin's safety again. At least, I felt confident that I wasn't a killer. That was an improvement from the way I felt upon awakening this morning. See, things were finally starting to look up.

*   *   *

The next day, Marcal gave me a ride to the federal building. I stopped by the crime lab, but Davenport and Ridley were out. From what I gathered, the footage was being scrubbed. Damn computers were never fast enough when I needed them. Annoyed, I stopped by Lucca's desk to say hello, but he was in a meeting. The fact that he'd taken over most of my caseload was appreciated, but I felt irrelevant and useless. I hated that feeling. Finally, I was out of distractions and knocked on Jablonsky's open office door.

"You showed up. Wonders never cease to amaze," Mark said. He glanced at the elastic bandage that I had wrapped around my wrist. "It looks like you've been busy."

"You knew." I should have been surprised, but since this began, I had the strangest feeling that Mark knew a lot more than he was letting on. "I don't like being kept in the dark."

"It was for your own good."

"Really? How?" The anger was uncontainable. "I'd love to hear what convoluted rationale you have this time."

"Easy, Agent," Jablonsky snapped. He focused on the open office door. "Don't you have an appointment?"

I slammed the door shut and crossed my arms over my chest. "I'm not going anywhere until you tell me what's really going on."

"I don't know." For the briefest moment, his gaze shifted to a folder on his desk. It had police codes and tabs on it. "The forensic experts weren't positive of the cause of your injury, and I will not put anything down in writing, even if it is speculation, because we don't know what the ramifications are. Plus, telling you anything could have caused further trauma or created false memories, and you don't need either of those things."

"Oh for god's sake," I growled, "did you hit your head and fall into some psychobabble alternate reality? You know I don't buy into any of that shit."

"Just because you don't see it as credible science doesn't mean it isn't." He leaned back in his chair. "I'm not your enemy, but we've done nothing but argue and fight. I know you're frustrated and scared which is why I've cut you some slack, but I will not allow you to continue to take it out on me. I'm still your boss, and you will act professionally, at least in the confines of this building. Is that understood?"

"Yes, sir," I said through gritted teeth.

"Good." He plucked a post-it from the stack and held it out. "Go talk to a professional. Feel free to bash the prick in charge that keeps pissing you off. It's confidential, so I won't hear about it."

"You would if it interferes with my ability to perform my duties."

"Well, then make sure everything you say to him doesn't conflict with what is expected of you. Dismissed."

Muttering curses under my breath, I went out the door and to the elevator. Dr. Weiler had been the Bureau shrink I'd been forced to talk to when my last partner died and I resigned. Quite frankly, Weiler was a large part of my need to leave this building and never come back. Perhaps Mark was trying to force me to leave again. Hell, it was a damn good plan.

Emerging from the elevator, I went down the hallway to his office, glanced up to make sure the Dr. Phil wannabe hadn't moved offices, and then cleared my throat. Weiler looked up, irritated by my presence. That made two of us.

"Agent Parker, have a seat," Weiler said. "I was surprised that SSA Jablonsky scheduled this meeting for you."

"You didn't know I came back?"

"I didn't know you wanted to." He gestured at the sofa.

"I've been informed of your recent incident. Have they made any progress?"

"The techs are working on it." I studied the couch for a moment. I'd had enough training to know the basics of body language and nonverbal communication. I also knew how Weiler worked. It was a chess game between us, or at least that's always how it seemed. Tired and annoyed, I lay down on the couch and stared at the ceiling, hoping to confuse him with this submissive position. "The hospital speculated I sustained a concussion. They aren't sure if my memory loss is caused by the physical trauma or something emotional, but they think I might remember some or all of it eventually."

"Have you remembered anything?" Weiler asked. He rolled his chair around from behind his desk to appear more open and picked up a pen and notepad.

"Bits and pieces. It comes in flashes. Sometimes in dreams."

"How can you be sure it's reality and not a fabrication of the mind?"

I shrugged. The short answer was I couldn't. The long answer was it felt different, but I couldn't elaborate my feeling into words. "Isn't reality nothing more than a fabrication of the mind?"

"I don't believe you were sent here to debate philosophy." Dr. Weiler dropped his glasses onto his legal pad and let out an audible sigh. "Agent Parker, this is for your benefit. Frankly, I have better things to do with my time. If you don't want my help, go away."

Biting my lip, I considered his words. "It's been a struggle, handling this." I turned my head and glanced at him. "I find it hard to trust people and myself. I've been arguing with everyone. I'm angry that this happened, and I'm even more enraged that I can't remember how it did."

"That's normal."

"Great, I'm normal. Can you write me a note or something?"

"How have you been sleeping?"

"Okay, except when I have a memory. It's like I'm reliving a snippet of what happened. It's not pretty."

He nodded, standing and crossing the room to the bookshelf. He skimmed through a few titles, pulled out a book, leafed through the pages, and returned to his chair. "Obviously, if you're remembering what happened, whatever trauma you endured is being repaired. In essence, your brain or psyche is healing. That's good."

"Wow, I was normal, and now I'm good. Next, you'll tell me I'm excellent."

"Sarcasm is a defense mechanism," he said, just to knock me down a few pegs. "Have you considered hypnosis to assist in recovering the missing pieces?"

"You just want to make me cluck like a chicken."

"That would be sarcasm." He closed the book and placed it on the edge of the desk. "You're afraid of what you forgot. Frankly, you ought to be. If your mind blocked it out, there had to be a reason."

"Thanks, Doc." I sighed. "Yeah, I know. Sarcasm, bad."

"Agent Parker, it is possible that injury or substance abuse could be the cause of your fog rather than repression. When you're asleep and your conscious mind is turned off, your subconscious continues to function. That may be the reason you remember things in dreams. In essence, your subconscious wants you to know what happened. Whether you like it or not, you'll probably recover most, if not all, of what happened. With hypnosis or some guided meditation, I can help you get there faster in a safe environment. It's up to you."

"Let me think about it." I sat up and eyed the book on his desk. "Can I borrow some reading material?"

"Absolutely."

FOURTEEN

"I can't believe I'm doing this," I said to my empty apartment. I'd read through a few chapters in the psych book and decided to follow the meditation advice listed. Frankly, if I completely lost it again, no one needed to be around to witness the mayhem, especially Dr. Weiler.

Locking my handgun in the safe, I scanned the area for other dangerous items. I was terrified. Luckily, I was alone. The chances of intentionally hurting myself were nonexistent. But I'd done a fine job clawing at my own bandages, so it didn't hurt to hide the sharp objects, just in case.

After leaving the OIO building, I called Martin. We had a conversation. It could have gone better, but needless to say, he was giving me space until my head was on straight. The sooner I got this over with, the sooner life could get back to normal. I liked the status quo. I'd give anything to return to it, even buying into this mumbo jumbo.

Taking a deep breath, I exhaled slowly and sunk onto the sofa. Closing my eyes, I concentrated on my breathing and heartbeat. Whatever thoughts entered my mind, I acknowledged them as nothing more than thoughts and allowed them to pass, making sure not to dwell on any of them. I couldn't force my memory to return. I had to be patient. After five minutes of trying not to think and failing because I was thinking about not thinking, I sat up.

"This is crap," I hissed, glaring at the book.

Flipping on the television, I channel surfed for a while, quickly growing bored. It was impossible to sit by and do nothing when there was a puzzle that needed solving. My notes were at Martin's, but I'd exiled myself from his place. Starting over, I took a vastly new approach and went with nothing but my gut. By the end, I hadn't reached any new conclusions. Someone was dead, and I had been there. That explained so much but left a million unanswered questions.

I needed to find the body. Taking a seat at the computer, I typed in a few search parameters, looking through a list of recent missing persons, murder victims, and unidentified John Does. At least my federal agent status was good for something. However, no one fit the bill of what I remembered. I dialed O'Connell and asked if homicide had been called to investigate any deaths involving GSWs. Of course, they had, but none of the bodies were encased in plastic wrap or fit the description I provided.

Hanging up, I remembered one shot, dead center, between the eyes. Come on, I coaxed my mind to obey, give me something else. Closing my eyes, I clung to that image, dismissing the irrational emotional response it elicited. I was safe. A memory couldn't harm me. The man was bound to a chair, but he was sideways on the floor. Blood ran from the head wound in a single line down his face. He remained unblinking in a state of absolute terror. I inhaled slowly, scanning my mind for other details.

"Oh, god." My eyes shot open at the image of his detective's shield. "He was a cop." From the way his jacket hung, it obscured his badge number. I didn't recognize him. From the angle, I must have been standing over him. A gun lay on the ground a few feet from his body.

"Knock, knock." Jablonsky's voice outside my front door startled me, and I screamed. "Parker?" he yelled from the other side of the door. "Parker, are you okay? Answer me."

"Hang on," I replied, hoping he wouldn't knock my door

down to get inside. "You scared me." I threw open the door, gave the gun in his hand a brief look, and hugged him.

"What's wrong?" He stepped inside, checking for intruders. "I figured after our tiff in my office, you wouldn't let me in. Did Weiler give you happy pills or something?"

"No," I closed the applications on my computer and dropped into the chair, "I was remembering details. We have a problem."

"Now what?"

"The dead guy, he's a cop. Was a cop." I rubbed my head. "He had a badge beneath his jacket. There was a gun, his gun, I guess, on the floor near him. I was standing over him."

"Are you sure you didn't find him that way?" Jablonsky asked, no longer pretending my memories were fictional misrepresentations.

"It's doubtful. The blood was still dripping." My stomach lurched, and I swallowed the bile that rose in my throat.

"What about the informant?"

"What?"

"You were meeting with a CI and his handler. Presumably, the dead cop would have been his handler. So where's the CI? He's probably our shooter." Mark looked at me. "He must have attacked you."

"Attacked?" I shook my head. "Back up a second. You believe me? You aren't insisting that I'm crazy?"

"You'll always be crazy. You have to be to do what you do, but that's beside the point." He removed a USB drive from his pocket. "We found you on the DOT footage. We know what happened to you before you ended up outside that parking garage. Davenport is backtracking further to locate your original location, but it's progress."

"Am I alone? Maybe we can ID the men with me and figure out who was killed."

"Alex," he plugged the drive into my computer, "it's just you. We have the plates. Lucca's running down the owner."

Before I could ask any further questions, Mark clicked on the video file, and black and white footage filled my monitor. Traffic and pedestrians were sparse, and I looked at the timestamp. It was almost two a.m. A dark colored SUV drove down the street. Without slowing, the back door opened, and something fell out.

Reaching over, Mark paused the footage, clicked on the magnification button, and hit play. "That's you."

"Holy shit."

I watched as my body hit the ground, bouncing and tumbling until the rolling came to a stop. The SUV didn't slow until it was half a block away. By that time, I had crawled out of view. The SUV abruptly stopped. But it had passed through the intersection, and with the changing light, it couldn't backtrack.

"They circled around less than two minutes later," Jablonsky declared. "They must have been looking for you. From the evidence inside that alley, you must have gone through there to get away from whoever was driving. Obviously, they didn't plan on your quick exit."

"The dome light," I said in awe as a rush of memories emerged. "I remember being preoccupied with a dome light. I was afraid it would light up and alert them, but they already knew." Biting my lip, I looked down at my hand. It was connected to the SUV, but I couldn't figure out how. Blinding pain shot through my skull, and I squeezed my eyes shut. "It's right there. I can almost see it." Slamming my palm against the desk, I let out a growl. "I don't remember his face. Too many pieces are missing."

"It's okay. We have a lot to go on right now." He looked at me. "I'm surprised you aren't more dinged up. Most people don't jump out of a moving vehicle and walk away with scrapes and bruises."

"I'm great at rolling. Can't you tell?" I rewound the footage and watched it a few more times. I remembered excruciating pain, a door handle, and the rough fibers of the floorboard. "Lucca's tracking the SUV?"

"Yes, and Davenport is working on tracking it through the city's grid. Hopefully, we'll know something solid tonight."

"What about the cop that was killed?" Now that I remembered him, I couldn't get the image of the blood from the gunshot trickling across the bridge of his nose out of my mind. "You should contact the PD. They might have a better lead."

Mark assessed me for a moment. "They'll want to question you. Are you sure you can handle that?"

"They have a right to know what happened. His family should be aware."

"It's been days, Alex. They must realize something's wrong. It's not like we have answers or hard evidence. What can you possibly tell them? Shit, we don't even know who was killed."

"I was there."

"Did you do it?" he asked, catching me by surprise. "Agent Parker, you say that you remember a man being shot and that he had a badge. Did you shoot him?"

"I don't know."

"Dammit, that's exactly why contacting the police at this point is suicidal. I know you have a few friends in the major crimes unit, but most of the cops remember you as a snitch that turned on one of their own. They won't offer you any favors, and until they have the person responsible in custody, they'll blame you."

I knew it was true. The system was flawed, and even my federal agent status wouldn't exempt me from the police department's need for justice. The worst part was I didn't know if I was responsible. From what I knew of the situation, the cop was on the ground and his gun was nearby. He could have failed to announce, and we exchanged fire. Although, that didn't explain why he was bound to the chair. Obviously, someone else had been nearby that wanted me dead, given the SUV that I narrowly escaped from. The cop could have been a casualty or the impetus for my capture and escape.

"You didn't kill him. We don't have hard proof, but the circumstantial stuff is all in your favor. Just give us some time." Mark gave my shoulder a squeeze. "Are you feeling better about things?"

"A little, I guess. It was bad enough when I was the victim, but the stakes are much higher now. We need to find the asshole responsible." I got out of the chair on shaky limbs. These revelations were proving to be too much for me. "Isn't there something we can do?"

"It would help if we knew why you were meeting with a cop."

"I don't know. I'll pull my notes, and we can see if something surfaces. I've gone through them, but that was before my memory started to return. Maybe I'll find something I missed."

"Let's get started. I'll order Chinese."

Rifling through my notes and documents, I searched for a clue as to why I needed a detective's help. Most of my current caseload involved analysis, monitoring surveillance updates, and performing the usual tasks that accompanied crimes. Frankly, the last couple of weeks prior to the incident had been rather dull. Lots of paperwork and hanging out in the office. The only open case on my desk with teeth dealt with Shade.

"Have we received any intel from the PD's intelligence or counterterrorism unit regarding Shade?" I asked.

"No, our intel suggests they're functioning outside our borders," Jablonsky replied, lowering the legal pad I'd used to list a network of their contacts.

"But DHS issued an alert of a possible impending attack. Wouldn't the locals be aware?"

"DHS always issues alerts of possible impending attacks. Frankly, I think the PD uses the news alerts as a drinking game." He chuckled. "We could do the same, but then we'd be too blitzed to get any work done."

I stared at him, not finding any of this amusing. "Is that a yes or a no?"

"If the locals contacted us, you didn't make a note of it."

"Who did you put on the intel besides Lucca?" I hoped to call someone and get a straight answer. This felt promising.

"Shade isn't a top priority right now. They haven't made any overt threats to national security. There haven't been any attempted plots or intel saying otherwise." He sighed. "I'll call the office and get someone to double-check, but I highly doubt the PD bothered to check with us about this."

While Jablonsky was on the phone, I considered his words. If the police department hadn't reached out, maybe

I did. But why? If Shade posed an imminent threat, I would have taken official action through the proper channels. Everyone would have been notified and on high alert. No, this was something else. None of my current cases required local law enforcement, and anything that dealt with my testimony in the Bard case would have involved Det. Heathcliff, not an unidentified cop. Maybe it was an old case, but those records weren't here.

"Hey, Parker," Jablonsky said, covering the mouthpiece, "when's the last time you took a side job?"

"I haven't lately. The last P.I. job I worked was for one of Martin's acquaintances, and it overlapped with that gambling ring we busted."

"And you haven't done anything since?"

It was no secret that I had spent my hiatus from the OIO as a security consultant and private investigator. My P.I. office had remained empty since my return to the OIO. Once my lease expired, I figured I'd close up shop and stick to a government paycheck. Jablonsky said I could take work on the side if I kept it below the radar, but my potential clients needed more time and energy than I could spare. Corporate work paid better, but it wasn't as fulfilling.

"No." I shook my head for emphasis.

"Well, that doesn't help." Mark removed his hand from the mouthpiece and turned his back to focus on the call. "Right, Lucca's working on it, but I need to find out if the police department contacted us after the DHS alert. It's in relation to a different matter."

Before the futile feeling returned, someone knocked on my door. "I'll get it," I declared, hoping the delivery guy remembered to toss in a few packets of duck sauce. Opening my front door, I took a step back.

"Agent Parker?" the police officer asked.

I looked at the two unfamiliar cops standing in my doorway. "I take it you aren't here to deliver my Chinese food."

"No, ma'am." He glanced inside. "We're Detectives Delaney and Collins. May we come in?"

"That depends. What's this about?"

"We have a few questions," Delaney said.

Jablonsky hung up the phone and stepped closer, subtly shifting his stance to make his OIO badge visible. "How can we help you, gentlemen?"

"Sir, this doesn't concern you," Collins said.

"The hell it doesn't. Parker is my agent. What's going on?" Jablonsky asked.

"Agent Parker's credentials and firearm were discovered at a crime scene. Can we please talk inside?"

"Fine," I stepped away from the door, fighting the urge to ask a dozen questions of my own, "what crime scene?"

The detectives exchanged a look but refused to answer me. Jablonsky caught my eye and shook his head. It was best that I keep my mouth shut. Talking would lead to trouble, and I already had enough of that in my life.

"Where were you Friday night?" Delaney asked. His eyes examined the bandage on my wrist and the few visible cuts and bruises. "It looks like you had an altercation recently."

"Friday night I was at work. Then something happened, and I woke up outside a parking garage the next morning," I said, watching the look of disbelief cross Delaney's face. "My property was reported stolen." I stared at him, shifting into interrogation mode. "Where did you find it?"

"You expect us to believe that you conveniently forgot what happened?" Collins spat.

"Do you want to see my medical report?" I asked.

"Perhaps later," Delaney said. "This is a courtesy call. It would be best if you tell us exactly what happened and what you remember. This will go a lot easier if you cooperate."

"I am cooperating," I said. Cold, hard bitch was my default setting when the shit hit the fan, and right now, it was getting flung around the room by an industrial grade cooling unit. "Where did you find my ID?"

"At the site of a double homicide," Collins said. "Ballistics is being run as we speak, but the clip in your gun was three bullets shy. From what the ME says, they're the same caliber as the bullets pulled out of," he swallowed, "our DBs."

"Who?" I asked, but Mark interrupted.

"You can't seriously be accusing a federal agent of murder," Mark growled, "especially one that was also attacked."

"Why the hell didn't we receive word of such an attack?" Collins asked. "Assault is a local crime."

"Not if it's an assault on a federal agent," Mark retorted. "We take care of our own."

"So do we," Collins said, and I knew that one of the bodies they discovered was the slain cop.

"Where were they discovered?" I asked, receiving a searing look from Mark.

"That doesn't matter. You weren't there, right? Just your gun, your badge, and perhaps some DNA or fingerprints, unless you were careful," Collins said.

"Get out," Mark ordered. "This conversation is over."

"We'll be back," Delaney said. He handed me his business card. "Think about it. If you weren't there, talking to us will clear you from suspicion. We want to catch whoever's responsible. Shouldn't you want the same thing since you claim you were also victimized?"

"I do want the same thing, but I can't tell you what I don't remember." A part of me wanted to unload everything, but it would confuse matters and shift the blame completely to me. I couldn't take that risk when we were so close to uncovering the truth. My colleagues were already following two promising leads. They'd get there faster than the police would. They had to.

"Fine, we'll go, but next time won't be so cordial," Collins warned.

FIFTEEN

"Relax," Mark said, shoving a container of Chinese food toward me, "they're performing their due diligence. At least we have some idea what's happened. I put a call in to Lt. Moretti. He'll get a copy of the report sent over first thing in the morning. In the meantime, we were making some headway, remember?"

"Sure." My appetite had evaporated as soon as the cops arrived. "Who do you think the second DB is?"

"The CI," Mark replied, jabbing his chopsticks into the container. "It's probably safe to assume that your gun was used in the commission of the crime. The police will be back with more questions, so we need to have some answers ready."

"Until something pans out, we can't be sure of anything." It didn't seem likely that I was the killer given the additional information we had about the SUV and my kamikaze leap from the moving vehicle, but it was possible. "I don't know who shot them. I can't even say with one hundred percent certainty that I didn't. I called and told you that I thought I killed someone."

"Well, we can spin it to be nothing more than hearsay. Shit, our connection was bad. Perhaps I didn't hear a word you said." He put the container down. "They don't need to know about our conversation or any of your cockamamie theories. Whatever you do, do not talk openly to the police until you're completely cleared from suspicion."

"I won't."

"Good girl."

He picked up the container and continued to eat, rereading my notes on Shade. While he was occupied, I took to pacing. When the silence threatened to break whatever was left of my sanity, I grabbed the cordless phone off the charger and dialed Lucca. It went to voicemail, and I hung up.

"Do you have the license plate number handy?" I asked. Since the boy scout wasn't neck deep in DMV records, I could at least do that much.

"Why do you want the plate? We identified the owner. Lucca went to have a chat with him. He and Cooper figured they might make more progress by pounding the pavement. Unfortunately, the vehicle was reported stolen."

"Big surprise." I sighed. "Did it have a security system or GPS? They might be able to track its location or previous locations."

"Parker, I might have told Marty that you are one of the brightest agents I've ever seen, but that doesn't mean that Lucca or anyone else in our department is incompetent. They know what to do."

"So why are you here?" I asked, realizing that Mark's appearance outside my door served no real function.

"You don't have a protection detail. I thought you could use the company. Plus, I updated you on our progress, and we touched base on your visit with the shrink. Don't blame an old man for being worried about you."

"I appreciate it." Slumping onto the couch, I didn't have the energy to pace any longer. "If the SUV has GPS, that information ought to make it easier for Davenport to trace the route it took and determine my original location."

"That's precisely what's being done." Mark glanced at the time. "Why don't you call it a night?"

"Are you sure they don't need an extra set of eyes on this? I'd be more than happy to help track down these bastards."

"You can't, especially now that the police have a vested interest. We need to avoid the appearance of impropriety, at least until we have the actual culprit in our crosshairs." He cleared the Chinese food off the table, stuffing it inside my fridge. "Get some sleep. I'll be back later after I check on their progress and make a stop at the police station. I'll take care of this, Alex. Everything will be okay."

"Right, and unicorns are real."

"They are the national animal of Scotland." Mark smirked. "I'll keep my phone on if you need me."

"Thanks."

After he left, I wound myself into a frenzy. Antsy and aggravated, my nerves were frayed, and I found myself jumping at the slightest creak. Eventually, the pacing and worry were too much for my mending body to deal with, and I conked out for the rest of the night, dead to the world around me.

* * *

The next morning, I felt calm. The questions from last night were manageable. Jablonsky was right; someone on the team would handle it. Everything would be okay. Whatever happened to me and those two lost souls would be determined, and the party responsible would pay. I needed to have faith in myself, my colleagues, and the police department.

Walking out of my bedroom, I jumped at the sight of a man rummaging through my refrigerator. "What the hell are you doing here?" I asked. "How did you get in?"

"Relax, Parker, you gave me your keys, or don't you remember?" Lucca asked. Holding up the container of orange juice, he added, "I hope you don't mind."

"I gave you my keys?" I narrowed my eyes, unable to recall that event. "Fine, whatever you say." Shaking my head, I took a seat at the island in my kitchen. "Why are you here?"

"Jablonsky said he briefed you last night." I nodded, so Lucca continued. "The owner turned out to be a bust. He reported the SUV stolen two days before you were attacked...or whatever we're calling it. We have no reason to believe he's involved. Our computer techs examined surveillance footage from the lot where the vehicle had been parked. Two unsubs broke into the SUV. We haven't had any luck identifying them."

"Great update," I said sardonically, "but it wasn't worth a glass of juice."

"No?" Lucca grinned. "You might reconsider. In fact, I'm thinking you're gonna owe me a top-shelf bottle of vodka to add to the juice."

"What did you find?"

He leaned back, taking a long sip from the glass. "You aren't working the case, so I'm under no obligation to tell you. Quite frankly, it's against protocol to discuss an open case with a civilian."

"I'm not a civilian."

"You're on medical leave."

"You will be too, if you don't start talking."

"Fine," he still had that self-satisfied look on his face, "Davenport tracked the SUV to a restaurant. Jablonsky wants you to see if any of it looks familiar." His eyes lingered on my pajama shorts. "You might want to change first."

"Brilliant assessment."

After a quick shower, I returned to the living room, stuck my nine millimeter into my shoulder holster, and donned a jacket. Lucca was at the kitchen table, helping himself to the breakfast cereal that he had mocked. I gave him a look, but he ignored it. When he was done, he washed the bowl and left it in the drain board to dry.

"Your presence isn't in an official capacity," Lucca warned. "You're a cooperating witness, so don't ask questions or take over the investigation like you always do."

"Fine."

He led us downstairs to his car. "Jablonsky said the police questioned you last night. Is there anything I should know?"

That question struck me as odd, and I turned to face him, wondering what he was thinking. "Like what?"

He shrugged. "Did you remember anything else? What do they know about our investigation?"

"I didn't say much. Jablonsky was there. I'm sure he gave you the play-by-play."

Lucca nodded, and the rest of the drive was in uncomfortable silence. At least, I was uncomfortable. I couldn't tell if it was because being around Lucca had that effect or if it was some odd familiarity about the path we were taking and our destination. An unsettling feeling crept its way into my belly, and when Lucca parked at a meter a block from the building, I knew I'd been here before.

"Parker," Lucca asked, "are you all right?"

I stared out the windshield. "I have the weirdest feeling of déjà vu."

"C'mon," he opened his door, "let's see if anyone remembers you. Maybe this is where you were."

Following him down the sidewalk, the anxious feeling in my gut grew stronger. Something was wrong. He stopped at the front door to Pepper, a local bar and grill. The hours were etched in the window. I stared at the frosty white script, but it wasn't familiar.

"I called ahead," Lucca said. "The manager agreed to let us check out the place before they open. It'll give you a chance to look around."

"This is the place?" I asked. "I was here?"

"I don't know. You tell me."

I didn't like the non-answer I was given. It sounded like the doublespeak Jablonsky had been using lately. I much preferred straight answers. Hell, even bald-faced lies might be a welcomed change. Certainty, that's what I wanted. Something had to change. We entered the establishment, and while Lucca spoke to the hostess who was rolling silverware in napkins in preparation for the afternoon opening, I surveyed the room.

It was a restaurant with a bar in the center, restrooms to the left side, and the kitchen around the back. The dining room was divided into four main sections. Moving through the room, I went to the far left corner, hoping that a different angle might jog my memory. Glancing around, I moved to the bar and took a seat at one of the stools.

Etched in the wood were the initials T.F. + J.C. I traced my finger along the indentions. Closing my eyes, I remembered doing that before. The martini glasses were stemless, and rum and coke was served in square glasses with artisan ice cubes. Intent on discovering if my memory was accurate, I went around the bar and checked the shelves of glassware. Stemless martini glasses and square highball glasses covered a few levels. The wine glasses were also stemless, but I didn't remember anyone ordering wine. What was I drinking? Was I drinking? I knew I shouldn't have been, and my initial thought was I had ordered a virgin rum and coke, but my tox report said otherwise.

I froze in place, pondering what I remembered. I saw the glasses on the bar — a martini glass, a highball glass, and a beer bottle. Noise surrounded us, and I traced the carved initials in the wood with my fingertip. Obviously, I hadn't sustained any splinters at that point. Faces, I needed to recall faces. Squeezing my eyes shut, I tried to visualize the rest of the room. Cash was laid on the bar, and a meaty hand pulled it away. There was a set of manicured fingernails tapping next to me, but that was inconsequential. Why couldn't I remember anything important?

"Dammit," I snarled at my own faulty memory.

A few of the nearby busboys and servers glanced up from their pre-opening prep to glare at me. Shaking it off, I crossed the room to where Lucca was speaking to the manager. The hostess had returned to rolling her silverware, but she remained close enough to eavesdrop. Excusing himself, Lucca took my elbow and led me out of earshot.

"Parker, does anything look familiar?"

"I've been here before."

"Good. What do you remember?"

"The kind of stemware they have at the bar." My eyes narrowed in at the wooden tables and chairs. "Did you notice the furniture?"

"Yeah." He waited, hoping that I would offer some

insight or fill in the blanks, but I had no recollection of being at a table or sitting in one of the chairs. "Give the place a final looksy, and we'll get out of here."

"Do they have a security system? What about receipts? How about the bartender? Someone might recognize me and be able to tell you who I was with."

"It's my investigation." He jerked his head to the side. "I'll handle those questions."

Deciding that arguing was pointless, I made my way through the different areas of the dining room, not finding any additional memory triggers. Moving toward the restrooms, I hoped I would remember something, but I didn't. The bar and the glasses seemed to be the only thing I recalled. Maybe I was a lush with a problem. Disheartened, I continued my walkthrough, ending up in the hallway to the kitchen.

From here, I could see white tile floors. Moving deeper down the hallway, I stood in the doorway of the kitchen. The neon red emergency exit sign was in the far corner of the room above a door. The room was nothing but white and stainless steel. Stainless steel tables, prep stations, cooking utensils, and shelves filled the space. It was clean and pristine, but something about this space felt sinister. My eyes roamed over the surfaces, tracing the grout in the tile and the sharp corners of the tables. Finally, my eyes came to rest on a drain in the floor.

"Oh my god." I stepped backward, knocking over a mixing bowl with a clatter that drew the attention of everyone inside the restaurant. I bent over and picked it up, suddenly feeling a sense of doom fill me.

"Parker?" Lucca asked, coming to see what the noise was, along with several of the restaurant employees.

Before I could say a word, my eyes locked on a busboy that had been lingering inside the kitchen while the cooks prepped for the day's meals. His gaze shifted from me to Lucca, and I knew in that instant he would run. He turned on his heel, bursting out the emergency exit. Without hesitating, I took off after him.

"Go around," I yelled to Lucca as I darted through the kitchen and out the door after the man.

SIXTEEN

Running from a federal agent wasn't advisable under the best circumstances, and these were far from stellar conditions. This was personal. I chased him out the door, ending up at the back of the building. The area was completely contained, or so it appeared. I slowed my pace, drawing my weapon in anticipation of the unknown. Where the hell did he go?

I moved forward; my gaze focused on the dumpster ahead while my peripheral vision monitored the surrounding area for signs of movement. Lucca hadn't followed behind, so I was right to assume that there was another way around. I considered the location of the restaurant on the block. Dumpsters lined the enclosed space, and doors lined either side. It must open up at the end of the block. If the busboy had enough of a head start, he'd run right into Lucca.

Why the hell did he run? I wondered, keeping my head on a swivel. A stray cat jumped down from the lid of one of the dumpsters behind me. Spinning, I focused my aim on the furry creature, but he seemed oblivious to his near-death experience.

Inhaling, I turned around, carefully flipping open the

nearest dumpster, but no one was hiding inside. Continuing on my path, I began to reconsider my direction, wondering if the cat had been spooked by someone besides me. I checked the first door I passed, but it was locked. I turned my head to check the opposite direction again. While I was distracted, the adjacent door swung open hard, knocking into my back and sending me sprawling. I landed spread eagle, barely maintaining my grip on the gun.

"Federal agent," I shouted, "freeze."

The busboy didn't falter. Instead, he gained speed, determined to get away as if his life depended on it. I pulled myself off the ground and ran after him. He wasn't a runner, and I was gaining on him. It helped that he was stuck in an enclosed space and there was only one way to go.

"I said freeze," I growled.

Barreling forward, I was almost close enough to take him down when a sharp pain shot through my body. The world blinked out for just a second, but by the time my focus returned, he had turned the corner and was on the main street. I continued after him for a few more seconds until my heart threatened to beat out of my chest and my body cried out for oxygen. Stopping, I bent over, forcing deep breaths down my throat.

"Parker," Lucca ran up, "are you okay?"

"Go," I pointed down the street, "go after him." My words came in between huffs, and Lucca hesitated before continuing pursuit. As soon as he was gone, I sunk to the ground. I needed to call for back-up, but I couldn't do anything aside from breathe. When the tunnel vision cleared and I was no longer gasping, I reached for the phone.

"Don't bother," Lucca said, trudging toward me, "he's gone." He offered his hand and helped me up. "What part of cooperating witness did you not understand?"

"All of it."

"Obviously. Do you have any idea who that guy was?"

"No," I considered the question, "I just knew he would run."

"Repressed memory or instinct?"

"Both, I guess. We need a name, an address, and I want security footage from the restaurant. Something went down, and that busboy knows what happened."

After an hour of listening to the manager stonewall most of Lucca's questions, we left the restaurant. Unless we had a warrant, Pepper refused to hand over security footage or receipts. The vindictive part of my psyche hoped that the manager was involved, and that we would have the joy of eventually arresting him. But it wasn't a crime to assert one's rights.

"So we get a warrant," I said, climbing into the car. "That shouldn't be too difficult."

"What happened during the pursuit?" Lucca asked, changing the subject. "You've never been outrun by a suspect. You're still not feeling good?"

"I'm recovering. It's a process. One step forward, two back, a little dizzy spell here and there, but I'm fine."

He gave me that annoying disappointed look of his. I should be immune to it by now since I got it often enough, but I wasn't. "You shouldn't have pursued. Even if you caught him, we'd have enough trouble explaining that."

"Oh, so it's better that he got away?"

"I didn't say that, Parker. Stop twisting my words. I know how displeased you are with the current situation, but you're putting yourself in harm's way. And you're putting me in danger too."

"He rabbited. That's on him. You told me to look around. I did. He must have recognized me and ran. That's not my fault."

"I guess not." He flipped on the signal light and headed in the opposite direction of the federal building. "I'm taking you home. You need to rest. You're not ready to be out in the field."

I wanted to protest, but I knew he was right. "Thanks for having my back."

"Yeah." He pulled to a stop in front of my building. "I'll let you know when we bring him in."

"And when the warrant comes through." I smiled at him. "I know I'm not on the case. You can't discuss that with an agent who's out on medical leave."

"I'll make sure you're in the loop."

"Careful, boy scout, your badge might get tarnished if you keep bending the rules."

"It's already too late. You're my partner. I have your back."

Giving him a bittersweet smile, I shut the door and patted the side of the SUV. Then I went up the stairs to my apartment. Truth be told, Lucca was a nice guy, but I had the habit of being a sarcastic bitch sometimes. Maybe I'd try to be nicer. I didn't want to be friends, and I knew I was close to crossing over to the dark side. My walls were up to protect myself from the potential pain of losing someone else that I cared about. But after this ordeal, I knew I could rely on Lucca, and he should be afforded the same courtesy. I just hoped that I wouldn't fail my new partner the same way I failed my old one.

After entering my apartment, I took off my jacket and slipped out of the shoulder holster, feeling a sticky dampness on my back. Great. Taking off my shirt, I soaked it in the sink and tried to get a look at my back. Martin was right; the bruises did look significantly worse than they originally had. Of course, my run-in with the car door, the parking pole, and our suspect today hadn't helped matters. The lacerations on my back had reopened, but once they were cleaned, they didn't appear much worse. I just needed to take it easy and not bump into anything for a week or two.

It was around dinnertime when Jablonsky knocked on my door. From the look on his face, I knew it wasn't good news. He entered, going straight to the liquor cabinet and pouring a couple fingers of whiskey. After knocking it back, he took a seat at the counter.

"The judge won't issue a warrant. He thinks it's a fishing expedition," Mark said, not meeting my eyes.

"Did you tell him that two men were murdered and an agent was injured?"

"Of course, which he interpreted as law enforcement's misguided need to subvert the system by infringing upon individual rights."

"It's a fucking restaurant."

"No shit." He looked at me. "Apparently a few hours after you and Lucca left, the police showed up to ask their own questions. They must have gotten the address off the SUV's GPS since they impounded the vehicle yesterday." He poured another glass and downed it. "The bodies were found plastic wrapped in the trunk. Two slugs in one and a single shot in the other. Your credentials were inside the trunk, and your gun was found in the back seat. GSR was all over the vehicle. The police won't release the identities of the victims, but Lt. Moretti did confirm that one of the deceased was a cop."

My lungs deflated, and I dropped into a chair before my legs gave out. I remembered the trunk, the sound of the gunfire, and the dead detective. I remembered too much and not enough. It wasn't fair. Inhaling slowly, I put my head in my hands. I had to silence that voice inside that said I was responsible. It didn't make sense, but it was how I was wired to feel. The weight of the world rested on my shoulders, or so Martin had said. Obviously, he wasn't wrong.

"What about the busboy?" I asked, attempting to distract myself with other information.

"His place is under surveillance, but he hasn't been back. I spoke with the police department, and they've issued an all points on Jacob House." Mark capped the bottle and returned it to the liquor cabinet. "Lucca said you didn't recognize him. But House ran, and you gave chase."

"Pretty much."

"Is there anything you forgot to mention?"

"No," I searched my mind, "but his name is familiar."

"How so?"

"I don't know." I bit my lip and crossed the room to my computer, searching through my files for a hit. The query came up blank, and I shook my head. "Do we have a profile on him? He must be guilty of something. He ran."

"He has a driver's license and a work visa on file at Pepper. However, we've run his ID through the database, and it's a fake. He might have run because he was afraid of getting caught."

"We weren't there to arrest him. He recognized me.

That's why he ran. He knows something or saw something."

"Then we need to find him before the police do. Their priority will be to get a cop killer off the street, and I'm not sure we can trust whatever an illegal immigrant says inside an interrogation room."

"Do you honestly believe the cops will try to pin this on me?"

"If I say yes, are you going to go on the lam again?" He glared at me. "That was the dumbest thing that you've ever done. Don't even think about it."

"I wasn't, but we both know the evidence points to me. It's either a setup or I was fortunate enough to escape."

"Your injuries and DOT cams suggest escape. House might have seen the actual killer. He might be able to clear you. I just think it'd be beneficial that we talk to him first."

"Are you sure he wasn't running from me because he saw me shoot them?"

"Parker, how the hell did you lift two grown men into the back of a SUV? You're strong, and you can fight. But I don't see you performing a two hundred pound deadlift. Practical reasoning is on your side, remember that."

"Well, it's not like I can remember much else."

"Oh for christ's sake, I'm sick of the self-pity. You're lucky. Those men weren't."

"I know, and that's why I'm so angry. I was there. I should be able to help. I want to help, Mark. I want to tell you what happened. I want whoever is responsible to pay. I just can't remember. And it kills me. It rips a hole through my heart every time I flash back to seeing one of their bodies. I can't stand the helplessness, the impotence, the," I raised my hands as if I were strangling an imaginary person, "the utter uselessness. God," I put my head in my hands, "I even spoke to Dr. Weiler and tried this hypno-meditation crap. It won't come, and it's my fault because I'm too weak or scared to remember it."

"Alexis," Mark said, crossing the room to be near me, "it'll come. Give it time."

A wave of nausea struck me like a ton of bricks, and I swallowed the burning bile, gagging slightly. "Get away."

"What?"

I pushed back, rolling my chair away from Mark and the desk. The smell of the liquor was stuck in my nasal cavity, and I couldn't shake it. It made me sick, and I remembered all the worst hangovers I ever had. None of those ever resulted in this type of lasting reaction.

"It's the whiskey."

He gave me a curious look. "Well, we know you're not pregnant. The hospital would have mentioned that. Is it just whiskey?"

"Scotch too, but they're incredibly similar."

"I want to try an experiment, but you won't like it." Mark went to the liquor cabinet and pulled out a few different bottles. "How about we start with vodka?" He uncapped the bottle and held it out. "Take a sniff."

SEVENTEEN

I couldn't remember the last time I'd spent the night with my head in the toilet. Then again, wasn't it two nights ago that I slept on the bathroom floor? This was not a pattern I wanted to repeat. My sides ached, and my throat burned. Jablonsky pushed a bottle of Gatorade toward me, looking apologetic.

"You ought to hydrate," he said.

"I should take that bottle and shove it up your ass," I hissed. Closing the toilet seat lid, I rested my cheek against the top and stared at him. "What time did I roll out of that SUV?"

"Around two a.m."

"So the alcohol was introduced to my system between eight p.m. and two a.m., and the hospital ran the tox report at nine a.m.?"

"That sounds about right."

"Which means I was fucking blitzed." I knew there was a way to calculate what my BAC had been at two a.m., but I couldn't remember the exact formula. Surely, the techs could determine that if necessary, but it was safe to assume I was well beyond the legal limit. I was probably near the alcohol poisoning end of the spectrum. "That's why I'm having trouble remembering what happened."

"Your body remembers better than you do," Mark said. "Do you have any idea what you were drinking?"

I'd reacted poorly to every bottle in my liquor cabinet. Honestly, I could have been drinking anything that night, but something told me it hadn't been by choice. Mark uncapped the Gatorade bottle and held it in front of my face.

"Drink this."

"Put that down. I don't want it," I said, not wanting to have a second viewing of the neon yellow liquid.

"Fine, do what you want. I'm not going to force it down your throat." He leaned back against the vanity. "For the record, I didn't expect you to get so violently ill."

"Yeah, well, my stomach is apparently my Achilles heel." I considered getting up, but the queasiness hadn't completely gone away yet. "Although, I haven't been sick like this in a while. I guess it was about time."

A thought crossed Mark's mind, and he stood up and went into the living room. "We might be able to retrace your steps. You must have gotten sick somewhere between Pepper and the parking garage." He sent a few texts and returned to the bathroom. "We'll see if that leads to anything."

"Okay." Braving the possibility of a relapse, I stood and rinsed my mouth in the sink. "Is it odd that I find this development reassuring?"

"What do you mean?"

"I finally have an explanation for why I can't remember things clearly, and it isn't because of some deep-seated trauma or repressed memory. It's because of the shit that some asshole force-fed me." The words came out of my mouth without any thought behind them, but I knew they were true. "We just have to figure out why."

"And who."

"Yeah." I returned to the living room. "Do me a favor and clear that shit out of here. I don't care what you do with it. Drink it, pour it down the drain, whatever. I just don't want to see it or smell it." Shuddering, I went into my room and flopped onto the bed. "Call if there are any updates."

"You do realize that you work for me, right?" Jablonsky asked, peeking around the doorjamb. "Because it sure as hell doesn't feel like it most of the time."

"Fine, what do you want me to do, boss?"

"Get some sleep. Clear your head." He entered my room and picked up the pill bottle. "Are you taking these?"

"Sometimes."

"They probably aren't helping with the fogginess." He put the bottle down. "Is Marty on his way?"

"It's just me tonight."

"All right. I'll unload whatever cheap liquor you still have in this dump, and then I'll camp out on the couch. If you need something, let me know."

I voiced numerous words to the contrary, but he waved his hand, dismissing my protests. While I remained in bed, staring at the ceiling and listening to the clink of the bottles being removed from the cabinet, my mind drifted over the recent facts. I considered giving the meditation thing another shot but decided that allowing my mind to wander was a better alternative. Once my front door opened and closed for the second time and the sound of the TV filled the silence, I relaxed. It was safe to let the thoughts come and the memories resurface.

Sleep came intermittently while I drifted in and out of the haze of memories. At some point, my own scream woke me, but Mark was used to such occurrences and didn't bother to check on me. By dawn, I had pieced together a few more vague recollections. Sitting up, I put my face in my hands and took a moment to become reacquainted with reality.

Wanting someone to talk to, I trudged into the living room. Jablonsky was snoring slightly on the couch, but after loudly clearing my throat, he shook himself awake and gazed at me. I curled up on the loveseat and waited.

"What now?" His voice was scratchy and rough.

"The detective was murdered in the kitchen at Pepper. I don't know who pulled the trigger. It could have been anyone, but I remember being near the doorway to the dining room. He was bound closer to the exit sign. That damn glow from the sign," I swallowed, "it might have been the only light in the room." I closed my eyes. "It's like I'm there now."

He sat up. "What else do you see?"

"Blood dripping down the drain."

"Alex, what do you hear?"

I squeezed my eyes tighter, nervous to experience more. "Men speaking. An argument maybe." I scrunched my brow and opened my eyes. "I don't know. Three gunshots, clear as day. That's about it."

He nodded. "What do you smell?"

"Cordite from the discharge and some kind of antiseptic or cleaner. It's almost like rubbing alcohol but different somehow."

"What about booze?"

"Ugh." My stomach twisted, and I glared at him. "My head was forced backward, and the bottle was shoved in my mouth. I couldn't breathe. I couldn't swallow. I was drowning and burning from the inside out." I covered my eyes with my hand and leaned my head back, inadvertently triggering more memories. "They bound me to a chair with my own handcuffs. I felt a nail or screw, something at the base of the chair." I opened my eyes and looked at my torn nails. "I pried it out of the wood."

"Shit." Mark grabbed his phone off the coffee table and hit one of his speed dial numbers. "Good morning, sir. This is SSA Jablonsky. Look, we need that warrant to search Pepper. We were rejected yesterday, but new information has come to light. It's imperative we search the property for blood residue, specifically in the floor drain of the kitchen, and we need to examine any damaged furniture. My agent remembers being restrained and clawing a nail out of the wood." He paused for a few moments. "Uh-huh." Another pause. "Sir, a LEO was killed. A federal agent was assaulted and nearly killed. This can't wait." Another pause. "Fine." He hung up, mumbling under his breath.

"What's the verdict?"

"Don't worry about that now. What else can you tell me?"

"I freed myself from the cuffs and struggled with

someone." The man's features were nothing but a blur. "My gun was drawn. It fired. I didn't want it to happen. I tried to stop it." My mind reeled from the sheer terror. It was the same memory I had when I awoke in the middle of the night at Martin's. "Someone was killed with my gun. My hands were on it. I thought he had it, but maybe, I did. Maybe I fired. I can't be sure." I frowned, realizing that the order of events was screwy. "Dammit."

"Was this before or after the detective was shot?" Mark asked, hoping to piece the puzzle together.

"I don't know. There were three shots total. During the struggle, one shot was fired. From the way I remember the gunfire, the two shots had to have been before I freed myself from the cuffs."

"What happened after that?"

"I have this sense of backward motion, pain, and then nothing."

"What's the next thing you remember?"

I thought for a moment, finally deciding on an answer. "A dome light."

"So you were at Pepper, things went sideways, and the perp stuck you in the SUV. What about the gift-wrapped bodies? Were they in the vehicle with you?"

"I don't know." My thoughts were breaking down into incomprehensible dribble. "I just can't make sense of it." I pressed my palms into my eyes and leaned my head back again.

"Hey, we're getting there. Look, I need to visit the judge and plead our case before the docket opens. We're going to get that search warrant, and the evidence will fill in the blanks. We'll get this son-of-a-bitch. In the meantime, why don't you go back to doing whatever it was you were doing that made you remember all of that? It looks like we'll need all the help we can get."

"I thought I wasn't working this case."

"Semantics," Mark replied. He attempted to shake the perpetual wrinkles out of his jacket and went to the door. "We'll nail this asshole. No one kills a cop and attempts to murder a federal agent and gets away with it. You did good. Now it's my turn."

"Good luck." I followed him to the door and locked it after his departure. "I know I'll need it." Returning to the bedroom, I climbed under the covers. Usually, I wished the demons away, but this time, I waited for them to come.

The events I recalled weren't in any logical order. How did I end up in the kitchen? Who bound me to a chair? And how did that happen without a fight? There must have been a reason — an impetus to keep me docile. How come no one noticed what was happening and called the cops? Again, nothing made sense.

Burrowing under the covers, I curled into a ball and started at the beginning. I walked to Pepper from the federal building. It wasn't extremely close, but it wasn't unreasonable either. Then again, I was on the phone with Martin during my trek. Our conversation hadn't lasted long enough for the entire trip, so maybe I was meeting the detective first.

Reaching across the nightstand, I grabbed the phone and dialed Lucca. "Did I walk into Pepper alone?"

"Parker?" He sounded groggy. "Do you have any idea what time it is?"

"I don't know. Six? Seven? Jablonsky's on his way to meet a judge. The law doesn't sleep, so neither do we. Did you see the footage? You said the techs placed me in the vicinity of Pepper. Was I alone? How did I arrive there?"

"Listen, I am going back to sleep for another hour and a half. When I get to work, I will find out, see if we've made any more progress, and get back to you." Silence ensued, and I thought he had hung up. Then he asked, "Why is Jablonsky meeting with a judge? We were denied a warrant."

"I'm starting to remember what happened." No response followed. "Lucca, are you there?"

"No, I hung up. Good night, Parker." The line disconnected, and I put down the receiver.

"But it's morning," I said to my empty apartment. I checked the time. It was half past six, and there was only one person I knew who would be awake right now. Dialing the familiar number, I debated if I should grovel or just cut straight to the chase.

"Why are you awake?" Martin asked in lieu of a greeting.

"I miss you, and I'm sorry." Groveling, it is. "Mark just left a few minutes ago. I've been remembering things about that night, and I need someone to help with the timeline."

"You don't like discussing this stuff with me. Work is separate, remember?"

"Can you rake me over the coals another day?"

"I wasn't, or rather, I didn't mean to. I just wish that we were having this conversation in person. You should be lying next to me, not half a city away." He sighed. "We'll figure this out eventually, so tell me what I can do to help."

"Why did we disconnect that night? We were arguing, but it wasn't a fight. I don't remember being pissed off at you. Maybe you hung up on me."

"I didn't hang up on you, Alex. You said you had to go. You were meeting someone."

"Did he show up?"

"I don't know. The way you made it sound was that someone else was there, so we couldn't talk any longer. Does that help?"

"It does." I bit my lip. "But I didn't mention a name or tell you where I was?"

"No, you just said you had a meeting with a CI. What happened after we hung up?"

"Have we ever been to Pepper?"

"The strip club?"

"No," I paused, "there's a strip club named Pepper? Have you been there?"

"We were talking about you," Martin insisted. "And no, there's no strip club here named Pepper." I was used to his double-talk which meant there was a strip club somewhere with that name that he had visited, but that was a discussion for another time.

"It's a bar and grill. It's a bit of a dive. They have stemless drinkware and square highballs with artisan ice. I have memories of the bar, but I wanted to make sure they weren't from some other outing."

"Well, if you were there in a social capacity, it must have been with one of your other suitors. I've never heard of it.

What do you remember about it besides the pretentious ice cubes?"

"Nothing good."

"Does this have to do with your nightmare the other night and why you won't sleep here?"

"Yeah, I also realized why I couldn't stand the smell of your scotch. Honestly, it might be quite some time before I can tolerate the presence of liquor. You should probably break up with me now."

"I'm not an alcoholic. I can live without it. What does scotch have to do with any of this?"

"It's the reason for my missing memories. I was highly intoxicated and not by choice."

"Were they spiking your drink?"

"No," I narrowed my eyes and went into the living room to see what Pepper's business hours were, "but they must have used some kind of leverage to make me comply."

"Sweetheart, I know you don't like it when I worry, but what happened? What did they do to you? Who are they?"

"I'm gonna find out."

EIGHTEEN

Pepper only operated between the hours of three p.m. and ten p.m. Most restaurants, particularly those with bars, stayed open much later. Frankly, that made me suspicious, but I had a vague idea of what had happened. I must have been meeting the cop and his informant at Pepper. It was a public place, busy enough that a chance encounter and conversation wouldn't seem out of the ordinary but cozy enough to afford some privacy. Then again, it was possible that the location was a key element for our meeting. Obviously, two murders occurred on the property, so Pepper wasn't exactly that warm and inviting.

Dialing the office, I waited to be transferred to the IT department and requested that they run a complete business profile on the restaurant. It must have some unsavory connection that needed to be fleshed out. In the meantime, I grabbed my notepad and started on a new timeline, deciding that I must have met with the cop, sat at the bar, and waited for the place to close before somehow ending up in the kitchen. Someone must have threatened me in order to gain access to my handcuffs and chain me to a chair without sustaining so much as a scratch. Then things got interesting. Shots were fired. I woke up in a

SUV, rolled out, and made my way to the side of a parking garage. Yeah, I was clearly missing a few steps.

Yawning, I fought the desire to go back to bed and anxiously stared at my phone, waiting for Jablonsky or Lucca to call. When the waiting became too intense, I showered and changed my bandages. The bruises were dark and painful, and I wasn't certain that they hadn't gotten worse since the last time I looked. Once that was done, I curled up on the couch and closed my eyes. I'd either give meditation another shot or take a nap. There was literally nothing else that I could do without further information.

The ringing I heard wasn't in my head. That was a plus, and I reached for my phone. A quick glance at the display meant Mark had news.

"A search warrant was issued yesterday," Jablonsky said.

"What? I thought it was denied."

"We were denied. The PD was not." From his tone, I knew he was pissed. "They had better reasoning. Apparently, the SUV containing the two victims also had telematic software equipped with the GPS. Once the police gained access to the tracking system, they discovered Pepper was the last known location. Suffice it to say, the judge thought they had probable cause to conduct a search."

While we were on the phone, there was a knock at the door. I answered, waving hello to Lucca while Mark continued to speak. Lucca raised an eyebrow, and I mouthed "Jablonsky" to him. He nodded and made himself at home at the kitchen table.

"At least someone is scouring the restaurant for evidence of what happened," I said.

"Great," Mark said sarcastically. "I'm outside the restaurant right now. Their crime team is tearing the place apart. It'll be a miracle if anything is salvageable for our case once they're through with it."

After disconnecting, I checked the time. It was noon, and Lucca was searching my kitchen for sustenance. The single file he brought with him was on the table. It contained a few printed photos from nearby traffic cams of my walk to Pepper. To the untrained eye, I appeared to be alone, but there was a man in close proximity.

"Do we have an ID on my shadow?" I asked.

"Negative." Lucca turned around. "Didn't I leave my sandwich here the other day?"

"It went bad. I had to toss it," I lied. "Help yourself to last night's Chinese food if you're hungry."

"That's okay. I'll grab something on my way back to work." He stood beside me and pointed to another photo. "You should have picked a better rendezvous point." He flipped to another shot, showing the unidentified man waiting at the side of the building for me. "I'm guessing that's the detective you were meeting."

"He's carrying," I said, analyzing the way his jacket bunched at the side.

"That doesn't make him a cop."

I looked at his face, flashing to the wide-eyed, muffled scream. "Yeah, it's him." I took a breath to steady myself and slumped into the chair.

"Facial rec should get us a name. I told Ridley to compare it to the PD's roster. Although, by now, I'm sure someone at the police department would be willing to talk. Word spreads when shit happens."

"Jablonsky's on it." The silence was unbearable, and despite my training to withstand torture and interrogations, I had to say something. "I ate your damn sandwich. Please, eat the Chinese."

"Parker," Lucca cocked an eyebrow up, "what's going on? You're acting strangely, even for you."

I filled him in on everything that I remembered, including the unsettling parts. "Where are we on identifying that busboy? Do we know his real name?"

"Yeah, Jakov Horvat. We ran the photo through the database, and he came back pretty quickly. He's a citizen, so I don't understand the reason behind his fake name and phony work visa."

"Obviously, he's up to no good, and he didn't want anyone from Pepper to identify him too easily. Have we grabbed him yet?"

"Our surveillance team might have been made. They thought someone matching his description had returned to the area, but before they could make a positive identification, the guy climbed into a cab and left. He hasn't been back since."

"I spoke to the IT department. Have you seen the business profile for Pepper? They must be a front for something. Who owns the place? Who runs the place? Why the hell haven't we arrested any of them yet? They should be wanted in connection with the double homicide and assaulting a federal agent."

"Alex, we're not beat cops. We're not homicide detectives. We're the FBI. Yes, you were assaulted, which makes this our case, but it's theirs too. They can handle it. We have other things to focus on." He looked at me. "Well, I do." He shook his head ever so slightly. "Shade's been moving a lot of cargo lately. We've received intel that at least one shipment has made it into the United States. We don't know what it is, but from the whispers we've been hearing, it can't be good."

"How was it shipped?" I asked.

"Cargo plane."

"Has it been searched by DHS?"

"The crate didn't make it to the airport. We have satellite imagery showing it being loaded onto the plane, but it wasn't there when they landed."

"Did you contact the FAA to make sure they didn't make any unplanned stops?"

"Yes," Lucca growled, annoyed by my rudimentary question, "I'm not an imbecile."

"Great, because that was my next question." I offered a playful smile, even though the topic was dire. "That means it had to be dumped somewhere before landing. Wouldn't that require parachute deployment and low altitude flying?"

"Yes, it would."

"Get their flight plan and figure out where it could be. Send the locals to investigate."

"Done and done." Lucca gave me a look. "They haven't found anything. The search is ongoing."

"It was probably picked up already. On the bright side, chucking it out of the back of the plane probably means whatever they dropped can't be that volatile. That should eliminate most WMDs. What do our intelligence gathering friends have to say about this?"

"They aren't saying much. I don't think they know anything more than we do. Frankly, Shade probably isn't one of their top priorities. I've put out feelers and checked with every agency I could think of, but I hoped you'd have some idea what they might be shipping in or where they might have taken it. You've been primary on collecting the intel for the last few weeks, so surely, you must have some theories."

I'd been so focused on my own problems that I hadn't given a potential threat to national security and potentially thousands of lives much thought. Talk about self-centered. After a few more seconds of internal scolding, I considered what I knew about Shade.

"It could be anything. I'm guessing small arms, drugs, or counterfeit goods. Honestly, I don't think what they dropped is the real issue. The problem is they have contacts here. Someone was already on the ground to pick up the package, and that means they have a functioning cell within our borders."

"It could just be a few buyers."

"It could," I agreed. "There's been a lot of activity at their base camp for the last few weeks. We'll need to identify the players involved and find out who might have been waiting for a delivery." I grabbed my jacket. "You might as well give me a ride back to the office."

"Parker, you're not cleared for desk duty yet. You can't be involved."

"Which is more important, Lucca? Protocol or preventing a potentially heinous attack?"

"Both. If they're planning something, we need to be able to grab them and hold them without some slimy defense attorney twisting things around. Your mental functions could be impaired which could affect your work. It could have legal ramifications down the line."

"So why the hell did you tell me any of this?"

"Because if getting your help saves someone's life, that's more important than the rest of this shit."

"You just contradicted yourself."

"You can coach from the bench, but you aren't being called in to play."

"That's why you came over. You wanted something from me." I snorted. "And to think, I was feeling guilty for eating your sandwich. Next time, bring me dinner too."

"Only if you come up with an original idea that I haven't already explored." He lifted the folder off the desk. "I'm glad your memory is returning. Hopefully, once it does, you can take point on this Shade shit." He went to the door, reaching for the knob just as a loud knock sounded.

"Police, open up," bellowed a voice from the other side.

"Friends of yours?" Lucca asked.

"My friends are too clever to announce themselves. They know I'd never answer if they did," I replied.

More knocking sounded, and Lucca opened the door. Detectives Delaney and Collins were standing in the hallway. They gave Lucca an uncertain look, but he stood his ground.

"Alexis Parker," Delaney called from the hallway, "we have a warrant." He pushed past Lucca and entered my apartment while Collins maintained a wary eye on my partner.

"For what?" I asked.

"Ma'am, you're under arrest," Delaney said.

"The hell she is," Lucca replied, stepping closer. Collins attempted to intervene, and Lucca practically growled at him. "I'm a federal agent. If you lay a hand on me, I'll arrest you for assault and interfering in a federal investigation. Is that clear?" Obviously, the interagency pissing match had begun.

"What are the charges?" I asked. He held the warrant out, and I read it. "This is bullshit. I didn't kill anyone."

"Your gun was found at the scene of a homicide. Your prints were also there, and I'm guessing that when the results come back, your DNA will confirm that as well," Delaney said. "Do you intend to make this more difficult than it needs to be? We can place you there. Don't bother denying it."

"I might have been there, but that doesn't mean shit," I said.

"She didn't do it," Lucca said. He snatched the paper from my hand and read it.

"That's for a jury of her peers to decide, now isn't it?" Collins sneered.

"Fine," I put my hands on my head and turned my back to them, "do your job, Detective."

"Alexis Parker, you have the right to remain silent," Delaney began, holding both of my hands in one of his while he performed a quick pat down. He continued to recite the Miranda warning while clicking the cuffs in place. I gasped at the sudden memory and the pain that shot through my sprained wrist which was now twisted and locked at an uncomfortable angle.

"C'mon, she's hurt. She's complying with your ridiculous demands. That isn't necessary," Lucca said.

"It most certainly is," Collins replied. "Did you know there's a jacket on Agent Parker? This isn't the first time that she's been wanted for murder, but we'll make sure this one sticks."

"Parker, don't say a word," Lucca warned, following us out the door with his phone in hand. "I'm calling Jablonsky. We'll have counsel meet you at the police station." He glared at Collins. "What precinct are you going to?"

"I don't remember. All those numbers blur together after a while."

"Fine," Lucca made eye contact with me as I was dragged down the hallway toward the stairs, "I'll be right behind you. We'll get this straightened out ASAP."

"It's fine, Eddie. This is just a misunderstanding. Tell Mark what happened. He'll take care of it," I said.

"Wow, even in handcuffs, these feds think they're calling the shots. They think they can do anything," Collins said to Delaney. "We'll see how things look when she's been sent through central booking." He smiled evilly at me. "Most cops don't do well in lockup. I'm guessing the same holds true for you." He narrowed his eyes. "You're already injured. The sharks will smell the blood in the water. Think about that on our drive. Maybe you'll reconsider keeping your mouth shut."

Delaney looked at me. "If you didn't do it, answer our questions. The sooner we can clear you, the sooner we can nail whoever is responsible. Talking to us can only help you."

That was bullshit. I knew they were playing good cop, bad cop. The evidence they had was circumstantial. Jablonsky would bring them the proof they needed, and this would be sorted out. Forcing myself to remain optimistic, I knew once I was cleared, their efforts would be focused on finding the real perpetrator, and then justice would be served for those two lost souls and my missing hours. It would be okay. It had to be.

NINETEEN

"Are you sure you don't want something to drink?" Delaney asked. I was sitting on the wrong side of an interrogation table. At least the pricks had been nice enough to remove the handcuffs. "It's the least we can do until this mess gets sorted out."

"I'm fine." I stared at him, pulling my legs up in the chair and resting my chin on my knees. "How are you doing?"

He gave me a look. "I'm okay."

"Really?"

"Agent Parker," he glanced down at the folder in front of him, "Alexis, why don't you take me through what happened that night at Pepper? We have your gun. Three bullets are missing from the clip. Ballistics matched the slugs we pulled from the victims to your weapon. Your prints are on the gun. Your prints are on the SUV where the bodies were discovered, and we found this." He slid a sealed evidence bag across the table. Inside were my OIO credentials.

"That picture doesn't do me justice," I said. I squished up my face. "Hell, are you sure that those are even mine?"

"Oh, so you're telling me that the badge number, your

photo ID, and your government-issued nine millimeter don't belong to you but rather some other OIO agent with the exact same name?"

I shrugged.

"And that person just happens to have the exact same fingerprints. How stupid do you think I am?"

"I know better than to answer that." I dropped my legs and leaned forward. "You're looking at this all wrong, Delaney. I understand why you think the things that you do, but you're missing the bigger picture. So am I." My words could be dangerous, and I was careful in what I said. "It has to do with the restaurant."

"What does?"

"I don't know."

"That's bullshit. You honestly expect me to believe that something bigger is going on here, but you don't know what it is? That's the biggest fucking lie I've ever heard. Prove that you didn't do this. Tell me why you were there, who you were meeting, and what the hell happened so we can both do our jobs."

"Honestly, I'd tell you if I could." I closed my mouth and returned to my previous position.

"I've seen your hospital admittance records, and I spoke to the EMT that treated you the following morning. Right now, your office is being subpoenaed to turn over everything relating to you and the condition they found you in. I'm sure you must have been covered in evidence. You should change your tune before we get it. Things will go a lot easier. I'll do what I can to extend you a professional courtesy but only if you talk to me."

"Really, you think that I'm responsible? I was lucky to escape with my life. What do you think happened?" I couldn't help myself. "You've seen enough already, so piece it together, Mr. Ace Detective."

He snorted. "Why should I? You won't answer my questions. Make this a fair trade, and I'll tell you what I think."

"I want my lawyer. This interview is over."

"You'll regret that." He went to the door. "I'll give you a couple of minutes to reconsider."

Resisting the urge to say something vindictive, I kept my mouth shut. Since being taken to the precinct, I'd been booked and held in an interrogation room. The accommodations were adequate, but the company sucked. What sucked more was the fact that I understood why they thought I was responsible. Frankly, I wasn't positive that I hadn't pulled the trigger on one of the dead men. The evidence pointed to me, but they should have realized that no self-respecting federal agent would leave a calling card at the crime scene or commit murder with her service piece. That would be idiotic. Hell, it was idiotic for a frame-up job, but I suspected that might have been what the actual assailant had hoped to accomplish. Too bad I didn't know who had done this. The only name I could provide was Jakov Horvat, and even that was a shot in the dark.

"Hey," I said, staring at the mirrored glass, "I changed my mind. I have something to say."

A few minutes later, the door opened and Collins entered. He must have been watching while Delaney questioned me. He took a seat and stared with cold, dead eyes in that intimidating way that only seasoned law enforcement was capable of achieving.

"So talk," he said.

"The arrest warrant left a number of blanks, and you and your partner haven't exactly been forthcoming. So maybe you'd like to tell me who was killed."

"You sick, twisted piece of shit," Collins spat, "as if you don't know."

"I don't know." I enunciated each word. "Who was killed? What were their names?"

He crossed the room and yanked me out of the chair and into the cinderblock wall. "You tell me. You set up the meet. You lured him to that place, and you killed him. Now you want me to believe that you forgot what his fucking name was?"

"I set up the meet?" My mind was focused on the new details rather than the irate cop. "Why would I have picked Pepper?"

"You fucking bitch," Collins screamed. That time, I heard the pain in his voice. He'd lost a friend. "How could you?"

"I didn't. I'm sorry."

He slammed me against the wall again, but I didn't struggle or fight back. I felt empathy for him and remorse for not saving his friend. The masochistic part of my mind considered that I deserved this.

"Collins, back off," Delaney said, entering the room with an officer at his heels. "Let her go."

"Greg's dead. She killed him. She needs to pay," Collins growled.

"I didn't kill him. I want to help you find the person that did," I insisted.

"Lies," Collins spat. He moved to throw a punch, but Delaney pulled him away before that could happen. "You won't get away with this. I'll make sure of it."

Delaney tossed another look my way while he led Collins out of the room. "Take her to holding. I want her out of our sight."

"Ma'am," the officer said, unsure exactly how to proceed, "come with me, please." He put his hand on my elbow and led me out of the interrogation room and down the corridor. Normally, I'd be cuffed, but I guess he wasn't sure due to the brace on my wrist and the encounter I'd just had with the detective.

"Parker?" Lucca called, quickly getting to his feet. "What's going on? Where are they taking you?"

"Back away, sir," the officer said. "She'll be held downstairs until her attorney arrives."

"That's insane," Lucca protested, but I gave him a sharp look.

"It's fine. I'll be fine. This isn't the first time I've seen the inside of a holding cell," I said.

The officer's grip tightened, and he pulled me away from Lucca and toward the elevator. He didn't speak again until he passed my sheet to the officer in charge and had the door to the cage unlocked. This particular police station was older than most of the others in the city and rather rundown. The women's holding cell was one large unit that had originally served as the drunk tank. I stood outside, staring at the dozen women. Based on looks alone, I'd say a couple had been picked up for solicitation, half might have been pinched for drugs, but four of them looked like they'd just lost a MMA fight. He gave my back a push, and I winced, feeling the impact of Collins' outburst.

"Are the accommodations not to your liking?" he mocked. "Did you make a reservation for a private room?"

"Something like that."

"We must have lost it. Too bad," he shoved me inside and slammed the door, "you had your chance earlier." He nodded at the officer on duty, who checked the lock. Then he waited for the other man to walk away before saying, "I guess you're used to swankier accommodations at the federal building. It's too bad none of your co-workers at the FBI thought to spring you." He said it loud enough that the women inside could hear.

"You son-of-a-bitch," I muttered.

Violence wasn't allowed in interrogations. It was considered police brutality, but letting someone else do the hitting was considered an accident or perhaps negligence. Keeping my eyes down, I took a seat on the end of the nearest bench, closest to the door, and put my back against the bars. The ache was getting worse, but this was the most strategic move that I could make. Then I placed one heel on the seat in front of me and rested my cheek against my leg, keeping my head tilted toward the ground. My peripheral vision monitored the area, but so far, no one had acknowledged me. That was good, but I didn't know if it would last.

"Hey," someone said, but I didn't look up. "Hey, girl, I'm talking to you." I suspected that I was the 'you' she was referring to, but I pretended not to notice. "Bitch, I'm speaking to you. Are you deaf or something? You got a broke arm. Do you have broke ears too?"

Slowly, I drew my head up, glaring in her direction. "What?"

"Is that shit true?" she asked, standing. Two of the other women flanked her. "You sure as hell don't look like any FBI agent I've ever seen."

"I'm not looking for trouble. I've got enough of it." I dropped my gaze, hoping she'd lose interest.

Unfortunately, she didn't. She crossed the cell and stood in front of me with her posse of reject fighters. "I just want to be left alone."

"Answer my question."

"Shit, you sound like the cops upstairs." I dropped my leg and looked up at her. "I don't want to get jammed up here. Neither do you. So I'll stay out of your way." There was the remote possibility that one of these women had been planted by the cops in the hopes of gaining information from me, so talking to anyone wasn't advisable.

"So why'd he say it if it wasn't true?" she asked, jerking her head at the empty corridor outside the cell.

"Because he has a small dick, and I wouldn't blow him." Jokes were usually the way to go in these situations.

"She's too tiny to be a fed," the woman beside her whispered loudly, "and she's dressed all wrong. She looks like a yoga instructor or pot dealer."

"Nah," my antagonist said, leaning over me and making exaggerated sniffing sounds, "she's got the stink on her. Ain't that right?"

"I won't say it again," I warned. "Leave me alone."

"C'mon," one of her minions said, grabbing her arm, "it's not our problem. We're already in enough trouble."

"Yeah, fine, she's not worth it," my antagonist said.

They went back to their previous spot across the cell and sat down. I felt her eyes continue to bore into me, but I kept my head down and my mouth shut. A few minutes later, another officer that I'd never seen before opened the cage to let one of the hookers out.

"Parker," he said, "your boss is on the way. We'll bring you upstairs when he gets here."

I didn't acknowledge him or his words, hoping to keep things calm, but my mouthy cellmate loudly asked, "Why the hell does she get out? What makes her so special?" Thankfully, the cop didn't say anything in return. My hope that she didn't realize I was Parker was short-lived when she barked more questions at me. "Who's coming here to get you out? Is it one of your FBI friends?" I remained silent, feeling the increasing tension build. "Answer me, bitch." She crossed the room and gave my shoulder a shove.

"Touch me again, and you'll regret it," I growled. Keeping a low profile was preferred, but being submissive was asking for trouble.

"Why? Are you going to arrest me?" She shoved my shoulder again. "It looks like you can't tell anyone what to do now."

"Fine." I looked up at her, seeing the two other women close in on the sides. If I stood, it'd be seen as an act of aggression that might lead to a fight. So I remained still, poised to move if the situation warranted it. "I'll mind my own business."

"Yeah, that's what you did every time you arrested someone, right? You were minding your own business. You never thought that they might have to do what they do in order to survive. That not all of us are pretty little things that have it easy." She shoved me again. Her anger was at the system and what it represented. Unfortunately, she decided that I was the embodiment of everything wrong with society and the criminal justice system. "That's why you're getting out of this hellhole because you're somebody that knows somebody."

"Lady, I don't have a beef with you."

"That makes one of us," she spat.

She moved faster than I anticipated and slapped me across the face. Glaring up at her, I stood, needing the space to avoid another hit. Unfortunately, I'd been boxed in by her two MMA pals. She shoved me backward, keeping me off balance when the backs of my knees hit the bench. She moved to throw a punch at my face, but I deflected it with my right arm, feeling the impact reverberate through my sprained wrist and along the microfractures in my arm. Dropping my injured arm, I followed through with a left hook to her jaw. She stumbled back, but the woman on her right charged into me, throwing me into the bars and punching me repeatedly in the stomach.

I twisted around, surprising her by reversing our positions and using the momentum to flip her over my shoulder and onto the floor. The other two came at me simultaneously, and in this compromised position, I was thrown sideways to the ground. While one of them straddled my hip and threw punch after punch at my face, I threw my arms up to defend my head while the other kicked me in the back.

"Get off of her," someone said.

I struggled to move, but I was pinned in this position. In my injured state, I was too weak to fend them off. Every blow resulted in white-hot pain, further diminishing my ability to get free.

"Hey," one of the hookers yelled, "get in here. They're gonna kill her."

I managed to shift onto my stomach, knocking the woman who was on top of me off balance. Her own momentum from throwing punches pushed her sideways, but before I could subdue her or retaliate, another hard kick landed on my previously bruised back. Rushed footsteps raced down the corridor, and I heard the sound of a gun being cocked.

"Stop," Lucca commanded, aiming at the women. The barrage stopped, and I shifted slightly, afraid to move. "Get this door open now," Lucca yelled to the cops who were slow to respond. "Now." The cage swung open, and the three women were handcuffed at gunpoint and pulled out of the cell. Lucca entered and knelt beside me. "We need a medic."

"No, we don't. I'm fine. I just suck at making friends," I said.

"That's an understatement."

My heart was pounding, and I was dizzy and shaky. It hurt all over, especially my back and side which were probably bleeding again. Luckily, I had a black t-shirt on that concealed the bloodstains. "I let them win. I didn't think I could afford to have assault charges added to my arrest record."

"The sad part is I believe you." Lucca gave the cops a stern look. "She's not leaving my sight. I want an explanation for this, and I want it now. Get Delaney and Collins down here."

"Forget it," I said. "No one did anything wrong.

Apparently, those ladies didn't like the way I looked or smelled." I grunted and placed my hand on the bench to steady myself. "At least I'll have defensive wounds this time."

"It's not funny, Parker," Lucca warned. "Stop protecting them." His eyes conveyed a message that I didn't understand. "I want her transferred somewhere else. There's an obvious bias, and her safety is in question."

From the appearance of a white shirt with bars, I knew the captain had come down to see what the commotion was about. Lucca left me for a moment, standing and speaking to the man in charge. Normally, that would be Jablonsky's job, but he wasn't here. At least my partner had my back.

After a few minutes, I pulled myself to my feet. Since I was standing, the police decided that my injuries weren't life-threatening. At Lucca's insistence for a transfer, Jablonsky was called and our meeting place was changed to the district attorney's office. The DA agreed to review the evidence personally and make a decision as to whether or not the police could keep me in custody. Transportation was readied, and I was handcuffed and led to the garage. An officer opened the back door of the SUV and helped me inside.

"We'll bring her right back here once the DA sees the evidence we have against her," the police captain said. "Regardless of your assertions, she's wanted in connection to the murder of a police detective, and that'll be taken very seriously."

One officer sat in the back with me, and two men piled into the front. Apparently being assaulted meant I posed a greater danger now than when I was originally brought into the station. Go figure.

"I'll tail you," Lucca said. "And if anything else happens to her between here and there, so help you." They grumbled a response, and off we went.

TWENTY

"Dammit, can't you take off these cuffs?" I asked. My hands were behind my back, and my entire arm ached. I felt panicky, and I contributed that to being bound. It was one of my triggers from previous trauma. A sheen of sweat covered my skin, and my breathing was coming in shallow gasps. I couldn't get enough oxygen in, and considering the way my heart was behaving, I suspected I might be hyperventilating. "I won't go anywhere. I promise."

The officers ignored me, so I inhaled deeply, shut my eyes, and slowly blew out a breath, trying to calm myself. As soon as my eyes closed, the dam broke, and my mind was flooded with images and lost memories. At last, I knew what happened.

I'd been at work that day, researching Shade. The increased activity at their base of operations had seemed suspicious, and I discovered an unknown shipment was destined for delivery soon. Unfortunately, DHS, the CIA, and the rest of the intelligence community had yet to determine what Shade was selling, but something about the passports had bothered me.

Evidently, one of Shade's leaders, Niko Horvat, had a

cousin in the United States. They looked extremely similar on their passport photos, and I suspected that could be how Niko managed to travel freely without triggering an alert. DHS had heard whispers that he'd been within our borders recently, but without any passport dings and no sightings on private or commercial aircraft, it seemed unlikely until now.

Horvat was the most common surname in Croatia, and no agency had taken the time to run down all of Niko's familial connections. However, I didn't have anything better to do. Leafing through the phonebook, I had scanned the pages and decided that a field trip was in order.

The small Croatian community was already being monitored by the closest precinct. Apparently, they'd received numerous reports from tourists of counterfeit goods being sold, thefts and robberies occurring, and some isolated incidences of what might be gang violence. Most of these claims were minor and unsubstantiated, but it never hurt to check.

After my trip to the prosecutor's office that morning, I detoured to the police station before returning to the federal building. Somehow, I'd forgotten this detail, and I considered the unnerving possibility that some of the fog had been due to an emotional aspect of the trauma. Shaking it off, I continued replaying the details in my mind, letting the flood of memories wash over me.

Upon entering the precinct, I'd been sent to Detective Greg Donaldson, robbery division. After briefing him on the possibility of a terrorist cell in the making, he contacted his confidential informant, Ivan, in order to aid in gathering additional intel. Ivan had been skittish, but after a bit of arm twisting, Det. Donaldson got him to agree to answer a few questions.

I'd left the OIO that evening, expecting to meet Ivan and the detective in some back alley. Instead, Donaldson met me outside the restaurant, told me that Ivan was tending bar, and that he had reason to believe that Niko's cousin was also working at Pepper. Apparently, a lot of the cooks and busboys were Croatian.

I entered the restaurant alone, took a seat at the bar, and waited for Donaldson to follow. A few minutes later, he sat down next to me. Ivan barely said anything to either of us, but he wrote notes on our napkins and placed them beneath our drinks. It was an odd way of asking questions, and I didn't feel right about being exposed with a potential target somewhere inside the restaurant. However, the detective had given me little choice since he hadn't provided any details about his CI other than a first name, which might have been an alias.

Pepper was practically empty by 9:30, and by ten, Donaldson and I were the only patrons left inside. It was a small operation, and Ivan told his boss he'd clean up. The servers bolted once the floors were vacuumed, and I didn't think any of the other staff remained. Ivan had gone into the kitchen to see if the chef or any dishwashers were straggling behind, and I had gone outside to wait.

From an onlooker's perspective, I was a single lady calling for a cab which might have been why I wasn't gunned down immediately. Someone had seen me talking to Donaldson all night and figured I was his girlfriend. It was a busboy or maybe a waiter that had come up to speak to me. That detail was fuzzy, but he had pushed me back inside without ever revealing his identity. He wore a hooded jacket that he kept over his head, and the shadows had concealed his face. His voice was nothing more than a few grunts. Upon reentry, the dining room was empty, and I didn't know what happened to Donaldson or Ivan.

Before I could say or do anything, a gun was shoved in my back. I was led into the kitchen where Donaldson was tied to a chair. Ivan was being beaten. The room was dark, and I couldn't make out details, just the silhouette of figures moving around.

"Let her go," Donaldson said. "She has nothing to do with this. She's just some woman I met. She doesn't know anything."

"We can use her," the man who was beating Ivan said. He left the nearly unconscious man on the floor and tossed Donaldson's cuffs to the man behind me. "Chain her to a chair. She might be useful."

Donaldson gazed at me, shaking his head. I didn't want to play along, but I didn't know what was going on. He did. Or at least I thought he did. I let the man cuff my hands behind my back around the chair, and while I sat there, listening to the sounds of Ivan being beaten and questions being asked in a language that I didn't understand, I felt the nail in the bottom of the chair.

For the next twenty minutes, I dug my fingers into the wood, gouging out tiny chunks and tugging on the stubborn piece of metal. When Ivan became completely unresponsive, likely unconscious, the man turned his attention to Donaldson.

"What do you want? Why are you here?" he asked.

"Do you have any idea who you're messing with?" Donaldson asked, full of moronic bravado. "I'm one of this city's finest."

I began tugging more frantically at the nail. Donaldson wasn't trained to deal with interrogations or torture. He hadn't dealt with this before, and he was going to get himself and the rest of us killed. I shouldn't have followed his lead. I should have done something sooner. I could have subdued the man who had me at gunpoint and stopped the shooter. Now, it was too late.

Questions and rebukes continued in rapid succession. I couldn't remember what they were about. Half of them weren't even in English. At some point, when Donaldson's lack of response had failed to appease the interrogator, the bastard crossed the room to me. He placed his hands on the seat of my chair and leaned over me. I could feel his breath on my neck. He inhaled deeply, letting out an amused sigh.

"You'll be fun," he said. Donaldson screamed a protest, and I heard a cry of pain come from Ivan who must have woken up. "Maybe I'll torture you first and see if that breaks his resolve." Pushing my heels into the ground, I made the chair teeter backward, but his grip on the seat kept me from going over. "Naughty, naughty." He waggled a finger in my face.

"She doesn't have anything to do with this," Donaldson repeated. "She's an innocent bystander. If you want to hurt someone, hurt me." Apparently, chivalry wasn't dead. It was just fucking stupid.

"Who is she?" the interrogator asked.

When Donaldson failed to offer a response, the man that had brought me back inside reached into my jacket. "Comrade, we have a problem."

Shit, my mind raced. He had spotted my gun. If he kept looking, he'd find my credentials too. My nails dug deeper, and I bit my lip to keep from screaming as the wood shards embedded themselves beneath my fingernails. He took my gun and held it out for Donaldson's inspection.

"Who are you?" the interrogator asked, turning back to me. "You're with him. Are you another cop?"

"Who the fuck are you?" I asked, finally prying the nail halfway out of the wood. "What the hell is any of this even about?"

"You have a mouth," he said. "This should make you more compliant."

He picked up a bottle of vodka from the top shelf where the cook had left it. He opened the bottle and leaned over me again. Grabbing my hair, he pulled my head back and forced the bottle into my mouth. The liquid burned, and I choked. I couldn't breathe, and my body took over, swallowing and gasping at the same time, hoping to find a way to clear the airway and get oxygen inside. When the bottle was empty, he released the grip on my hair and threw the bottle into the wall. It shattered, and he picked up a piece of glass, returning to Ivan and Donaldson.

I was drenched in vodka and dizzy from the ordeal. Taking a few breaths, I continued working on the nail, hearing voices and mumbles fill the room. My mind was drifting, and I felt disoriented. As soon as the nail was free, I manipulated it around, placing the end into the keyhole in the cuffs and struggling to unlock them.

The interrogator crossed the room, angry and irate. He held the muzzle of my gun to my temple, barking questions at Donaldson. I felt the metal of the handcuffs release, and I dropped the nail, moving the metal link outward so I could get my hand free. The man turned the gun toward Ivan and fired twice before I was able to get my hand onto the gun. We struggled, and another shot went off.

The other man, who had held me at gunpoint, tackled me from behind. He pinned my arms at my sides and forced me back into the chair. My gaze was locked on Donaldson, seeing the aftermath of the bullet that had gone through his skull. I vomited on the interrogator's shoes, seconds away from my own oblivion.

"You stupid pig," the interrogator said, grabbing the back of my neck and slamming my head into the nearest counter.

Everything went black, and the next thing I knew, I was being dragged outside. An SUV was parked close to the building, and inside the trunk were two plastic covered corpses. Then darkness returned.

Opening my eyes to the sound of voices, I realized someone else was driving. The man who had conducted the interrogation was above me, sitting on the back seat, and my eyes stared at the dome light in the ceiling. It took a few moments before I realized I was lying on the floorboard. They were speaking Croatian, but from what I gathered, they were going to kill me and dump the bodies. That or we were all going to the Russian tea room. Even in my impaired state, I didn't think this was about tea. The asshole noticed I was awake and pointed my own gun at me. I managed to sit up, and I stared at him.

"Are you going to do it?" I asked.

He aimed, and I grabbed the gun, shoving the webbing of my hand between the hammer and pin. He pulled the trigger, but it didn't fire. A yelp escaped my lips, and he jerked the gun upward, but I refused to let go. We fought over the gun, and he snapped my wrist back with a pop. This time, I howled. He aimed again, and I grabbed the door handle, tumbling out of the vehicle before he could fire.

I didn't feel the impact. The alcohol acted like a numbing agent, and the pain from my wrist blocked a lot of my other nerve receptors. I must have blacked out momentarily, but when I opened my eyes, the violent spinning had made everything unbearable. When it finally stopped, I crawled out of the street. I had to get away.

They'd be back in a second. They would kill me, and I couldn't let that happen. I had to get help. Without knowing where I was or even cognizant of what I was doing, I stumbled forward. I had to get to the cops before the men could get to me. Someone had to survive to tell the police what happened to Detective Donaldson.

A sudden squeal shook me out of my memory and back to the present. I was inside the police vehicle being brought to the district attorney's office so the allegations against me could be assessed. Holy shit, who were those men at Pepper, and how could this be happening? The police vehicle veered to the right like the entire truck was off balance.

"Radio for back-up. We're under fire," one of the cops in the front said. "Who the hell is shooting at us?"

Suddenly alert, I sat up straight. "What's going on?" I asked.

Before anyone could answer, something exploded at the side, and the vehicle tipped over onto the passenger's side, sliding along the asphalt with a metallic shriek before coming to rest a few dozen yards away. Gunfire echoed outside, and glass broke. Shit. A few shots ripped through the truck, and I heard a groan. No one returned fire, and I managed to right myself from where I'd fallen against the side door. The man next to me was unconscious. His head had collided with the window, and I didn't know the extent of his injuries. The other cop seated on the passenger's side was in similar shape. The driver had been shot, but he was breathing. Thankfully, it didn't look like a fatal wound since I wasn't in any condition to help anyone.

Dammit, my hands were bound, and I was stuck between the two sets of seats. Finally, I slipped one leg down against the door and righted myself, inching sideways toward the cop beside me.

"Hey, officer, look alive," I said, hoping he was. "Wake up." He grunted but didn't move. Flipping onto my back, I wriggled around, lifting my legs until my feet touched the opposite door, and I could slide my hands down past my butt and upward. Bending my knees, I rolled forward, landing on my face but freeing my hands from behind my back. "At least that's a start."

The growing sound of gunfire made my panicked state worse. Prioritizing my actions, I awkwardly felt for his pulse with my handcuffed hands. After finding a steady rhythm, I searched through the unconscious officer's pockets, but I couldn't find his cuff key. So I took his service piece, figuring I needed it more than he did at the moment. I leaned into the front seat. But with my bound hands and the sideways vehicle, I couldn't maneuver around to check the vitals on the man riding shotgun. The windshield had sustained a few bullet holes, and one of them had gone through the driver. It pierced his chest on the right side below his collarbone. He was gasping.

"Hey, take easy breaths," I said. "I'm gonna get you out of here."

He looked at me through the rearview mirror. "My leg's jammed. I can't get free."

"Okay, what's your name, buddy?"

He laughed, a gurgling coming from his throat. "The last time I heard that line was when I was in Kandahar. Come to think of it, that's also where I was the last time I hit an IED."

"Someone needs to take away your driving privileges." From what I could tell, there wasn't an exit wound. "Apply pressure. It'll hurt like hell, but I can't see an exit wound, so you need to stay still and slow the bleeding." I looked out the cracked windshield again, but I didn't see anything. "Do you have a cuff key?"

"Tell me something, Agent Parker, did you kill a cop?"

"No, but I was there when it happened. I've been having trouble remembering it." I looked at the three men and the state of the vehicle. "Now's really not the time for twenty questions. You either trust me or you don't."

He took his hand away in an effort to gain access to his pockets, and the bleeding increased. "I can't reach it." Instead, he grabbed the radio, but it let out a burst of static.

"Forget it. Just focus on you. Are you sure we hit something?"

"I don't know. I thought so. Shots were being fired, but I don't know where they came from. If someone's out there, we're fucked."

"Story of my life. Hang tight. If you see someone, shoot first. I'm gonna get help."

I slid backward and tried to get out the side door, but the accident had jammed the locks. So I repositioned myself, and after a few strong kicks, I knocked out the rear windshield. Giving the downed officer next to me another look, I hoped for the best and prepared for the worst. Crawling out of the wreckage, I didn't know what I'd find on the outside.

TWENTY-ONE

Pulling myself out of the SUV, I took cover behind the police vehicle. Glancing in the direction we had been traveling, I didn't spot anything amiss. The police vehicle was sideways on the pavement. It had skidded and blocked part of the shoulder and most of the lane. We had just gotten off an overpass and were on the exit ramp. We were far enough down the ramp to not be seen by vehicles on the main thoroughfare. A black sedan was parked behind us, and I fought to steady my breathing and my hands as I held the gun two-handed, hating how restrictive the cuffs were.

The shot had to have come from somewhere, and I looked upward, wondering if shooters or an assault team were above. How did anyone know where we'd be? Why were they shooting at us? A man stepped out from behind the sedan, and I aimed my gun at him. His weapon was trained on me, but he held up a hand.

"Parker, what the hell's going on?" Lucca asked.

"We took fire." That tingling feeling of impending doom was coursing through my body. "The radio's out."

"They're using a jammer," Lucca said. "Cell phones are down too."

"How do you know they're using a jammer?" My pulse

was in my ears, and my hands were shaking.

"Common sense." Lucca had yet to lower his weapon. "Alex, what's wrong?"

"Where were you?"

"What?"

"You said you were following behind. You must have seen what happened, but you didn't come to help. Instead, you were behind your car. What were you doing?"

"Following protocol and assessing the situation. Are you okay?"

"I remember what happened."

"Now's really not the time." Lucca's eyes kept glancing around. "Do you know who killed the cop?"

"I don't understand how he knew Donaldson was a cop or that he'd be there. It felt like a setup. There were two men. I never got a look at one of them. He just shoved me back inside and held me at gunpoint. He never searched me. He never came into view. He didn't speak." My breathing was coming in shorter, more frantic spurts.

"We'll figure it out. Maybe there's a mole." Lucca moved closer to me, sidestepping around the sedan so he was directly in front of me. "Are you okay? We need to get out of here. Are the cops okay?"

My mind was reeling. Nothing was making sense anymore, and from my body's reaction, I wasn't sure I could trust the man holding a gun on me. "How'd you get the bruise on your side?" I asked.

"What?"

"After our altercation when you woke me up, I saw a bruise." My thoughts began replaying everything. "You found me that morning. You called me. You kept saying that I was imagining things. That this was some drunken mishap or PTSD. You said I fell down some stairs."

"Parker, stop."

"Lower the gun, Lucca."

"You first," he said, and I felt my heart break at the possibility that he had betrayed me. My hands shook. "You're not gonna shoot me, Alex. Stand down. You're reading this wrong." Gunfire rang out behind me. Suddenly, without warning, he focused his aim and fired.

The shot whizzed past me, and then Lucca tackled me to the ground. "Bogeys at twelve o'clock." We took cover behind the police vehicle, and Lucca edged around, checking to see if they were advancing.

"Get these cuffs off of me," I snapped. Blindly, he handed me the key, and I freed my wrists. "How many?"

"I don't know. At least three."

I cautioned a glance around the SUV. A Hummer was parked at the exit to the ramp, effectively boxing us in. Trembling and sweating, I leaned my head back, remembering the officers trapped inside the metal box that we were using as cover. I didn't know who these shooters were or how they'd found us, but it didn't matter.

"You have to get help," I said, hoping that my instincts were wrong. At the moment, everything was telling me I was under attack from all sides. Unfortunately, I needed help, and Lucca was the only one in a position to provide it. "We're low enough that you could probably go over the guardrail and make a run for it."

He looked at me for a long moment. "You go. I'll hold them off."

"The hell you will. You have a family."

"You're faster."

"I can't." I blinked a few times, trying to shake it off. "I won't make it. Just go. I'll distract them."

He looked at the unsteady grip I had on the gun. "You better be here when I get back."

"Where else would I go?" I asked, switching positions with him so I could provide a distraction while he ran for help. I hoped the angle of the police transport would obscure him from the attackers' view, but I couldn't be certain. "On three."

He nodded, and we silently counted down. On three, I fired a few shots in their direction, and Lucca vaulted over the guardrail to the ground below. I wasn't positive how high a drop he had to make, but it was our only shot. Return fire ensued, but I barely glimpsed the man who was firing back. We were disabled. Why weren't they advancing on our position?

As if answering my question, I heard a sound that I'd

only ever experienced during advanced weapons training. Oh, god. I ducked down, feeling the peripheral effects of the explosion. We didn't hit an IED. We had been struck by the projectile from a grenade launcher. The grenade exploded too far to the left to cause severe damage, but I imagined their aim would improve.

Inhaling, I ran at a crouch along the side of the sideways police unit until I was near the front of the vehicle. Even from here, the curve of the ramp partially obscured the Hummer. The police officer that had been shot signaled to me and punched the barrel of his gun through the bullet hole in the windshield. He planned on providing assistance in the form of a distraction. Nodding my understanding, I darted to the far side of the ramp and waited for him to fire.

The first shot edged the assailants back, and I rushed forward at a crouch. When the man with the grenade launcher stepped to the side of the vehicle, believing he was in a cover position, I fired on him. I was a decent shot with my left, but I didn't kill him. He went down, and one of the other men grabbed his collar and dragged him backward. They shifted their gunfire toward me, and I bolted across the ramp again, unable to find a cover position.

Sliding next to the sideways police vehicle, I rested my head against the tire and checked the clip in the gun. I had nine shots left. For a moment, I thought I might be having a heart attack, but quite frankly, I didn't have time for that luxury. Dizzy and unsteady, I gulped down some air and listened for sounds of the next barrage.

The officer inside the vehicle fired a few more times, and I thought I heard a faint shriek. Forcing myself away from the vehicle, I fired as well. I hated westerns and how the hero always went down in a blaze of glory. It was stupid. This was equally idiotic. Thankfully, their aim hadn't improved either. We continued exchanging fire until my clip was empty.

The officer inside the vehicle fired a few more shots, but he'd be out pretty soon. While I was contemplating my options, a car slammed into the Hummer. Throwing caution to the wind, I stood up straight, seeing Lucca exiting from the driver's side of a crashed minivan. He had his gun out and was barking orders to the men.

Moving down the ramp, I found two of the shooters facedown. The one I shot had three wounds and was on the ground. The other one, that I assumed the officer shot, had his hands in the air while blood trickled from a hole in his shoulder down his back. The other man, Lucca had already slapped cuffs on.

"They have a grenade launcher," I said.

"Yeah, I noticed." Lucca didn't take his eyes off the men. "Cover him."

I moved closer. "I need your spare clip."

"Fine, but don't shoot me."

He kept his gun trained on the men but opened his stance so I could take the extra magazine he had stowed in his jacket pocket. I reloaded my appropriated weapon and pointed it at the cuffed man while Lucca put a spare set of cuffs on the one with the shoulder wound.

Sirens sounded, and I relaxed slightly. Two police cars arrived on scene first, followed by Jablonsky and Agent Cooper. An ambulance and fire truck arrived a few minutes later, and the Hummer was rammed out of the way so the injured officers could be pried out of the vehicle by the fire department.

"Give me that," Lucca said, taking the gun from my hand. "You're technically still in police custody, so you don't need to get hit by friendly fire."

Jablonsky joined us as the shooters were loaded into a second ambulance and accompanied by Agent Cooper and a few police officers to the hospital. This was serious shit. No one could declare war on a police vehicle, shoot at officers, and expect to walk away with nothing more than a slap on the wrist.

"Sir," I said, teetering, "I remember what happened. It came back. All of it."

"Parker, go sit in the car and wait for me," Mark ordered. "And don't say a word to anyone about this." Media vans were circling the scene like vultures. Some had already gotten out and had begun live broadcasts. "Go." He pointed to the nearest government-issued SUV.

Obeying, I climbed into the car. I was used to adrenaline surges, but whatever was going on with me was a hundred times worse. It was getting harder to focus, and I was nauseous, hot, and dizzy. Something was seriously wrong. I rolled down the window, hoping that the air would help, but things were getting hazier. Opening the door, I barely managed to loop my arm through the open window before crumpling to the ground.

"Parker," Mark yelled, running to me with Lucca at his heels. He grabbed me before I landed face first on the asphalt. "We need a paramedic. Now." He felt for my pulse. "Hurry." I looked up at him, wanting to articulate whatever was wrong but not knowing how. "You'll be okay." I blinked out for a few seconds. "Alex, I'm right here. Stay with me."

TWENTY-TWO

I couldn't remember much of what happened after that, but I didn't care. Jablonsky was there. He could go into specific details if I wanted to hear them, but I didn't. Frankly, I was happy it was a blur. That was over now. All of it was over now. The only thing to do was move on. The world would keep spinning, regardless of anything else. Life was a cold, heartless bitch sometimes. It was my job to make it suck a little less, and thus far, I'd failed miserably. It was time for a change.

Waking up, I looked around the room, taking comfort in the familiar surroundings. Martin was speaking, but I couldn't comprehend his words. Shifting my focus, I stared at him, waiting for the world to make sense again. He smiled and concluded his phone call.

"Hey, beautiful." He crossed the room and climbed into bed.

"Were you speaking German?"

"Ja," he replied.

"Did I know that you speak German?" I asked, and he shrugged. "How many languages do you speak?"

"Five."

"That explains it. For a second, I thought something

short-circuited in my brain."

"I take it you're still feeling wonky." His features contorted into sadness.

"Don't look at me like that. I don't want your pity. I'm okay. You've been lingering nearby for almost a week. It's creepy. Obsessed stalker creepy. How long will it take before you get it through your thick skull that I'm gonna live?"

"You better." He leaned back and put his arm around me. "But given your recent track record, I think it's wise to make sure you adhere to the strict bed rest guidelines. Emergency surgery because of internal bleeding isn't something that needs repeating." His grasp tightened.

"Well, you don't need to work from the bedroom." I glared at the desk that he'd moved into the corner of the room. "Just because I'm stuck in this room doesn't mean you have to be too."

"Neither of us can afford a repeat of that night we spent on the bathroom floor," he pointed out. "I don't want to replace the carpet again. And you aren't supposed to lift anything over five pounds, so I'm pretty sure that means taking a frantic tumble out of bed is also frowned upon."

"Stop talking to me like there's something wrong with me."

"Sweetheart, there is something wrong with you," he said, and I lifted my newly casted arm and punched him in the stomach. Frankly, with his ridiculously toned abdomen, I probably hurt my arm more than him. "Do I need to point out that you had numerous internal injuries and were bleeding into your adrenals? You could have bled out. You could have arrested. You could have suffered a clot or permanent organ damage. Alex, you nearly died."

"Don't you think I know that?" This wasn't exactly an uncommon occurrence, but this was the first time that my stubbornness was the root cause. Based on the bruises and the extensive internal damage, the doctors suspected that my initial injuries had gotten progressively worse with the numerous beatings I'd taken. Unfortunately, my body waited until I was under heavy fire to send my already overloaded system into overdrive. "Those moments before

I passed out were the most terrifying seconds of my life." I swallowed. "Honestly, I can't think about that now. I just can't." A dark understanding had settled over me within the last few days, but it was too unnerving to verbalize just yet.

"Hey, you'll be okay. I will do everything in my power to make sure of it. I'd move heaven and earth for you." He nuzzled against my hair, hoping to lighten the mood. "See, I've already moved the desk. How hard could the rest be?"

"I don't know. Didn't Mark help you move the TV in here?"

He clutched his chest. "You wound my masculinity."

"It's been a while, but from what I remember, that's not where you keep your masculinity."

"Apparently, you're confusing it with my manhood." He smirked. "I understand your confusion since they are both massive."

I laughed. "Just like your ego."

"That's why I'm a triple threat."

"A triple threat who needed help moving the TV. Didn't Mark hold the mount while you screwed it in?"

"Obviously, your memory isn't quite up to snuff since I've never needed any help screwing anything in," Martin said, causing me to laugh harder. "I'm glad you're entertained, even if it appears to be at my expense." I snorted and wheezed, choking on my own laughter. "Okay, enough of that or I'm taking you to get another MRI to make sure you didn't pop a stitch or blow an artery or blood vessel." My laughter turned into quiet chuckles. "For the record, once you're back in fighting shape, I'll make sure you have no reason to laugh at me in bed."

"There's that ego again," I teased. "You and that swelled head of yours."

"Two, but who's counting?"

I rolled my eyes. Normally, I'd blame him, but I was the one who started in on the juvenile jokes this time. Perhaps it was a side effect of the medication I was on. At least, that was the rationale I kept using for why I'd been sleeping so much. Truthfully, I felt like I was at the end of my rope, and I needed to either hang myself or step away from the ledge.

"Did the lawyer call?" I asked, forcing myself to return to practical things. This was about putting one foot in front of the other.

"Yours or mine?"

"Either." I sighed. "Which is worse, jail time or a six-figure settlement?"

"Money's just money, but I already told you I won't let anything happen to you. There hasn't been any word yet from your lawyer, but Mark said the DA didn't believe the cops had a case against you. They were planning on dropping the charges, but after those shitheads tried to blow you to kingdom come, the police opened a new investigation to determine if you orchestrated the attack. It's bullshit. The officer driving made it extremely clear to everyone that you're the only reason he's alive today."

"I could say the same thing." My mind went back to Lucca and the mistrust I'd felt toward him. One thing stuck out in my mind clear as day: *you're reading this wrong.* What the hell did that mean? "When's Mark getting here?"

"He'll be by around lunchtime. He tends to show up when he smells food."

"It's because he's trying to catch a glimpse of you wearing the apron." I smiled. "It's a crowd-pleaser."

"I'm glad I please you."

"Always," I whispered, sinking deeper into the pillow. "So what's the latest on the Francesca front?"

"Do you really want to know?"

"It's only fair. Plus, if it gets too boring, I'll probably just fall asleep."

"Gee, thanks a lot." He lifted my casted arm and slipped a pillow beneath it. Then he filled me in on his legal strategy.

They were about to enter the discovery phase, and the Martin Technologies' legal team believed they had sufficient evidence to prove that MT held the intellectual rights to the disputed technology. The secondary issue, which would be more difficult, was figuring out a way to rebut the claims that they had gained the rights through emotional and psychological manipulation. It sounded like bullshit, but Martin had been engaged to Francesca more than a decade ago. That would make an impartial party raise an eyebrow, and then to top it off, he had a sexual history with numerous employees, including yours truly. It gave a certain level of credence to the claim of hostile work environment, but on paper, there was no evidence backing Francesca Pirelli's claims. Suffice it to say, she was being vindictive and putting the screws to him. At least Mark wasn't holding the mount for her.

"If discovery goes well, we'll file for a summary judgment and hope to get it dismissed before it goes any further," Martin concluded.

"Have they made any other attempts at a settlement?"

"No, that has my attorneys slightly worried."

"What about the Germans? Are they planning an invasion if the shit hits the fan?"

"What?" He glanced at the phone on the desk. "No, that was about a distribution issue. We've lost our Eastern European supplier, and it directly affects that branch of MT. That's just normal business shit."

"Why am I under the impression that there was a time in your life that issue alone would have stressed you out and resulted in at least another dozen phone calls and a few angry e-mails?"

He shrugged. "Maybe you don't know me that well."

"Go," I jerked my chin at the desk, "make your calls, send your sharply worded e-mails, and don't do it from this room."

"Am I bothering you?" he asked, pretending to be insulted.

"Yes, now get the hell out of here." I pulled myself up and whispered in his ear, "I'll miss you while you're gone."

"Liar." Mumbling protests, he got out of bed and went to the desk, collecting his various work paraphernalia. "Laptop or tablet?" he asked.

"Laptop and my notepad." He picked them up from the edge of the desk and placed them on the bed. "Oh, and the pack of colored pens."

"Anything else?"

"Not at the moment."

"Fine," he gave me a look, "I'll be across the hall in my office if you suddenly decide that you need something else." He went to the doorway. "How come you get to work from our bedroom and I don't?"

"I've been trained in manipulation techniques. You haven't, despite what Francesca asserts. However, maybe I'll throw some pointers your way." I winked.

"Not funny." He continued out the door, leaving me to contemplate the recent developments concerning a possible terrorist cell, Det. Donaldson's murder, and the three men that were keen on preventing me from making it to the DA's office alive.

The OIO and the PD opened a joint investigation following the assault on the police vehicle. After what happened, the two branches of law enforcement didn't have a choice. It was a local crime, but the threat of terrorism was a federal matter. The men that attacked us would likely face both state and federal charges, but I was less concerned with what would happen to them and more concerned with what might happen if we couldn't get them to talk.

The police department had granted my colleagues access to Detective Donaldson's records. Anything that mentioned Ivan or Pepper was in review. Mark insisted it was a stall tactic, but reviewing the PD's intel could be helpful. Jablonsky griped and complained, but it was currently our analysts' main priority.

While the police department appeared to be sharing with us, it was obvious that they were examining the role I played in Donaldson's death and the assault on the police car. Luckily, the three officers that were assigned to escort me to the DA's office were set to make full recoveries, and the driver insisted that I had nothing to do with it. I knew they wouldn't find any evidence to suggest otherwise, but given my spotty past with the PD and the altercation in the holding cell that likely caused or contributed to my recent stint in the hospital, it was difficult to assume they'd reach the proper conclusion. In the meantime, I had to be patient and wait for the verdict. The police had taken the assailants into custody, and so far, the OIO hadn't been given access to them. However, Jablonsky planned to take custody soon.

It was in the PD's best interest to clear me, and from what I'd been told by Mark and the OIO's legal staff, I would find out today or tomorrow what the state had in store for me. As usual, I wasn't good at taking things lying down, even if I was actually stuck in bed. So I was reviewing Homeland's file on Shade. I'd read through it before, but now that I knew there was a local connection, I had been spending my downtime cross-referencing names and associates with Pepper and the local immigrant community. Shade was a small organization, but it wasn't tied to just one nation-state. Its membership spanned the Balkans and most of Eastern Europe, particularly the former Soviet Union. Membership was estimated to be less than fifty people, ten of which were in charge, but it only took one determined, desperate individual with resources to make a big mess.

Despite the fact that the men who fired on the police vehicle were yet to be identified as members of Shade, I couldn't imagine that another random group had taken a hit out on me or the police. Coincidences didn't happen. The men with the grenade launcher wanted to take me out to make sure that I couldn't clear myself of Donaldson's murder. Someone wanted the double homicide to be wrapped up in a nice neat package and the federal agent to take the rap and be sent away as a raving lunatic. That hadn't happened, at least not yet.

Picking up my notepad, I grabbed a pen and worked on the physical description of the shooter from Pepper. Based on the way he acted, he was either in charge or took his orders directly from whoever was in charge. Unfortunately, most of the details concerning his looks eluded me. It had been dark in that kitchen, and I wasn't in any condition to make determinations like height or weight after I was skunked out of my mind. But I figured he was average height and fairly lean. He was strong though. Strong enough to snap my wrist in one quick move.

Biting my lip, I replayed the struggle over the gun. He must have been trained, perhaps former FSB or Spetsnaz, or whatever special paramilitary entities existed near Shade's HQ. Then again, he might have been a street brawler that picked up a trick or two to avoid getting his face blown off. However, if he was military or paramilitary, that would explain the use of the grenade launcher. Normal civilians didn't have access to military weapons.

Scribbling a note on the sheet, I thought about the Hummer and the weaponry. It was classic military, so I performed a search for security specialists in the area. It wouldn't be the first time one of these private organizations had ties to terrorism. After all, selling weapons, tech, and soldiers was a lucrative business, and not everyone had qualms about which side paid the bills. Money was money.

Copying down a list of potential companies to investigate, I checked the time and started with the first one I jotted down. A few clicks provided some biographical information and a résumé of sorts, so I began researching each company for a connection to Shade's area of operation. I'd cleared three companies from my list when Martin returned to the bedroom.

"Jablonsky sent a text. He just pulled in."

"Thanks." I put the computer on the bed and pushed myself up. "I'll get changed and cleaned up."

"Okay," he watched warily as I crossed the room to the dresser, pulled out a pair of jeans and a t-shirt, and went into the bathroom, "do you need help?"

"You just want to watch me change."

"Maybe." He lingered outside the bathroom door, waiting for me to emerge. "If Mark plans on hanging around, I'll head to the office for a while."

"Good." I opened the door. "Have fun, just be safe."

He gave me an odd look. "So I should take condoms to work?"

"I meant stay safe, you jerk. Things have been precarious lately, at least for me." I tried to shake off the foreboding feeling that continued to fester. "For the record, keep it in your pants."

"I plan to." He kissed me. "The legal team would murder me if I didn't."

"So would I."
He smiled. "I know."

TWENTY-THREE

"The district attorney dismissed their claims. The police don't have a case against you. All charges have been dropped. It was circumstantial at best, and in light of recent events," Jablonsky surveyed the bedroom, skimming across the work I'd done, "your involvement is no longer a question that needs answering. We have bigger fish to fry." He gave me a look. "You're white as a sheet. Shouldn't you be resting?"

"You just said we have bigger problems."

"Parker, you're sitting this one out." He made himself comfortable in Martin's desk chair. "Lucca's on it. Everyone is on it. Honestly, you're benched for the next couple of weeks until medical clears you. Why don't you focus your efforts on recovering?"

"I can't let this go." Walking away held an unbelievable level of appeal, but I wasn't wired to leave things unfinished. "We could be dealing with a large-scale attack. Can you say with complete certainty that you don't need my help?"

He huffed but didn't say anything to the contrary. Leafing through my notepad, he pulled out his own and made a few notations. Then he pocketed the information, picked up a pen, crossed out some of my scribbles, and placed the notepad on the bed beside me. I read through the changes, realizing that they'd already explored the list of private military contractors.

"Analysis is complete on the grenade launcher and the firearms that the assault team possessed. They're Soviet made. Old. And most likely, black market imports. Interpol is assisting us in tracing their origin. Most of the old Eastern Bloc was controlled by warlords at one time or another. A few are still around, even today, but the gear is dated. Any dealers left in the area are probably selling more advanced weaponry by now, so we're thinking it came from an old weapons cache that had been stockpiled since the Cold War days. Hell, it might have been dug out of some underground doomsday bunker."

"Damn, that is old. It must remind you of when you were a young whippersnapper cutting your teeth at the OIO."

"Don't be cute. I'm old, but that's before my time. The good news is the bulk of the assault team's equipment, like tactical vests and close range weaponry, came from the same era as the grenade launcher, so we think it must have been provided by the same seller. Assuming he has more to sell, we'll eventually be able to track down the supplier and force him to give up his clientele."

"That seems like the long way around. Have the assholes been questioned yet?" I didn't even know what to call them besides derogatory names.

"They're under local jurisdiction. Director Kendall wants us to make as much progress as possible beforehand, so we have leverage to use against them."

"It's a gamble. The longer we wait, the harder it'll be to stop an imminent threat."

"So you believe the three men in custody are members of Shade?" It wasn't a question so much as asking for affirmation on a theory.

"I don't know. I do believe that they are connected."

"Explain." Mark leaned back in the chair and waited.

"I'm guessing the lost shipment from that cargo plane made it to its destination. It might have contained the weapons that the assault team possessed, or it could be something else entirely. Shade must already have allies within our borders. Those allies picked up the shipment and did everything in their power to make sure we didn't know about it. I'm guessing Pepper is a front for something heinous. Ivan must have seen something since he was reporting unusual activity to the police. Donaldson thought it was gang related." I sighed. "He didn't know what he had stumbled upon. Someone else must have realized Ivan was a snitch, and they waited and followed the rat back to the big cheese. Maybe it was my fault. I requested that meeting. Perhaps something about our presence that night tipped our hand."

"You can't think like that. Whatever happened probably had nothing to do with you and everything to do with Ivan or Donaldson," Mark said. "From what you've told me, the man performing the interrogation had no idea you were a federal agent. So you weren't the one acting suspiciously. It's not on you."

"Yeah, but it doesn't change anything." I bit my lip. "I don't think the shooters from the highway assault were the same men involved in the kitchen interrogation."

"So we're dealing with at least five men with suspected ties to a terrorist organization. That worries me."

"Yeah, me too." I stared at the ceiling. "What about Jakov Horvat? Didn't you say he was picked up?"

"Yeah, TSA nabbed him at the airport late last night. He bought a one-way ticket to Croatia under a fake name. His passport didn't pass muster, and he was tagged by security. Homeland is detaining him, but we'll get a crack at him later today."

"All right." I propped myself up on my elbows. "He worked at Pepper with Ivan. His cousin is highly placed in Shade. We have to convince him to talk."

"Agreed." Mark looked at his watch. He and Martin had been trading off to stay with me. On a few rare occasions when they were both busy, Marcal, Martin's valet, had stayed nearby, but it was obvious Mark wanted to get back to work and Martin was nowhere to be found.

"I'm fine," I said. "I won't do anything stupid. I promise.

You can leave me by myself."

"Yeah, right." He ignored me and opened the laptop, starting a new search. "The police sent the crime scene file. Do you want a copy?"

"Yes."

He copied the data from his office inbox and saved it on my hard drive. "It's a bit gruesome, but it contains a lot of data concerning the search of Pepper and the location of the abandoned SUV and the bodies. Maybe you'll notice something that they missed or didn't think was important. You can take a look after I leave."

"Sure."

"Right now, we have something else to discuss," he said. "Eddie Lucca."

"What about him? Did the boy scout get reassigned?"

Mark held up a hand to silence me and pressed his lips together to compose himself. "Explain to me why the man who might have saved your life at least three times in the last few weeks has voiced concerns over your continued partnership."

"I'd say three's pushing it. Once, maybe. And even that's a bit of a stretch."

"Parker, answer me."

"I can't. You haven't told me what his concerns are. If it has to do with my ability to follow orders, well, that's not anything new. If it's my ability to stay alive and reasonably healthy, well, shit, it's been a tough couple of weeks. And if it's because he suddenly realized that being in close proximity to me ought to warrant hazard pay, that's on him because he's been slow on the uptake."

"He's concerned that you've almost fired upon him on two separate occasions." Mark stared at me, wanting to understand. "What the hell would possess you to think he was the enemy?"

"I don't trust him," I admitted.

"What more does the man have to do? Hasn't he proven himself to you, especially in light of recent events? I trust him. The federal government trusts him to uphold and protect the law. What makes your opinion superior?"

"For the record, I didn't plan to shoot him the first time.

I wasn't cognizant of what I was doing. I was asleep, remembering Donaldson's murder in the kitchen. It came to me in a dream, and Lucca was attempting to wake me from it."

"And the second time was in the middle of the firefight with possible terrorists. How do you plan to explain that away?"

"I'm out of my mind," I snapped, sarcastic and annoyed.

"Be honest with me. What is it?"

"A lot of things didn't make sense in that moment. Lucca didn't come to my aid after the police vehicle was disabled. I kicked through the back windshield, emerged under hostile conditions, and was subjected to the barrel of his weapon. Did he mention that?"

"He said he was assessing the situation. The scene warranted having his weapon drawn. He was facing the attackers. You were facing him."

"He had bruises."

"Bruises?"

"The morning he claims I tried to kill him. I saw them on his torso, deep blue bruises like he'd been in a fight. And then everything he had said and done, the fact that he phoned me that morning, that he found me so quickly after the call was made, it was like he knew I wouldn't be in to work that morning and knew precisely where to find me. And then he just kept dismissing everything I said like it had been an accident and I was raving mad. Even when we went to Pepper, Lucca didn't run down Jakov, and our only suspect got away."

"Whatever you think, just spit it out, Alex."

"It's possible that Lucca could be part of this."

"You're telling me that Shade has a mole in the OIO, and that person just happens to be your partner?"

"I'm not telling you anything." Taking a deep breath, I wanted to be able to do something to let out the frustration, but I couldn't. "I don't know, Jablonsky. I don't have a fucking clue. I just know that something is off when it comes to Eddie."

"Didn't he stop the assault in the holding cell? Didn't he call for help and then put himself in danger to apprehend the team that seemed intent on killing you and the police officers? If you don't trust him, why did you send him to get help?"

"I knew I wouldn't have made it. I didn't realize I was bleeding out at the time, but I knew that physically I wasn't capable of making a run for it. And he did save me, which confuses matters. Like I said, I don't have any idea what's going on, but there's something strange going on with him." I looked around the room. "I don't want him here. I don't want him to have access to Martin or this house. Is that understood?"

"Yeah, okay." Jablonsky sighed. "I think you've been through a lot lately. Is it possible that it's clouding your judgment?"

I knew he wanted me to agree, so I shrugged. If Lucca wanted me dead, he had ample opportunities. Obviously, he wasn't all bad, but I had a feeling the boy scout wasn't as honorable as he initially appeared.

"Just be careful around him. We can't afford a leak on the Shade intel. We have to find these guys. We have to figure out if they are plotting something and what that is, and we gotta stop it."

Jablonsky laughed. "You do realize that I'm in charge of the team. I'm the one who says that shit. You're the one causing trouble and being a pain in the ass. Hell, I never expected it would be worse with you as a victim instead of an investigator."

"Face it, I'm both, so you get twice the trouble for the same price."

"Lucky me." He narrowed his eyes. "Is there anything else going on that I need to know about?"

"No." Mark had an uncanny knack for knowing when something was bothering me, but I'd already come off sounding like a paranoid loon with control issues. That was enough for one day. "So, tell me what to do, boss."

He crossed the room and picked up the remote on the nightstand. Turning on the television, he flipped to one of the world news channels for a few minutes, caught the headlines, and then turned to a sports channel. After a few minutes, he grew bored of the highlights.

"Want some chow?" he asked. "Marty said there was a leftover roast in the fridge."

"I'm not hungry."

"Yeah, he said you'd say that too."

Mark moved the remote to the desk, so it would be out of my reach and went downstairs to make lunch. While he was occupied, I opened the police file and scanned through the inventory list and forensic analysis of the SUV where Donaldson and Ivan had been found. Ivan's full name and personal information weren't included in the report, but someone in the police department must have known the true extent of Ivan's helpfulness.

"Hey," I called, hoping Mark would hear me despite being two floors away. A few minutes later, I heard footsteps on the stairs. "Hey," I tried again, "have you spoken to anyone in the police department's counterterrorism unit about Ivan?"

"Not yet. The commander in charge was asked to join our task force. That meeting is scheduled later this afternoon when Homeland drops off Horvat."

"Can three law enforcement agencies share intel without driving each other crazy?" I asked. Then I began humming the theme song to the *Odd Couple*.

"Cut that out."

"I will if you take me to the meeting."

"No."

"C'mon, Mark, pretty please." I batted my eyelashes at him. "I want to know what's going on. Plus, I might possess valuable intel. As far as anyone knows, I'm the only person who can identify a possible Shade operative."

"You said it was dark and you were too impaired to get a good look when the opportunity presented itself. You've done all you can. You found the connection to Ivan. Unfortunately, Detective Donaldson won't be able to answer our questions. However, his notes and files might shed some light on the matter. His CO will be in attendance as well. We can handle this. You compiled the footage and intel on Shade's suspicious activity. DHS and other intelligence agencies have provided surveillance footage and satellite images. We have this under control.

The FAA is tracking the cargo plane's course. We'll find the drop site. We'll find the cargo. And we'll find these fuckers." He put a plate on my lap. "You've done all you can. Now eat your lunch."

TWENTY-FOUR

"Alex, stop fidgeting," Martin said in a tone that I most definitely did not enjoy.

"Don't tell me what to do, and do not for one second act like my caretaker. I'm not a child."

"Fine." He threw up his hands and walked away. "You figure it out."

"Pretentious piece of shit," I mumbled under my breath after he was gone. I glared at my reflection in the mirror. "You're such a bitch, Parker. Snap out of it." Well, at least I had been fair and called us both names; although, it did nothing to reinforce my claim that I wasn't a child.

It had been ten days since the roadside firefight. The injuries I'd sustained prior to that had healed enough that bandages were no longer required. The incisions made during surgery were tender. But the glue holding me together had dissolved, and I remained in one piece. The prescribed bed rest was now an irritant. I wanted to go to work. I wanted to see how things had progressed.

Four days ago, Jakov Horvat was transferred into OIO custody. The assault team was now being questioned by the federal government, and due to the Patriot Act, Jablonsky had taken a creative license with their civil liberties. If they were innocent or had been racially profiled, I would have wondered if we were the good guys, but that wasn't the case. They'd fired on us and would be charged with multiple counts of attempted murder, aggravated assault, assault with a deadly weapon, and whatever else we uncovered. There was no question about their guilt, just about how far reaching their criminal activities went.

Lucca had phoned twice since my conversation with Jablonsky. The first time, he had asked how I was. The second time, he had provided an update on the progress that had been made concerning Pepper. Since the police department was now an active entity in gathering intelligence on Shade and any potential plots, progress was being made. The restaurant was shut down, and the owners and manager had been taken into custody.

Inside the freezer, a crime technician discovered a trap door that led to a walled-in storage area. The freezer was the only access point into the room. Inside the storage area were cases of Kalashnikov rifles, Makarov pistols, PPS submachine guns, Dragunov sniper rifles, and an assortment of knives, grenades, and other small incendiary devices. Given the location, it was obvious the employees of Pepper had access to the stockpiled artillery, so multi-agency surveillance teams were keeping a watchful eye on the twenty-seven employees. But I didn't know if any of them had been brought in for questioning.

Despite doctor's orders, Jablonsky was on his way to pick me up. It'd been approximately two weeks since Donaldson was killed. My memory concerning those events hadn't changed. The details remained vividly the same. The questions I initially couldn't answer upon remembering the event remained unanswerable, but the task force wanted to bring me in for another debriefing which was why I was fidgeting with my button-up shirt which wouldn't fit over the cast on my arm.

"Screw it." I balled up the shirt and threw it into the hamper. Then I went into the bedroom to find Martin typing at his computer. "I suck." He ignored me and continuing clicking keys. "I hate this. I hate the way I feel. I hate that you've been forced to take care of me. I loathe being taken care of."

"Yeah, I got the message loud and clear." He glanced back at me, cocking an eyebrow in surprise. "Are you still planning to go to work?"

"Yes, and I hate that I want to be there. I do, and I don't. And I don't know what's wrong with me." I slumped onto the bed. "Your girlfriend is a psycho freak."

"Yes, she is." He stopped typing and spun the chair around. "You do realize that you've had these meltdowns a lot since we've been together. And I mean *a lot*. I've lost track since I've run out of fingers to count on. At first, I thought maybe it was me, but then I realized it's you."

"Did I mention I'm a bit psycho?"

"You're stressed. This isn't good for you, and this definitely isn't good for us." His gaze continued to linger on me. "You haven't said what's so urgent that it can't wait until you're fully healed. Alex, you don't need to set yourself back. You go stir crazy and then just crazy, and," he shook his head, "everything spins out of control from there. What's going on? Talk to me."

I snickered. "This might be the first time I've ever said these words and had them be absolutely true, but I am not at liberty to discuss it. It is a matter of national security, and it scares the hell out of me." Something else was also scaring the hell out of me, but that was another discussion for another day.

"I don't like it." He rubbed his eyes and leaned back in the chair. "You're just answering questions. Why can't you do that here or over the phone?"

"Security issues," I said, finding some peace after verbalizing my feelings. My normal methods of dealing with stress had all been taken away. I couldn't run or workout or even pace. Hell, even drinking was barred for now, so talking was my only release. "Damn, I need to get laid." I winked at him, and he chuckled.

"That makes two of us." His eyes traveled down the length of my body. "Is that why you're wearing nothing but dress pants and a bra? Are you hoping to seduce one of your colleagues? I'd like to point out that since you told me I had to keep it in my pants at work, I'm requesting that you do the same."

I looked down. "My work clothes won't fit over the cast. And this is important. I really don't want to show up in a sweatshirt or t-shirt to talk to these people. So what do I do, Mr. Fashionista?"

Martin crossed the room and opened the closet. He sifted through the racks of clothes and found my suit jacket. Like most things, it had been tailored and didn't have a lot of extra sleeve space for a bulky cast. Replacing it on the hanger, he picked through the rest of the clothes in the closet, but I didn't have any short sleeved work items. Finally, he shifted to his side of the closet and removed one of his freshly pressed shirts from the hanger.

"Here," he said, handing me the light blue shirt, "but for the record, I want it back."

"We'll see." I grabbed a black tank top and went into the bathroom to change. It wasn't exactly work appropriate, but I didn't have a choice. I left Martin's shirt unbuttoned, tied a knot at the bottom, and returned to the bedroom so Martin could roll up the sleeves for me. "How do I look?"

"Like you're trolling Wall Street for some tail."

"Great, high-end hooker, just what I wanted."

"Hey, you said you wanted to get laid." His face contorted into mock horror. "Does this make me your pimp?"

"Shut up."

"I thought the pimp called the shots."

"Martin," I whined.

"Hey," he pulled me into a hug, trying hard not to cringe at the state of his once neatly ironed shirt, "make sure that you're well enough to do this. If you need to come home and Jabber's busy, call me. Okay?"

"I thought you agreed not to take care of me anymore."

"It's not you I'm worried about. It's my shirt."

* * *

Upon entering the conference room, a chill traveled down my spine. The mood in the room was bleak. Several serious faces remained focused on the projection in front of them. Lucca cast his eyes in my direction and offered a welcoming nod. Jablonsky pulled out the nearest chair for me before taking his seat.

I'd met with the DHS agent earlier when he'd first delivered the file on Shade to us, but I couldn't remember his name. The woman seated beside him was Bethany Tinsley, the commander in charge of the police department's counterterrorism unit. She'd delivered her fair share of press conferences, and so far, her record was perfect. Hopefully, we'd keep it that way. Agents Lucca and Cooper were on the opposite side of the table with our Interpol connection, Patrick Farrell. The other two people must have been from other agencies, but it would have been a waste of time to guess which ones.

"Special Agent Parker," the DHS agent said, "I'm Assistant Director Stuart Behr from the Department of Homeland Security. We met briefly."

"Yes, sir." I nodded, feeling my brainwashed training kicking in. "What can I do to help?"

"We appreciate your willingness to assist, given your condition." His eyes traveled to my arm, and I retracted the wounded appendage from sight. "Our speculation that the organization we've dubbed Shade might be a terrorist cell has led to numerous unsettling discoveries over the last few weeks." He glanced down at his notes. "You showed concern over the increased activity at their base of operations. From your reports, it appears that contraband has traded hands. Our sources indicate that Shade supplied a domestic faction with military grade weaponry. As of now, we do not know the extent of these weapons, but in light of recent discoveries, we believe they are dealing in Soviet era arms."

"We've tested the cargo plane, the restaurant, and other possible transaction sites for radioactivity, chemical residue, and biological components. So far, the scans have been within normal parameters," someone else added.

"Agent Parker, what can you tell us about the night you were attacked and Detective Donaldson was murdered?" Behr asked. Before I could speak, he added, "We've read the initial reports, the police account, and we've spoken extensively to SSA Jablonsky and Agent Lucca. There's no need to rehash old news."

I blinked a few times. "With all due respect, I can't help you." I leaned back in the chair. "That's everything."

"Please," Behr implored, "you must have found some indication that led you to seek police assistance."

"Niko Horvat is highly placed in Shade. The last I heard, we don't know who's in charge, but Niko might be. We've speculated that he has plentiful connections, and he's been added to the watchlist. Since we've attempted to monitor his travel plans, I figured there might be some way he was subverting the system. Fake papers can be bought for a price, but since we have our feelers out for that type of activity, I did some more checking which led to Jakov Horvat." I glanced at Jablonsky. "He's in custody." Mark nodded. "That was the connection I found. He had similar features to his cousin, Niko."

"Jakov's immediate family is under surveillance. We've examined his phone records. There have been no communications between him and Niko, so how did you come to that conclusion?" Tinsley asked.

"It was a hunch," I admitted. "Their passport photos were practically identical, and Horvat is an incredibly common name. It would be understandable why the authorities wouldn't realize the connection or ping Jakov. However, Jakov has made a couple of suspicious trips from the Balkans to the U.S., but I suspect that it was actually Niko who made the trek instead."

"How did Niko obtain Jakov's passport?" Behr asked.

"I don't know. I never said he did. I just think he might have," I said.

"The passport records indicate that Jakov made a return trip from Serbia to the U.S. However, there was no record of him having ever left the United States," Jablonsky said. He rifled through the stack of papers and pushed one across to Behr. "My people know their shit."

"So you pulled Jakov's records, found out where he lived and worked, and went to the police department?" Behr asked, the accusatory tone in his voice. "Why didn't you report this to your superiors or to me?"

"She did," Jablonsky growled. "She left me the passport information."

"But that was after she approached Detective Donaldson and set up a meet with his confidential informant," Tinsley said, scribbling down a note.

"I had nothing to report at that time. It could have been a glitch or an oversight. Thousands of people travel daily. I needed to make sure that Jakov Horvat hadn't been returning from a trip out of the country," I said.

"Then why didn't you speak to Jakov directly?" Behr asked.

"Because if he was involved, it could have tipped our hand on the investigation into Shade," I argued.

"Alex," Mark hissed, and I fell silent.

"I guess the next question is why did it take you so long to remember these details? You didn't write a report on Jakov or your intentions to monitor his activity," Behr said.

"I don't know how things are done at Homeland," Lucca replied, "but here, we do the work first. Actions speak louder than words." I glanced at the boy scout, wondering when he grew a pair. Something was definitely off. "Why would Parker report something if there was nothing to report? It could have been nothing."

"Except it wasn't," Behr said.

"Stuart, I didn't realize you wanted to crucify my agent for bringing this shit to your attention and giving us a fighting chance to stop another attack on American soil," Jablonsky barked.

Behr swallowed, clearly indignant and pissed. "I'm just trying to get the facts straight before moving forward."

"Are they straight enough for you?" Jablonsky asked.

Deciding that we shouldn't be at war with each other, I cleared my throat. "I'll answer your question, but my reasoning is nothing more than a restatement of previous facts. During the struggle that resulted in Detective Donaldson and his CI being killed, I'd been forced to consume a large quantity of alcohol and sustained a concussion. You can read my medical reports yourself, but it screwed with my mental capabilities."

"Are you still impaired?" Behr asked.

"I don't believe so," I replied.

"And the reason for your extended medical leave is due to...?" He raised an eyebrow.

"Severely sprained wrist and doctor's orders following surgery after nearly bleeding out on an off-ramp," I snapped. "But this is more important than any one person. This is certainly more important than me. We took an oath to defend this country from all enemies foreign and domestic, and I can't stand by when a threat of this magnitude looms overhead."

"I guess that means you're back to work, Agent Parker. It looks like your doctor's gonna be pissed," Behr said.

TWENTY-FIVE

Lucca placed a cold bottle of water in front of me. After the debriefing, Assistant Director Behr had returned to DHS to update his cohorts. Lt. Tinsley remained in the conference room. She had asked me a few questions, wanting elaborations on precisely how Donaldson had been subdued and why I hadn't intervened. The more she asked, the more I doubted myself. Truthfully, I knew I could have done more to stop it from happening. I should have. Maybe those two men would still be alive and that asshole would be in custody. Then we'd know how the weapons came to be inside the storage area beneath the freezer and what Shade was planning. I failed epically. What was worse was the fear that my inaction could lead to mass casualties.

"Are you okay?" Lucca whispered. "The last time you looked like that we had to rush you to the hospital."

"Don't remind me." I leaned back in the chair.

Tinsley hadn't heard our exchange or was pretending she didn't. She swiped the images on her screen to the left, circling and making notations as she went. Photos of Pepper and the hidden storage area were visible, but she didn't offer to share.

In the quiet, I read through the updated file and the numerous transcripts from Jakov's interviews. He swore he didn't know anything, but he ran. I scanned through the questions, but he never provided a reason for evading us or attempting to flee the country. He had to know something.

"Can I see the complete profile on Jakov?" I asked.

"Sure," Lucca said, getting up to search through one of the file boxes. He found the file and placed it next to me. "We need to break him."

"Why don't you have him moved to one of the interrogation rooms, and I'll give it a go," I offered.

Agent Cooper was across the table, skimming through the data on Shade's known connections. He looked up at me. "I don't think that's the best idea. We've been given strict guidelines to follow while interviewing him."

"By whom?" I asked.

"Behr," Cooper said.

Tinsley snorted in displeasure but kept her head down, focused on the work in front of her. I glanced in her direction, realizing she must have thought Behr was a bureaucrat first and foremost. Although, I assumed that the lieutenant in charge of counterterrorism was also a brownnoser.

"Can you gentlemen give us the room?" I asked.

Lucca looked at me uncertainly. He probably figured I'd come to blows with the cop over my mistreatment or I'd shoot her since he tended to believe that my goal in life was to put holes in my allies. Thankfully, he didn't have to worry about the two of us trading gunfire since I wasn't armed or permitted to carry at the moment due to the medical mandates. Perhaps she'd fire upon me. After all, she'd made it very clear that I was to blame for Donaldson's death and the predicament we found ourselves in.

She looked up, intrigued by my request. "This ought to be good."

"Boys," I said, not looking at them, "just give us two minutes."

Cooper stood up, making an exaggerated stretch. "I could use a break."

"Behave yourself, Parker," Lucca whispered in my ear before exiting the conference room and intentionally leaving the door opened.

"You don't like Behr," I said.

"Am I that obvious?" she asked sarcastically.

"No. Not at all. It must be woman's intuition." I crossed my arms and assessed her. We'd either be best friends or bitter rivals. My money was on the latter, but this was important. This wasn't a competition. Lives were at stake. "Did you know Donaldson personally?"

"Not well."

"I'm sorry for your loss."

She sighed. "It's not just my loss. It's this city's loss. He was good police and a good man. I can't fathom why he'd put himself at risk."

"Did he ever mention anything about Jakov or Shade to anyone in your unit?"

"No."

"But he must have been on to something. He had Ivan keeping watch at Pepper. Look, I'm well aware of the code of silence and the us versus them mentality. I know we're nothing but feebs to you. Frankly, I get that. We're a bunch of pencil pushing morons that sit in our tower away from the real world and dictate how everyone else should do their jobs. We're assholes. We pretend we're perfect, but we miss things. And when we do, people die."

"So you admit you screwed up?"

I looked her in the eye and said, "I've screwed up a lot, but I didn't kill Donaldson. I didn't put him into that position. Somehow, they were already on to him. My guess is that Ivan fucked up somewhere, asked too many questions, and made someone suspicious. Donaldson tried to save me. He didn't blow my cover. He begged them to let me go. That's probably why they focused their attention on him, and it gave me time to get out of the cuffs. But by then, it was too late."

"Have you seen the crime scene report?"

"Only the sanitized version that the police department shared."

She smiled. "I see you've dealt with my people before."

She flipped through the pictures and turned the tablet around. "The bodies were posed. The scene was set. Everything was placed. It was too perfect. Even the most incompetent feeb would be smart enough not to leave her credentials inside the SUV and use her service piece to murder a cop."

"Thanks, I think."

"They roughed you up pretty good while you were in custody."

"Yeah." I stared at her.

"And you let them." I didn't say anything, but we both knew it was true. You couldn't be a female in this line of work and not be able to defend yourself. "Was that to prove your innocence? Or was that to alleviate your guilt?" she asked.

"I don't know."

She nodded. "Behr's an ass. He wants to pretend this isn't happening, and he wants someone to say they screwed up and fabricated the entire thing in order to clear it off his plate. That's not how things like this work. I'm afraid if he doesn't pull his head out of his ass soon, it'll be too late."

"Then we have to work together to pick up his slack. I need you to believe that I'm not responsible for this mess. We have to find common ground."

"Jablonsky already gave me this speech," she said. "He has my cooperation. I'll get the rest of my unit on board, but you need to understand something, the FBI and OIO aren't calling the shots. Neither is DHS. This is a collaboration. Is that clear?"

"Yes, ma'am."

"Okay, I guess that means I'll tolerate you and your pals for the time being."

"Hurrah," I deadpanned.

She turned off the tablet and shoved it inside her bag. "C'mon, let's take a ride." She glanced out the doorway. "Do you need to ask permission first?"

"What do you think?"

"That's how you ended up in this mess."

She led the way out of the conference room and to the elevator. Lucca caught sight of us and came over to see what was happening. He put his hand against the elevator door before it could close.

"What's going on?" he asked.

"I'm taking Parker to Pepper. It's about time your side gets a firsthand look at what we've discovered. Do you want to tag along?" she asked.

"I'll meet you there," he said, releasing the door and disappearing from sight.

"That's your partner, right? Is he always this protective?" she queried.

"Not usually."

"Eh, close calls can do that to a person." She dismissed his odd behavior easily, and we fell into a comfortable silence until our arrival at Pepper. After parking at an angle in front of the building that partially obstructed the far right lane, she marched to the front door, knocked, and waited for the officer who was guarding the place to open the door. "Simmons," she said, nodding to him, "is the stuff on ice?"

He snickered. "Yes, ma'am. We left it in cold storage."

"Anything to report?"

"No, ma'am," he said. He stepped away from the door, allowing us to enter.

"Agent Lucca will be along shortly. Let me know when he gets here," she said before leading the way toward the kitchen and freezer. "Parker, you still with me?"

"Yes, ma'am," I said, mocking Simmons. Personally, I despised the term ma'am, but I had my reasons. If Tinsley was cool with it, then good for her.

"Good." She stopped short the moment we stepped inside the kitchen. "Since we're here, I'd like you to show me where everything went down. Just so I'm clear."

I did my best to hide the glare, understanding that had been her primary motivation for taking me to Pepper. It wasn't so we could make progress; it was so she could decide if she believed my version of what happened. I walked through the kitchen, pointing to places of interest and doing my best to remain emotionless. Flashes of Donaldson sideways on the floor with blood dripping from the bullet hole in his head and the look of horror permanently etched on his face was hard to bear, but I did it anyway.

She knelt down at the drain, taking out a pen and hooking the tip into one of the holes in order to pry it loose. Once it was free, she examined the drain with her penlight and made a note to have it swabbed for blood residue again. Then she replaced the drain cover and stood.

"Agent Lucca," she smiled warmly, as if she hadn't just used the last few minutes to torment me, "we were just about to check the freezer."

"Lead the way," he said, eyeing her crouched position. "Our crime lab is on standby to examine the items you've discovered."

"Didn't you receive our reports?" she asked.

"Yes." A brief smugness crossed his features. He liked putting the screws to her, and at the moment, I was also enjoying it. "But it's time we share more than just reports. You've been given access to our evidence and suspects, and you promised Jablonsky complete cooperation. It's time we put this interagency task force to use."

"Agreed," she said, crossing through the frigid air and lifting the thick rubber mat out of the way. "Why don't you start by helping me lift this door?"

Lucca bent down, and they opened the hatch. A narrow staircase led to a warmer, decently lit room. It reminded me of the laundry room in the basement of my college dormitory, except instead of washing machines and dryers, a dozen wooden crates lined the walls.

"Everything's been searched and cataloged, but we haven't moved the bulk of the weaponry yet. Samples have been taken from each crate and sent through our labs for analysis. You do have the reports," Tinsley said. "However, we didn't want to move the crates themselves just yet. We've been occupying the restaurant for the last few days, but in case our efforts have been monitored, we were hoping to let the terrorist operatives believe that we haven't found their stash in the hopes it would delay them from acquiring more weaponry."

"They'll assume that the longer you're here, the better the chance is that they'll be discovered," I said. "Has anyone stopped by or been snooping around?"

"Simmons didn't have anything to report," Tinsley replied.

"Still," Lucca lifted one of the lids and examined the contents, "even if we delay their acquisition temporarily, they'll find another source."

"What if we use the stockpile as bait to lure the players out of hiding?" I asked.

"That's what I was thinking," Tinsley said, "but it's been days. It could be too late."

"We'd need approval," Lucca said. "The last thing we need to do is put these weapons back in the hands of terrorists."

"What if we removed the firing pins?" I asked. "We could leave boxes of ugly paperweights behind and set up a sting to grab whoever comes to get the weapons."

"It's not without risks," Tinsley said. "It'd be easier to obtain firing pins than it is to obtain the actual artillery. Plus," she lifted the box on the incendiaries and grenades, "we can't necessarily disarm these."

"Our people need to see this," Lucca declared, "and whatever plan you want to implement needs to be approved by DHS and Director Kendall, not just your superiors."

"My superiors?" Tinsley asked, and I knew she was seconds away from chewing him out.

"Uh, guys, we have a bigger problem," I said.

"What?" Tinsley and Lucca both asked.

"Jakov's in custody. He's involved. Whoever he speaks to and contacts must be wondering why he's gone radio silent. He might have been planning to meet someone once he arrived at his destination, but we stopped that. They already know we're on to them. The question is what they're planning to do about it."

TWENTY-SIX

"Parker," Jablonsky said, "what are you doing?"

"Thinking," I mumbled from beneath the blanket. Upon our return from Pepper, Mark had requested a private chat in his office which had been a thinly veiled excuse to give me a much needed break. I'd curled up on his couch and hadn't moved since.

"You're not up to this," he said. He dropped the reports he'd been reading and stared at me. "I'll cover for you if you go home. Stuart Behr can kiss my ass."

"No," I sat up, "I'm all right. Have you seen the armaments that these assholes have? Pepper has to be a front for Shade. Can't we do something? The Patriot Act should allow us to detain and question the employees. It isn't ideal, but we can't disregard the danger either."

"Our techs are scanning the surveillance footage. We need to narrow down the list. I don't honestly believe that every employee is involved. Tinsley is supposed to be working on Donaldson's records. Once we have verification of Ivan's true identity and what he was reporting, we'll have a better idea of where to go from here."

"We shouldn't be waiting. We've waited long enough. It took me long enough to remember, and even then, I didn't see the connection." I sighed. "How did I forget that I'd gone to see Donaldson about Shade? Anything else wouldn't have mattered, but that mattered."

"You can't change it." He went back to reading reports, and I closed my eyes for a few more minutes. Without warning, he slammed his palm down on the stack of folders. "Dammit, we don't need everyone else involved. They dumped this shit in our laps, and then they tie our hands before we can clean up the mess. Homeland didn't want to deal with the threat. It was beyond their scope, but now that we've made progress, they want to step back in and fuck up our progress."

"Tinsley said the same thing."

"Well, she's not an idiot. She's also not helping matters." He scratched at his mustache. "Do you want to take a crack at Jakov before calling it a day? I could use the assist."

"Sure." I'd been dying to question the man since he recognized me inside Pepper. "Cooper said we were given strict instructions on what was allowed inside the interrogation room."

"Yeah, well, that's Cooper. Sometimes, it's better to ask for forgiveness." Mark smiled. "Plus, you weren't here for that meeting. You don't know any better."

"If I get suspended, you're subsidizing me."

"Hey, I gave you a comfy couch and blanket to nap on. It's the least you can do."

He picked up the phone and requested that Jakov Horvat be moved into one of the interview rooms. After that was completed, we discussed various techniques and topics that needed addressing. The goal was to finger the Shade operatives and pull them off the street. In the meantime, the foreign FBI offices were monitoring Shade HQ for questionable activity. In the event we screwed the pooch, they'd be in a position to intervene, or so we hoped.

"You take point," Mark instructed. "I'll weigh in if it becomes necessary."

"Great." Since the night of the attack, it felt like every move I made was being scrutinized by someone. First, it was Lucca, then the police department, and now Jablonsky. Frankly, there was no reason to beat myself up over this anymore since everyone else was taking turns. "Am I getting graded too?"

"Yes, and I expect you'll do me proud." He twisted the doorknob and pulled the door open, allowing me to enter.

The interrogation room was bleak, more so than the one I'd been forced to tolerate at the precinct. Even the lights appeared dim. Jakov Horvat was seated in a metal chair at the metal table with his hands bound and secured in front of him. He didn't look like much, so I couldn't fathom why my colleagues hadn't broken him yet. I must be missing something.

"Do you know me?" I asked without so much as a greeting or acknowledgement of my credentials.

"What?" Jakov asked, focusing on my face. His expression didn't change, but his pupils dilated ever so slightly, a sign of recognition.

"You know me, right?" I waited, but he didn't say anything. "You recognize me. At least I think you did. That's why you decided to run, wasn't it?"

"I don't know you. Who are you?" he finally asked.

"Let me make sure I have this right. You don't know me? You have no idea who I am?"

"No. Should I know you?"

I shrugged. "Well, if you knew me, you'd know the answer to that." I took a seat across from him, seeing Jablonsky take to leaning against the door. "Do I know you?"

"No," he said, becoming more bewildered by the moment.

"Are you sure about that, Jakov?" My odd, slightly friendly and albeit utterly frustrating line of questioning just turned a little darker.

"So you know my name. Big deal. You all know my name. It doesn't make me guilty of anything."

"Your name doesn't, but that thing you did, you know, that thing, it makes you guilty."

"What the fuck are you talking about?"

I sat back in the chair and studied my nails. Time was on my side. With any luck, he'd crack under the pressure he was placing on himself.

"Answer me," he demanded, but I glanced up at him and smirked. "What the hell is she talking about?" he asked, swiveling to face Jablonsky. "I've told you that you have me confused with someone else. That I want a lawyer, and now you send this psycho in here instead. What is she talking about? I want to know the charges against me."

"Resisting arrest," Mark said in a neutral tone.

"But why were you arresting me in the first place?" Jakov growled, exasperated.

I let out an audible, exaggerated sigh. "Because of that thing you did."

"What thing?" he bellowed, frantically spinning to face me again. "What did I do?"

"You know what you did," I said. This was my personal version of *who's on first*, and it was utter hell for Jakov. At least I was amused, and I suspected Mark was too.

"Fine, I'm not saying a word. I'm entitled to a lawyer. I want a lawyer," Jakov insisted, staring across the table at me. "You can't deny me my civil rights. You have to get me a lawyer."

"No, we actually don't," Jablonsky said.

"Why the hell not?" Jakov spat.

"Because of that thing you did," I volunteered. "Now, you said you weren't going to say a word. So don't."

He went slack-jawed, alternating his gaze between Mark and me. "Then how the hell do I get out of here?"

"You start talking," Jablonsky said.

"No, remember, he said he wasn't saying a word," I pointed out.

"Oh, right," Mark said.

We fell silent, and Jakov began to fidget. Then he got the look. I'd seen it before. I'd actually seen it on Jakov's face before. He was considering his options. He planned to bolt, but there was nowhere to go.

"It's a good thing you don't know me," I said, distracting him from whatever dumbass plan he was formulating that would likely get him hurt, "but you are wrong about one thing."

"What's that?" he asked, giving the door another furtive glance.

"I do know you." My words were dark and sinister. "Your chances of making it out of this room are miniscule, but if you do, I can guarantee that you won't make it out of the building."

"You don't know that," he replied, his tone more confident and a tad menacing. His look changed. The dumb act just went out the window. He grinned, staring at me or possibly through me. He truly believed he was superior, that he knew something we didn't, and he would be victorious.

"I'd bet on it."

"You'll lose. You have the wrong man, but my family will come for me. They'll stop at nothing." He looked around the room. "This is the reason that you are hated."

"You don't know me, so how can you hate me?" I asked.

"I know enough. You were supposed to die in that kitchen with the other rats," Jakov said.

"Thanks," I gave him a big phony smile, "that's what I wanted to hear."

His confidence wavered slightly, realizing he'd admitted to something, but he was too arrogant to give up that easily. "It's not a crime to hear things."

"What else did you hear?" Mark asked, standing straighter.

Jakov snorted. "I want a lawyer. You can't keep me here. You can't question me without one."

"Damn," I said, leaning back and realizing this would take a while, "did you already forget that we are keeping you here? It's been days. You're not going anywhere, and you're not getting a lawyer. Now stand by your word and shut the fuck up." I kicked the table, jolting him slightly.

He cursed and muttered in his native tongue, but I ignored it. And the waiting resumed. Leaning back, I resisted the urge to close my eyes for an extended amount of time. It was important to appear relaxed, but it'd be unprofessional to fall asleep while conducting an interrogation. However, in the event I was ever on the other side of the table again, I might actually attempt it to halt the questions.

"I want to go back to my cell," Jakov finally said.

"We don't give a shit," Mark replied. "You insist that you've done nothing wrong, but unless you tell us something useful, we're gonna sit in this fucking room from now until kingdom come."

"Fine." Jakov wanted to be stubborn, so we waited him out. It took nearly an hour before he spoke again. "Do your bosses know you're doing this?"

"He's my boss," I said, jerking my head at Jablonsky. I stared at Jakov. "He doesn't like it when his underlings are supposed to die, and he really hates it when an asshole like you gloats about it."

"I didn't touch you," Jakov said. "I wasn't there."

I smiled. "Of course not. Clearly, you don't know me, and you most definitely didn't recognize me the day you bolted from Pepper."

"You have it wrong," Jakov insisted.

"Then tell us how it is," Jablonsky snapped. He was losing his patience.

Jakov looked at the door again, rolled his eyes, and stared at the floor. The time lapse had done nothing to loosen his lips, so I kicked the table again. He glared angrily at me, so I kicked it harder this time.

"Stop it," he growled. I kicked again. His chair was bolted to the floor, and he was hooked to the table, completely susceptible to the vibrations from my kicks. "Stop."

"Maybe I will if you beg," I snarled, keeping my voice low on the off chance that we were being monitored. "Or maybe I should knock you to the ground and kick you instead of the table. It didn't do anything to anyone, but you're a different story."

"I didn't hurt you," Jakov yelled.

"Who did?" Jablonsky asked, taking a few steps closer and motioning that I should stop rattling our captive.

"I won't betray my family," Jakov insisted.

"Your family?" Mark reached into his jacket and pulled out photographs. "Like your cousin Niko?" He pulled out a printout of the two passport photos. "Or is that really you? It's hard to tell. You can see why we're confused." He cocked his head to the side, making every effort to soften his voice. "Maybe we do have the wrong man."

It was the opportunity that Jakov wanted. Unfortunately, we'd only given it to him as a condition of pointing the finger at Niko and providing us with actual evidence that he was innocent. Jakov narrowed his eyes at the photos and shook his head.

"Those are doctored. They're fake. You altered them in order to pin the crimes on me and my family," Jakov argued.

"Bullshit. You already admitted that your family will come for you and stop at nothing. We know who Niko Horvat is. We've had our eyes on him for some time," I volunteered, hoping that he'd open up. "We can overlook some things, like if you sent your cousin your passport to use. Since you insist that we have the wrong man, why don't you prove it?"

"I am no rat." Jakov practically bared his teeth. "You've seen what happens to rats." His lips pulled back into a snarl. "We kill the rats and their source of cheese."

"I'm guessing that sounds better without the English translation," I mocked. "Either that or your attempt to sound like a badass needs major work."

"I don't have to sound like anything. I have done nothing. You're blaming me for having relatives," Jakov argued.

"Actually, you just admitted to multiple counts of murder and the attempted murder of a federal agent. My federal agent," Mark spat. "For all we know, you could be Niko."

"You have my identification," Jakov said.

"Right, because there's no way that could be a fake." Mark rolled his eyes. "Wait, you were arrested for attempting to use a fake passport, and you provided Pepper with fake work documentation. Surely, you must realize the irony of your statement. This is it. Tell me what happened Friday night, two weeks ago, inside the kitchen at Pepper." Jakov opened his mouth to say something, and Mark slammed his palm onto the table, rattling Jakov's bindings again. "And let me make it real clear, if you don't answer the question truthfully and to my satisfaction, I'm going to take this file and these photographs, light them on fire, and shove them down your throat. Now talk."

Jakov turned his anger on me. He hissed, practically spitting in my direction. His gaze was meant to intimidate, but I wasn't frightened. His eyes darted to the cast on my arm, and he slowly drew them back to my face. Then he smiled wickedly.

"You were there," I said. It wasn't a question. Truthfully, I didn't remember seeing him that night, but from what he'd said and the way he acted, I knew it was true. "Pull up his sleeves." Jablonsky didn't ask why I'd said that, but he roughly shoved the long sleeves up to Jakov's elbows. "Like I said, you were there."

Jakov studied his arms, not finding any visible marks that would explain my comment. He had a tattoo, but only the slightest trace of it was visible at the crook of his elbow. He narrowed his eyes.

"This proves nothing," he insisted.

"No, it's everything. You were there that night. You know what happened. A police officer and a civilian were gunned down in the kitchen of that restaurant. The bodies were moved, and I would have ended up dead if I hadn't escaped. Why wasn't I killed when they were?"

Jakov huffed, searching the room for a way out. "It would be impolite to kill a woman. Maybe someone thought you might be useful."

"How?" I asked.

He licked his lips, considering his options. "It doesn't matter now. It's obvious."

"What is?" Jablonsky asked.

"Niko's aware that you're monitoring him," Jakov said, leaning as far back as he could and looking smug.

TWENTY-SEVEN

"Parker," Jablonsky called, stopping me at the elevator doors, "hey, what was the deal with his sleeves? If that means something to you, tell me now. We don't have evidence. He won't talk. He refuses to help. I need something."

"It was a bluff," I replied. "At first, I thought that there could be bruising or scrapes from struggling over the gun, but it's been too long. They would have healed by now. Then I thought maybe if he had some kind of identifying mark, that would be something, but I don't have anything."

"He thought you did. That's why he said as much as he did," Jablonsky said, stepping into the elevator with me. "We can work with that. Expand. Just tell me the part he played and what you remember."

"You don't get it." I spun so we were face-to-face. "I don't remember him from that night. He could have pulled the trigger for all I know, or he could have been hiding inside a broom closet. I don't remember."

"Okay, take it easy."

"No, don't handle me." I put my hand up for him to stop and immediately began pacing inside the elevator. "I don't want to try hypnosis or more therapeutic techniques. It was dark. I was scared and drunk. He could have been the shooter."

"Do you remember the man's voice?" Mark asked. "We could have him say some of the things you remember, and maybe the voices will sound the same."

I bit my lip, searching my memory. "I don't think it was him. He might have been the man that brought me into the kitchen and cuffed me to the chair. Or there could have been an unknown number of other people inside that I never saw or don't remember seeing."

"So you took a gamble that he'd break?"

"It didn't work."

"It helped," Mark insisted. He watched me stalk the floor in front of him. "Okay, you said the man that snapped your wrist was the same man that shot Donaldson."

"I think so."

"Someone else was driving the SUV."

"Obviously."

Mark nodded slightly, lost in thought. His eyes darted back and forth for a few seconds while he processed through whatever scheme he concocted. "But you're positive that Jakov was there?"

"He ran. He knows what happened. He knows me," I insisted.

"All right. I'll coordinate with Tinsley. The security footage from Pepper is already being scrubbed. I'll make sure they pinpoint Jakov's position inside and outside the restaurant. We'll figure out where the bastard was and what he was doing."

"He said now Niko knows. The clock has started. We don't have the luxury of wasting time with this asshole."

"I know." He looked grim. "Speaking of time," he glanced at his watch, "you've been here for almost ten hours. I can't afford to risk your health and have you benched at a time like this."

"We don't have time to waste. I'm okay to hang around here. Maybe I can help."

"You're useless to me. Go home and sleep on things. Tomorrow, I want to know how we can break Jakov."

"You might need to hire a psychic for that one."

"Go home," he ordered, abandoning me outside the elevator while he marched down the hall to the conference room.

"Sure, just as soon as I find a ride."

Calling Martin for help didn't hold any appeal, so despite logic, I grabbed my car keys and went to the garage, enjoying the freedom of self-reliance that I'd so desperately been missing. Thankfully, Martin was too preoccupied to notice how I arrived home.

I took off his shirt, leaving it draped on the kitchen chair while I searched the fridge for sustenance. After heating a bowl of soup and polishing off a bottle of water, I gave the staircase a dirty look. Our stupid bedroom was on the fourth floor. How moronic. Settling onto the sofa, I ate my dinner and tried to focus on Jakov, but I had no recollection of him from that night. I attempted to force myself to logically assess the floor plan of Pepper and the likely locations where Jakov might have been. My thoughts kept returning to his haunting words. Niko knew we were monitoring him. That could mean he had surveillance equipment set up near or around Pepper, or Jakov's incarceration had set plans in motion.

Eventually, I gave up and climbed the stairs to bed. Martin came in a few minutes later, carrying his laptop and a few thick binders. He gave me a look but refrained from asking how today had gone. The answer was written all over my face. Without a word, he brought me the TV remote and sat down beside me, letting my viewing choice drone in the background while he worked.

A few hours later, I opened my eyes. My face was firmly planted against his stomach, and he was sitting sideways since I was stretched out. The TV had turned itself off, which was what had woken me, but he was buried in one of the binders and hadn't noticed. For a moment, my morbid sense of humor laughed. In the event all hell broke loose, it was absolutely pointless to worry about ridiculous lawsuits or work. It was a waste of precious time. But then the saner part of my mind took over, and I shook away that thought. Work mattered to Martin. It was his company, his creation, his empire. Regardless of whatever Niko and Shade planned, the world would keep spinning, at least most of it would. I had to have faith that we'd find a way to sabotage their plans. If we couldn't crack Jakov, there was another path to take. We just had to find it.

My thoughts and dreams remained fluid throughout the night, running from facts and problem solving to nonsensical whims. Upon waking, I wasn't hit by an epiphany. It was just the unsettling revelation of my own mortality that greeted me, as it had done every morning since the incident. Going back to sleep and remaining in denial was the best course of action, but the bed was cold. Martin was gone, and work needed to be done.

Throwing on a pair of jeans and a t-shirt, I decided that professionalism was overrated and returned to the office. When I got there, Lucca and a platoon of agents and techs were hard at work in the conference room. There was no sign of our fearless leader or any of the other head honchos from our joint task force.

Taking a seat at my desk, I checked for notes or case updates, but I didn't have any. Even my e-mail was empty. I stared down at the cast, knowing that I shouldn't be here. I had nothing to contribute. I wasn't cleared to be in the field. I posed a danger to myself and others due to the plaster hindrance covering my arm. I also knew that my left-handed firing capabilities were decent, but protocol was protocol. Or that was just my current excuse. Sometimes, it was hard to separate reality from the lies I told myself.

"Good morning," Lucca said. He looked at my blank computer screen and empty desk. "Is everything okay?"

"Peachy. Where's Jablonsky?"

"He's with Tinsley. The police have a lead on Jakov's whereabouts at the time of Donaldson's murder. They're checking it out."

"Have you heard anything concerning Shade's movements? Last night, Jakov made it sound like an attack might be imminent."

"We're working on it." Lucca glanced back at the occupied conference room. "Shouldn't you be in bed?"

"Behr wants me on this. Weren't you paying attention

during the meeting yesterday?"

"Yeah, but what exactly can you contribute? You don't remember anything, do you?"

"Thanks, Lucca, I appreciate that vote of confidence." I rolled my eyes. "You can't even muster a single word of gratitude since I schlepped all the way here."

"You aren't cleared to drive. Did you walk? Because that would be impressive."

"I can drive. I'm off the pain pills since I need to be sharp." I also didn't have much of a choice.

"If I were you, I'd take advantage of the medical leave, especially with the way things are right now."

"How can I?" I narrowed my eyes at him. "How could you even suggest something like that? This is an all hands situation. Would you really step back if you were in my position?"

"I don't know, but we can do this without you, Alex."

"What the hell is your problem? You went to Jablonsky and accused me of assault or attempted murder or something. You've wanted me out of the way this entire time, and even now, when I've been ordered back here, you still want me gone. It's not like we're working together. I'm not cleared to be in the field, so my presence isn't a safety risk to you. So what the hell is your problem?"

"Lower your voice, Agent Parker," Lucca hissed, glancing behind him.

"Don't tell me what to do, boy scout. Are you afraid I'll tarnish your reputation by calling you out for the shit you've been pulling?"

"Alexis, please," he whispered, "now's not the time to get into this."

"What else is new? It'll never be the time. Just tell me what the problem is, and I'll stay out of your way."

"It's not you."

Before I could respond with a snappy comeback, my desk phone rang. "This isn't over," I warned, lifting the receiver. "Parker," I said.

"Alex, drop whatever you're doing and meet us at the precinct. Grab Lucca and have him join us as well," Jablonsky ordered.

"Yes, sir."

"Who was that?" Lucca asked, eyeing the phone.

"Jablonsky. We've been summoned to the precinct." I snorted. "Sorry, I guess I was wrong. You are going to be stuck with me in the field."

"A police station is hardly the field," Lucca retorted. "Then again, with your recent track record, I'll be prepared for armed combat." He shouted across the room to Agent Cooper and the others inside the conference room that he'd be back later, and then he palmed his car keys. "C'mon, let's go."

That uneasy feeling returned, and I swallowed. "Maybe we should drive separately," I suggested.

"For god's sake, Parker, how many times do I have to come to the rescue before you decide that I'm not going to hurt you? I'm not out to get you. I didn't have anything to do with what happened to you. If I did, don't you think that I'd be off this case?"

"Probably." I got up from behind my desk, and we walked to the elevator. "But a lot of what happened still doesn't make sense."

"One of these days, it will." Lucca pushed the button for the garage. "Can you trust me, Alex, at least for today?"

"Sure, just don't make me regret it." Despite the words, I didn't trust him, and he knew it.

The silence inside the vehicle was too much for Lucca to take, and he cleared his throat, eyeing me out of the corner of his eye. When I failed to fill the silence, he took a deep breath and licked his lips.

"You scared me that day on the off-ramp," he said, breaching the most uncomfortable subject I could think of. "You were so shaky, but I thought it was from the crash. I didn't realize it was more than that until you went down." He snorted. "Jablonsky wouldn't let you go. The hospital was a mess. It's the closest I've ever come to losing someone on the job."

"Lucky you."

"I didn't mean it like that. I mean, literally, it was the closest I'd been in proximity to the action."

"Lucky you," I repeated. "How about we go back to that

silence thing we are so good at?"

"I just don't understand how, after that, you could doubt my allegiance." He shifted his gaze to me. "Even now, you're afraid to be alone in a car with me."

"Well, I imagine the feeling must be mutual."

"What I said was for your own good. Not mine." Lucca shook his head. "You're right, let's just forget this. Silence is great."

"Yep." I glanced at him before shifting my gaze out the windshield. I had missed the point of the conversation. I wasn't sure if it had been an apology, a peace offering, or some weird thing to lull me into a false sense of security. I turned my head toward him again briefly and looked away when he looked at me. "What were you working on in the conference room?"

"Monitoring Shade's recent activity. Niko Horvat's financials have gone haywire. There have been numerous six figure transfers in and out of his accounts. We suspect that he's selling weapons and then transferring the funds to other accounts to keep them off the radar."

"What if he's using the money to buy something else?"

"We're checking into it. The forensic accountants are tracing everything, but it looks like he's been dealing with the Colombian cartels and some crime syndicates. So far, we don't believe that he's selling to any of the larger terrorist organizations."

"Maybe Shade doesn't like the competition," I suggested.

"That could be. The analysts think that Niko has a specific goal in mind, and once he obtains the means necessary to make it happen, he'll green light his operatives."

"How many operatives are we talking? We pegged Shade as having less than fifty members."

"It could be larger. You saw the firepower that was hiding in Pepper. They must be arming someone, and that would supply a small army."

"A small army that's already stateside." I bit my lip. "Y'know, it wouldn't hurt to drive a little faster. The clock's ticking."

"Yes, ma'am."

"Asshole," I griped, smiling at him for the first time today. If he didn't kill me, we'd find some way to work out our differences.

TWENTY-EIGHT

"There," Tinsley said, pointing to the screen, "we can place Jakov Horvat at Pepper during the time of the murders."

"First, you have to prove that Donaldson and Ivan were murdered inside Pepper," I muttered under my breath.

"The drain," Jablonsky offered. "CSU swabbed it, and the DNA results finally came back. It contained human blood belonging to Donaldson and an unknown party. A positive comparison hasn't come back to Ivan yet, but I'm sure it will."

Tinsley nodded absently. She frowned and continued watching the footage from one of Pepper's exterior cameras that happened to cover the emergency exit. She fast-forwarded, noting the plate number on the SUV and the timestamp.

"How come we never see the bodies being loaded into the trunk?" Lucca asked. "Shouldn't that be on the footage?"

"Angles," Tinsley said, cycling through again while her eyes remained transfixed on the monitor. "We're lucky we even spotted Jakov." She picked up the printed image and held it out to Jablonsky. "Do you honestly believe that this will make him talk?"

"No," Mark replied, "but it's better than nothing."

"Where are we on Ivan?" I asked, feeling like this was a waste of time. "Do we know his actual identity yet?"

My question garnered her full attention, and Tinsley looked up, scanning the room for signs of intruders. "Ivan Novak," she replied. Standing abruptly, she headed for the door. "Parker, with me."

Mark nodded, and I followed her down the corridor and to a darkened office. The nameplate on the door indicated it was hers, and she unlocked the door and pushed inside, not waiting to see if I was behind her. She rolled her chair to the side and hefted a box onto the seat.

"You were there," she said as if that was explanation enough. "You spoke to Donaldson and Novak. The information in here might mean something to you, but I don't want it leaving this room. I trust that you can determine what might be pertinent to our investigation and if any of it can help identify a cop killer. I've reviewed it from a counterterrorism perspective, but I don't see a link between this and Shade. Obviously, you did. So find it."

"Has Jablonsky or anyone from the task force gone through this?" I asked, flipping through the pages inside the box.

"I have." She swallowed. "Look, I'm sure your team is great, but this is police business. This is a detective's private files. It contains information that out of context could draw some of his decisions into question. Ivan Novak is not a good man. The fact that Donaldson was willing to overlook a number of offenses in exchange for intel means that there's something more going on."

"I found it once. I'll find it again."

"That's what I like to hear. Good luck." She moved toward the door, but I stopped her before she could leave.

"Whatever relevant information I find will be shared with the task force, despite how it might make Donaldson look," I warned.

"I understand that." She stared at me for a long moment. "I hope I'm not wrong about you." Without another word, she closed the door and left me in the dark office to review Donaldson's notes, files, and reports concerning Ivan Novak.

Mr. Novak had been an enforcer for a crime syndicate. His arrest record was impressive. He'd served a nickel for aggravated assault. At the time, he had drugs on him, enough that the police felt he had intent to distribute, and I agreed with that assessment. Illegal gambling, assaults, robberies, and drug offenses littered the sheet. Frankly, I was surprised that there weren't any homicides listed. Then again, he might not have been caught.

My recollection of the bartender didn't match up with this description of Ivan Novak. From what I remembered, he hadn't been covered in prison tats or had a particularly intimidating demeanor. Then again, a white button-up shirt and black apron could do a lot to a person's physical appearance.

All of Donaldson's notes concerning Ivan and the intel he'd provided were in relation to gang activity, or so it appeared. Ivan had handed Donaldson a number of large-scale burglaries, drug busts, a weapons raid, and a few illegal poker games. From Donaldson's notes, he was waiting for Ivan to lead him to a big fish. Someone was behind these crimes, and Donaldson believed it was some Croatian Mafioso don. Unfortunately, no hard evidence linked the intel Ivan provided to a single entity. Frankly, these offenses could have been random, and Ivan might have been doing nothing more than pulling Donaldson's chain. The proof was in the pudding, and we had no pudding. No wonder Tinsley was worried about sullying Donaldson's name. It looked like he'd been gullible and jerked around by a common thug who decided to get paid while the police turned a blind eye to his criminal activities.

Picking up a pad and paper, I made a list of the players that Ivan had ratted on. There was no mention of Jakov or Niko Horvat. Frankly, none of the names correlated to the list we had of suspected terrorists. However, there was one glaringly obvious truth. Ivan Novak worked at Pepper, which appeared to be a front for Shade. The connection had to be somewhere.

Dammit. Why couldn't I remember our interactions more fully? Sure, I'd met Donaldson prior to the meet, but it was a blur. Somehow, I persuaded him to let me speak to Ivan. But how did Ivan get on my radar? I practically laughed at my own stupidity. It wasn't Ivan that I wanted to speak to. It was the inside connection to Pepper that I sought, and since Donaldson believed that Pepper was the stomping grounds for a crime syndicate, it made logical sense that he believed our cases overlapped. I must have agreed.

"Hey, Tin Man," a sergeant said, knocking as he entered the room, "I have that — oh, sorry, you're not the lieutenant."

"No, I'm not."

"Who are you? Does she know you're in here?" he asked.

"Agent Parker, and yes, Lt. Tinsley left me in here to organize her files. I think I'm being punished."

He laughed. "Any idea where she is?"

"The last I heard, she was watching surveillance videos."

"Okay," he gave me another uncertain look, "stay put, just in case."

"Aye, aye, Sarge."

If I had broken into her office to steal files or intel, why would I stay put? It seemed moronic, but I let it go as I tried to get back to what I was doing. My train of thought had fractured, and I emptied the box again, remembering I was looking for information on Pepper instead of Ivan. Surely, Donaldson had some kind of notes on the restaurant in here.

"Parker," Tinsley called from the doorway, "this is Sergeant Evers." The man who had just barged in smiled and nodded. "He pulled Donaldson's notepads from records. They might be relevant to our investigation." Evers placed a large sealed bag on the desk in front of me.

"Thanks, Sarge."

"No prob, Tin Man," he said, backing out of the room and leaving us alone.

"Tin Man?" I asked.

"I'm a heartless bitch." She cracked a mirthless smile.

"Some asshole started calling me that in the academy, and it stuck. My colleagues think it's cute."

"I'm glad I don't have your last name." I opened the bag and sifted through the contents. "If I only had a heart." I snorted. "At this point, I'd much prefer having a brain."

"I'd rather be the man behind the curtain who knows everything that's happening." She looked down at my notations. "I take it you haven't found anything solid yet, Scarecrow."

"It's not about Ivan. It's about Pepper. I needed an in at Pepper, and Donaldson gave me Ivan. Unfortunately, that didn't work out very well for any of us."

"See what you find in his pads, and I'll update Jablonsky."

"What about Lucca?"

"Your partner went back to the OIO to get a jump on interrogating Jakov."

Nodding, I turned my attention to the handwritten pages. Donaldson wasn't a meticulous note taker, but the notes he bothered to make had dates, times, addresses, and names listed with the recorded facts. Most weren't relevant to our Shade investigation, but since I didn't know who might be involved, I had to read through everything. Deciding that I needed a list of Pepper's employees, I texted Agent Cooper, who was kind enough to forward the twenty-seven names to me. I read through the list and then tackled Donaldson's notepads, hoping to find a few matches.

Squeezing the bridge of my nose, I blinked a few times and checked the time. I'd been reading and rereading Donaldson's notepads for the last two hours. Five names matched. Ivan had provided intel on five of the Pepper employees. Two were cooks, one was a busboy, another was a waiter, and the last was an assistant manager. They all had access to the hidden room beneath the freezer.

I stared at the last page from Donaldson's most recent entry. *Speculation that Pepper is base of ops. Details to follow.* After that, he had noted the time of our meeting. I ran my finger over the indentions on the page, feeling a pang of sorrow and guilt. Then I went in search of Sergeant

Evers.

"Knock, knock," I said, standing in the open doorway, "I have a quick question."

"Shoot," he said.

"Where was this?" I held up the final notepad with the police insignia on the cover. "It's the newest."

"We found it when we cleared out his desk." Evers looked pained. "We skimmed through it and added it to the stack. Is something wrong?"

"No, I just didn't know if he had it on him when things went sideways."

Evers shook his head. "Greg was a stickler for protecting his assets. Half the time, he wouldn't even meet with an established asset with his badge. He was always afraid that there'd be a double-cross, and he'd compromise himself and his people." Evers scoffed. "Stupid son-of-a-bitch." He sighed. "You were with him at the end?"

"Yeah."

"Did he give those fuckers a good fight?"

"Yes, he did." I wanted to explain how I failed his brother in blue, but the words wouldn't come. "I'm sorry," I choked out, "I should have done more."

"Hey," Evers stood, "are you okay?"

"She's fine," Jablonsky said from behind. "Right, Parker?"

"Yes, sir." I clamped my mouth shut and composed myself. "I was verifying that our sleeper cell didn't have access to Detective Donaldson's notes." I rubbed my eyes with the back of my hand and turned around. "We have five possibles inside Pepper based on the intel Donaldson received from Ivan. Jakov's right. Shade knows. They've been under our noses this entire time. We need records, profiles, and to pull these assholes off the street before they can act."

"You heard the lady," Tinsley said, appearing behind Jablonsky. "We'll round them up."

I passed her the list of names, and she went to order the arrests be made. Since the Pepper employees were already under surveillance, federal agents were on standby to offer assistance. At least we knew who was involved, or so I hoped.

"Parker," Jablonsky pulled me into Tinsley's empty office and shut the door, "I'll yell at you later for attempting to take the blame on Donaldson. Right now, I want to know how you decided these are Shade operatives."

"Ivan informed on them to Donaldson for drugs and weapons. Shade has the armory beneath the freezer. It stands to reason that they're connected."

"Logical." Jablonsky didn't look wholly convinced. "What if we miss someone?"

"What choice do we have?" I asked. "Unless Lucca magically makes Jakov talk, this is the only thing we have to go on. We can't exactly ask Ivan about it."

"I don't know." Normally, Jablonsky wasn't this wishy-washy. "Something doesn't smell right." He crinkled his nose. "We've had the owners and manager of Pepper in federal custody, but they're practically spotless. Ridley and Davenport scrubbed every bit of footage we could get from inside Pepper, and nothing indicates it's a base of operations for Shade. The weapons we found don't exactly scream out terrorist plot. They scream out black market dealings and stolen goods, which would explain why a burglary detective was involved." He shook his head. "It doesn't seem that the stash beneath the freezer was worthy of an overseas airdrop."

"The food delivery trucks," I said, pulling out my phone and clicking keys while I spoke, "that must be how they moved the cargo into Pepper without anyone noticing. It came in along with the food shipments."

"Enabling them to move it into the hidden room beneath the freezer during normal hours of operation without anyone being the wiser," Jablonsky said. He removed his own phone and dialed Ridley. "I need to know when Pepper received deliveries and what other restaurants or stops the trucks made."

"I have a list of food service providers," I said, handing my phone to Jablonsky. "Most serve the tri-state area. Shade could have disguised a truck to resemble one of them, or they have someone on the inside to make their illicit deliveries."

"Ridley, get me what you can off the footage." Jablonsky disconnected, dialing Lucca next. After barking more orders to search through Pepper's records for their providers, he hung up. Glancing at his watch, he took a deep breath. "It's probably best that you stay here. After Tinsley has our suspects brought in, I'll need someone to coordinate with the PD. With any luck, we'll be getting actionable intel soon."

"Fine." That annoying sinking feeling returned to the pit of my stomach. "We found one restaurant and five potential terrorists. What if it's bigger than we think?"

"Then we'll find the rest." Jablonsky went to the door. "Shade isn't al-Qaeda, Hezbollah, or even ISIS. It's a rinky-dink operation with some shitheads that want to be big and bad. Disbanding them shouldn't be that difficult, so don't psych yourself out."

"They killed a cop. They're not afraid of consequences."

"I'll make sure everyone keeps that in mind," Jablonsky promised, heading out of the office to pass word along to Tinsley.

TWENTY-NINE

The five employees had been brought to the precinct for questioning. They were being held in separate interrogation rooms, secluded from one another and forced into complete radio silence. A few had squawked about their right to make a phone call and to speak to an attorney, but we were keeping them on ice for the time being. Jablonsky had kept me busy with secretarial duties. I'd phoned various members of the task force to update them on our progress. Then I spent another couple of hours on the phone with Davenport, Ridley, Lucca, and Cooper, making sure that Jablonsky and the PD weren't left in the dark on the OIO's recent developments. Agent Parker, switchboard operator, at your service.

I went to the fax machine in the corner of Tinsley's office and picked up the information on Pepper's delivery trucks. The restaurant had several different suppliers, giving us four potential companies to track. Cooper and a few of the other agents were working to crack that angle, so a team had been sent to each trucking company. They would determine which drivers delivered to Pepper and then drag those individuals in for questioning. Since we didn't have the names yet, we couldn't compile any profiles. It was just a matter of waiting.

"Parker," Jablonsky said, stepping into the office, "I just spoke to Behr. Given what we don't know, he's ordered that the evidence from Pepper be taken into custody. He's afraid that securing the restaurant isn't enough to prevent the terrorists from trying to gain access to their weaponry."

"Where the hell are they going to put it?" I asked. Numerous crates loaded with weapons weren't the easiest things to move. Granted, I'd seen bigger busts, but safety and security were at issue. The movement of that much evidence would require a lot of additional support. "Who's taking possession?"

"The police department performed the initial search. It's theirs for the time being. We'll worry about the rest later." He glanced at the notepad I'd been using to keep track of our agents. "At least we won't have to reassign anyone to get this done."

"I guess not." The tension was making me antsy. "Have you spoken to any of our suspects yet?"

"Yeah, and I'm not convinced that we have the facts straight." He picked up one of Donaldson's notepads. "I'm gonna ask Evers if there are any transcripts from the detective's communications with Ivan."

"I doubt it. Evers said Donaldson was paranoid about his CI's safety. He wouldn't have done anything to jeopardize it."

"But he took you to speak to his CI inside the lion's den." Mark shut the door to ward off eavesdroppers. "Does that make any sense to you?"

"I hadn't thought about it." I had but not in practical terms. I bit my lip. "Donaldson must have thought the threat was too great. He wanted me to see the place and the people. He wanted Ivan to put faces to the names and aliases he'd been informing on, but it was a risk."

"Ivan was already compromised even though no one knew it at the time. Did Donaldson express any concerns or give any indication of how that might have happened?"

"No, but I'm guessing someone overheard Ivan talking or saw him texting or something," I considered it for a few minutes, "unless they were using Ivan to pass word along to make sure the police stayed in the dark. But why would they kill Ivan if he was giving the cops misinformation?"

"He knew too much," Mark speculated, "or they weren't positive of his betrayal until Donaldson showed up at Pepper. Maybe they thought Ivan brought the cops there to make arrests or search the place."

A thought crossed my mind. "I don't know how Ivan and Donaldson ended up inside the kitchen. By the time I was taken to the back, Donaldson was already restrained and Ivan was being beaten." I swallowed. "Do you think Ivan knew about the stash and had taken Donaldson to see it?"

"That could be, but it's pointless to theorize unless it's noted somewhere or buried in a recording or transcript."

"The bulk of Ivan's information was against Pepper's employees. Someone inside that restaurant must have wanted to know how much Ivan knew and who he had told."

"According to Donaldson's records, we have a busboy and waitress dealing coke. We have the cooks in the back taking part in gang activity, and we have the assistant manager who was bringing in shipments of something. It sounds like drug trafficking for a cartel, doesn't it?"

I nodded. That's how it read. That's how Donaldson read it. Shit, that was how Tinsley read it too. "Are we certain that Shade isn't working for a cartel or starting their own drug empire?"

"They don't have a supply line. They can't be a cartel. They could be middlemen, but what's the incentive for a cartel to funnel through them?"

"Maybe Shade is supplying the cartel with weapons in exchange for some of their product," I suggested.

"The barter system doesn't normally work long-term with drug dealers," Mark replied. "Eventually, they want more than tail." He sat behind Tinsley's desk and flipped through the pages that the OIO had sent over. "You said Shade was a terrorist cell. You were one of the first agents assigned to gather information, so it's your call, Alex. What do you think?"

"I think we underestimated them. They're here. They have a plan. They have leadership. They're organized.

They're armed, or at least they were." My mind backtracked to the incident on the off-ramp. "What we found inside Pepper is probably a drop in the bucket." I shuddered at the thought. "I need to start over. We need to figure out what their mission is and the kind of rhetoric they've been spouting. We need to identify their target." Jakov's words were now a haunting threat. "They have something planned, and it's already in motion."

"Call Director Kendall and have him put every spare agent on this. We need the assault team questioned again. If they still won't talk, we'll make them. We need to break Jakov, and we need more eyes to comb over what we've already gathered. Ask the director to have our analysts and forensic psychologists review everything," Jablonsky ordered, marching toward the door. "In the meantime, I'm gonna get answers."

He slammed the door behind him, and I made the call. Afterward, I sat in the stillness, wondering what I'd missed. How did we end up here when a few hours ago we didn't realize things were nearly this bad?

I had read through everything concerning Shade and Niko Horvat, and my priority had been tracking their movements in the Balkans. The extra activity triggered an alert, and I'd passed it along the pertinent channels. Then I'd taken it a step further and sought help from the police department. However, not once did I bother to figure out potential targets. Our sources said that Shade was isolated and small. They didn't have the manpower or resources to launch an attack, at least not one in the United States, but it looked like we might be wrong.

Performing an internet search, I bookmarked everything I could find posted about Shade. Then I dialed Davenport and had her guide me through what I needed to do in order to access the dark web, correctly figuring the crime lab tech had picked up a few extra skills here and there. The dark web was a place that I rarely ventured. Normally, if we needed that type of access for a case, a former hacker now a federal techie would surf through the depraved underbelly and hand over the relevant information. However, my usual go-to, Agent Lawson, was busy, as was the rest of the cybercrime division, so I was on my own since everyone else had more important roles to fulfill. It was a good thing I hadn't taken Lucca's advice to sit this one out or else who would have ample time to search the darkest recesses of the hidden internet to unearth terrorist plots? Damn, my life was turning into a cheesy spy novel. I just needed to bed a sexy double agent and get captured by the enemy and interrogated. Oh wait, I had basically done the latter, but Martin wouldn't be too keen on the former.

After scanning through the data, chatting with a few dark web hackers and getting responses to my questions that didn't resemble English or any language I'd ever heard, I dialed Davenport again. "Hey, Sasha," I said, "I'm out of my depth. Why the hell isn't this thing more user friendly?"

"It's the dark web. It's meant for those computer junkies with mad skills," she responded.

"Yeah, not me. I think I might have found someone that's offered to help, but I don't know what this means." I read the illogical pattern of numbers and letters to her. "Any thoughts?"

"Repeat that," she said, this time writing it down. "It's an address. Give me a sec." After a minute, she returned to the line. "It's a hidden site." She started to explain how the picture contained information and after entering a specific sequence of keys, it led to a log-in page that required a username and password, but I was getting more frustrated by the moment. "Look, I can probably crack it, or one of the guys upstairs can. It'll just take some time. Is this a priority?"

"I don't know. Shade is a priority, and I'm hoping to pinpoint a list of their potential targets. It appears they might have a larger following than we thought. There could be sleepers positioned anywhere, or I'm just a paranoid lunatic."

"We're all paranoid lunatics when it comes to national security and terrorist plots. It's why things are the way they are. We live in a post-911 world. We try to make the best of it, but the only way to save lives is to thwart plans. This will be first on our list after we get everything done for the director. I'll call you back when we've broken into the site."

"Thanks."

"No sweat, Alexis."

With nothing else to do, I went back to the list of bookmarked websites. If Shade was anything like most organizations, recruitment was a top priority, and since they had physical weapons and hadn't unleashed any known cyber attacks, I didn't believe their membership was open only to the world's most elite computer junkies. They must have their mission statement and information readily available somewhere.

Most pages I discovered were obscure news articles listing new and upcoming threats with no real information or sources. Obscure mentions and footnotes were all the media provided. Numerous law enforcement websites had issued warnings and cautionary statements, but I'd read through this jargon before. It was just like the warning memos that DHS distributed. The majority of the threats never panned out, and for that, I was grateful. However, reading similar statements from various government organizations and official policing sites did nothing but waste precious time.

Finally, after typing in numerous search parameters which often led to window treatments, some unknown garage bands, and information concerning the dangers of unprotected exposure to sunlight, I came across a message board. It was a simple type and post system that didn't require user verification or any type of credential. The design was basic, cheap, and would deter most people who were looking for the more common searches for Shade. The fact that the website wasn't in English probably aided matters.

Downloading a translator key, I ran the site through the software and copied down the link. After forwarding it to the OIO's techs, I read through the rough translation. Without usernames, it was impossible to tell who posted the comments. The IP addresses were encrypted into the page, so I'd need someone to run them in order to acquire the posters' actual identities. Sending off a quick text to my favorite tech guy, Agent Lawson, I hoped he could help a girl out. Feeling as if the ball was rolling on a new front, I read the words.

One of the posters frequented the site more than the others. He used typical inflammatory language that would incite anger and urge readers to a call to action. I suspected that it probably belonged to Niko Horvat or one of Shade's other higher-ups. The message board provided a brief overview of Shade, boasting that it wasn't a hierarchy and that all were equal. No one should be subjugated or forced to conform to ridiculous radical notions. Pot meet kettle, I thought before forcing my internal dialogue into silence. The ranting went on to speak out against every major nation of the Western world. Democracy was a lie. It was an excuse that the democratic nations used in order to control the smaller, weaker countries. Money was key, and by exuding monetary influence and power, the West would use its various police forces and military to conquer the poorer nations, strip them of their resources, and destroy millions of lives, extinguish rich cultures, and otherwise annihilate the current world order. Shade wanted to put a stop to that. It encouraged others to join and stand up to the oppressor. From the rhetoric, it made every Western nation sound like 1940s Germany.

While the world had a lot of problems, I liked to believe that it wasn't as sinister as Shade made it sound. The truth was Shade was relying on cult mentality. It pointed to problems and offered a solution. This garnered followers because people wanted to feel as if they could take control of things that were beyond their capabilities. Whoever posted these messages had done a nice job to point out various incidents to twist the truth in order to gain additional support.

After suffering through the incessant large-scale bitching, the focus of the posts switched to tactics to infuse oneself into the system in order to destroy it from the inside out. There was a metaphor to a virus destroying the host from the inside, but I didn't believe that Shade intended to use biological warfare. They weren't suicidal like a lot of groups. They lacked a religious element, meaning that promises of rewards in the afterlife weren't part of the package.

The focus of Shade was to improve the here and now. Hell, at times, it sounded like they might have gotten a political campaign speechwriter to help bolster support. However, they didn't want to improve life for everyone, just the few who had been displaced due to wars, disasters, political persecution, and dissolution of nation-states. It was an issue that many in various regions of the world had faced, but for Shade's purposes, the focus was on the Balkans. That's how they gained support.

Continuing reading through the back and forth, Shade seemed to have an axe to grind with the United States due to our interference throughout the 1990s. While to some that might seem like ancient history, to the members of Shade, it was how they lost parents and family. The wars in that region were horrific. Despite the fact that there were numerous claims of genocide, from what I recalled, the International Court said that there wasn't enough evidence to prove it in several cases. But that much destruction and hatred often lead to a backlash. So even decades later, the echoes of the past continued to shape the present.

Niko, or whoever the primary poster was, wanted someone to blame. He decided the fault lay with the Western world. The countries with power. The ones that stepped in to help but somehow failed him personally. After all, the road to hell was paved with good intentions. And from the feel of his words and the limited size and resources of Shade, this felt like a personal vendetta or a perceived slight that someone wanted to air on a grand scale.

The good news was that I didn't think we were dealing with a giant terror organization. We were most likely dealing with a small group of individuals with adequate resources, probably a few million in total, that hoped to expand their monetary reach in order to inflict the most damage as quickly as possible. I kept reading, but it didn't sound like they had settled on a target. The United States as a whole was far too large and out of their reach, and it didn't sound like our current officeholders were a focal point for Shade's vengeance.

The main poster was pissed at the soldiers that failed his family. I considered military outposts, bases, training facilities, and other typical targets, but military intelligence, both domestic and foreign, was normally outstanding. They didn't know of any threats. No, whatever Shade planned was an isolated attack. It was personal which meant that this could be worked like any other case. Once I had the identity of the poster, we could go through his history, determine his motive, and that would lead to determining Shade's target. Despite the claims, this wasn't an organization with equality for all; this was one man, or a select few, hell-bent on getting revenge.

While I skimmed through the rest of the message board posts, I dialed Agent Lawson again. I needed verification that Shade was being run by Niko before I could do anything else. Before the phone connected, the building shook with a reverberating boom.

THIRTY

"What the hell was that?" I asked, peering into the hallway at the police officers who acted like a reverberating boom was commonplace.

"Water delivery," a detective offered from the bullpen. "Paolo drops the hand truck every time. Dumbass kid." He rolled his eyes.

I shifted my gaze to the elevator at the end of the corridor where a young man was struggling to get two large water bottles back onto the fallen dolly. A uniformed officer was helping him, but before the bungee cord was secured, the lower bottle rolled to the left. The elevator doors started to close, banging against the sides of the bottle. Apparently, this was the usual comedy relief that the officers enjoyed. However, I was not amused.

Returning to my call, I filled in Agent Lawson on my latest discoveries. He promised to coordinate with Davenport to crack that hidden site and to get a name to go with the IP address ASAP. Hanging up, I was almost out of ideas.

"Hey, does anyone have a background on Jakov Horvat?" I asked. The police officers ignored me. "Sure, don't trouble yourselves, I'll find it myself."

Heading for the interrogation rooms, I hoped Tinsley or Jablonsky could be of some help. I entered the observation room, noticing the current interrogation was well underway. Jablonsky was doing that see-into-your-soul stare. He'd broken quite a few hardened criminals with nothing more than that look and a few calmly worded threats. The busboy seated in front of him didn't appear to be a stone-cold killer; he looked like a scared young man. Of course, tears and snot could make anyone appear weak.

"The kid's not talking," Tinsley muttered from the corner. "I've gone at him. SSA Jablonsky's been working him hard, but the kid won't talk. He says he doesn't know anything about the weapons beneath the freezer."

"Did he say anything else?" I asked.

"Yeah, he said he wants a lawyer. He might have also said that we're mean." She shrugged. "I've been in counterterrorism for ten years, and this is the first time that a suspect's cried. They normally get aggressive or defensive or refuse to talk at all. This is new."

"I'm beginning to think they aren't terrorists. Well, some of them aren't," I clarified.

"That kid, probably not. Unless he's a new recruit. Maybe he hasn't sat through the interrogation classes yet." She glanced at me from the corner of her eye. "Did you need something?"

"Yeah," I tore my eyes away from the window, "I was looking for Jakov Horvat's profile."

"Can I leave your boss alone with the suspect, or is that gonna be a problem?"

"Jablonsky's by the book," I assured her.

"Okay, let's see where I put that." She led the way to the file room. "What'd you get from reading through Donaldson's notes and shit?"

"I'm not sure. It reads like drugs."

"That's what I thought." She pulled out a folder and held it out. "The assault team's prints came back. They're private military contractors from Yugoslavia, Chechnya, and Belarus. We'd probably have more luck getting solid leads from them than some chump busboy." She assessed me for a moment. "I take it no one bothered to tell you that."

"No, they didn't." I blew out a breath and took the folder from her. "The last I heard, they weren't talking either."

"Is there a reason that the lead agent on this case is being left out of the loop?" She glanced at my belt. "And isn't carrying?"

"Don't tell me I left that darned gun somewhere again. Crap." The sarcasm was biting.

"Despite what Behr ordered, your superiors won't clear you from medical leave, will they? Damn. That's fucked up." She sighed. "Why the hell are you bothering with any of this shit?"

"I've been asked that question a few times. I'll let you know when I come up with an answer. In the meantime, I'm waiting for an internet address to come through. From the rhetoric I just found, it appears that this is a personal vendetta. The target will probably be small and isolated. If we can figure out what Shade wants to hit and why, we should be able to stop it and arrest those involved."

"That makes more sense than this being the work of a terror group. The only downside is they have a name, leadership, and a couple dozen members. If they're successful, it could become a terror group in the future, and I don't want to contend with that. Get back to work, Parker."

"Yes, ma'am." I turned on my heel to leave.

"One last question," she said, stopping me in my tracks. "How come the agencies that provided the initial threat assessment didn't bother to investigate the rhetoric and the speaker behind it?"

"I don't know. I just took the intel and went from there. It didn't occur to me to backtrack."

"In the future, always check your sources and do the work yourself. It makes a difference." She offered a grim smile. "Then again, that might have been how you ended up unconscious outside a parking garage." I gave her a confused look. "I read your file and the relevant incident reports. I like to know who I'm working with. You aren't one to cut corners. You found the connection to Pepper. It sounds like you were trying to build a case from the foundation up. Maybe when this is over, you'd like to transfer over to counterterrorism. We could use a federal liaison."

"I'm not interested." Continuing on my way out of the room, I made it past the interrogation rooms before my phone rang. "What do you have?" I asked, recognizing Lawson's extension.

"You're right. This tracks back to Horvat. His computer posted those messages. It also designed the hidden website. However, we haven't been able to crack the password yet. Numerous protections are in place to deter hackers, so it might take a bit of time. How urgent is this?"

"I don't know. Tell me what's on the site, and I'll let you know its level of importance."

"Understood. I'll get back to you when it's done."

I had just put the phone back into my pocket when it rang again. This time, it was Agent Cooper. The delivery trucks had made deliveries to several other restaurants in the vicinity. The drivers were being questioned, but as of yet, no one had been formally charged with any crime. He was hoping to gain more intel before showing our hand. In addition, search warrants had been signed for the other restaurants. Since illegal firearms had been delivered to Pepper, it stood to reason that there could be other crates inside the other eateries.

"Is ATF on it?" I asked, wondering how many other agencies we'd have to deal with before everything was said and done.

"No, DHS is overseeing that personally. Behr has an in with a judge, which is probably how the search warrants even got signed. When I contacted Director Kendall about it, he wanted us to wait until we had a solid lead from one of the drivers. Obviously, we at the FBI must be doing something wrong."

"Yeah, we're letting Homeland jerk us around," I retorted, and Cooper laughed. "Keep me apprised. I'll pass word to Jablonsky and Tinsley."

Ducking back inside Tinsley's office, I closed the door and sat behind her desk. I needed a minute to regroup. How the hell could my fellow agents fail to inform me that they uncovered the identities of the men that nearly killed me and three police officers? That seemed like pertinent information, especially since the assault team was a group of private military contractors. Someone must have paid them to execute a hit, but who would have known my whereabouts? My mind drifted to Detectives Delaney and Collins who had been placed on administrative leave since the mishap inside the holding cell, but I doubted that the detectives would jeopardize their own people. Lucca had been acting strangely, but that seemed farfetched too. Regardless, it would be beneficial to focus on who paid the assault team to stop us.

In between phone calls and catching up on information that I had just received, it soon became apparent that the private contractors had been paid through a wire transfer that linked back to one of Shade's accounts. Shade hired the team to clean up the mess left behind by their own people. That meant the assholes we had taken into custody must know the identities of their employers and would be able to blow this case open for us. So why the hell weren't we questioning them instead of the dumb schmucks from Pepper?

"Lucca, what have you gotten from the assault team?" I asked as soon as he answered.

"Nothing. I told you I was working on cracking Jakov."

I clenched my fist around the phone, barely resisting the urge to slam my casted arm against the desk in frustration. "Lt. Tinsley was kind enough to tell me that they were hired mercenaries. I've read the financial reports. They were paid through one of Shade's accounts. Why aren't you questioning them?"

"Behr has them. He had them transferred days ago. There's nothing I can do."

"That's insane. They could identify members of Shade. We need to speak to them. What the hell is Behr doing with them?"

"Your guess is as good as mine. He's in charge of the task force, and he thought it'd be best if they were moved to a secure site for questioning."

"That's bullshit."

"That's bureaucracy, Parker. Look, I gotta go. It's a madhouse here." Without waiting for my response, he hung up.

"Bastard." I slammed my phone onto the desk. Homeland was making things more difficult, and I was tired of doing things the hard way. I wanted easy answers and for this to be over. I couldn't take it anymore. I couldn't do this anymore. "Chill," I whispered, struggling to fight off the overwhelming feeling. Now wasn't the time.

For the next few minutes, I did nothing but read Jakov Horvat's file. I read it cover to cover. He had been orphaned and adopted by an American family. He'd lived in the United States since his eighth birthday. His juvie record had been unsealed due to the nature of the threat, but aside from an arrest for tagging, he hadn't been a troubled kid. Once he reached the age of majority, he had a citation for smoking pot in public. Obviously, the officer had taken it easy on him instead of bringing up charges for possession or public intoxication probably due to the ever-changing laws. Other than that, there was nothing.

I placed a call to his adopted parents, but they didn't answer. It was probably for the best. It's not like Jakov had been given his due process, and we didn't need concerned parents contacting some civil rights attorney and turning this into a circus.

I grimaced at what we'd been forced to do. Our actions were rather atrocious, but I took comfort in knowing that Jakov was involved. He had been at Pepper that night. Perhaps he hadn't participated in murdering Donaldson and Ivan, but he didn't try to stop it either. He didn't call for help. He didn't report it, and he refused to cooperate. All he had done was make veiled threats. However, that didn't make our actions right either. I hated it. I hated this job, and the things it made us do. What I hated more was the things it made me want to do. One day, I feared that I wouldn't be able to look myself in the mirror, and that day was getting closer and closer.

Someone opened the door. "Parker?" he asked.

"Guilty," I replied, lifting my eyes off the page. "What do you need?"

"These were just faxed over from the FBI." He held up the cover sheet with the words *Urgent. Give to Agent Parker Immediately* scrawled in Lawson's handwriting. "I thought it'd be best to do what it says."

"Thanks." I took the sheets.

"Ma'am, if you have a lead, Lieutenant Tinsley should be made aware of it."

"I don't know what I have," I flipped through the printed pages, "but feel free to let her know the OIO just sent over some new information."

He gave me an annoyed look, like he wasn't around to be my servant, and left without another word.

The pages were printed copies of the hidden website. The information wasn't necessarily that helpful. Most of it was more of the brainwashing rhetoric from the message boards. However, there were a few sheets that contained a list of seemingly random words and numbers. The tech geeks were working on cracking that code. The last page contained a list of contact information found on a hidden page within the hidden site. It contained a few local numbers. Lawson had written notes in the margins to let me know that reverse lookups and traces were being established. It was progress. The OIO was handling the situation. We'd figure this out. It was just a matter of time, but no one knew when the clock would run out.

Deciding that my time would be best spent focused on a single angle instead of barely brushing the surface on all of them, I considered my options. The private military team hired by Shade was a dead end unless Homeland decided to share their toys. I could only get so far by reading through Jakov's profile, so I nixed that idea. My best bet was to continue working on determining Shade's targets. Unfortunately, I didn't know how to determine that. When in doubt, start from square one.

Clicking through the police case files on Tinsley's computer, I found the photos of the evidence cataloged inside Pepper. Flipping through the pictures, the scenes of the kitchen and drain did nothing but bring back bad memories, but the photos of the dining room and freezer might be key. The crates and weapons had no discernible identifiers, and the dining room looked the way it had when Lucca and I visited. Pepper wasn't the target, but it probably was a stash house or safe house for Shade operatives. That's why the five suspicious individuals whom Ivan had informed on were currently being questioned. Too bad they hadn't cracked under the pressure since I was beginning to think I might.

Curiosity got the best of me, and I opened the next file. Inside were photos of the double homicide involving Detective Donaldson and Ivan Novak. Their bodies had been wrapped in plastic and left inside the trunk of the SUV. The interior photos from the back seat were of my nine millimeter, and the forensic experts had marked a bullet hole in the roof. A flash of the struggle over my gun and the sound of my wrist snapping reverberated in my mind, and I cringed. My gun had been discovered partially hidden beneath the seat. Fingerprint powder covered the vehicle, but nothing usable was found.

The next file I opened contained photographs from the off-ramp shootout involving the hired PMCs. An extensive list of items found inside the Hummer and on the assault team was cataloged. The list was extremely similar to the items discovered beneath the freezer at Pepper. At that moment, there was no doubt left that Shade hired and armed these men. The remaining question was whether these military contractors were hired to perform a service or if they were actual indoctrinated Shade operatives?

Keying in a new set of search parameters, I figured I'd work backward from the contractors to Shade in order to find the connection. Keying in Niko Horvat's IP address, I searched for any postings he might have made that I hadn't yet discovered. After narrowing the search and sifting through results, I found something. It was a private listing on a classified ads site that Niko had used to contact the mercenaries. It contained more cryptic language and code words, but it answered my question. The PMCs had been hired to do a job, and I had a feeling I knew who their target was.

THIRTY-ONE

"Lucca, so help me if you hang up again," I said when he answered.

"What is it now?"

"I just e-mailed you a link. Niko Horvat hired the assault team. I'm guessing Shade airdropped the weapons for the team's use, and the delivery trucks stashed them inside Pepper. Given the quantity, there could be more hired mercenaries out there, so get on the horn with Behr and find out everything you can about the hitmen for hire."

"All right. Hang on." He clicked through a few things. "I'm passing this board posting to our cybercrimes division to verify its legitimacy and track down the party that responded to the ad." He went silent for a few minutes, reading through the translated version of the site. "It looks like they have an axe to grind with the police department. Any idea how some Eastern Europeans chose our city's finest to be the recipients of their hatred?"

"Not yet. Maybe someone should ask Jakov about it," I snapped.

"He won't talk. You've been inside the interrogation room with him. What do you want me to do? Do you think roughing him up is going to get us anywhere?" Lucca sounded just as frustrated as I felt. "We've been keeping him on ice, and it's not working. He wants a lawyer, but even if we get him one, I don't know that it'll help."

"No, you're right. We should get him one." The thoughts swam through my mind. "Contact the prosecutor's office and tell them what's going on. They've dealt with this type of issue before."

"Did Jablonsky okay it?" Lucca asked.

"He will. Don't worry about it. Just do it."

"Parker," Lucca hedged.

"Fine, Jablonsky okayed it. I said so. It's my ass. Now make the call, boy scout."

After we hung up, I pushed away from Tinsley's desk. We finally had something, and Mark needed to be brought up to speed. Hell, it might even give him a leg up while conducting the interrogations. My mind was reeling. Why did Shade plan to attack this city? My city. It made no sense. We were a world away. What had we done to warrant the wrath of Niko Horvat? I shook my head. There was no point trying to decipher crazy, but it bothered me. Obviously, this maniac had a deep-seated hatred for law enforcement and military, probably due to growing up in a war-torn country. But how did that translate into attacking us? It wasn't that he hated the United States or wanted to see the country fall, just the city. According to the classified ad, he wanted the police force to crumble and quake.

"Hey," I said, stopping briefly to speak to Sergeant Evers, "have you received any threats lately?"

"Me personally?"

"No, the police force in general."

"I can't count them all. You're talking tens of thousands of police personnel which are typically disliked by the general populace. We get threats often." He glanced at the paperwork in my hand. "Is there something I should know?"

"Check with the brass and see if the commissioner's office has been made aware of any credible threats lately. I have to speak to Jablonsky first, but I'm sure Lt. Tinsley will be by to brief everyone shortly."

"Agent, failure to communicate is what led to these

problems in the first place," Evers chided.

"Fine, from what I've read, it sounds like Shade is planning an attack on the police. I don't know anything other than that." Without waiting for his other questions, I continued down the corridor.

Jablonsky and Tinsley were inside a different interrogation room, speaking to the assistant manager. I knocked on the door and poked my head inside. Mark glanced at me, and I gestured that he join me in the hallway. Then I closed the door and waited.

"What's up?" he asked, shutting the door behind him.

"Homeland had search warrants signed for a few other restaurants to check for additional weapons. Cooper's talking to the truckers. Lucca's doing something. Jakov won't crack, but I found this." I handed him the printed pages Agent Lawson had faxed over. "The IP traces back to the last known physical address of Niko Horvat."

"Shit," Jablonsky cursed, reading through the intel. "Do we know where or when Shade's planning its next attack?"

"No idea. We have people working on it."

"That whiny ass bitch. I'd love to strangle that arrogant weasel."

"Jakov?"

"Jakov, Fuckoff, whatever his name is," Mark growled. "He knew about this. I don't know how he fits into it, but he does. He's said just enough that I'm positive of that fact."

"Aren't we all," I retorted. "I...um...told Lucca to contact the AG's office. Since Jakov wants a lawyer, we ought to give him one."

"On whose authority?"

"Yours," I said, wondering if I was about to be the recipient of Jablonsky's anger.

He nodded. "Fine. Let's hope it's the right call." He flipped through the pages again. "Anything else of use?"

"Behr took custody of the hit squad. He hasn't offered any insight into what he's learned, but since it looks like they were hired, they should be able to hand us Niko and the leaders of Shade on a silver platter. We need to force the other part of this joint task force to share what they have."

"I'll handle Assistant Director Behr. For now, why don't you take a break? Tinsley and I will give a briefing, and I want you on hand just in case there are questions. After that, you're going home."

"But, sir—"

"Until we know more, you're standing on a landmine, and you aren't cleared for action. You've done enough today, Parker." He offered a slight smile. "We've finally made real progress. Well done."

Turning, he went back into the interrogation room, and I headed for the kitchen which was next to the bullpen. It had been a long day. Evers didn't notice my reappearance, and the other cops were busy doing what they did best. Taking a seat at the table, I glanced at the nearly empty coffeepot, but it still held no appeal. Settling for a bottle of water, I dialed Detective Nick O'Connell. He had never gotten back to me, but I wanted to give him the heads up to be vigilant in the event Shade made good on its threat to attack the entire police force.

"You're telling me that it's open season on cops?" Nick asked. "How exactly is that different from any other day?"

"It's not, but some Eastern Europeans hired private mercenaries to carry out the threat. I'm sure that you'll be briefed shortly. Right now, Jablonsky is updating the head of the counterterrorism unit, but what kind of friend would I be if I didn't tell you first?"

"You realize that you're breaking a few rules by doing this," O'Connell chided. "Apparently that partner of yours hasn't rubbed off yet."

"Don't call him that."

"Sorry, but man-slave has negative connotations." He went silent for a moment. "Thanks for the warning."

"Sure."

"I'm sorry I couldn't get you anything on that CI."

"Eh, you'll just owe me."

"You have a strange way of keeping score."

After the call, I considered pestering Davenport, Lawson, and Lucca for updates, but I didn't believe that they had learned anything new in the last thirty minutes. If anything, we had an information overload at the moment. It was nice to have some answers, but every single one of them had led to dozens of questions. At least we knew where to begin, and I was certain that my colleagues were doing everything they could to find those answers as quickly as possible. Obviously, there would be contingencies and protocols in place to safeguard the police and the city from this very real threat. We'd do what needed to be done. We'd find a way to survive, and the person or persons responsible would pay. It's what we trained for.

Another loud thud sounded, shaking the table. Letting out an agitated sigh, I capped my drink and stood up. How clumsy could people be?

"Again with the freaking water bottles?" I muttered, opening the door to the hallway. Seeing the assault rifle, I barely had time to dive to the side before the man opened fire. Instinctively, I reached for my firearm. "Fucking A."

Seeking cover inside the kitchen, I took a deep breath and glanced out into the bullpen. Two guys in full assault gear were conducting a sweep, firing every few seconds to deter the dozen armed police officers from successfully retaliating. From what I could tell, no one had been seriously injured yet.

Another barrage swept the kitchen above my head, and the coffeepot shattered. Okay, now this was personal. The sound of return fire emanated from the rear of the bullpen. One of the assailants tossed a concussion grenade toward the back of the room and followed through with heavy fire when the police officers hurried to escape the explosion. The grunts and screams were unmistakable.

I couldn't stay in this room while people were being shot. Running at a crouch from inside the kitchen, I took cover behind the first desk I came upon. The two assailants remained back-to-back, so they could keep an eye on their surroundings and avoid an ambush. The nearest cops were positioned at their desks or inside their offices, taking potshots at the assailants in between hoping their cover positions remained intact.

At the sight of their brethren being gunned down, a few

were inching closer from the sides, hoping to box in the assailants. From what I could see of the hand signals, they were planning some kind of distraction and physical takedown. Glancing in the other direction, I spotted Evers on the radio. Back-up would be arriving soon.

Feeling naked without a gun, I slid open the bottom drawer, working my way upward through the desk in the hopes of finding someone's spare weapon. No joy. More gunfire rang out, and I checked the progress the police were making on their advancement. This wouldn't end well. They were sorely outgunned, but they had to try. They couldn't stand by and let their friends and co-workers die. I swallowed, knowing that I couldn't sit back and watch it happen. I had to do something to help.

Scanning the area, I spotted an alcove in the hallway about twenty feet behind my current position. Twenty feet wasn't that far. I could make it. Edging backward, I wished I wasn't an outsider and that I knew the cops and their plays, but I didn't. And at the rate things were going, I never would.

"Hey, assholes," I bellowed as soon as I made it to my feet. I'd backed up nearly five feet from the desk, making the distance less to travel. "Drop your weapons."

Of course, one of them fired at me, and I dove toward the nook in the wall. Pockmarks appeared on the edge of the wall before I made it to safety, but I didn't think I was hit. And if I was, the adrenaline would keep me numb and moving for now.

The gunfire continued, hammering the wall and crumbling the edge. I didn't dare peek out to see what was going on. Instead, I pressed my face against the farthest corner and covered my head with my arms, waiting for the barrage to stop. The faintest click sounded, and I knew one of them had to reload.

"Agent Parker," Evers hissed. His office was a few feet from my current position on the other side of the corridor. "You alive?"

I didn't move from my position, fearing that once the gun was reloaded the attack would continue, but after a few seconds, I untucked my body and glanced out. The police had taken one of the assailants down, but the other one had somehow backtracked to the elevator. He tossed another two grenades to either side of the room and held his position, firing as the cops were forced to flee their positions. At least two more officers were hit. The blood spatter covered one of the walls, and I didn't want to process the possibilities.

"Where's back-up?" I asked, the rage over the violence making me bolder by the second. Leaving the alcove, I joined Evers in his office. "I need a weapon."

"Tactical is on the way. Additional support is en route. We have an ESU team inside the building, but from the chatter, these assholes have breached every department inside this building."

"What about the other precincts?" I asked, listening while I searched his office for useful items.

"I don't know. Dispatch isn't responding." He reached into his ankle holster and held out a snub-nosed thirty-eight. "How can you shoot?"

"With my other hand." I shook off the question, loaded one into the chamber, and took a deep breath. "How do you know support is en route if dispatch won't respond?"

"Someone else made the call before I did. I picked up the radio chatter," he replied. He pushed me away from the door, taking up the primary position to glance outside. "If you know anything that might help, now's the time."

"They're mercenaries, probably from the Eastern Bloc. Shade supplied them with weapons." Putting the gun down, I removed my cell phone from my pocket, but the circuits were overloaded, preventing outgoing calls from connecting.

"Shit," Evers replied, "that's why they're here." He looked back at me. "We had the stockpile brought to the precinct for evidence cataloging." Another scream sounded and a few grunts. "It's those damn grenades." He swallowed. "I can't leave my people out there to die."

"There's only one left." I took a deep breath. "There's a lot more of us."

"We don't know how many more are inside the building," Evers said. "Hell, we don't even know how many are on this floor."

I looked at him. "Then let's go kill that son-of-a-bitch and get your people some help. We'll count these shitheads after they're dead."

More shots were fired. This time, it was the police. Evers edged out of the office, hugging the wall and keeping me behind him. Ten steps later, we could see the entire bullpen. It looked like a massacre. Desks were charred. Paper, shrapnel, and who knows what covered the floors and walls. One of the assailants was cuffed and unconscious, and the other was clearly dead.

"I need some help over here," someone called, and I saw the remnants of the bloodbath.

Evers took off toward the sound, just like the rest of the police force that had been scattered during the attack. I was on his heels when I heard another thud in the distance. Jablonsky, I thought, remembering Evers warning that every department was under attack. Reversing course, I raced down the corridor toward the interrogation rooms.

At the juncture in the hallway was another two man assault team. They were scanning the area for targets, and I was half a second away from being spotted. Unfortunately, there were no cover positions or unlocked doors.

At this distance, there was a good chance I could take out one of the men before being seen but not both. Taking aim, I used my casted arm to help steady my shot, and I fired. The headshot looked clean, but with the helmet, I couldn't be certain. Then the man dropped. Without waiting, I ran toward the second target, firing haphazardly. Shots rang out, but I didn't slow or stop. It was harder to kill a moving target, and I couldn't let him make it back to the bullpen. Enough damage had already been done.

The shots were getting closer, and I slid like a baseball player, hoping to knock the man off balance before he could shoot me. My leg kicked into his shin, but he didn't go down. I rolled to the left, going deaf in my right ear from the closeness of his latest shot. I fired at him again, hitting his body armor with no effect. I had to make a headshot or else the bullets did nothing.

He kicked the gun out of my hand, and then he stomped

down on my side to hold me in place. I screamed, opening my eyes in time to see the barrel of the long gun inches from my face. Squeezing my eyes closed, I was hit by an incredibly heavy weight, vaguely aware of the sound of a single gunshot. Apparently they were wrong; you do hear the bullet that kills you.

"You motherfucker." The weight eased slightly then dropped down again. "You piece of shit." This time I recognized that the voice belonged to Tinsley. The weight was dragged off of me, and I gasped, opening my eyes to see the world hadn't rid itself of me just yet. "Don't move, Agent. You've been hit."

I pushed my palm against the blood, dropping my head back against the tile floor and forcing air into my lungs. "No, I'm okay. They need help in the bullpen. Go. Evers said there are more inside the building. Tactical and back-up are on the way."

"Go, help your people," Jablonsky said, kneeling next to me. "We're okay."

"Be careful," she said, heading toward where I'd come from.

"I'm okay," I repeated, taking Mark's offered hand and getting up.

"Good," he gave me an uncertain look, "we're to hold tight until help arrives. I've locked the prisoners inside the interrogation rooms. We think the gunmen might be here to free the hostages."

"Perhaps, but Evers said they moved the weapons cache into the building from Pepper. He thought that was the impetus for the attack."

Jablonsky looked at me. "This is what Shade planned. Total pandemonium. God knows what is happening out there while the police are busy fighting to stay alive in here."

"We can't just sit here and wait for help to arrive. We have to do something to even the odds."

"You're sure you're good?" He lifted my shirt. Blood ran from the wound, but I disregarded it. Jablonsky pulled a first aid kit from the wall and taped a bandage against the injury. "It looks superficial, but I'm no doctor."

"Great." I tugged my shirt down and checked the clip in my gun. "Let's help the police retake the building."

THIRTY-TWO

"Stay on my six," Jablonsky insisted, taking point as we moved toward the staircase.

We'd removed the weapons from the two dead assailants, so at least we wouldn't be overpowered. Between the two of us, we had four frag grenades, two AKs, and a few extra magazines. It wasn't ideal, but it might save our asses.

Tinsley and the uninjured police officers had secured the elevator, so Jablonsky and I were securing the stairwell. That would sufficiently block off the floor, but it did nothing to assist the rest of the cops inside the building. He opened the door to the stairwell and stepped onto the landing. I waited at the door, holding it open with my shoulder.

First, Jablonsky checked the stairs leading from the upper level. Once he was sure no one was immediately heading down, he focused his attention on the lower level. Muffled gunfire could be heard, but given the acoustics, it was hard to tell from which direction it was coming.

"How many casualties did counterterrorism sustain?" he asked, stepping backward but never letting his eyes stray from the stairs.

"Too many."

"Parker," he snapped, cautioning a brief glance at me, "focus. Are you sure you're up for this?"

"Yeah, I just don't know. At least three grenades went off before they were subdued. The walls were painted red. I can't be sure. There were a lot of injuries. We can't just stand here and do nothing."

"I agree." He swallowed. "There are three floors above us. I'll go see what's what. You stay here. I'll be right back."

A long, interminable wait followed. I wasn't particularly patient, and these were extraordinary circumstances. My gaze kept snapping from one flight of stairs to the other, unsure of whom or what might be coming from either direction. The sounds of gunfire had died down, which I hoped was a good sign.

Heavy steps sounded, and I edged backward, using the closed door as cover. Four men came down the steps wearing ESU emblazoned body armor. Slowly, I cracked the door open and raised my hands, spotting Mark at the back of the group. He nodded to me, and the five of them stopped on the landing.

"Agent Parker," the ESU commander said, moving next to me, "the top floors have been cleared. Is this level still secure?"

"As far as I know. Tinsley should have the elevator locked up tight," I responded.

He nodded. "The lifts have been taken out of service." The radio chirped, and from the message he received, it was apparent that the Shade operatives had broken into the evidence locker and established a stronghold inside. The weapons cache was still live since the firing pins and mechanisms hadn't been removed prior to the transport. "Any injured?" he asked, somehow ignoring the dire message he'd just received.

"Too many to count."

He nodded, signaling two of his men to go inside. "Ambos are nearby, but we can't let anyone inside until the threat has been eliminated." He turned to Jablonsky. "We could use all the help we can get."

"Then lead the way," Mark replied. On our way down

the steps, he finished briefing the ESU team on what we knew of the attackers and the types of weaponry at their disposal. "What else was inside the evidence locker?"

"The usual suspects," the commander replied. We made a brief stop on the next floor, and two ESU team members went to scout the floor. They returned with additional police personnel to assist. "The rest of the tactical unit is working from the ground up. They haven't made it past the fifth floor. That's where these assholes have boxed themselves in, but we'll flush 'em out."

After repeating the process a few more times, we emerged through the stairwell door on the fifth floor. The hallway looked like the scene of a drive-by. Another six men were positioned behind a barricade near the door to evidence lockup. We crept behind, and brief introductions were made. On the floor was a blueprint of the room and estimates of where everything was.

More gunfire sounded from a nearby floor, and I spun toward the staircase. The ESU team remained focused on their task, and Jablonsky put a hand on my shoulder.

"Three additional emergency services units have arrived. They'll secure the other floors," Jablonsky whispered. "We just have to handle this."

"I thought we got them all." I blinked a few times. "Damn." What was happening was beyond my comprehension. How many of Shade's soldiers had ransacked the building? How many cops were dead because of it? Shit.

"Agents," the commander barked, "we're ready to move. You've seen the crates, so you know what they look like. Once we get inside, I want the two of you to secure them. We don't know if any friendlies remain inside. Two officers normally work the desk, but it's protocol to secure the armory and evidence locker if under attack. So don't get trigger happy. We move on three." He looked at his team. "Fan out. Stay low. And stay alive."

They moved as a unit toward the doors. I watched the signals being exchanged and the positions modified. Then the doors were kicked in, and the tactical team entered two at a time. Jablonsky moved ahead of me.

"Stay behind me," Mark growled.

We entered low, remaining hidden behind the counter while the ESU team continued through the metal gate into the evidence storeroom. No one fired a shot. The only sounds were the footfalls of the tactical team. The silence was unnerving. I edged along the counter, following Jablonsky through the gate. This was the operatives' stronghold, so they must be hidden deep inside the storeroom.

Turning, I checked behind the counter, seeing a dead police officer. Rage boiled inside of me, but I kept moving. The shelves were crammed full. The newest additions should be somewhere easy to spot. They wouldn't have been cataloged yet, so they must be in a specific place to separate them from older evidence.

The storeroom looked like it could go on for miles. The shelves were fully packed, numbered, and categorized based on date, case, and possibly department. The shelves went practically to the ceiling, destroying visibility. They stood at least five across, creating various paths and hiding places. How the hell were we going to find the boxes in a room this large that contained numerous unfriendlies?

"We'll check the perimeter," Jablonsky whispered, reading my mind as we continued moving at a crouch.

The tactical team hadn't said a word as they continued to spread out, checking between the shelves for signs of the enemy. I expected gunfire, not total silence. I heard a noise behind us, and I spun around, sweeping my aim 180 degrees. But I didn't see anyone.

"Where are they?" I asked. "I thought this was their stronghold."

"I don't like this," Jablonsky said when we were halfway through the evidence store.

He held up his hand to stop our procession and lay flat on the floor. At the base of the shelving was a few inches of space, and he was using that space to check the next aisle for signs of an ambush. Silently, he stood up. Holding up two fingers, he signaled that I go back the way we came while he continued forward.

Nodding in agreement, I backtracked our steps. Coming

to the opening, I edged to the corner and peered around. The men he spotted were two of the tactical team members. One of them noticed me and gave the all clear signal. Jablonsky came around and joined us.

"Where the fuck are they?" I whispered.

The tactical team shook their heads. "We're looking. Have you located the weapons?"

"Not yet," Jablonsky said. "Any idea where you store the newest arrivals?"

"For a large shipment like that, probably in one of the corners. It gets cataloged before getting shelved, so the evidence piles up somewhere," the ESU guy said. "Find it and stay with it. We'll find you." The tactical unit resumed its sweep, leaving us to continue the search.

We returned to the outer edge of the storeroom, continuing our check of the perimeter, but I felt eyes on me. They were here; the mercenaries that Shade recruited were close. They were watching us, probably laughing at us. Any second they'd make their presence known.

Jablonsky stopped, pointing to a large assortment of boxes, folders, and evidence bags that littered the entire side wall in front of us. We'd already walked the other two sides of the storeroom, so this had to be it. I recognized the five crates from Pepper. We'd found them.

The feeling of impending doom returned with a vengeance, and I studied our surroundings. The shelves across from the crates were fully stocked, leaving no spaces for an ambush. The area directly in front and behind us appeared clear, but it felt like a trap.

"Mark," I hissed, "wait." He had taken a few steps toward the crates to make sure we'd found the right ones. "Something's off."

He nodded, leery of the opening between the shelves a dozen feet away. Bypassing our prize, we continued down the aisle, checking for signs of the enemy. Jablonsky dashed across the opening, and we both took up corners, checking to make sure the next aisle over was clear. When no danger presented itself, we returned to the crates.

At the far end of the last aisle, two ESU team members emerged. They spotted us, not showing any signs of having located their targets. Maybe the radio chatter had been incorrect. Perhaps the mercenaries had already ransacked the storeroom and left. It'd explain how they had been so heavily armed, assuming they hadn't arrived with a boatload of artillery on their persons.

In the distance, the ESU commander called out "clear", and the rest of his team began echoing the sentiment. Jablonsky lowered his gun and reached for the crate, giving the heavy lid a shove. I heard the grenade hit the ground before I saw it.

"Grenade," I shouted. We dove for cover at the end of the row of crates, knowing that the rest of the aisle was devoid of protection. Thankfully, the grenade didn't explode; it emitted thick plumes of opaque smoke. "It's an ambush."

From the sounds I heard, I couldn't tell where the enemy was coming from. But they were coming in force. Wood splintered, and the lid on the crate shifted. Through the thick plumes, I couldn't tell what was around me. Jablonsky was at my side. His measured breaths reassured me that he hadn't moved, but we were blind.

Gunshots ripped through the air. They were close. Too close, like they had been fired from right next to me. The smoke was beginning to dissipate, and I cautioned a glance over the top of the crate. A man was firing from behind my cover position. I lunged, tackling him to the ground. He used the rifle to knock me off of him, but Jablonsky grabbed the barrel of his gun and tore it from the shooter's hands. Then he swung the butt at the guy's head, connecting with a resounding thud that put the assailant down for the count.

"Trojan horse," Jablonsky whispered. Visibility wasn't ideal, which was why we weren't returning fire. I suspected that ESU was being extremely judicious with their shots as well. "We need to get away from here to improve our odds. Let's move."

Remaining ducked, Jablonsky led the retreat to the end of the aisle. Visibility greatly improved, and he turned to make sure I was behind him. In that split second, I didn't see the shooter, but I saw the AK aiming at my boss.

"Down," I screamed, loud enough that shots were fired from every direction at my location. I moved to intervene behind the shelf, and the AK fired, narrowly missing Jablonsky who had hit the deck. My boss came up firing, and the impact of his bullet made a wet, crunching sound, followed by a thud. "You good?" I asked.

"Yeah," Jablonsky said, kicking the gun from the dead guy's hands while we took cover at the end of the shelving.

I tightened my left-handed grip on the thirty-eight and took a deep breath, sensing that the Shade operatives were moving in on us. They had been concealed by the smoke a few feet away, so it'd only be a couple of seconds before they found us. Jablonsky had an assault rifle in both hands and peeked around the edge.

"ESU wanted us to stay put. They might as well have asked us to be sitting ducks," Mark commented. "Can you handle the right?"

"Sure." I braced my cast against the metal frame of the shelf and leaned over. As soon as I did, gunfire broke out.

Pulling away from the corner, I inhaled deeply. This wasn't good. I didn't know where the attackers had been hiding or how many we were dealing with. So far, we'd taken down two. And with the dozen ESU members patrolling the room, the odds should be in our favor, but it didn't feel like it. The shots were getting closer, as were the sounds of footsteps.

Sneaking another glance, I saw a man creeping along, pressed against the side of the shelf. I spun around, keeping as much of my body protected by the boxes and corner while I stretched my left arm straight against the side and fired directly at him. The move surprised him, and I made a shoulder shot. The attacker stumbled, and someone shot him from behind.

Not waiting to see if he had been killed by his own team, I spun back into a cover position, hearing more shots ring out. Jablonsky fired several rounds before making a move to the endcap on the next aisle. He caught my eye and signaled that three more were heading for us.

Scooting over, I peeked around the edge where Jablonsky had been, seeing ESU perform a couple of takedowns. Jablonsky glanced back around, firing again. It was only after he lowered his gun that I realized just how loud the battle had been. There had been commands being shouted, but I hadn't heard anything besides the gunfire.

"Clear," someone from ESU yelled. "Target down."

"Affirmative, targets down," someone else responded.

The smoke had abated, and near the crates were five dead and one unconscious terrorist. Or were they mercenaries? Dammit, I still hadn't figured out exactly what these assholes were.

More gunfire was heard at the other end of the storeroom followed by "clear."

"Clear," Jablonsky added, stepping away from the men he killed. We stepped out of our cover positions, surveying the damage. Large sections of evidence had been knocked off the shelves and strewn across the floor. "They were using the evidence boxes and shelves to hide their positions."

"That's fucked up," the ESU commander said. He exchanged looks with his team. "What's the final count?"

"Eleven," one of his team members responded.

"Eleven?" I asked, and he nodded. I'd only seen these assholes move in pairs. It should have been ten or twelve, not eleven. We missed someone. I voiced my concern, but I was met with shrugs.

"There are officers outside. If someone got past us, they didn't get far," the commander stated.

Jablonsky looked uneasily at the weapons crates. "Check the rest of the crates and make sure someone isn't hiding inside."

We waited while the crates all opened and searched, but we didn't find anyone inside. From what we gathered, they'd repositioned the boxes on the shelves and the row of crates to conceal their positions behind the evidence, not inside of it, but it didn't hurt to check.

The doors to the evidence room burst open, and another ESU team entered. The rest of the building had been successfully cleared, and medical teams were triaging the victims. Jablonsky and I made our way out of the room and back upstairs to the counterterrorism unit, but something continued to nag at me. I was positive that we'd missed a target.

THIRTY-THREE

"Oh, god," I said, reading through the latest count, "this is brutal." Thirty-nine police officers had been killed, and another hundred and sixteen had been injured. I wasn't entirely sure how severe the injuries had to be in order for them to make it onto the list, but I assumed it meant that at least a paramedic checked them out. "How did this happen? How could I let this happen?"

"You didn't, Parker," Lucca insisted. In an uncharacteristic move, he stepped behind my chair and rubbed my shoulders. "This is entirely Shade's fault. Not yours."

"Do you remember being at Quantico? Do you remember the exercises and drills we had to perform in the event of a terrorist attack?"

"Yeah." He swallowed. "We can't always win."

"That's bullshit. We could do better. We could try harder. We should have figured it out sooner. I should have remembered. I could have stopped this." He let go of my shoulders and spun my chair around. Then he knelt down and hugged me. "Ouch," I hissed, pushing him away. Whatever alternate reality this was, I didn't care for it.

He let go, and I turned my chair away from him. "This is

not your fault. Blame Behr and those fucks at Homeland that dumped this in your lap without properly assessing any of it. Blame the asshole cops that arrested you and had the living daylights beaten out of you. Blame me for not reading the intel sooner and not breaking Horvat, or blame the cybercrimes unit for taking forever to hack into Shade's website and message boards and find out they had PMCs preparing a strike. Because honestly, Alex, there's enough blame and regret to pass around to everyone."

I shook my head and went back to writing my incident and after action reports. After the shooting started, everything became a blur of nonstop action broken up by brief periods of inaction. I had to recount how I'd acquired Sergeant Evers piece and precise locations of shots fired for the incident reports. The logistics to determine what happened would be a nightmare, and I wasn't sure what agency would be tasked with reviewing everyone's account. The paperwork would be a beast. At least that wasn't my problem. My problem was recounting everything that happened in the last few hours in my shell-shocked state.

Finally, I hit print, spinning my chair away from the desk. Lucca was working at his desk, but he seemed keenly aware of my movements. He stopped what he was doing to watch me retrieve the hard copies from the printer.

"It was easier to type these things with two hands," I said, hoping for some levity.

"Seriously, Parker, how are you holding up?" he asked.

"Much better than 155 police officers." There was that dark, morbid sense of humor.

"Jablonsky said you were shot," Lucca said, failing horribly at keeping things lighthearted.

"Not really. Bullets were fired, followed by a physical altercation, and then there was some blood." I held out my report. "Do you want to proofread this for me?"

He took it from my hand, scanning through the pages of details. "What'd the paramedics say? Maybe you're one of the 116 on the list."

"Great, that narrows the count to 154." I sighed. "You didn't pop up for a routine checkup or anything, did you? Maybe we can knock this number down even more."

Lucca handed the reports back to me. "Did they think you were shot?"

"They said it was a flesh wound." I didn't want to bother getting triaged with those who actually needed help, but given my recent track record, Jablonsky insisted. The paramedics cleaned it with some antiseptic, but it was little more than a scratch. "It was probably the result of the physical altercation, but they happened in such close proximity to one another that Lt. Tinsley thought I'd taken fire. Jablonsky just went with her assessment."

Lucca nodded. "Good, I was afraid you had sugarcoated something in your report."

"Now I lie in my reports? Thanks."

"Parker, stop." He looked exasperated. "It's been a long ass day. Go home."

"There's too much to be done. We don't know if another attack has been planned. Anything could happen. This is an all hands situation."

"And you are on medical leave," Jablonsky said, stepping out of his office and into the middle of our conversation, "so all hands doesn't apply to you." He offered a mirthless smile. "You saved my bacon already today. Twice, maybe. I can't keep count anymore. Go home before it becomes three, and I'm forced to resign."

"What about the men we've taken into custody?" I asked. "They need to be questioned."

"That's being handled. The entire Bureau is on top of that." Mark glanced around the room. "Anyone who might be involved has been taken to a black site. We'll get answers. In the meantime, cybercrimes and our tech wizards are monitoring everything for suspicious communications. If we hear anything, I'll call." He studied my face for a moment. "The news story hasn't broken yet about the attack. We've managed to keep the media outlets from reporting yet, but the dam will break soon. Once that happens, none of us will be able to slip away without notice, so you should go now."

"Okay."

Truthfully, I didn't know how any of us were still standing. Today had been devastating. I imagined it was the muscle memory from our intensive training that was keeping us going, and I marveled at the brave men and women who had endured much worse in recent years but persevered. They were real heroes.

Despite my acquiescence, I remained at my desk. I didn't know how to leave. This wasn't a nine to five job. I couldn't just call it quits because it was late, especially not tonight. Not after everything that happened. Without realizing it, I spent another two hours at my computer, reading through the initial reports and reevaluating the facts that we already had. However, my mind was shot.

"Alexis," Lucca said softly, "you should be at home."

"So should a lot of people." The grief was setting in. "There's gotta be something here to keep this from happening again."

"I hope so." He pulled on the back of my chair. "Come on, I'll walk you to your car. I need to stretch my legs."

"Eddie," I growled.

"Alex," he admonished, "you're done for the night. Even Jablonsky's taking a couple of hours to regroup. No one expects the two of you to deal with this. You already spent several hours being debriefed and even longer writing reports." He glanced at my computer screen, making sure that it didn't contain anything new, and hit the power button. "Let's go."

"Fine." I grabbed my belongings and pushed away from the desk. We took the elevator down to the garage in silence, and when the doors opened, Lucca waited for me to exit. "You better find a way to put an end to Shade. This can't happen again."

"It won't."

"How do you know that?" I asked, feeling my emotions transverse the entire map.

"No one here will let it happen." He glanced around before leaning close, like he was sharing a secret. "Behr ordered a raid on Shade's HQ. It's going down tonight. A team has been formed and is being briefed. It looks like our agents abroad will be seeing some action soon. Keep it under wraps. This is supposed to be handled quickly and quietly."

"So I should disavow any knowledge?"

"Precisely." He winked. "Now get some rest. You look terrible."

"Screw you, Lucca." I opened my car door and got inside. It was time to go home.

* * *

Upon entering the house, I was met with the bright glare of the living room light. It was nearly midnight, but Martin was holed up in his office. After trudging up another three flights of stairs, I headed straight for the bathroom. I locked the door, turned the water on full blast, climbed into the shower, and at some point, began to sob. It wasn't one of my finest moments, but it was all I could do. People died today for no reason. I killed at least two men, adding more tallies to my sheet. And the only thing I could do was cry. It was a joke, a sick, pathetic expulsion of empathy and remorse. It didn't serve any purpose. It wouldn't change things or bring back any of those lost souls. My mind ran straight to the pity party and self-flagellation, but I knew that I couldn't do this right now. Right now, I had to be strong and focused. Our job wasn't done yet.

After a few steadying breaths, I forced my mind to compartmentalize today's tragedy. Tomorrow was already here. I needed to eat and sleep, so I'd be ready for whatever challenges were to come next. Stepping out of the shower, I towel-dried my hair, changed into one of Martin's t-shirts and a pair of pajama shorts, and returned to the kitchen for dinner.

Martin had cooked, so I reheated whatever was in the container and wolfed it down. Then I knocked gently on his office door. He turned around and smiled.

"When did you get home?" he asked.

"A few minutes ago." I picked up his phone from the corner of the desk, knowing that he received local news alerts, but nothing about the attack from today had been mentioned. "Can I turn off your phone for the rest of the night?"

"If you want. Are you afraid some early morning calls are going to wake you up?" he teased.

"Something like that." I waited for the phone to power off before placing it back on the desk.

"Sweetheart, is everything all right? You look exhausted. I know it's been eleven days since the surgery, and you aren't on forced bed rest anymore. But you shouldn't be running yourself ragged either."

"So I've been told." I moved across the room at his beckoning and curled up on his lap. Martin wrapped me in a tight embrace and kissed me. "You shouldn't do that. I'm likely to stay here all night."

"I'm not complaining." He loosened his grip slightly, keeping one hand on my back while picking up the financial statement he'd been reading before my entrance.

The silence was nice. It allowed my mind to shut off, and I rested my eyes. Martin was rubbing random patterns against my skin while he worked, but I barely noticed, too numb from the day to feel much of anything. The chair swiveled again, and I pressed my cheek more firmly against his shoulder to keep my head from lolling.

"How was your day?" I finally asked.

"Busy," he replied, and I snorted. "What?"

"Nothing."

"Something's wrong." He leaned away, so he could see my face. "What is it? What happened?"

"I can't go into it." He continued to stare as if he could see into my soul. "Please, get the hell out of my head, just for tonight."

"Is it that bad?"

"Worse." I was torn between disentangling myself and going into another room to hide and staying where I was. Frankly, I was too spent to move, but talking would be far more taxing in the long run. "A lot of people died today." I swallowed. "I'm going to bed."

"Alexis." He reached for me, but I had already left my perch and headed for the bedroom. He didn't say another word. Instead, the chair swiveled again while he went back to making notes for his morning meetings.

I tossed and turned, dozing occasionally while my mind

remained blank. Normally, thoughts and questions would race through my skull, but my circuits were fried. Too much had happened. Eventually, Martin came to bed, and I blindly reached for his arm, wrapping it around me. Normally, I didn't like feeling confined or suffocated, but tonight was a different story. I needed the comfort of another human being.

Morning came, bringing with it bright sunshine. Obviously, the weather didn't get the memo that the forecast should be doom and gloom. The crushing reality of yesterday weighed heavily on my heart, but my mind took issue processing and coping. It needed to get with the program.

"Martin," I croaked, my throat was dry and sore from the hysterics in the shower last night, "are you awake?"

"Uh-huh," he mumbled.

"Yesterday, the police department was attacked."

"Is Nick okay?"

"Yeah, as far as I know, his precinct wasn't hit. There might be more attacks. More targets. I just really need you to be careful today. There's no indication that businesses or the business district is a target, but shit happens."

"I'm glad you're not a cop," he whispered, snuggling against me. "At least I don't have to worry about you being caught up in the middle of this."

"Sure," I replied sadly. His breathing deepened, and I knew he had gone back to sleep. "There's nothing to worry about. Nothing at all." The blatant lie somehow made the direness of the situation more obvious. It jumpstarted my brain, and yesterday played out in my mind's eye in extreme detail. New questions were raised, and I glanced across at the nightstand to check the time. I ought to be back at the office by now.

Shrugging out of Martin's grasp, I grabbed my clothes and went to get ready. When I opened the bathroom door a few minutes later, Martin was gone. Incorrectly assuming that he had gone downstairs to get a jump on his morning workout, I put on my shoes and strapped on my shoulder holster with my back-up nine millimeter. There wasn't a chance in hell that I wouldn't be packing today, regardless of whether or not I was cleared to carry on duty. I doubted anyone would give me shit about it, and if they did, I'd direct them to Jablonsky. Mark owed me.

Going down the stairs, I was stunned to find two federal agents waiting in the living room. Martin was wearing a robe, bewildered and confused.

"Alexis Parker, we need you to come with us," one of them said.

I shifted my gaze from Martin back to the two of them. "Who the hell are you? And what is this about?"

They flashed their badges, and I immediately recognized the Homeland Security insignia. "This is about yesterday's attack. Please, Agent Parker, time is of the essence. We'll brief you on the way."

THIRTY-FOUR

I wasn't a fan of undisclosed locations. The process of being taken to one was akin to being kidnapped, or so I imagined. It didn't help matters that these DHS agents had found me at Martin's house. How the hell did they know where I was? Obviously, they'd tracked my phone or gotten the information from Jablonsky, but their abrupt appearance didn't sit well. Of course, time was of the essence. It sounded like a clichéd line from every bad action movie I'd ever seen, but in truth, the possibility of another attack remained extremely real.

"Agent Parker," Behr smiled tightly, "nice to see you this morning."

"Sorry, I can't say the same." I stared at him, glancing around the room. "Is anyone else joining us?"

"SSA Jablonsky is in the other room. I trust that you're up-to-date." He shifted his focus to the agents that had brought me into the building, and they nodded. "Since you discovered most of our current usable intel, it's only fair to include you in the interrogation."

"What happened this morning in the Balkans?" I asked. The DHS agents told me a raid had been conducted, and air support had been called in. The likelihood anyone survived was slim, but then again, an airstrike was a great way to cover our tracks and disseminate misinformation if it furthered our agenda. "Did we nab any HVTs before fire rained down?"

"Aren't you poetic?" He smirked. "All that matters is Horvat's in custody."

"Civilian casualties?"

"Who the hell are you? The Congressional oversight committee?"

"I'm someone with a conscience, and even more than that, I know that the more we fuck with them, the more they're gonna want to fuck with us. And yesterday, we took it up the ass. We didn't expect it or see it coming." I clenched my one good fist and fought to keep the anger contained. "Isn't this over, Assistant Director Behr? Who's left to orchestrate another attack?"

"It's not over yet." He picked up a folder marked confidential and leafed through the pages. "No reported collateral damage. However, Shade's hierarchy has been wiped out. Niko Horvat is in custody and is being interrogated as we speak."

"Then why am I here? It sounds like you've dismantled a terrorist cell. What aren't you saying?"

"I'll get to that." Behr's eyes burned with a passion I hadn't seen before. "This is what *I* do. Dismantling a cell isn't atypical for me or my people. What is unusual is the fact that our intel was so far off. We turned over the intelligence gathering to you because Shade didn't pose an immediate threat, but something happened that moved up their plans. They slipped through the cracks, and we lost American lives on American soil. That is unacceptable, and I want an explanation." He slammed the folder down on the desk. "You determined they were planning something. You took action. Maybe it moved up their timetable. Maybe it didn't." He pressed a button, turning the conference table into a computer display. "How did you find Niko inside that restaurant?"

"Jakov," I corrected. "He was employed at Pepper. When I started digging into Shade's leadership, it led me to the local Croatian community and to Detective Donaldson, and you know the rest."

"No, Agent Parker, the man you believe to be Jakov is actually Niko Horvat."

"That's not possible. You just said Niko was taken into custody." My head was spinning.

"He was. We arrested him at the airport. You spoke to him. The OIO questioned him. Niko Horvat is in the next room."

"He said he was Jakov," I protested. "He was fingerprinted. His identity matches the records we have on file."

"Does it?" Behr tapped on the glass, shifting the images and files around. "These prints passed muster through the local database but not through the international one. What does that say?" He pointed to a side by side comparison.

"They're a match. How did Niko trick the fingerprint database?"

"He probably hired hackers, or he's been planning this for far longer than any of us realized. Perhaps the juvie record was actually Niko's. It's possible he was here on a visit, and when he was arrested, he decided to impersonate Jakov."

"That was ten years ago. How is that possible? Who runs a long game for that length of time?"

Behr stared at me. "Have you watched the news in the last two decades? People hold grudges."

"So when did Niko and Jakov switch places?"

"It's hard to say. Based on passport usage, I'd say that it was a couple of months ago. Niko probably had his subordinates continue to post the rhetoric online using his computer and location. Meanwhile, he was here. He made the cargo pick up, and he enlisted the help of the private military contractors. They aren't local either, but it's harder to track movements if seemingly unconnected parties meet at a neutral location. It might also explain the fake work documents for Jacob House on file at Pepper."

"So Niko shipped over the weapons and the men he hired to use them." I watched the video feed of the man I thought was Jakov being questioned. "Horvat kept saying we had the wrong man. Finally, he slipped and said his family would come for him. That they would make us pay. Does that mean cousin Jakov is planning his own attack?"

"Niko didn't slip, Parker. You pushed his buttons. It seems you have a tendency to do that. That's why I wanted you here. We've issued an alert for Jakov. Everyone is scouring the city for the bastard, especially the police. We're hoping to bring him in alive and use the Horvats against one another."

"If the police get a hold of him, he won't be taken alive."

"They'll keep him breathing if it means saving one of their own from the same fate that so many met yesterday," Behr declared. "In the meantime, we need to rehash the night Detective Donaldson was murdered. You don't remember much about the assailant, but I want you to watch some footage."

He scrolled through some files, selecting a video. Hitting play, I watched the silhouette of a man move through a small, enclosed space. At the other end of the room was another man. I couldn't tell what provoked it, but the first guy hauled off and hit the man. The movement was a bit jerky, but he kept going. One, two, one. The same combination over and over. Then he stopped, jerking his chin upward, like he'd just bested his opponent. He shuffled to the right and hit the man again.

"A lot of people probably use that same combination," I said. He rewound, and I watched the footage again, wondering if I'd seen that somewhere else. It was the odd jerky movement that got me. Most fighters moved fluidly. This guy wasn't a fighter. He was a bully. A hitter. It could have been Donaldson's killer, but I wasn't willing to jump to conclusions.

Behr dialed up the audio file, and I heard the voice. My blood ran cold. It felt like the oxygen had been sucked out of the room.

"I know that voice. He killed Donaldson and Ivan. He nearly killed me. Who the hell is that?" I pointed to the man on the screen.

"Niko Horvat."

"That's bullshit. We questioned Niko. He doesn't sound anything like that," I argued.

"Maybe he does when he isn't pretending to be Jakov," Behr said smugly, opening a file containing Niko's psych profile and splaying it across the table. Niko had dissociative tendencies, was borderline bipolar, and a sociopath. "I want you to conduct his interrogation. You've been briefed on what occurred in the last twenty-four hours. Hell, you were at ground zero yesterday, and you know what happened a few weeks ago at Pepper. Use it to your advantage to push his buttons and get answers. He made this personal, so you deserve the chance to do the same." Behr turned off the computer display and led the way to the holding cell where Niko was being questioned. "The only stipulation is I need your firearm before you go inside." He held out his hand, and I stared at his palm, not comprehending what was happening.

"I want to speak to Jablonsky first."

"Go right ahead. He's already inside," Behr replied, disarming me and unlatching the heavy door.

At the sound of the metal grinding as the door opened, Jablonsky glanced at me. His eyes darted to the wall in the corner, and I understood the unspoken meaning. Without saying a word, I slunk into the darkened corner of the room.

Niko noticed my presence immediately. He didn't say anything, but he didn't look pleased. That made two of us. I gave the terrorist my death stare, finding it increasingly difficult not to cross the room, rip out his tongue, and strangle him with it.

"Why?" Jablonsky asked.

Niko smiled. "Now they know how it feels. I wanted them to hurt." His eyes shot to me briefly. "Did they hurt like that detective?"

It took every ounce of restraint not to react. Instead, I remained completely impassive. Jablonsky scratched his neck, somehow keeping himself just as emotionally detached.

"No one told you?" I asked. Stepping away from the wall, I made an amused snort. "We found your ancient weapons in the freezer. We tracked down the delivery source and followed the breadcrumbs." I shrugged and closed my mouth, waiting. Horvat didn't say a thing. He studied me, searching for the lie. "Soviet era weaponry is a joke. Newsflash, Niko, the United States won the Cold War. You should have armed your men better or, I don't know, paid for the upgraded package when hiring mercenaries to carry out your dirty work. It would have been smarter to have them buy their own weapons. Then they might have actually kept them from being confiscated."

"If my plan failed, you wouldn't be here now," Niko rationalized. "Were they all killed?"

"The only people who were killed yesterday were your people," Jablonsky said. He went to the table and opened the folder, carefully picking up each photograph from the destroyed Shade HQ and placing them on the table facing Niko.

Niko paled, staring at the destruction. "This isn't true. You're liars," he screamed. "You're liars, just like the soldiers that invaded my country. You Americans do nothing but lie. You claim to help. That you're humanitarians, but you killed my family." He looked up with anger and tears in his eyes. "You killed my family." Then he let out a rage-filled scream and violently began thrashing in an effort to free himself from the restraints. "You'll pay. I will enact vengeance. You'll all be dead. Dead." The shrieking threats reverted to his native tongue, so Jablonsky and I waited. "This isn't over," Niko hissed, spittle running down the side of his mouth while sweat covered his face from the exertion of attempting to free himself from the restraints. "You won't be able to stop what's in store next."

"More outdated weaponry?" I asked, casually taking a seat across the table from him. "More hired hands that owe loyalty to the highest bidder?" He stared with venom in his eyes. "Let me ask you a question, not about any of this," I waved my hand at the disturbing photographs, "but about your little act. You see me at Pepper, and you run like a little bitch. And then you hide like a little bitch. But you get stupid, and you get arrested."

"Like a little bitch," Jablonsky muttered, joining in with the annoying commentary that would probably elicit a response since Niko had shown a sensitivity to irritations in the past.

"And then you lie like a motherfucking coward," I concluded. In a whiny, high-pitched voice I said, "I'm Jakov. You have the wrong man. I'm a good guy. I would never do any of the things that you say." My expression hardened. "You're a chicken shit. You hide behind your computer screen like an internet troll, thinking that you can say and do anything, but once you're out in the real world, you don't care to send others to do your bidding just as long as you're safe, right?" He continued to glare. "Fucking coward."

"Is that what it looked like when I put a bullet into the detective's skull?" he asked, his voice deeper and more menacing just like it had been the night he killed Donaldson and Ivan. "I should have put one into you inside the kitchen instead of waiting." He scoffed. "Women are weak and fragile." His eyes focused on the cast on my arm. "You were lucky I let you live as long as I did." He sneered. "You'll die, just like the rest of them."

"Really?" I asked, cocking my head to the side. "How do you plan on achieving that? Have you not been paying attention?" I pointed to the photos. "You're in here. You're not gonna get away, so how are you going to do it?"

"My family will enact vengeance. We are righteous. You will pay and suffer."

"Suffer?" Jablonsky asked in a lethal tone. "I'd say there's enough suffering to go around." He moved next to Horvat's chair and punched him hard in the gut. "Does that make you feel more righteous?"

Horvat began muttering again in his native tongue. He looked up at Mark, smiling disconcertingly. Then he focused on me and said something that, despite the language barrier, came across loud and clear. Obviously, we'd pushed Niko's buttons, but I didn't know how to get him to talk. His life was destroyed, so no amount of threatening would work. And he had no incentive to bargain or cooperate. We were at a stalemate. Niko would talk if it served his purposes, and that was it.

THIRTY-FIVE

"You're done for now," Behr said, opening the door. "We'll take it from here."

Jablonsky grunted in acknowledgement, never breaking eye contact with Niko. "Now the fun begins," Mark warned. Then he left the room, not breaking stride.

I stared at the shackled man, not understanding what led us here. Images from inside the police station ran through my mind. Grenades exploding, people screaming, bullets flying, the death count and casualty list, those things were because of this man, and we'd just spent the last few minutes trying to convince him none of it happened.

"Parker, move it," Behr snapped.

"Yes, sir." I gave the table a good kick and smiled wickedly at Niko. "Game over. You lose."

"We'll see," Niko replied, watching as I left the room.

"What the hell did that accomplish? You wanted us to crack him. Isn't that why you dragged me here to conduct an interrogation?" I asked as soon as the door slammed shut. "He didn't give us anything."

"I wouldn't be too sure," Behr said. "My Slavic language skills leave a lot to be desired, but that madman's ramblings provided a few hints about the next attack." He looked at the translator who was transcribing the conversation from the recording. She gave him a thumbs up. "See, we got something."

"What?" I asked, fearing a repeat of yesterday or something far worse.

"Not yet," Behr said, ushering us away from the DHS agents. "We'll evaluate it first."

"The hell you will," Jablonsky said. "This is a joint venture. Director Kendall was told that he'd receive your full cooperation. It's the only reason he agreed to help. Now I want to see that intel you have on Niko. We've waited this long already." Mark glared at Behr. "Or should I call Kendall so you can explain to him what the holdup is?"

"Fine," Behr glanced at both of us, "you can set up in conference room C. I'll have someone bring you the intel."

After we were left alone, I turned to Jablonsky. "What the hell is going on? DHS agents came to Martin's house to pick me up. They said it was time sensitive and a matter of national security. Then I get here, Behr screws around for a bit, tosses me into the interrogation room completely unprepared, and flips the entire investigation on its head."

"Jakov is Niko. We missed it. Call it a clerical error or a computer glitch, but that was on us. He was in our custody until Behr took over with updated intel. If you ask me, the CIA or one of the other fifteen intelligence gathering agencies gave it to him. He wouldn't have found it on his own."

"What does it say?"

"Aside from the fact that Niko was impersonating Jakov, I don't know. Supposedly, it's beyond my clearance level."

"Then what are we about to see? Behr's vacation slides?"

"Director Kendall made a few calls and had us both granted temporary top-level security clearance on this matter. Behr's annoyed that Kendall went over his head. He's also annoyed that this shit happened on his watch. Suffice it to say, he's gung-ho about foiling Shade's next attempt in order to claim the victory and blame us for not stopping yesterday's attack."

"Politics."

"Yep." Jablonsky shrugged. "Frankly, that's the least of our worries."

"I agree. How could we have been duped into thinking one cousin was the other? Maybe we really are incompetent."

"Shush," Jablonsky said, silencing me a second before the files were brought to us.

For once, it was nice to be able to read through the intel without having to deal with the redacted bits. Those were always distracting and a bit troublesome. The information was highly detailed, containing a complete profile of Niko, his family, background, and the origins of Shade.

Niko Horvat was orphaned as a result of the war. The war claimed the life of his father, who had been a soldier. While Niko's mother, brother, and grandparents attempted to escape the siege, the entire village was destroyed. A firefight broke out between the insurgents and U.S. forces that had arrived on a peacekeeping mission. Neighbors, friends, and extended family were killed while trying to flee. Unfortunately, many civilians were caught in the crossfire, and Niko's mother was killed. The U.S. soldiers took Niko and his brother to a refugee camp, but they were of a tender age and didn't fully comprehend what happened. All they knew was their mom and dad had been killed by soldiers.

Eventually, other aid workers arrived. Peace was temporarily restored, and Niko and many other boys were sent to an orphanage. According to the records, two of the peacekeeping soldiers repeatedly brought supplies to the boys. A brief profile was provided for the troops that Niko encountered, but one profile stood out. One of the peacekeepers had taken a leave of absence from his job at the police department in order to serve overseas.

"R.J. Cook," I read the name aloud. "This was roughly twenty years ago. If he's still around, he's probably retired from the force."

"He's the commissioner's driver," Jablonsky said. "How do you not know that?"

"Why would I know that?"

"Because you're like a friggin' badge bunny. Every time I turn around, you've made a new friend in blue." Mark rolled his eyes. "That's why Shade targeted our city and our police force. Niko must blame Cook for losing his family and tracked him down."

Jablonsky flipped through the file, finding a transcript of an interview Behr had conducted with Cook yesterday. While he read that, I continued leafing through Niko's history. After the war, a well-off family showed an interest in adopting a son, but they only wanted one. The administrator altered the documents, saying that Niko and his brother were cousins, not siblings, in order for Jakov to be adopted.

"Holy shit, Jakov's his brother." I reread the words on the page. "His twin brother."

"Damn, when did our investigation turn into a daytime soap?" Mark grumbled. "Hey, get this." He held up a page from Cook's transcript. "Cook doesn't remember the boys specifically, but he remembers being stationed over there and seeing so much destruction. Families were broken apart. The place was a mess. It was total anarchy. He said he used to save whatever rations and candy bars he could and bring them to the kids at the camps and in the orphanages. He regaled them with tales of being a policeman in the United States and the importance of maintaining law and order to protect the people. He told the children that he and the other soldiers were there for their safety. I guess he thought he was improving U.S. relations. It's too bad young Niko took that to mean that our people should suffer too."

"Jakov might be the only living blood relative Niko has. We have to find him. He's the leverage we need to get Niko to spill on his next plan."

"I agree we need to find Jakov but not for that reason. Jakov was brought to the U.S. after his adoption, but there's every indication that Niko indoctrinated his long-lost brother with Shade's ideals." Jablonsky flipped to a financial assessment. "Shade's hierarchy was comprised of Niko's fellow orphans, and damn, if one of them hadn't done exceptionally well for himself." Mark shook his head. "This mogul could give Marty a run for his money. Shade at one point had an estimated net worth of nearly six million dollars, ninety percent of it coming from a single source. Niko must have convinced his fellow orphan to invest his money in creating Shade. They did a good job of hiding their assets. None of our intel came close to this."

"So we bring them in, track the cash, and get them to talk," I said, hoping to find another avenue.

"As of six hours ago, Shade's commanding body was declared dead."

"Dammit, who's still alive?"

"Niko and Jakov. Everyone else was identified at Shade HQ and eliminated."

"That means it's up to Jakov to carry out Shade's mission."

The door to the conference room opened, and one of Behr's lackeys stepped inside. "Agents, your presences are needed in the command center." She held the door, waiting for us to leave the room. I was certain it was so they could hide the information from us again.

"You summoned," Jablonsky said, sounding incredibly displeased once we were back in the central room of the black site.

"As I was saying," Behr said, not even glancing in our direction as he continued to speak to the team assembled, "they planned a multipoint attack on key precincts and station houses. Firearms and small incendiaries were delivered to three area restaurants throughout the city. The FBI confiscated the remaining two shipments last night, and the police have the original shipment at the site of yesterday's attack. Niko Horvat hired private military contractors from Eastern Europe to travel here and orchestrate the attack. At the present, we are unsure how many contractors were hired. We have several in custody. Keep in mind that yesterday wasn't Shade's first attack; it was their second. The first attack occurred against a police transport that was escorting a prisoner to the district attorney's office."

"Prisoner?" I scoffed, and Behr gave me an icy glare.

"The weaponry that these contractors used was provided by Shade. Therefore, we're assuming whatever Niko Horvat has planned will continue to rely on weapons that Shade personally obtained," Behr continued. "Our interviews with the private contractors reinforced this theory. However, we have yet to determine how many men were hired."

"Have you tracked their compensation?" Jablonsky asked.

"We didn't meet success following the money. The parties in custody said the funds were sent to a trust that would be transferred to their families in the event of their demise. It involves foreign banks with closed policies. Despite our insistence that these funds were provided by a terrorist organization, no country is willing to turn over their information or assist in our endeavor," Behr said. "Scolari and Cleaver, let me know when the private contractors have been broken." Two agents nodded, waiting for the dismissed order before leaving the command center. "Brotherton, is the translation complete from Niko's earlier interview?"

"Yes, sir," she said, reading a very obscure message. "That's the literal translation, but based on cultural and slang references, it roughly translates into meaning 'stomping on the memory of the dead and spitting on their graves'."

"Sweet," I mumbled sarcastically.

"He also had quite a few imaginative things to say about you, Agent Parker," Brotherton said, "but I don't believe any of that bears repeating. It wasn't particularly useful."

"Neither is this," Jablonsky said. "He didn't give us anything, and we have no leverage to break him."

"We could quite literally break him," Behr retorted, "but given his psychological profile, it's unlikely that would provide results." Behr picked up the translation, reading the words again. "Niko's a self-centered egomaniac with delusions of grandeur. He truly believes that his plan would work to fall the police force." Behr flipped through the pages, muttering to himself.

'Fall the police force,' I mouthed to Jablonsky, who

sighed and shook his head. I wouldn't doubt that Assistant Director Behr was also delusional and self-centered. Edging to the corner of the table, I picked up a copy of Niko's psych profile and skimmed through it again.

"He doesn't know what to believe," I said, causing all eyes in the room to turn to me. "Until I told him that his plan failed, he believed that yesterday was a success. Obviously, he hired the trucking company or delivery driver to store his weapons around the city. That's three different locations. Does anyone have a local map?"

"Here," Scolari said, handing me a city map. "The marks are the locations the weapons were found."

"And each one is close to a different police station. However, we discovered Pepper first. That's why the attack yesterday happened so quickly. The mercenaries didn't have time to organize or plan. The other two locations were probably supposed to happen at a specific date and time, but hopefully, we pulled the plug," I said, verbalizing my thoughts as I went.

"Have these precincts been alerted?" Jablonsky asked, pointing to the map.

"Affirmative," someone replied. "The police department is being incredibly vigilant right now."

"As they should be," Behr said. He put the translation down. "Agent Parker, you were saying something about Niko believing his plan of action worked. Please elaborate."

"Actually, something doesn't jive. Niko's been in custody. How would he know that the police confiscated the weapons from Pepper? Why would he assume that the last twenty-four hours were a vital turning point?" I stared at Behr. "Hasn't he been incommunicado?"

"You tell me. Did your people keep him deaf and blind?" Behr asked.

"The transfer tipped him off," Jablonsky said. "He's smart. He knew something was up. Hell, we almost gave him access to the outside world a couple of hours before the attack went down." Jablonsky turned to the translator. "Did he mumble anything about the first phase being completed or anything like that?"

She thought about it. "I don't know. He rambled a lot in

metaphor and allegory. It's possible."

"What do you think?" Behr asked.

"He wants to spit on their graves. Regardless of if any of the precinct attacks were a success, Niko could be certain of one thing. At least one cop's dead," Brotherton said.

"Donaldson," I sighed, "which means there will be a cop's funeral."

"All right, people," Behr said, "let's investigate this theory. Sniff around and see if it stinks. If we can't find fault with it, we'll begin prepping for that possibility. There's no doubt that the police department will hold a huge memorial after yesterday's incident, so we need to have actionable intel before anything else goes down. We'll reconvene in two hours. Dismissed."

THIRTY-SIX

"Jakov's our best bet," I said. "If we can locate him, we might be able to sway him to give up Shade's plan."

"You mean give up his brother's plan," Mark corrected. He chewed on his bottom lip and flipped through the updated police reports. "That'll be a hard sell."

"Jakov was raised here. He has no record of violence. There's nothing to suggest he's unstable. Have we contacted his adopted family?"

Mark snorted. "His mom and dad won a month long cruise, or so they were told. We haven't been able to locate or reach them."

"Then how do you know that?"

"Tickets were purchased in their names on one of Niko's accounts. He probably wanted to remove the stabilizing influence from Jakov's life. For all we know, they might be dead. Regardless, we have people sitting on their house and at every single place that Jakov has visited in the last two months. We should have never called off the BOLO."

"We thought we had him. How the hell were we supposed to know they were identical twins?" I glared out the door of the conference room. "It's not like Homeland bothered to share their information."

"They didn't have it at the time," Jablonsky said. "The time codes printed on the sheets matched two days ago. They're not our enemy, Alex. We all screwed up. That's why we're gonna fix it."

"How?"

"By getting out of this secret facility and back to the real world." Without another word, Jablonsky left the conference room. A few minutes later, he was back with a couple of Homeland agents that were being forced to deliver us to the federal building. "It's time to go."

As soon as we were back at the federal building, we hit the ground running. Within ten minutes of our return, our team was convened inside the conference room and updated on the situation. The biggest threat was Jakov Horvat. Teams were continuing to scout the area for signs of his presence. Our tech geniuses had access to every public camera available and had the facial rec running through the incoming data for sightings of Jakov. It was an incredibly expensive and tedious procedure, but the city was under attack. We had no choice.

"I want agents sitting on those three restaurants and the trucking company," Jablonsky said. "If someone so much as coughs within a hundred yards of there, I want them brought in. These private contractors should be hungry for weapons, so they'll come sniffing."

"How do we know there are more soldiers of fortune out there?" Cooper asked. "Based on yesterday's reports, it's possible they've all been wiped out."

"Until you can guarantee that with absolute certainty, we're working under the assumption that more will come. Passport records are being reviewed. Since we have photos and fingerprints of the men involved in yesterday's attack, it should make it easier to pinpoint others who traveled into the country around the same time. Based on what Homeland has to say, the mercs probably entered the country in waves," Jablonsky stated.

"What about the half a dozen or so that were apprehended yesterday after the assault on the police station? Why aren't they being questioned?" Lucca asked.

"They are. The police department is handling that until

orders are passed along from Homeland. I didn't see any reason why we needed to enter the pissing contest to take custody when there are much better uses for our time," Jablonsky said. "Lieutenant Tinsley has agreed to give us transcripts and recordings of the interrogations they conduct."

"The cops need to stay off the streets," I said, "since they're the targets. What can we do to pick up the slack?"

"Find Jakov, bring him in, and find out what else Shade has planned." Jablonsky looked around the room. "Look, people, yesterday hurt. We don't have time to mourn or to process. I know you're angry, scared, and possibly homicidal," he cracked a slight smile, "but we push on. The best thing we can do is stop this from happening again. If anyone has any idea how to find Jakov or any clue how to track down the hired guns, speak up. I'm all ears."

No one spoke, but an errant thought kept running through my mind. I cleared my throat. "Donaldson's CI file might be key. The restaurant employees that Ivan was ratting on should know something. You and Tinsley were questioning them yesterday before shit blew up. They might have known Niko's true identity or something else relevant to stopping another terrorist attack. We need to speak to them again, and we need to review all of Donaldson's notes again for any discrepancies or odd information that didn't fit before."

"Okay," Mark nodded, "Lucca, take a team and head to the precinct. Request a transfer, but if that fails, question them there. We don't need to waste time."

"Yes, sir." Lucca looked at me. "Are you coming?"

"Actually, there's something else I want to follow up on." I focused on Mark, shaking my head slightly instead of sharing it with him.

"Then let's get to work. Dismissed," Jablonsky said, leaving the conference room and hitting the elevator without missing a beat.

Taking a deep breath, I waited for the rest of the room to empty, and then I stepped out of the conference room. Everyone was determined and desperate to end this, and so was I. Swallowing, I took the elevator to a different level and wandered down the dreaded path that I had come to despise years earlier. Knocking on the door, I licked my lips, hoping that Weiler was out.

"Enter," he called, looking up as I opened the door and stepped inside. "Mandatory counseling?"

"No." I snorted. "Not yet, anyway. We need your help."

"The behavioral analysis unit is working on a psychological profile for Jakov Horvat based on the latest information. Forensic psychology isn't my area of expertise. I doubt I can give you anything faster or more useful than they can."

"Okay, well, it turns out Niko killed Detective Donaldson. He could've killed me, and frankly, given what we know, it makes no sense why he didn't."

"He didn't kill you because you're a woman."

"So he's sexist?"

"Possibly, but he saw his mother gunned down in front of him. It's unlikely he'd intentionally put himself into a position to revisit that trauma."

"But he planned to kill me," I argued.

"Maybe someone else was going to do it. You said Niko was in the back seat, so there must have been a driver. Maybe he was told to kill you."

"Thanks, Doc. That makes me feel so much better."

"You asked for help. I'm just giving you my honest opinion." He picked up the copy of the reports and files that the FBI had received concerning Shade. "I find it hard to believe that you came down here yourself just to ask for a rudimentary profile. Why are you really here, Agent Parker? Do you want to talk about yesterday?"

"No," I growled, struggling to keep my annoyance to a minimum, "we need a lead, which means I have to remember who else was in the kitchen helping Niko murder two men." I sat on the end of the couch and hugged the pillow. "Hypnotize me, but so help me if you make me cluck like a chicken."

"Apart from the fact that hypnotherapy is nothing like a vaudevillian act, I can't just snap my fingers and make you remember something that your psyche suppressed." He came around the desk and sat in the chair across from the couch. "First of all, for you to be open to any therapeutic technique, you have to feel safe. It's apparent you don't."

"Cut the bullshit. Just talk me through the Kantian or Freudian hullaballoo."

"Fine, but I don't expect this to work."

"We'll see."

"Shut your eyes," he said, flipping on the white noise machine, "and take a deep breath. How do you feel?"

"Frustrated," I opened one eye and looked at him, "let's just cut to the chase."

He sighed. "Talk me through that evening, just whatever sights, smells, and tastes that come to mind. Describe them. Focus on them. The facts aren't important; you've gone through that information with the investigators. So just concentrate on immersing yourself in the memory."

I remembered the chime when I first entered Pepper, the smell of thyme and garlic, the sizzle of a skillet, and the low roar of people talking and laughing. I remembered the indention of the carving on the bar beneath my fingertip and the sound of Donaldson's voice. Ivan was harder to remember since he stayed in motion the entire time. He didn't spend a lot of time speaking to us, instead whispering a few phrases or pointing out employees between serving drinks and writing notes.

"Okay, let's move on to after the restaurant closed. Focus on that," Weiler instructed.

The frigid breeze against my skin, the smell of the cold, and the prickles on the back of my neck when that man approached. He stayed concealed, ushering me back inside and into the kitchen. It was a rush. A blur.

"I never got a look at him," I said.

"Keep going," Weiler insisted. "You have to work past what happens next. Just remember, you're in a safe place, Alexis. No one can hurt you here."

I snorted at the condescending words. "No shit, really?"

"Focus."

"It's dark. Everything has a red tint to it from the exit sign." I closed my eyes tighter. "I can see Donaldson. There's a body slumped in the corner. It has to be Ivan."

"You're not sure?"

"I was, but now it's hazier. I know it's him though. His body was found alongside the detective's."

"What about the other man? Is he in the room?"

"He's behind me. He's keeping out of my line of sight. He follows Niko's orders but doesn't speak much. He cuffed me to the chair and held me at gunpoint. Shit." I bolted upright on the couch. "During the interrogation, Niko said he should have killed me, and you just said that he would have avoided the act if he could."

"What are you getting at, Agent Parker?"

"In the back seat of the SUV, the man pulled the trigger." I held up my casted arm, knowing that the damage to the webbing of my hand was a result of the failed attempt to fire. "I recognized him as the interrogator, but if what you said is right, it was Jakov that planned to shoot me. Niko must have been driving." I stood up, heading for the door. I had to see the surveillance footage from outside Pepper again. Lucca said that they spotted Jakov on the feed, but it might have been Niko since they didn't see Jakov loading the SUV with the bodies. Perhaps they were both there that night. At the moment, I couldn't figure out if that would hurt or help us in the long run.

Once I found the file, I watched it play through with Agent Lawson peering over my shoulder. He adjusted the sharpness as best he could, but the glimpse of the man we believed to be Jakov Horvat was nothing more than a quick pass. It was enough to place either him or his twin brother at Pepper the night of the murder, but I doubted we'd need the solid evidence. I was there. I remembered seeing at least one of them. Dammit, maybe my double vision from the booze was actually twins.

After thanking Lawson for his continued patience with my off-the-wall requests, I detoured to the behavioral analysis unit to find out if they'd finished their profiles. They were briefing a crisis negotiator and SSA Jablonsky on the details when I appeared. Mark waved me over, and I listened in. Apparently, they believed that Jakov was the meeker brother, but he was bullied and guilted into helping Niko with his vendetta.

"They both suffered the same loss, but Jakov's world

rebuilt itself. His understanding of the world was painted by the love and support his adopted parents provided. However, they both have a shared history. Jakov probably repressed it until he came face-to-face with Niko. Based on the communication logs we've seen and passport records, it's only been in the last ten years that the two were reunited," the analyst said.

"That's because Niko wanted to have things in place before he recruited the final piece of the puzzle," Jablonsky said. "He couldn't be sure how Jakov would take it, and in the event his brother betrayed him, he wanted to be able to carry out his plan before the authorities could stop him."

"Probably," the analyst agreed.

"Do you think Jakov suffered some kind of episode?" I asked. "Normal people don't turn into killers overnight, but I'm fairly certain that Jakov was the man who attempted to murder me." Mark raised a brow. "That's the verdict Weiler and I reached a few moments ago."

The analyst mulled it over for a few minutes. "If the juvie record belongs to Niko and not Jakov, which would explain the fingerprint discrepancy, then I'd say that the brothers weren't reunited until their mid-teens. By then, the shock would have shattered Jakov's self-image. His entire foundation would have shifted. It's possible that everything he's done since was to earn Niko's approval or to make up for being given a life that his brother was denied. Jakov's been manipulated into feeling like he abandoned his brother and is struggling to make up for it. Niko's aggressive, dominating attitude, emotional manipulation, and attempt to isolate his brother from rational outside forces have molded Jakov into the perfect vessel to carry out Niko's mission."

"So he's been brainwashed?" the negotiator asked. "How can a situation be deescalated if the subject is in a semi-delusional state?"

"It's not delusion," the analyst argued, but Jablonsky interrupted before this turned into a lot of big words and not much useful information.

"Does this make Jakov more dangerous than Niko?" Jablonsky asked.

"That's hard to say. Jakov will do anything to win his brother's affection, perhaps to the point of suicide. You need to approach him with extreme caution, and if you attempt to talk him down, choose your words carefully," the analyst said.

"Parker, what do you have?" Jablonsky asked as we went back to the elevator.

"Nothing. I thought if one of the restaurant employees had been helping Niko, we might be able to find out what Shade's next target is, but it was his brother, who we can't locate."

Mark narrowed his eyes. "I bet they pulled a switch a time or two. It's probably how the weapons came to be beneath the freezer. Yesterday, someone said that there were times that Jakov acted like he didn't recognize him. Someone else said he spoke differently. I thought maybe it was his psychosis, like the way he changed when you kept kicking the table, but now I think it's because they were reenacting *The Parent Trap*." He pulled out his phone. "Let's see how Lucca's doing. Are you up to revisiting the precinct?"

"If we must."

"You can bow out, Parker. I probably would if I had the option. It's not even twenty-four hours. That was some crazy shit yesterday."

"I'm fine. Send me where you need me."

THIRTY-SEVEN

After several long hours, we were convinced that the staff of Pepper wasn't part of a sleeper cell of Shade operatives. The police weren't as quick to jump to that conclusion, and everyone was being held in custody until further notice. A sympathetic judge had signed arrest warrants for all of them, and given the extreme circumstances, the employees were denied bail. However, from Detective Donaldson's records and his informant files, the restaurant was a front for gang activity. The information and case files had been turned over to narcotics and gangs to sort through. Even if they weren't terrorists, those involved would pay for something. After all, it was the initial illegal activity that led Donaldson to Pepper in the first place.

"What about the other restaurants?" Lucca asked.

"We've run backgrounds on everyone. Homeland even checked our work, but aside from a few minor violations, everyone's clean. No ties to the Balkans, terrorists, drugs, guns, or the Horvats. The same can't be said for that trucking company," Jablonsky offered. "One of the drivers made a lot of money recently. He's offered up everything he knows."

"Doubtful," Tinsley muttered. We were inside the roll call room, sharing updates on our progress. "He knew he was transporting something illegal. He should have reported it sooner. He's just as guilty as the rest of them."

"What'd he think was in the crates?" I asked, understanding her anger.

"Exotic ingredients," Jablonsky said. "We know that a man matching Horvat's description approached him during a routine delivery at Pepper and told him that if he loaded a few dozen extra crates onto the truck and dropped them off at the restaurants without saying a word, he'd be handsomely rewarded."

"Where'd he get the crates?" Tinsley asked.

"They were left outside the warehouse. It was timed. Surveillance footage is being collected and analyzed," Jablonsky replied. "Look, the point is we're too late to stop what's already been done, so we need to concentrate our efforts on grabbing Jakov."

"I think it was a ploy," Lucca said. "Niko made sure he'd get caught, so we'd be caught with our pants down."

"Fool me once," Tinsley snarled. She stormed across the room and slammed her palm against the map. "Police are canvassing the area. We'll track down this son-of-a-bitch."

"No uniforms," I said.

"No." She agreed. "Even our patrolmen know to wear civvies. We're under attack, so we're gonna blend in. If they want to fight dirty, so will we. The entire city is on alert. We've removed our visible presence from most of the neighborhoods. We're better safe than sorry."

"Are we sure that isn't what Niko wants?" Lucca asked. "He could be hoping for anarchy."

"I doubt a riot is going to happen just because the beat cops are out of uniform," I retorted.

"The commissioner expects an increase in criminal activity, but we're still patrolling the neighborhoods. And the regulars know what we look like. They won't do anything that stupid," Tinsley said. "So until this manhunt is over, none of us with a shield can rest easy."

"You have the OIO's full support," Jablonsky said. "We have agents monitoring every possible location that Jakov might visit, and we have teams at the airports, bus terminals, and roadblocks set up on the roads leading out of the city. He won't disappear. We'll find him."

"What about the soldiers that Shade hired?" Tinsley asked.

"Their records have been carefully examined, and Homeland is in charge of their interrogations," Lucca said. "Based on our latest update, Assistant Director Behr believes that roughly forty men were hired. From the casualties and arrests that occurred yesterday and that day on the off-ramp, it's possible we've eliminated the threat completely."

"They work in teams of four," I surmised. "Three to carry out the mission and one to coordinate from an op center. So maybe ten teams."

"What are you basing this on?" Tinsley asked.

"I know a private contractor that operates like that. It makes sense. Plus, there were three shooters trying to take out the police vehicle. Someone removed from the line of fire was controlling things from an outside location."

"It's speculation," Jablonsky said, "but we work with what we have."

She nodded. "Do what you can, and I'll do what I have to." She offered us a grim smile. "Thanks for helping out yesterday."

"Sure," Mark said, and I nodded.

After she left the room, Lucca cleared his throat. "There's nothing else we can do here." He focused on Mark. "What do we do next, sir?"

"How the hell should I know, kid?" Jablonsky shook his head and looked around. "Dammit." He picked up a chair and heaved it across the room. "We find that little shit, and we end this by any means necessary."

*　　*　　*

"You're home early," Martin greeted when I entered the kitchen. "After the men in black kidnapped you this morning, I wasn't sure I'd ever see you again." It didn't sound quite like a joke, but I managed a polite chuckle anyway. "Have you seen the news?"

"Uh-huh."

"That's why you turned off my phone last night." He put the spoon down that he was using to stir whatever he was cooking and reached for me. "Is everything okay? The reporters said it was a coordinated attack and there might be more."

"Yeah," I swallowed and looked up at him, "that sums it up." I wanted to cry, but I shoved my emotions down into the pit of my stomach. "What's for dinner?"

"A shrimp and rice dish. It's a variation on gumbo. Is that okay?"

"It's great," I stepped away from him, "but don't wait on my account. I have some stuff to do first."

The OIO was at a standstill. The city was on pins and needles, waiting for the danger to pass, and I had never felt more helpless in my entire life. Honestly, ever since my first encounter with the Horvats, I'd been feeling this way, and in the peace of the darkened bedroom, the thought that I'd been avoiding screamed through my psyche: *This is it. You're done. It's over.*

My chest felt tight, but I tried to ignore it. I couldn't eat. I couldn't sleep. I wanted it to go away. I wanted to feel something besides what I knew my late partner had felt. I remembered that day clearly. Carver had been shaken. After that close call, he never bounced back. He planned to resign from the OIO. If he had done it immediately, maybe he'd still be alive today. Instead, he waited, and things happened. God knows I blamed myself for it, but some asshole's booby-trap killed him. And deep in my soul, I felt like this job was going to claim me next.

"Alex?" Martin said, entering the bedroom several hours later. "Is it my birthday already?"

"Well, if you don't remember, that means you've gone senile."

Somewhere in the midst of my insanity, I'd slipped into the white and silver lingerie Martin had bought for some occasion or another. I had never worn it, like most of the slinky gifts he thought were romantic, but I needed my mind to turn off. And he could make that happen.

He crossed the room to me and brushed his lips against my neck. With one hand, he untied the sash on the silk kimono, and the other traced my cheekbone. Once the robe was open, his free hand slipped inside, gently caressing my side while his lips found mine.

"What are you doing hiding in the dark?" he murmured. His hand stopped on the bandage, and he pulled back, confused. "When did this happen?"

"It doesn't matter," I said, becoming agitated. "Focus on the rest."

"Well, you color coordinated to your bandage at least."

"Martin, stop." I tugged on the opened collar of his shirt, pulling him closer. Then my fingers went to work on the buttons and yanking the hem of his shirt free from his pants. This was a much harder feat with one arm in a cast. "C'mon, I'll make it worth your while. We can even do that thing you like. Come on. Please."

"Damn, I should have taken lessons from you on sexual harassment." He gently grabbed my hand and kissed the back of it to lessen the sting. "Tell me what's going on first. Then I'll do that thing that you like." He winked.

"You'd rather talk than have sex?"

"I'm screwed regardless of what I say."

"Apparently not." I folded my arms across my chest and turned my back to him, staring out the window. It had been several hours since I'd come home, but I'd accomplished nothing. "I've completely lost my mind. This was stupid."

"It's not stupid." He rubbed his hands along my shoulders. "I just like to know that you're okay before things heat up."

"I'm not okay," I snapped. I spun around to face him, and he stepped back. "I'm terrified." He looked dumbfounded and took a seat on the edge of the bed. Swallowing, I took a deep breath. "I'm not supposed to get scared, or rather, I'm not supposed to let it control my actions. We're trained, y'know, that no matter what, we have a responsibility to uphold the law. At times we're the only ones that can make a difference. Our lives don't matter."

"Alex—"

"No, it's true. That's how it is. We can't think of ourselves first. Our instinct for self-preservation has to come second to serving the greater good. So I can get scared, but I can't let it stop me from doing my job. But I've seen it happen before to a lot of agents. The smart ones get out. Hell, I don't even remember how many recruits left during training or within the first two years. Others get burnt out later. It happened to Michael."

"Your late partner?" Martin was doing his best to follow along, but my narrative wasn't exactly coherent.

I nodded. "He got spooked. Hell, the smart ones take private sector jobs, claiming that the pay bump is the real reason, but it isn't."

"You tried that yourself, but your OIO career turned into a revolving door. Are you telling me that you want to quit again? Because I don't care. You can do whatever. It doesn't matter. I'd just like it if you'd make up your mind and stick with it. We don't handle adjustment too well."

"Even if I wanted to, and I'm not saying that I do, I can't. Not now. I can't walk away. Lives are at stake. I'm just scared. I've been afraid since this began, and now, it's turned into a madman's vendetta to seek vengeance against the police. I can't let that happen. I couldn't let it happen to complete strangers, and I definitely can't sit back and do nothing when my friends are out there with targets on their backs. Think of O'Connell, Thompson, Heathcliff, and everyone else that we've met along the way. They could become victims. I can't just quit."

"I wasn't telling you to quit."

"I know. Everything's overwhelming me right now. Before you came up here, I was thinking of all the ways people can die. There are so many random acts of violence, and crimes of passion, cold-blooded murders, war, bombings, suicides, famine, drought, biological weapons, chemical warfare, viruses, bacteria, genetic issues, diseases, genocide, shark attacks, natural disasters, killer storms, asteroids."

"Okay, no more disaster movies for you."

"I'm serious. Anything could happen at any time. In fact, there are so many possibilities that I can't believe that any of us live for more than a few days at the rate things are going."

"Well, first things first, stay out of the ocean and away from aquariums, and you can mark shark attack off your list of fatal threats." He sat up a little straighter, sensing that the reason for my lunacy was due to recent events. "Sweetheart, tell me how you got that new gash on your side."

"I was inside the police station when forty hired mercenaries stormed the building. I'm okay." I batted his hand away. "But 155 cops aren't, and it's not fair. I was primary on the investigation, but it got jumbled and confused in my head. I didn't remember a lot of things. Even now, new details keep coming to light, but it's too late for them to help."

"It's not your fault," Martin said quietly.

"I know. For the first time in my life, I understand that. But that just means that I can't control any of this or stop anyone from doing something much worse. I can't stop a meteor or a shark either. I can't come up with a cure for an incurable disease or usher in world peace. It's useless. It's too big. Everything is too big. And I'm worried about what's going to happen, but even more than that, I can't shake the thought that I'm living on borrowed time, that I shouldn't have survived that evening in the restaurant." A bitter laugh escaped my lips. "And to top it off, the voice inside my head keeps telling me that my own well-being should be at the bottom of this damn list."

"Well, it's at the top of mine." His voice was stern, and he pulled me onto the bed and into his arms. "Listen very carefully to what I'm about to say. Shit happens. It's out of our control, and we have two choices. We can fight against it, or we can let it steamroll us. Fighting against it doesn't mean we'll win, but we have to try. You're a fighter, so you fight."

"I know. Like I said, this is stupid. I'm being stupid."

"No, you're not." He hugged me tighter. "I've said it before, but I want you to really hear the words this time. I will do everything in my power to move heaven and earth for you, or I'll storm through the gates of hell. If you lose your will to fight, then by god, I'll fight for you."

"Martin, shut up and kiss me."

THIRTY-EIGHT

It was early. Too early for the sun to be up, but I was. Staring out the window, I couldn't see past my own reflection in the glass, but I wasn't looking for anything. I wasn't sure what to do. During a brief period of sleep, I'd dreamt of the SUV and Jakov Horvat. Martin had said a lot of passionate things to reassure me, and they weren't empty promises in order to win my love. He already had it. But Jakov wanted to win his brother's love, so whatever he was willing to do would be extreme. Initially, I'd considered that he'd attempt a prison break, killing all law enforcement officers that were in the vicinity of Niko's incarceration, but Niko was off the grid. He was being held at a black site that I had visited and didn't even know the location of. That wasn't feasible, so what else could be Jakov's grand gesture?

"Come back to bed," Martin whispered, propping himself up on his elbows.

"I shouldn't. It feels like a waste of time. Everything I've been doing is nothing but a huge waste of precious time." But despite my words, I knew sleep would improve my cognitive function and possibly my mood. I took a few steps closer to the bed, and he grabbed my arm and pulled me against him.

"Then let's stop wasting time." He kissed the top of my head as I settled into the cozy spot against his chest. "Marry me, Alexis."

"Okay," I replied, too fried to say anything else or think too much about the words and what they entailed.

He didn't say anything else either. Instead, he rubbed random patterns against my shoulder blade while I drifted back to sleep.

* * *

"We have another sighting," Lawson said. "Bravo team's the closest."

"Notify them," Jablonsky said. "I'll get on the horn and see if anyone else is nearby. This bastard isn't giving us the slip again."

Within the last eighteen hours, the city's CCTV feed picked up Jakov Horvat three different times. By the time a team was dispatched to his first location, he was long gone. The second sighting was soon after, but he eluded us again by jumping into a cab amid the sea of taxis during morning rush hour. This was our third hit. They were coming more frequently because Lawson was doing a superb job of tracking the footage in the vicinity in which Jakov was traveling.

"Parker, figure out his target," Jablonsky ordered.

Quickly, I crossed the op center and pulled up the maps. Lucca was at the computer with the three-dimensional rendering of the city grid, including the subway lines, streets, and walking paths. He scooted his chair slightly to give me access.

"I don't see anything," he said. "He's not near any police or government buildings. No landmarks or historic sites in close proximity."

"What about restaurants?" I asked. Digging through the intel, I found the list of delivery sites from the trucking company. "He'll need to gear up before he can carry out his plan." The nervous energy coursed through me. "If we can stop him before that, we can end this without any more casualties."

"That doesn't make sense," Lucca said, even as he began marking the deliveries on the map. "The news outlets are still reporting on the precinct under siege. Everyone knows that the weapons and the men hired to carry out the massacre are in custody."

"Then we missed something else. Maybe there's a fourth location. We need to determine the weight differential on the cargo plane. They dumped something out the back, and we've been functioning under the assumption that it's the crates of guns. If the weight of all of that doesn't explain the sudden lightness when the plane landed, then we missed something."

"You'd have to account for fuel usage too," Lucca said. "I don't know that the records would help. It's not like a weigh station for trucks."

Pushing away from the screen, he crossed the room to ask about something while I searched through the data that the FAA had sent over. Unfortunately, he was right. While there were calculations and logs indicating the weight at takeoff to ensure balance and adequate fuel, nothing was recorded upon landing.

"What about the crew?" I asked, continuing to search through the paperwork. Unfortunately, the crew manifest was full of fictitious people, and we never managed to track down anyone involved in the cargo drop. "Dammit."

"Hey," Lucca said, reclaiming his chair and adding more highlighted areas to the map, "this was the location where Donaldson's body and that CI were found." It was close to Jakov's last known location. "He might have a hideout nearby."

"They ditched the SUV. They probably wanted to lie low until the coast was clear. Let's check it out," I said, scribbling the information on a piece of paper and handing it to Jablonsky. He read it, nodding approval while waiting for some other agency to verify that they had a team in pursuit of Jakov.

"Do you remember if there was anything in the vehicle?" Lucca asked as we made our way to the garage.

"No, I don't remember any biohazard or radiation

warnings on anything," I retorted. "Honestly, aside from the dome light and the door handle, I have the briefest recollection of a plastic-wrapped corpse, but that's it."

"After murdering two men and abducting a federal agent, the Horvats must have been smart enough to know that Pepper was compromised. If there was anything particularly useful or valuable on the premises, they would have taken it with them. And if it was large enough, they'd have to stow it somewhere safe until they could go back for it. It's not like they could walk onto a city bus with a RPG over their shoulder."

"Didn't the police search the area?" I asked.

"Yeah, but they were looking for evidence and clues on the murders. They found you." He jerked his chin at the glove box. "Grab that map and make a grid. We'll start a search. Let's just hope we find it before Jakov does."

"Hell, I'd be happy finding Jakov first," I said. Giving Lucca a sideways glance, I asked, "Do you think we're actually on to something?"

"We have to be. There aren't any other rocks left to overturn."

Arriving near the former crime scene, Lucca parked the car and cautiously stepped outside. The area was deserted. It was near the waterfront, but the ground was rocky and polluted. It wasn't a picturesque scene. It's where dope dealers and street-walkers perfected their craft and where runaways came to disappear. It was a shitty spot to leave a SUV.

"How come no one jacked the vehicle?" I wondered.

"It was gutted. It wasn't going anywhere." He shrugged. "Hell, maybe it didn't start out that way." He set off in a direction, and I followed, keeping my head on a swivel for signs of Jakov or anything amiss.

After searching four of the squares on the artificially created grid, we hadn't found anything of use. Lucca was on the phone with the original police crime scene investigators, asking what had been in the vicinity at the time. They'd forwarded photos to his phone, but the place looked about the same.

"I got something," I said, pointing to a large, rusted

dumpster near the edge of our search area. Sprinting over to it, the first thing I noticed was the new steel lock. Why would an old rusted dumpster have a shiny new lock? "Do you want to shoot it off, or do you have bolt cutters in the car?"

"Lock picks would be easier, Annie Oakley," Lucca said. He scanned our surroundings while he patted down his pockets. "You didn't happen to bring a set, did you?"

"Yeah, I shoved 'em up my cast." I glared at him. "Dammit, boy scout, the one time that I needed you to be prepared."

"I left them in the car. Just stay out of sight, and keep your eyes peeled for Jakov. If you spot him, call for back-up before you make an approach."

"Yes, sir." The sarcastic tone earned a glare before Lucca double-timed it back to the car.

The dumpster was probably half a mile from our original location, so it shouldn't take Lucca more than six or seven minutes to get there and back. In the meantime, I examined the exterior of the nearest building. It was old with no windows facing this way. A single steel door stood at the corner, but it was also locked. This wasn't the best place for hiding spots.

The next nearest building had a basement, and I glanced down the exterior steps. At the bottom were two, dirty, half-asleep teenagers, probably runaways or junkies. They didn't look like they were in any condition to make a move, so I cautiously crouched down at the top of the steps to wait.

"Whatcha doing," the girl asked. "You getting out of the rain?"

"Yeah," I said, glancing at the sky which was clear. "Storm's pretty bad."

"Shit, I know," she said. "I always come here to get out of the rain." She leaned her head back, closing her eyes. "Do you think it'll pass soon?"

"Maybe." I glanced back at the two of them. Her junkie boyfriend or john, whatever he might be, was pawing at her, and she was giggling. "Do you guys hang around here a lot?"

"What's a lot?" he asked, eyeing me. "Are you a cop? If you're a cop, you have to tell us. That's the law."

That was the dumbest thing I'd ever heard, but it had filtered through our culture and media so much that I suspected everyone believed it. Morons. "I'm definitely not a cop. I just got picked up two weeks ago."

"You working or buying?" the guy asked. "Because I can hook you up, baby. I'll set you up with some coke for a little three-way action." He waggled an eyebrow and stared with glassy eyes at me. "You look like you're in need of a pick-me-up." Finally, he noticed my attire. "You normally buy on the northside, right? That's where you corporate types feel safe, but we ain't scary over here."

"Really? Weren't two people killed like right around the corner a few weeks ago?"

"Nah, they arrived that way. Those weird dudes did them in before dumping 'em, but they haven't been around much since." He stood up and moved up the stairs until his crotch was at eye level. "A blow for some blow?"

"Tempting. Can I see it first?"

"Whatcha wanna see?" He smiled through heavy lids. With one hand, he reached into his pocket and pulled out a dime bag, and with the other, he grabbed himself.

"Impressive," I scanned the area, but there were no signs of Jakov or Lucca yet, "you just tried to solicit sex and sell narcotics to a federal agent. Now sit your ass back down there." I shoved him backward. There weren't that many steps, and he fell back, making an oomph sound when his body hit against the brick wall at the bottom. "I have a couple of questions. As long as you answer them, I'm willing to forget this ever happened."

"But you said you weren't a cop," the girl said. "You lied."

"Lady, I hate to break it to you, but it's not raining either," I replied, going down the steps. Doing a quick frisk, I took a revolver out of his ankle holster, and I found a knife beneath the blanket they were using for things I didn't want to think about. Other than that, they were clean. On closer inspection, they were probably in their late teens. Runaways most likely trying to eke out a living through whatever means they had available to them. "So you remember the SUV and the weird foreigners that abandoned it. Do you remember if they had anything with them, like a package or a gun?"

"I'm not telling you shit," he said. "This is extortion and entrapment."

"Those are big words. Do you even know what they mean?"

"They mean I'm not telling you shit," he repeated.

"Those guys are dangerous. Have you seen the news lately? They keep mentioning terrorists and a reward for any information that could help the police find them."

"They're terrorists?" the girl asked, her mouth dropping open. "OMG, he stuck something big into that dumpster across the street. Is it a bomb? Oh my god, I don't wanna die."

"Babe, you're not gonna die. This is bullshit. This bitch is just trying to shake us down. I bet she's not even a cop. She probably works for Sal and was hoping to find out where my dealer keeps his stash. I've seen him use his girls to get that information out of other guys before." He was growing increasingly more brazen. "I can take her."

He stood up again, bent over like a bull, and charged. In the narrow staircase, I didn't have much room to maneuver, barely managing to turn sideways to keep from taking the full brunt of his momentum in the stomach. He knocked me backward into the rail and hit me hard in the side. He tried to race up the stairs to escape, but I grabbed his pants leg with my good hand, tripping him.

Once he was down, I grabbed his wrist and twisted his arm behind his back. The girl let out a scream, and Lucca appeared at the top of the stairs with his gun pointed at us. Ignoring my partner, I tightened my grip, wishing that I had my other hand free to secure the guy's other wrist.

"Federal agents," Lucca announced, slowly coming down the stairs. "Stay on the ground. My partner is going to let go of you, and when she does, I want you to slowly put your hands on top of your head. Do it now."

"Thanks," I said, stepping back, so he could cuff the guy. "I'll call for the police to pick them up."

"Didn't I tell you to find somewhere quiet to hide?" Lucca asked.

"You did, but there aren't many options, and the one I found was occupied." I looked back at the girl. "Look, if you tell us everything you remember, we'll let you scram before the cops get here. What else do you remember about the two men and what they were carrying?"

"I don't know," she hesitated. "It was dark that night, and they were arguing about some girl that got away. The one in charge blamed the other one, or I think there were two. They looked exactly alike. Maybe it was one guy talking to himself." She shook her head. "Anyway, he had this like duffel bag thing. It had wheels like the stuff people use at the airport, but he carried it."

"How big was it?" Lucca asked. "Like the size of a backpack?"

"No, it was more like a refrigerator."

"A refrigerator," Lucca repeated, giving me a skeptical look. "That's really helpful. How could some guy carry a refrigerator?"

"It wasn't a fridge. It was the size of a fridge. Y'know, those little ones. I had one in my dorm before I dropped out." She sniffed, either from the cocaine or because she was growing nostalgic. "He tossed it in that trash thing." She pointed toward the top of the stairs. "I saw him come by again to check on it. He took something out and left." She sniffed again. "I got curious, so me and Xander went to check it out, but it was locked tight. We was gonna crack it open, but that seemed like too much trouble."

"And this is Xander?" Lucca asked, nudging the cuffed guy.

"What's it to you?" Xander growled. "We didn't do anything wrong. She didn't tell us she was a cop. She has to do that. If not, it doesn't count."

"Did you hear that, Parker?" Lucca smiled. "It doesn't count."

"When's the last time you spotted the terrorist guy?" I asked, trying to keep the questions simple.

"Two days ago, I think. He hasn't been back since," she said.

"What about you, Xander? When did you see the guy last?" Lucca asked.

"Two days ago. We were down here when he came by. We heard the dumpster lid slam, which is why we noticed him," Xander said, struggling against the cuffs. "C'mon, man, this is bogus, and we all know it. Just cut me free."

"If I do, the two of you need to clear out of here," Lucca said. "Is that understood?"

"Yes, sir," the girl said. "I don't want to stick around and get blown up by a big bomb."

"Did you see a bomb?" I asked, distracting them while Lucca sent word to the police department to send someone to pick up our eyewitnesses.

"No, just the duffle thing with the wheels. It was the size of those little fridges." She gasped suddenly. "Could that be a bomb?"

"We'll check it out, but you should clear out. I'll tell you what, we'll have someone come and make sure you weren't exposed to any harmful materials before you go," I promised.

As soon as the undercover officers arrived, I stepped out of the alcove and briefed them on the situation. Quietly, they went down the stairs and removed the two runaways. Lucca looked at me and shook his head. He then sent another few text messages, stowed his phone, and sighed heavily.

"That stunt could have cost us," he said.

"I know, but they were here. I had to find out if they knew anything. What if they knew what he was planning or where he hid it? We couldn't let that opportunity pass us by."

"It was a gamble." He glanced at his phone again. "Do you think we need to call the bomb squad or hazmat to check it out? That would be protocol."

"It won't be quiet, and if Jakov spots them, he'll definitely go to ground. We can't risk it. Do you concur?"

"Yeah, I'll go check it out. You stay here."

"No, we both go."

After several tense minutes of carefully assessing the entire dumpster, removing the lock, and slowly lifting the lid, we found the large crate that was bungee-corded to a luggage cart. The crate was opened, so we had no way of knowing what might be missing. Lucca slipped on a pair of gloves and slowly sifted the contents around. Inside were dozens of photos, maps, and schematics for something.

"We'll need the lab to verify, but I think I know his next target," Lucca said, holding up a photograph.

THIRTY-NINE

"This better not go sideways," Lt. Tinsley said. "What's happened to my precinct is bad enough. The entire city's practically on lockdown. We're afraid, and everyone else is too. I can't imagine how much worse it'll get if you fuck this up."

"We won't," Jablonsky said. "Behr's verified our intel as accurate. Everything we have points to total dissolution of the hired mercenaries. Our cybercrime team has been monitoring the communications, and everything's quiet. Jakov's on his own, and there are a lot more of us."

"There better not be any surprises," Tinsley warned. She blew out a breath. "I'll pass word along about our radio communication. We're on cell phones until Jakov's been taken down." She walked to the conference room door, turned, took two steps back, opened her mouth as if to say something, shook her head, and went back out the door.

"You heard the lady," Jablonsky said. "We can't screw up. All eyes are on us. If the news outlets get a whiff of a memorial, they'll come out in droves. The commissioner and a stand-in for the mayor will be there. This is a huge event. It's precisely what Jakov wants, so we're giving it to him. Just remember what the stakes are."

He took a moment to look at each of us. Every available agent and team was tasked with monitoring a specific area. HRT would be stationed at various points, prepared to deliver a death shot if the situation warranted it. Jakov brought the fight to us, and by god, we were going to win.

"Who else is in play?" the HRT commander asked.

"Homeland's coordinating the rest, but there will be a lot of federal agencies on-site. Everyone's in plainclothes. We aren't showing off our Kevlar. Vests underneath your jackets, people. And keep your eyes peeled. I want everyone going home tonight, understood?" A round of ayes and affirmatives went through the room. "All right, let's stop this asshole."

I gave the maps another glance. I felt just as able-bodied as my fellow agents, but Jablonsky wanted me benched inside. The last time I'd been left to coordinate, things had gone horribly wrong. I didn't want to be here, and I nudged Lucca with my elbow.

"Parker, we found what he was hiding. We have the photographs and maps. Jakov Horvat knew precisely what the PD would do to honor one of their fallen. He plans to make a mockery of the funeral procession, so we're throwing him off his game by blowing it way out of proportion."

"Wouldn't someone inside Shade have assumed that there would be a city-wide memorial service after they decimated the largest precinct we have?" I asked.

"Contingencies," Lucca surmised. "They didn't count on you and Donaldson showing up at Pepper and wrecking the plan. The Horvats must have figured that their plan was wrecked, so they moved on to plan B. Step one, kill the bitch that escaped. Step two, make a large show with disposable soldiers. And step three, convince the cops they won, wait for the funeral, and blow them all to kingdom come."

"There's no indication Jakov has a bomb. Hazmat checked that dumpster, so did the bomb squad and the dogs. We even checked the three restaurants and the trucks. No bomb-making materials to report," I argued.

"Parker, I wasn't being literal." He patted my shoulder.

"I get it. We're all on edge. The intel suggests heavy artillery. It goes along with what we already know, and the CIA located the weapons dealer and has him detained. So far, the only weapon unaccounted for is a PKM and plenty of extra rounds. It stands to reason that is Jakov's intended method of delivery."

"And a shooting spree in a densely populated area by a lunatic with a machine gun is supposed to make me feel better?" I asked. "Why in the world did we encourage this memorial service?"

"We have to lure him out. This is new. It's happening too fast, and he'll be unprepared. That's how we'll stop him," Lucca said.

It wasn't the actual memorial service. It was a ploy that the police department planned in order to trap Jakov in a secluded area. A number of brave men and women volunteered to be decoys while the rest of us diligently worked to locate and apprehend Jakov Horvat. Since this was such a grandiose gesture, the police commissioner agreed to partake. He wasn't one to hide in his ivory tower while his people were massacred, and Assistant Director Behr had found a lookalike for the mayor.

As part of the plan, we hoped to get Niko talking by showing him some doctored news coverage of a massacre at a police funeral. Unfortunately, the bastard did nothing but smile and cheer. Agents were working around the clock to break him for information on how Shade planned the massacre, but Niko wouldn't talk. I suspected that our phony footage didn't convince him of anything since the psychological profile indicated that he'd take the opportunity to gloat. Behr should have thought about that before sending Mark and me to convince Niko that Shade's prior attempt at the precinct had failed. Shame on us for attempting to fool him twice.

"I'm going," Jablonsky declared. "Keep your eyes peeled. The second you spot him, I want a team surrounding his location."

"Yes, sir," Lucca and I said simultaneously.

As the calls came in, Lucca marked the location of our teams. The fake ceremony would be a procession from the precinct to the cemetery. The photos we'd found inside the dumpster were of other police memorials and the location of the gravestones and vantage points behind trees. Based on the data we had, Jakov would slip into the cemetery once the procession arrived and open fire. He was smart enough to know that the area would be scouted ahead of time, so he wouldn't be able to lie in wait.

The road leading from the precinct to the cemetery could be used to target the cops, but without the help of his hired team of assassins, it wasn't feasible for a single gunman to do vast amounts of damage to speeding vehicles. He would have to wait for the cops to be left unprotected. Just in case, we had agents on foot and in vehicles on both sides of the street, on the side roads, and around the cemetery. This time, Jakov wouldn't catch us unprepared.

"Bravo team's checked in," Lucca announced, lighting up another patch of ground that we were covering. "Charlie and Echo are go. Did you field a call from Delta team?"

"No, Tango and Foxtrot," I said. "Should there be this many unaccounted for?" I looked at the screen. Nearly a quarter of the map hadn't had any reported check-ins. "Something's up. What team was Cooper assigned?"

"Alpha," Lucca replied. "He and Jablonsky both." Picking up the phone, he dialed Agent Cooper. "Let me see what's taking them so long." After almost two minutes, Lucca put the phone down. "That's odd."

"I'll see if I can raise Mark." Using my cell phone instead of the office phone, just in case we had a circuit jam, I hit my speed dial and waited.

After three rings, he answered, "I'm on my way. Anything to report, Parker?"

"I don't know." I squinted at the computer screen. "We're waiting on quite a few teams to verify their locations. Do you have eyes on the area?"

"Not yet. I'm about five minutes out from the rendezvous point. Our agents along the way are in place. No signs of Jakov or a shooter. Everything appears normal," Jablonsky continued. "Have you tried calling them?"

"Lucca tried raising Alpha team, but we had no love," I said.

"Contact the closest sniper team and see if they have a visual," Jablonsky ordered.

I passed word along to Lucca who started dialing while Mark waited patiently on the other end of the line. Once the call was answered, Lucca asked the question. Turning, he gave me a thumbs up, and I relayed the news to Jablonsky.

"It could be a communication problem," Jablonsky said. "I'm almost there. I'll see what's wha—" The line crackled and cut out. Glancing at the dropped call message on my screen, I double-checked the map. A second later, my phone rang. "Sorry, I must have hit a dead zone. Breathe, Parker. You haven't even said a word, but I can tell you're panicking."

"I'm fine."

"It's probably all this damn granite and tree cover interfering with the cell signals. I'm going to check in with each team, and then I'll check back with you. If anything happens, contact HRT. They're our eye in the sky." Mark disconnected, but that annoying itch was scratching at the corners of my mind.

"What is it?" Lucca asked.

"We're having communication trouble." I narrowed my eyes. "How'd you know they were using a cell jammer on the off-ramp?"

"My GPS cut out, and I had no signal on my phone." Lucca looked worried. "I'll get HRT to investigate."

"It'll blow our cover. We can't have them move out of position."

"So you want our people to be sitting ducks instead? What choice do we have?" Lucca picked up the phone and began dialing. Reaching over, I put my finger on the hook. "Move your hand, or your casts will be symmetrical."

"Jablonsky said it might be a dead zone. He's going to check in with the teams. If we start moving too many people around, Jakov will know something's wrong. Since we haven't spotted our terrorist yet, we can't spook him before he arrives, or he'll give us the slip again. I'll go check it out."

"You have orders to stay here."

"I don't care. I'm going. Give me ten minutes. If you don't hear from me or Jablonsky when time's up, call HRT." I checked the clip in my side arm, struggling to make sure a round was chambered. "Ten minutes."

"How the hell are you going to get there in ten minutes? It took the rest of our teams nearly three times that long."

"I'll take a shortcut. Seriously, Lucca, ten minutes."

He sighed. "Go. The clock's ticking, but I don't support this decision. And you damn well better come back because I'm documenting this in my report."

Racing down the stairs, I burst out the front door of the federal building and hailed a cab. I'd been forced to navigate this city in the pouring rain while barred from normal methods of transportation, so I'd picked up a trick or two. Telling the driver to get me as close to the park as possible, I impatiently waited in the back until the car came to a stop.

Without bothering to pay the man, I opened the back door and ran through the streets, into the park, dodging the strollers and dogwalkers while I beelined away from the path. Checking the GPS on my phone which had a point amidst a large beige blob, I kept moving. Eventually, I hit street again, crossing quickly, until I found more wooded areas. By the time I made it to the iron fence, I was too winded to speak.

Placing my palms against my thighs, I bent over, hoping oxygen would make it to my brain before I passed out. Thankfully, the black bubbles cleared from my vision, and I dialed Lucca.

"Can you hear me now?" I asked through deep inhales.

"Where the hell are you?"

"Outside the cemetery. I'll go around the side and edge over to the dead zone. Have you heard from Jablonsky or any of our unreported teams yet?"

"Jablonsky phoned. He's made about half the rounds so far. Everything looks in order. You've been told to return immediately to the federal building."

"Yeah, fine." I continued walking the outer perimeter of

the fence. Snipers were positioned inside the mausoleum and on the roofs of surrounding buildings. There was a good chance that a sight was focused on me at the moment, but I didn't think I'd be confused with Jakov Horvat. "I just want to check one other thing, and then I'm gone."

"Now, Parker."

"Damn, your impression of Mark is really good. You should do that at the next office party. It'd be a hit."

As soon as I found the side entrance that the groundskeepers used, I pushed the gate open and ducked inside. In front of me was a stretch of perfectly aligned headstones with some random trees and shrubbery dispersed throughout. A few paths and stone benches littered the otherwise green expanse. As if fear of my own mortality hadn't been commanding enough attention lately, this otherwise serene scene threatened to wreck my already bruised psyche.

"Hey, Eddie," I said, my voice barely above a whisper, "in the event something unforeseen happens, will you do me a favor and make sure someone tells Martin that I'm sorry we wasted so much time?"

"Parker, what's wrong? What's going on?" Lucca sounded overly concerned.

"Nothing." I scanned the area again, seeing a cluster of 'mourners' in the distance. On both sides were a large scattering of undercover agents. "Everyone looks like they're in place on the ground. No sign of the commissioner or the mayor yet, so I'm guessing that Jakov is waiting for them before he moves in."

"From the Horvat file, I'm sure that R.J. Cook must be a named target, so Jakov won't risk exposure until Cook's on scene. The appearance of the commissioner's car will probably signify the beginning of the assault."

"Is Cook going to be here?"

"No, we found a decent body double. Mr. Cook is actually in protective custody until this is over," Lucca said condescendingly. "Weren't you listening during the briefing?"

"I must have missed that part."

"Parker, stop stalling and get your ass back here."

"Did we check the groundskeeper's building?" I asked, suddenly spotting a tiny shed positioned off to the side, secluded from the rest of the cemetery by a few tall trees that blocked it from view of the gravesite.

"HRT did a brief sweep before our teams began arriving but found nothing. DHS scouted it prior to that and determined that it provided no vantage point and wasn't in close enough proximity to be used for effective implementation of incendiary devices. Three-quarters of the building is made out of cinderblock. It was cheap construction with thick enough walls to insulate a blast from spreading."

"But it would be a great place to hide a cell jammer. I'm gonna check it out." I started moving toward the building, and a burst of static shot through my earpiece.

"Say again, Parker." The message came over garbled, just barely decipherable.

"Shit, Lucca," I moved quickly toward the door, "the procession just cleared the front gate. Do you copy?"

The call disconnected, but I didn't have the time to backtrack and phone again. Stuffing the phone in my pocket, I hurried to the door, glancing skyward. The trees surrounding the side of the building kept it from our sniper's view, and there were no buildings near this side of the cemetery that would provide perches for our sniper teams. This would be where I'd stage my attack if I were Jakov Horvat.

Tightening my grip on my gun, I reached out with my casted arm and pulled the door open. The place was little more than a storage shed with a few shovels, some flower holders, and random tools piled along the sides. The floor was made of dirt and covered in dead grass and leaves. Entering, I didn't spot anyone inside, and there weren't any visible places to hide. Perhaps I was paranoid.

Deciding that the room was clear, I tucked my gun into my holster and checked my phone. No signal. A large toolbox sat on a workbench along the back wall. It would be large enough to hold a cell jammer and could have been missed by our teams who were scanning for explosives and weapons. Opening the lid, I found the tiny electronic device hidden inside an old candy bar wrapper. How the hell did it get in here? Turning it off, I picked up my phone and dialed Jablonsky.

"Horvat's already here," I said. "I'm in the shed." I fell silent, hearing a creak. Placing my phone on the table, I pulled my gun just in time to see the end of a machine gun poke out of the ground.

It looked like the earth had cracked, and it took a moment before I realized that a metal hatch was hidden beneath the dirt and dead foliage. Jakov Horvat didn't fire. Frankly, I wasn't positive why he didn't until he cleared the small staircase from the underground storage unit. Strapped to his chest was a bomb vest. He had thought of everything. He knew we wouldn't risk firing upon him for fear of detonating the C4. I didn't see a trigger, but that didn't mean it wasn't there.

Aiming at his head, I wasn't convinced that my left-handed shot was good enough to take him out with one bullet before he opened fire or detonated the bomb, so I held back. He eyed me, recognition dawning on his face.

"I know you," he said. "You were inside Pepper with that cop and his snitch. I was supposed to shoot you, but you jumped out of a moving car." He cocked his head sideways. "That should have killed you. Then the PMCs we hired should have killed you."

"Why did you hire PMCs?" I asked, hoping to distract him. "I thought you and Niko hated the military for what happened to your family."

"I hate *your* soldiers. The peacekeepers," he sneered, "they destroyed."

"What's the difference?"

"Why do you care?" He narrowed his eyes, sensing this was a trap. "You won't be around long enough to tell anyone anyway."

"They were former Soviet soldiers. Just like that shitty weapon you're holding. Are those C4 bricks also from the Cold War?"

"Shut your mouth."

I knew the line on my phone was open; I just didn't know if Mark could hear me. I had to say as much as I could. Don't focus on the consequences, Parker. I let out a sigh.

"Well, that's a relief. They probably won't even explode. And that hunk of junk, it's probably too rusted to fire."

"Let's find out," Jakov said. His finger tensed over the trigger, and I centered my shot.

"You'll be dead too, and what will that accomplish? Your brother, Niko, is in custody. Shade and the rest of your terrorist friends have been eliminated. What's the point? No one's left."

"I'm setting things right." He studied my posture and aim. "Now lower your weapon."

"Why? You're going to kill me. I thought I'd return the favor."

"This vest will be triggered if my heart stops beating." He held up his wrist which had a heart monitor and some wires attached to it. "There's enough explosive to take out the entire funeral."

"Isn't that your plan with the big gun?"

"I want to destroy the police. The family is innocent. I'll let them go. It's up to the peacekeepers to allow them to flee. We shall see what they do." His rationale was twisted. He'd take out as many as he could but assumed that the officers would kill him, thus killing everyone else. In his mind, the fatalities would be due to police action and not his fault. "The rest will suffer." He stared at me. "You will suffer."

"Funny, Niko told me the same thing. Your brother's an asshole. I can see the family resemblance."

"Silence."

My words hit a nerve. He pulled the trigger but didn't expect the recoil from the automatic weapon. It fired wildly, hitting high, and spraying the entire back wall while I hit the floor. Suddenly, the door burst open.

"Don't shoot," I yelled over the gunfire. "He has a bomb. It'll detonate if he dies. Clear the area." The tactical unit and Jablonsky immediately pulled back, but their appearance didn't go unnoticed.

The gunfire stopped, and Jakov smiled at the damage he'd done. He announced something in his native tongue, which I could only imagine must have meant something like "this will be fun" and turned toward the now closed door. He planned on using my team for his target practice.

"Yo, Fuckoff," I growled, pulling myself off the ground, "don't you want to stay and chat some more? Maybe you need to reload. You're probably empty by now." He didn't even turn around, muttering that I had wasted enough of his time. "Come on, you said you wanted to make me suffer. So do it. Or aren't you man enough? Your brother was too much of a chicken shit to murder a woman because he was too busy crying over your dead mother."

"Do not speak of them," he screamed, spinning around to face me. This time, I knew he wouldn't miss.

"Fuck you." Pulling the trigger, I hoped that enough of the area had been cleared. It'd only been a few seconds since I told the team to clear out, but Mark had been monitoring my call the entire time. With any luck, the loss of life would be at a minimum. Jakov fell to the ground, his gun firing a random, nonstop spray behind him as his muscles tensed and the last of his synapses fired.

This was it. I shut my eyes. Unlike my partner, I knew the explosion was coming. It wouldn't be a surprise. My eyes filled with tears, and I thought about the night before with Martin. Our last night.

FORTY

Mark was the first one through the door when the gunfire stopped. Two members of HRT and a bomb expert were at his heels. The PKM was taken from Jakov's dead hands. The bomb expert was analyzing the vest, wondering why it hadn't detonated yet. Jablonsky grabbed me in a bear hug and dragged me out of the shed and away from the crisis zone.

It took Mark nearly an hour to calm me down. The hysterical sobs were the least professional thing that I'd ever done, but I couldn't stop. I wasn't dead. The vest had been a ploy. The C4 had been bricks of clay, and the wires connected to the heart rate monitor were nothing but decoration. The PKM machine gun was real and so were the hundred rounds fired inside that shed. Surprisingly, none of them hit me, but three of the tactical team that had been outside preparing to breach had taken stray fire after I killed Jakov. None of the injuries were life-threatening, but from the way I acted, an onlooker might have thought everyone had been slaughtered.

Assistant Director Behr, dozens of Homeland Security agents, ATF agents, and every other federal law enforcement agency were on-site, scouring the cemetery for evidence, additional weapons, and anything that might be of use. The police department was present in full force, and Lt. Tinsley was coordinating a grid by grid search to make sure we didn't miss anything.

Lucca arrived to escort me back to the office where I was debriefed by Director Kendall and left to write my after action report and incident report. It wasn't pretty, particularly the obvious refusal to obey orders. But it was done, and the consequences be damned. I didn't care what they were. I didn't care if my presence at the cemetery was appropriate or warranted. I knew the shooting was justified. Given the intel I had at the time, I didn't see any other choice, and I said as much to Kendall and in my reports.

"How are the three men from HRT that got hit?" I asked when Lucca reappeared at his desk a few hours later.

"They'll live. Harmon's gonna be on crutches for a while, but the other two should be back at work tomorrow." He looked around the room. "You're insane. You could have gotten yourself and everyone else killed. What the hell were you thinking?"

"That I didn't want to die."

"You have a funny way of showing it. Why did you open fire? You didn't know the bomb was a decoy."

I blinked hard, hoping to keep it together. "They didn't deserve to die." I swallowed. "The cops who volunteered to be machine gun fodder and our colleagues that had no choice but to try to stop this, none of them deserved to die."

"God, you have the worst martyr complex I've ever seen." Lucca shook his head. "No wonder you have that damn commendation on your record and they let you come back to work after all the shit you've done. It's ridiculous. You have a problem."

I nodded. "I can't do this anymore, Eddie. I didn't want to. I swore that I was done, but I got dragged back. And I'm not even sure how or why. It just happened." A stray tear fell, and I wiped my cheek with the back of my hand and laughed. "I'm a fucking mess. Completely unstable. Write that in your report. Write all of this in your report. Put me out of my misery. Please, Lucca. You keep saying you don't want to work with me. You don't trust being in the field with me, so get rid of me. Help me get out of here."

"Alex," he looked around the bullpen, seeing far too many people standing by, "come on, you don't mean that. I didn't mean that. We need a minute in private."

"Are you going to snuff me out?"

"Don't tempt me." He led me down the hall and into Jablonsky's empty office. Mark had left the door unlocked, so Lucca ducked inside and closed the door behind me. "It's time you know what's really going on." He cleared his throat. "What I'm about to say can't leave this room. Only Director Kendall and SSA Jablonsky are aware of what's been happening. It's the reason we're partnered together. You've never liked working with me. We've had our differences and spats, but I trust you. The reason I voiced concern to Jablonsky was more for your safety than mine." Lucca licked his lips and looked around the office "Do you remember why you were reinstated?"

"Because there had been a data breach and undercover agents had been compromised."

"The security breach goes beyond a computer hack. I was planted at the OIO to investigate the breach, and within my first two months of being here, it became apparent that there's a mole. I don't know who it is, but sensitive information has been going missing. Evidence has been compromised. A few cases have crumbled. Witnesses have disappeared. It's bad. Frankly, you're the only one here that I can trust."

"What makes me so special?" I asked, wondering if this was some elaborate tale to jerk me out of my pleas for help escaping this job.

"You weren't here when this occurred. You had retired or went on sabbatical or whatever the fuck it is you were doing for two years. Hell, none of this even happened until after your last consulting gig ended. You're clean, and you have an airtight alibi."

"Because I wasn't here?"

"Pretty much."

"So this has nothing to do with me. I shouldn't be here. Everything about today made that abundantly obvious. You wanted to have me reprimanded, so do it. Don't chicken out just because you think you need an ally in your mission to find a mole."

"Parker, I think the leak is the reason the police transport you were on was attacked. Hell, at first, I thought it was the reason for Donaldson's murder and your near miss, but you never filed a FD-209 to say you were meeting with an unofficial criminal informant."

"That's why you've been acting so strange this entire time?"

"I hoped that we'd flush him out, but it didn't work." Lucca sighed. "I never meant to give you the impression that I didn't have your back or that I posed a danger to you."

"Just a danger to my career."

"You do that to yourself," Lucca said. "You're reckless, just like today. Why? What makes you think that you deserve to die?"

I didn't say anything, but Lucca was determined to wait me out. Finally, the door opened, and Jablonsky stepped inside. He gave us both a look, asked if our reports were completed, and kicked Lucca out.

"Parker, are you out of your fucking mind?" Jablonsky growled. "I just came from Kendall's office. As of this moment, you are on medical leave. Following that, you'll be suspended for two weeks, pending an internal review."

"Why don't you make it a month?" I retorted.

"If you mouth off again, I will." He glared at me. "Zip it. It's also been mentioned, that there will likely be an award for bravery added to your file for your actions today. Your asinine, suicidal, insubordinate actions."

"Permission to speak freely?" I hated when Jablonsky turned into a hard ass.

"Denied." He leaned back in his chair. "If I so much as catch a glimpse of you anywhere near this building, I will make your suspension a month. You're going home and staying there. We have your reports. There's nothing left to do. Homeland is cleaning up the mess. It's another day."

"Are we positive Shade's completely dismantled?"

"Unofficially, yes. The official report is under consideration by the powers that be, but we're confident it's over." He offered a tight smile. "You had a lot to do with it." I opened my mouth to speak, but he held up a finger. "No, I don't want to hear whatever lame thing you're about to say." He softened slightly. "You scared the shit out of me today, Alex. Don't do that again."

"I'll try not to." I gave him a grim smile. "I can't help it if that's how the pieces fall."

* * *

After leaving the federal building, I waited impatiently at home for Martin. Then we made love for most of the night. It was early morning when I opened my eyes, looking around the bedroom. We were on the floor, propped up against the foot of the bed. I wriggled out of his grip, and he opened his eyes, wondering what was going on.

"My leg's numb," I said, shifting off my side to get the blood flowing again.

"I love you too," he chuckled. "I take it from the way you pounced the second I came home, that you're not feeling much better than you were last night." He put his arm around me, pulling the tangle of sheet around us. "I shouldn't have taken advantage like I did, so I'm taking the proposal off the table for now. I had no right to ask that when I knew you were emotionally compromised."

My heart sank. I hadn't even processed it yet, but standing in that shed, I wanted nothing more than to be with Martin. Marriage wouldn't be so bad. It'd make him happy. Hell, it might even make me happy.

"Emotionally compromised?" I repeated, hearing the lawyer speak behind his words.

"Yeah, I don't ever want to trick you into something that you don't want to do."

"Isn't that how you convinced me to move in with you?"

"That was supposedly your idea, but we both see how well that worked out." He snorted.

"Let me guess, Francesca's lawyers are claiming that you manipulated her into the contract because you took advantage of her emotionally compromised state."

"Something like that, but it got me thinking that's what I did to you. Maybe that's something that I've always done in order to win business deals and get what I want. I don't know." He began trailing kisses along my collarbone. "I want you to say yes without coercion or any doubt in my mind. And I want to ask when there are no fringe benefits aside from you being naked. It's possible that part of the reason I asked when I did was to prevent you from being able to testify against me."

"Which of us were you trying to protect?"

"Both, I guess." He stared into my eyes. "But I'm telling you now, I'll ask again soon, so you should be prepared."

"Why would you want to spend your life with an emotionally compromised lunatic who's out of work for the next six weeks or so?"

"Medical leave?" he asked, ignoring my question.

"Yeah, and my reward for helping end this reign of terror."

"Good. That means we'll have time for a lot more mind-blowing sex, and you'll get a preview of the fringe benefits you'll enjoy on our honeymoon."

"Aren't you afraid that you're being coercive?"

"In this instance, I'm willing to risk it."

LOOK FOR CRISIS OF CONSCIENCE, THE
ELEVENTH NOVEL IN THE ALEXIS PARKER
SERIES.

NOW AVAILABLE IN PRINT AND AS AN E-
BOOK

ABOUT THE AUTHOR

G.K. Parks is the author of the Alexis Parker series. The first novel, *Likely Suspects,* tells the story of Alexis' first foray into the private sector.

G.K. Parks received a Bachelor of Arts in Political Science and History. After spending some time in law school, G.K. changed paths and earned a Master of Arts in Criminology/Criminal Justice. Now all that education is being put to use creating a fictional world based upon years of study and research.

You can find additional information on G.K. Parks and the Alexis Parker series by visiting our website at
www.alexisparkerseries.com

Made in the USA
Columbia, SC
24 November 2020

25348803R00202